THE VANISHING ENCORE

CAROLYN RUFFLES

THE VANISHING ENCORE
First Edition
AUGUST 2021

Copyright©2021 Carolyn Ruffles

Publisher: Carolyn Ruffles
ISBN 13: 978-1-9163913-3-8

Sisters share a unique bond. As children, this bond can be tested by bitter rivalries and divided loyalties. But, as we grow older, it offers the unbreakable strength of treasured memories, fierce support and enduring love.

*For Ros and Sara
and for sisters everywhere.*

PROLOGUE

Overhead lights snapped off, plunging the room in blindness. Someone screamed. Nervous giggles rippled through the audience before fading into throbbing silence. The walls shivered in anticipation.

'When's the musician coming?' A young boy's voice wobbled the mounting suspense.

'Ssh ... *magician*.' An irritated hiss from Pandora Pilkington-Brown. It was her party.

More silence. A cough. The hush of twenty-five children holding their breath.

A sudden explosion of light shook the room. Thick smoke snaked in spirals as a creature shimmered into view – a man, resplendent in a swirling, multi-coloured cape and a tall, red hat like a pillar box.

'Behold!' he announced, his voice deep and hypnotic. 'You see before you ... Magical Marvo. Prepare to be amazed!' Beneath the cape, he whirled his arms. Slowly, with the artistry of many performances, he unfolded his long, thin fingers to reveal a squirming, white mouse.

'Ooh,' gasped the children.

'Watch carefully. I shall now make it disappear.' The magician turned his huge hands inward, fingers closing and reopening. The mouse was gone. An adult at the back of the room began to applaud; the children followed suit. 'Thank you.' Magical Marvo surveyed his audience. 'For my next trick, I require a special assistant.' Several hands shot into the air, unseen in the blackness. 'Is there someone here called ... Pandora?'

'Yes, me!' A young girl squealed with delight. She skipped to Marvo's side, blonde pigtails dancing in the spotlight, plump, pink cheeks flushed with excitement.

'Behold ... Pandora!' Another flourish and more applause. 'Today, Pandora will show you some true magic. She will *disappear!*'

'If only,' a girl whispered. The younger sister beside her sniggered. It might be Pandora Pilkington-Brown's birthday but she was a complete pain in the backside. Their invitation to her party had been issued under sufferance because their daddy worked for her daddy.

The magician wheeled forward a large, black box emblazoned with 'The Magical Marvo' in gold letters. 'Now, Pandora will step inside the box.' He opened a forward-facing door so they could see the empty space inside. It looked quite small.

'Do you think she'll fit?' The older sister muttered in her sibling's ear.

'Ssh!' giggled the younger.

'This is dangerous magic, children.' Marvo lowered his voice to a dramatic rumble. 'Do *not* try this by yourselves. To make a person vanish, a magician has to spend years practising.' Pandora gave the audience a smug smile before spinning around and stepping into the box. She sat, crouched, facing out, her candy-striped, party dress scrunched around her. 'Are you alright in there, Pandora?'

'Yes.'

'I'm going to close the door.' The audience watched, eyes wide in anticipation. 'Don't worry,' Marvo smiled, 'she's still in there. I haven't said the magic words yet. Do you want to see?'

'Yes,' called the children.

The birthday girl was revealed and she gave the crowd a cramped wave. 'Right, Pandora. Are you ready to disappear?'

'Yes.'

Once more, he clicked the door shut and stood in front of the box. 'It's time to summon the magic.' He swung his cape in the manner of a bullfighter. 'Repeat these words after me. *Magical Marvo, make her go!*'

'Magical Marvo, make her go,' chanted the children.

Another twirl of his arms. 'Let's see. Has the magic worked?' He flung the door open, displaying the empty space inside. As promised, Pandora had vanished. The audience uttered a collective gasp and clapped enthusiastically while Marvo bowed. Excited voices increased in volume as the spectators turned to each other in wonder. The magician smiled at the appreciation and bowed even lower. 'Thank you for your help, children. That's the end of my performance. I hope you've enjoyed it.' More clapping ensued, accompanied by confused mumbles.

'Aren't you going to make her come back?' a small voice, tinged with anxiety, called from the front row.

Marvo feigned puzzlement. 'Oh, I don't know about that. That would need a very powerful spell. I hadn't realised you wanted her to reappear. Oh, very well. I'll see what I can do.' He scratched his head, pretending to be thinking hard. 'Right. I've got it. You'll need to shout these words as loudly as you can if we're to summon the lovely Pandora back with us.' The children watched, spellbound 'Here we go. Repeat after me. *Marvo Mack, bring her back!*'

'Marvo Mack, bring her back!'

The box opened. Gasps splintered the air as the white mouse scuttled out. Marvo swept it up and dropped it in his pocket before clasping his hands to his face. 'Oh no!' he moaned. 'Wrong words.'

'Have you changed Pandora into a mouse?' It was the same voice, her younger brother.

'No, no, never fear; Marvo is here. I'm sure she's fine.' He flashed a reassuring smile. 'Let's try again. I've remembered the words now. This time, shout them really loudly.' His arms swept through the air, conducting his orchestra. '*Marvo Mora, show Pandora!*'

'Marvo Mora, show Pandora!' yelled the children. The box opened and out she stepped, beaming at her reception. As the audience cheered, she gave a low curtsey, giggling as Marvo spun her around.

'An incredible performance of magic, young lady. Well done!' His giant hands clapped together, echoing the applause.

After Pandora had returned to the seat next to her brother, Marvo continued his act. There were card tricks, a seemingly never-ending string of silk hankies extracted from his red hat and assorted items produced from thin air, behind children's ears and from up their sleeves. The party-goers were enthralled.

'And now, for my final trick, I shall perform the most dangerous magic of all ... I shall make myself disappear. In a few moments, I shall get into the box. When you shout the magic words, I shall reappear from the back of the room.' Heads turned as if they expected to see him there straight away. 'The magic words this time are ... *Magical Marvo, it's time to go!*' He spent a few minutes rehearsing them. 'You've got to get it right or the magic might go wrong,' he informed them solemnly. 'Now, I need another helper. Perhaps ...' he surveyed the group, '... you!' He pointed at the two sisters and the eldest jumped to her feet. 'What's your name?' he asked as she approached.

'Scarlett.'

The audience sniggered and someone called, 'That's not her name!' Marvo frowned but chose to ignore them.

'A lovely name. Now, Scarlett ...' More titters. 'I want you to check there's no trickery going on. Can you scrutinise the box, please, to make sure that this door is the only way out?' She walked around it, taking her time, inspecting every part of it. 'Do you want to check underneath?' She nodded and he tilted the box forward so she could see. 'Now, can you confirm that this door is the only way out?'

'Yes,' she replied with a confident swish of her long, dark hair.

'Now, please stand close to the box as I go in so you can shut the door behind me. When I'm inside, I want you to count to three and then everyone must shout the magic words. Let's practise that, one more time.'

At last, he squeezed his frame into the box, the girl pushed the door shut and counted to three.

'Magical Marvo, it's time to go!' roared the children. As Scarlett threw the door open to reveal the empty box, a bang resounded from the back of the hall. The audience turned, as one, to see Marvo heading towards them, arms outstretched.

'It worked!' he called. 'Well done everyone! You were amazing.' More rapturous applause. The children babbled in excitement and awe. 'Remember my name and tell your friends ... Magical Marvo! The best magician in the world!' A final, deep bow and, while exclamations continued, the lights dimmed. Seconds of darkness ticked by until the sudden glare of the main lights shocked the children to silence. Blinking as their eyes adjusted, they scanned the hall for Marvo but he was nowhere to be seen.

His place was taken by Pandora's mother, a stick-thin, blonde woman in a designer dress and gold, hooped earrings.

'The birthday buffet is ready. Would you like to take your seats?' She gestured towards a long trestle table, laden with party food, and grimaced at the immediate scramble for chairs. The two sisters found themselves separated at opposite ends of the table and it wasn't until much later, on their way home, that they were able to discuss the magic act.

'Why did you call yourself Scarlett?' the smaller one asked. 'That's not your name!'

'Because it's fun pretending to be someone you're not. And, anyway, I'd like to be called a cool name like Scarlett. That will be my stage name when I'm a famous magician ... Scarlett Starlight.' She flounced her arms, as Marvo had, thumping her sister on the side of the head.

'Oi, careful you idiot!'

'Sorry. I'd love to be able to do magic like that.' The older sister leaned back into her seat and closed her eyes, a dazzling future unfolding before her. 'I'd love to be able to disappear ... poof ... just like that!' She clicked her fingers.

The younger sister shot her a look of pure scorn. 'I wouldn't,' she exclaimed. Her face became serious as she considered the prospect and its implications. 'It's all very well disappearing,' she said slowly, 'but what if ...?'

'What if *what*?'

'What if you *never* came back?'

CHAPTER 1

Lily

There is a man who wants me dead. My whole adult life has been spent looking over my shoulder, jumping at shadows, wondering when I'll feel his breath on the back of my neck and know my time has come. It never goes away. Sometimes, I forget, and I laugh like a person who doesn't have a death sentence hanging over her. Sometimes, I relax, live for the moment, let my mind float free from that shackle of fear. But it's always there, festering, a malignancy eating away at my spirit, holding me back. Time helps. With the passing of months and years, the terror fades, like an old photograph, losing colour and clarity. Then, something happens to bring it back into sharp focus ...

I stare at the smiling face on my tablet. *It's him – I know it's him.* With trembling fingers, I click on the link to the accompanying news article. It's entitled, 'Winner of the Family Business of the Year Award,' and trumpets the success of Turner Packaging, a company who have 'revolutionised the world of packaging with innovative, environmentally-friendly solutions.' I read through to the end of the piece but my mind is too numb to absorb the details. Of their own volition, my eyes flick back to the photograph. I study the face for a long time, while worms of dread burrow deeper. Beneath the snap is a caption, 'Chairman David Turner and his son-in-law, Nick Georgiev, Managing Director of Turner Packaging.' *Nick Georgiev.* It's an Eastern European name. The face is thinner, older, still good-looking in an arrogant kind of way. He's wearing the smile which had us all fooled. And he's married. I do a swift calculation in my head. He would be late fifties now; that matches the man in the photograph. *I'm sure it's him.*

I google Turner Packaging and discover the company is based in Essex but also has sites in China and Bulgaria. *Bulgaria – the country of his birth.* My stomach clenches as I sit alone in the living room. The TV is on, a cooking programme I enjoy, but I'm not watching it. Upstairs, Todd is working on his novel. I long to talk to him about this, about all of it, but I can't.

My mind is racing and I'm trying not to panic. Essex is close, too close for comfort. *He doesn't know where I am.* I repeat the mantra, over and over, in my head, until my breathing calms. Then, I force myself to confront my options. I could do nothing; pretend I haven't seen the article; maintain the illusion I'm currently living. A part of me longs for that. Todd makes me happy. Maybe, one day, there will be a time I feel safe, when I'm no longer fearful for myself and those closest to me. Maybe …

I continue to sit, staring into space. I can't ignore this; I have to act on the knowledge I now possess. This man has destroyed my family. He should pay. And anyway, I'm sick of being a victim, hiding away, giving him power over me. It's my turn to seek vengeance, my chance to act. I have to take it.

***

My resolve grows and hardens overnight and through the following day. Late afternoon, after work, I head to my small flat in the town centre. My excuse – should I need one – is that I need to pick up more clothes and check my post. I'm staying over at Todd's most nights so it would make sense to give up the flat but I'm reluctant to do so. If my nemesis is finally behind bars and I have the answers I seek, I'll be free to make the commitment Todd wants … that I want. For the first time, I allow myself to hope.

Having completed my housekeeping chores, I drag out the box from the bottom of my wardrobe. It contains my past: birth certificate; old photos I took from the family home; my one-eyed teddy, Angus; other sentimental mementoes from my childhood. I sift slowly through them, unable to pass some of them by without holding them close to my chest. There is a photo of my sister and I, so alike, both smiling, which always breaks my heart. I remember Dad taking it. We were on the beach at Hunstanton, shivering with cold but determined to swim in the sea. Afterwards, we sat draped in towels, huddling together on the sand, laughing at something Dad said. I wish I could remember what it was. In my dreams, I imagine finding my sister and showing her the photo, rediscovering the moment because she can recall it too. The thought fires my determination and I keep looking through the jumbled pile of papers until I find what I'm searching for. It's a card bearing the logo of Norfolk Police. On it is printed a name – Kate Bell, Family Liaison Officer – and a telephone number. I remember Kate giving it to me at the children's home, Happytrees, before I went to live in Kent. 'If you need to talk to me about anything at all, just call,' she said. 'Especially, if you think you may be in any danger.' I'd rung it once before, after I finished university, when I saw him in Canterbury that time. Back then, nothing had come of the sighting. This time, it will be different.

I take the card through to the kitchen and find my phone. Taking a deep breath, I key in the number. It rings but no-one answers. Voicemail kicks in, asking me to leave a message. I don't. First, I need to consider what I'm going to say. Instead, I save the number to my contacts, pack up the box and restore it to its hiding place. As I'm locking the flat, my mobile rings.

'DI Kate Bell.' Her voice is terse. 'You rang this number?'

'Yes ... um ... hi, Kate ....' I tell her who I am. My real name feels strange on my tongue after all this time. We exchange brief pleasantries before I launch into my reason for calling.

'Right.' She checks the details with me again, her tone non-committal. 'We'll look into it and I'll get back to you as soon as I can.'

She ends the call and I drive to Todd's house, expecting to feel like a burden has been lifted from my shoulders. The sensation doesn't come.

***

It's ten days before she rings again – ten days of enduring the daily agony of expectation, hope and disappointment. I pay close attention to the news, searching for an announcement that police have raided the home of successful businessman, Nick Georgiev, and arrested an unnamed male suspect ... or something like that. It hasn't happened. *Yet*, I tell myself.

Kate gets straight to the point. 'I'm sorry but, so far, he checks out. His history, his background, his paperwork – it's all legit. The Essex team could find nothing at all which links him to your sister's disappearance or which suggests he's anything other than the man he says he is. Are you absolutely sure it's him?'

'Yes,' I say. Furious disbelief surges and I don't trust myself to say more.

She sighs. 'OK. I'll ask them to keep digging but, I have to warn you, they're not treating it as a priority.'

'But it's definitely him,' I insist. 'There *must* be something they can find. They're not looking hard enough.'

'I know you're disappointed, but they already feel it's a dead end. I'll tell them you're certain but, as I said, they won't be treating it as a priority.' She might as well say, 'They've wasted enough time.' The scepticism in her voice is vinegar sharp. She thinks I'm mistaken.

My pent-up hopes evaporate. I sit clutching my phone, bereft, my future unsure. He's still out there ... not far away ... and untouchable. That thought brings bile to my throat. Somehow, I have to prove the police wrong. There has to be a way.

Then, the very next morning, I see my own name and photograph in *The Gazette*, an online news site. Just like that. No warning. A minor incident at work, something which happened months before, has suddenly merited media attention. I can't believe it when I receive a text from a friend, congratulating me. Urgently, I scour the online news and find the report mentioned by my friend. There's a headline proclaiming, 'Teacher heroine just doing her job'. At least, I'm barely recognisable from the photograph they've printed – the same one which was in a local paper, *The East Anglia Chronicle*, just after it happened. When I can't find anything on the other news sites, I breathe more easily. With luck, that will be it. Nevertheless, my pulse is fluttering with trepidation as I drive to the school where I work as a teacher. When I round the final bend, my heart plummets. People with cameras are gathered on the pavement – poised, alert, ready to strike. As my car slows, they surge forwards, a collective thrust of faces at my windows, lens clicking, bulbs flashing. I stamp on the accelerator and screech through the gates. Voices yell, 'Miss Nichol!' I tear around to the staff carpark, safely out of their reach. My hands shake as I fumble my seatbelt loose and step from my car. I fear I'll see a stampede of reporters charging around the corner and scurry, head down, into the building.

'Here she is, the celebrity!' Dave Parker, a member of the school senior management team, sneers. He doesn't like me much but, to be fair, I don't like him either.

'You're famous!' Sarah Peters exclaims. 'They'll be wanting you to do *Strictly* next!' Her smile turns to concern. 'Are you alright, Lily? You're very pale.' She takes my arm and leads me away from Dave. 'Are you OK with all this?'

'Not really. I didn't want any publicity.' My heart is thudding wildly and my classroom blurs. I sink onto a chair.

'Fair enough. I'll speak to Michael. There must be a safeguarding issue, anyway, with them all outside the school gates like that. I'll tell him to get rid of them.'

I try to smile but I know it's too late. The damage has been done. The man who wants me dead will know where to find me.

CHAPTER 2

Todd

Friday. Not even the driving rain could dim Todd's high spirits as he let himself into the house. *The start of the weekend and the holiday.* Tomorrow, they would set off for the Cotswolds – him, Lily and Charlotte. He couldn't wait. Whistling the song which had been playing on his car radio, he dropped his briefcase by the door and kicked off his shoes. His overcoat was dripping wet and he slung it on a hook. *Bring it on!*

'I'm home!' he called, pausing to listen for a response.

Nothing. The house was eerily silent. Frowning, he called again. No Lily; no Charlotte. That was strange. Usually, his daughter would run to greet him and Lily would follow closely behind, smiling, her hazel eyes locking with his, full of promise. He checked his phone. No messages. He put the kettle on and struggled to remember what he'd forgotten. Was something happening today – maybe something at school? Lily often accused him of not listening when she was telling him things. God, if so, he was going to be in trouble. She'd been in a weird mood anyway this past week and had snapped his head off when he asked what was wrong. He couldn't blame her. The answer was obvious and he was an idiot. He knew it had upset her, big time, a few days back, to find her photo plastered all over the papers. Eventually, she'd been persuaded to give a statement to the press and, after that, the furore had died down. He thought she'd got over it but perhaps he was wrong. Tonight, he'd devote all his efforts to cheering her up. Anyway, it was the end of term and they were all looking forward to their holiday, their first together, as a family. Getting away was going to be good for them.

Buoyed by that prospect, and still mulling over whatever it was which might have delayed Lily and Charlotte's return, he headed for the kitchen. It was small but tidy; everything in its place. Reaching to pull a mug from the cupboard, he stopped in his tracks, brow furrowed. That was odd; something was missing. Lily's coffee machine had been moved. His eyes roved the worktops lining two of the walls but there was no sign of it. *Weird.* As he took his first gulp of tea, cursing as the hot liquid scalded his tongue, he pulled his phone out from his trouser pocket to ring her. No answer; his call went straight to voicemail. Shrugging, he perched on a kitchen stool and scrolled through his WhatsApp messages instead, chuckling at a joke from one of his mates. Still, Lily and Charlotte failed to materialise. After trying her phone once more, with no success, he decided to make a start on tea. That would score him a few brownie points. Checking the menu list on a pinboard on the kitchen wall, he saw that tonight was lasagne. Lily was an organiser and liked meals planned in advance so that whoever was home first could start cooking.

Right. He pulled a saucepan from a cupboard ready to fry off the mince and opened the fridge door. There, where he expected to see the mince, was a lasagne, ready-made. He wondered when she'd had time to do that. Probably last night, after he'd gone to bed in a huff. They'd had a bit of a row, something which had never happened before. It was almost as if she'd been picking a fight, needling him about the fact that he'd got home late the night before. She was the one who had told him to take Lee out for a drink, for God's sake.

'He needs a friend right now,' she'd said. 'Try to get him to talk about things over a beer or two.' Lee, a friend from his schooldays, had been having problems with his wife, Callie, and they'd recently split up. The poor chap was devastated, missing both his wife and their three children. She was right. Lee did need someone to talk to. And yes, maybe it was after eleven when he returned and he'd had at least two beers too many. But still ... it just wasn't like her to give him a hard time about it. The whole thing had been totally out of character.

He slid the lasagne out of the fridge and switched the oven on, wishing he knew what time to expect them home. Best to get it cooked. It would keep in the oven if necessary. The salad was also ready, in the fridge, covered with clingfilm. Perhaps that was Lily's way of admitting she'd been in the wrong last night. The thought cheered him and he headed upstairs. He might as well take advantage of the solitude and get some writing done while he waited. There wouldn't be time for that during their fortnight away.

His study was a tiny boxroom with a desk, a chair and his laptop computer. There were no windows but he didn't mind that. It meant no distractions. He switched on the light and thought, for the thousandth time, that he must get a lightshade. The bare bulb suspended from the ceiling had been irritating him for too long.

The distance between the door and his desk was barely one stride. And, it was there, on the grey surface, layered with dust, that he found the note ...

BEFORE

CHAPTER 3

Saskia
March, 2003.

7:13 a.m. My departure for school is much earlier than usual but I hope no-one will notice. As I creep through our front room, I stumble over a ridge in the threadbare, patterned carpet. My bulky backpack lumps against sun-bleached floral wallpaper with a loud thunk. I gasp, my breath clogging my throat, as I strain for any sound coming from upstairs. Nothing. Andrian is a heavy sleeper and never rises before nine. Mum rarely surfaces at all. Tension thrums through my body as I prepare to make my escape.

The front door is stiff, reluctant to admit the outside world, unwilling to disgorge my quivering body. As I push it open, its rotten frame rattles and shakes, traitorously heralding my exit. Again, I hold my breath and listen. Upstairs remains silent.

I've left Mum a note, tucked in her favourite handbag, explaining everything. It's hidden away in her wardrobe so Andrian won't find it. I'm hoping it will be a few days at least before they clock that I'm missing.

Outside, the day is spiky with cold. Head down, eyes averted from the tired, ill-kept terraces along the street, I trudge along the pavement. The roads are already humming with traffic; the pavements less so. The steady slapping of footsteps behind sends a dart of adrenalin down my spine. Turning my head, I scan the murky street. A jogger. I step aside to let him pass, a flash of lycra-clad sinew to a soundtrack of heavy breathing. A few more strides and he disappears around the corner ahead. I doubt he'll remember seeing me.

Cars splash through water pooled by the side of the road, sending up showers of tiny droplets. The past few days have been monotonous with rain but it's now stopped; that's something. My coat is cheap, thin, offering little protection against the elements. Despite that, I can feel the clamminess of sweat on my back as I march on. I'm wearing several layers of clothing, my way of taking as much as I can with me when I hadn't been able to fit it all in my backpack. I don't know when I'll be coming back.

My mind is numb, tired from trying to process the conversation I overheard a few days ago. I was at home, unexpectedly, in the afternoon, having left school early with a migraine. That was the moment my world fell apart, when I heard the nasal tones of a man I trusted, chatting on the phone – so calm, so matter-of-fact – talking of killing as if discussing the weather. I couldn't believe what I was hearing. *Don't think of it now; focus.*

At last, I'm away from my neighbourhood, unlikely to see anyone who recognises me, but I'm taking no chances. My long, brown hair is bundled under an old, woollen hat of my Mum's, dirty pink with circular, purple stripes, my pathetic attempt at disguise. I wouldn't be seen dead in it in normal circumstances. *Dead.* The thought makes my heart thump and I picture my lifeless body discovered in a ditch somewhere, still wearing the awful hat. I swallow down my fear and march on.

It's a forty-minute walk to the train station. I know because I timed it yesterday in a dummy run after school. Kaz was miffed. I was supposed to go to her house and help with her maths homework. It's something I often do. Her house is warm and there's always a choice of cake or biscuits. Kaz and I have been best friends ever since those first days at Thorpe High School. I recall the morning we met, me feeling self-conscious and painfully aware that, unlike most of my peers, my shoes were scuffed and old. I remember tucking my feet way back under my chair, trying to hide them. Kaz and I were in the same form group and she was new, not from any of the local feeder schools. She sat alone, biting her lip, twiddling her long, black plait around her finger. I could tell she was a rich kid, from the pristine smartness of her uniform and the cool watch she wore on her wrist. Not at all like me! But there was a vulnerability about the way she pretended to ignore the rowdy greetings going on all around her which tugged at my heartstrings. I caught her eye across the room and smiled. When she smiled back, I moved to sit next to her. From that moment on, we just clicked and that was that.

I glance at my watch. 7:40 a.m. Kaz is probably having breakfast right now, unaware she won't be seeing me down at the bus stop where we meet every school morning. A car horn blares and, instinctively, I swivel my head. A pedestrian, a middle-aged man in a suit, phone clamped to his ear, raises his free hand in a gesture of apology as he steps back onto the pavement. My eyes turn to the driver – brown hair, thin face, scowling. *Oh God, it's Mr Turnbull, Head of Science.* My heart somersaults in my chest and I snatch my gaze away. The car drives past, a dark green Subaru. It's OK; I don't think he's clocked me; it might not even have been him. I force myself to relax and hurry onwards.

The station is up ahead, an impressive, red-bricked building with arches at its entrance. I know I won't be able to catch a train for a while. This is prime commuter time and I have to wait for a cheaper slot. I bought my ticket yesterday with money I'd saved from my Saturday job, helping out at *Just a Snip*, the hairdresser on our estate. The rest of my savings is split into small wads and hidden in different places, some zipped up in my coat pocket, some in my bag and some tucked into my sock. Just in case. The next part of the plan involves peeling off and dumping my school uniform and, maybe, getting a drink. Kill some time. Then I'll sit, perhaps with a magazine if I can find something cheap, in the waiting room. Anonymous. Blending in. I've got some food supplies in my backpack: biscuits, an apple, a pack of Tesco's own chocolate wafers. It will be enough to keep me going.

The station is a flurry of activity, smartly-dressed men and women scrambling through the doors leading to the platforms. A train is waiting and London commuters are jostling for the best seats. I'm surprised how rude they seem, pushing past, far too busy and important to worry about holding a door for anyone else. I could never be like that.

'Manners cost nothing,' Dad used to say. He always held the door open for Mum. Treated her like royalty, even when she didn't deserve it. My lips tighten at the memory. What would he think of her now?

I head for the loos and remove the Thorpe High School sweatshirt and grey trousers, before wrapping them in two separate, plastic bags and discarding them in different waste bins. The disgusting, woolly hat goes too. My next layer consists of another sweatshirt and faded jeans and I think I could pass for a college student. I brush my hair and leave it loose which makes me look older. Next, I apply mascara, eye liner, foundation, blusher and shiny lip gloss. I take my time, aiming for that sophisticated look I've seen in magazines when flicking through them at the hairdresser's. By the time I'm finished, the overall effect isn't half bad. I take a moment to imagine Darrell Parkinson's face if he saw me like this, tarted up. He'd probably say something rude about piling on the slap but inside, I reckon, he'd be thinking 'phwoar' or whatever boys think when they see a girl they fancy. My heart aches a little bit at that. I've always liked Darrell Parkinson.

Critically, I inspect my face once more. I might've overdone it. It's a bit OTT for this time of the morning. I want to look older than my fifteen years but the blusher looks garish in the harsh, artificial light. I find a tissue and wipe some of it off. That's better – more natural-looking. It'll have to do.

My stomach rumbles, reminding me I've eaten nothing since a piece of toast when I got home yesterday evening. Time for a cup of tea and one of those biscuits. The coffee shop is warm and clean, empty but for a middle-aged couple at one table and a thin man wearing a dark blue suit and metal-framed glasses at the counter, buying a coffee and a sausage roll. My mouth waters at the pastries on display but I stick to my plan and order a pot of tea for one. I carry it on a tray to a table in the corner and pile three teaspoons of sugar into the white, china teacup.

I take my coat off and unzip my phone from the right-hand pocket. It's an old Nokia, a cast-off from Kaz. No messages yet. 8:07 a.m. It won't be long. I leave the phone on the table and take the first sip of my tea, savouring the sugary warmth. It's tempting to take another sip straight away but I make myself wait. Eke it out. I'm catching the nine o'clock train – 9:03 a.m. to be precise, Platform 2. Plenty of time.

The middle-aged couple leave and, for a while, it's just me and the blue suit. He's reading a copy of the Financial Times as he eats his sausage roll, crumbs of pastry falling like confetti at his feet. Then, there's a flurry of customers: a group of women, loud with lipstick and laughter; a couple with a toddler; a young woman with a ponytail; a lad in a hoodie.

Feeling conspicuous suddenly, I stand and head for the door. My phone pings from the table.

'Hey, you've left your phone!' Ponytail girl hands it over with a smile.

'Thanks,' I mumble, looking at the floor. I scurry to the safety of a magazine rack before I check my phone. As expected, it's a text from Kaz.

Where ru? U ill?x

It's the obvious assumption when I hadn't turned up at the bus stop, especially as I'd sown the seed yesterday by feigning a headache when I called off going to her house. All part of the plan – a way to give me a few days of respite before people at school start asking questions.

Feel terrible. Prob flu. Tell Batty will you?

Batty, Miss Bateman, is our form tutor. The reply comes quickly.

OK. Poor u. Get well soon. Darrell asked where u were!

Kaz is well aware of the romance budding between Darrell and me and I wonder if she made that up. She knows it would give me a boost. It does too – a fuzzy tingling warms my chest. I switch off my phone. Depending on what happens, I may have to get rid of it at some point like they do in crime books. Not yet though.

I decide not to buy a magazine after all. Their glossy covers seem fake, all glamour and no substance. Waste of money. I toy with the idea of getting a book, something to take my mind off things on the train. For a while, I pick up the titles on the bestseller table, read the blurbs, waiting for something to grab me. One is a thriller about a missing child and I read the first few pages of that one before replacing it. The cover claims it was based on a real-life event. Maybe, someday, someone will write my story: *The Girl Who Ran Away*. I stifle a laugh. 'Don't be so dramatic,' Kaz would say. She doesn't know the half of it.

I walk out of the bookstore and across to the *Ladies* once more. I need another wee. The pot of tea, I justify to myself. *Nerves*, says the voice in my head.

I *am* nervous, there's no denying it, like a skittish kitten, outside on its own for the first time. 'You'll feel better when you're safely on the train,' I tell the pale-faced reflection in the mirror. The blusher comes out of my bag once more. Something *is* needed on my cheeks unless I want to resemble the walking dead.

8:41 a.m. Not much longer. I head for the waiting room. A woman with iron-grey curls is sitting on the right-hand side, halfway through a Danielle Steel novel. She doesn't look up as I enter and I take a seat in the far left-hand corner. My stomach rumbles again. Time for a snack. Fumbling through my bag, my fingers locate the apple but push on past until they find the pack of chocolate wafers. That's more like it. The foil covering crackles in the silence but my companion remains engrossed in her book. I envy her ability to switch off so completely and wonder what it would take to get her to look up. It's the same on buses – everyone wrapped up in their own worlds, on their own journeys, avoiding interaction. Sometimes, I deliberately make eye contact with someone, strike up a conversation, just to buck the trend. Not today though. Definitely, not today.

'The 9.03 train for London Liverpool Street is now at Platform 2.' The announcement issued by a metallic, male voice jolts me into action. I gather up my bag and stride out of the waiting room, relieved to be moving once more.

It's time. I'm going to London. Yes, I'm running away but there's more to it than that. I have to find my sister.

CHAPTER 4

Todd
Eighteen months ago

Todd Matheson sat next to his wife, struggling to control his embarrassing physical reaction to the woman opposite. This was his first, school parents' evening and it was promising to be memorable for all the wrong reasons. The problem was Charlotte's teacher. She was smoking hot – 'a babe', as his friend Lee would say – from her shoulder-length, blonde hair curling in waves all the way down to breasts which made him lose all rational thought. Another surge in his groin forced his gaze upwards, to a pair of arresting, hazel eyes, almond-shaped, framed by long lashes and a mouth which mesmerised him – full, gently-smiling lips which he longed to crush beneath his own and ...

With effort, he wrenched his attention away from his lust and focused on what she was saying. Miss Nichol – wasn't that what Reggie had called her?

'Charlotte's made an excellent start.' Her voice was low and melodic. 'She's settled in really well and made friends.' Todd saw how her face lit up whilst she was talking about his daughter. 'She loves books and has made great progress with her reading. In class, she listens well and tries her best with every task she's given. I'm very pleased with her.'

'Yes, but what about the bullying? What are you doing about that?' Reggie snapped, her face tight with displeasure.

Miss Nichol's eyes narrowed slightly but her professional smile remained intact. 'Bullying?' she queried politely.

'Yes, last Tuesday. She was crying when the childminder picked her up. A boy had hit her. Robbie, I think his name was. What's being done about that? I won't tolerate my child being bullied.' Reggie was snarling now. As a barrister, she'd earned the nickname 'Rottweiler Reggie'. To his own cost, he knew she deserved it. Once she had something between her teeth, she wasn't going to let it go. Fortunately, for the most part, that was no longer his problem.

'Last Tuesday you say ...' For a moment, Miss Nichol looked puzzled and then her face cleared. 'Ah yes.' She treated them both to a reassuring smile and Todd felt his loins tighten in response. 'That was just a minor incident. Charlotte and Robbie were arguing over a book at the end of the day. They both wanted to take the same one home and were wrangling over it. Then, Robbie let go suddenly and the book hit Charlotte in the face. I think Robbie laughed and told her it served her right. That's what upset Charlotte. She wasn't hurt. I'm sorry she was a bit upset. I *did* tell the childminder what had happened.'

'That's not good enough. I want to know if the other child was punished for laughing at her. In my book, that constitutes mental abuse.'

'Reggie, I don't think ...' Todd tried to intervene but Miss Nichol was up to the task.

'It really wasn't necessary,' she explained pleasantly. 'I followed it up the next morning and spoke to them both together. Robbie apologised for laughing and I saw the two of them playing happily together in the role play corner later.' She gestured towards the 'farm shop' at one end of the room. 'Again, at the end of the day, I *did* tell the childminder it had all been resolved.'

'Yes, well ...' Reggie's tone was still aggressive, 'unfortunately, *she* didn't pass it on to me.'

There was a brief pause before Miss Nichol moved on to Charlotte's progress in other areas of the Foundation Stage curriculum. It appeared their child was doing very well. Todd tried to relax and left it to Reggie to ask any questions, wincing as she struggled to regain the upper hand, treating the parents' consultation meeting as if she were in court, engaged in the interrogation of a witness. He was impressed by the calmness with which Charlotte's teacher had dealt with his difficult wife. Technically, they *were* still married as the divorce had not yet gone through but they had been apart for the last two years. She was now living in a swanky house in the heart of Suffolk with a mild-mannered barrister from the same law firm, whilst he languished in a small, terraced house in Bury St Edmunds. That had always been the problem in their marriage – what she termed 'his lack of ambition.'

They'd met at law school, were immediately inseparable and married shortly afterwards.

'I think you're making a mistake,' his sister, Grace, told him in her no-nonsense, blunt way. 'You and Reggie love each other now but you want different things from life. I don't think, in the long run, you'll make each other happy.'

She was spot on, although it took them a long while to admit it – a whole ten years enduring the slow misery of a disintegrating marriage. Charlotte, though, made it all worthwhile. She was an angel child, the brightness in Todd's otherwise nondescript life. He wished she lived with him full-time and treasured the weekends they spent together. In reality, he probably spent more time with her than Reggie who spared her only brief moments from her busy working schedule. Currently, their daughter was being raised by a succession of nannies or childminders, a situation he was trying to resolve. He worked by day as a lawyer in a small firm but spent his nights writing, in the hope of becoming a full-time author. So far, he'd published two novels, both crime thrillers, which had achieved mediocre success, and was currently researching his third, hoping against hope that this might be the one to achieve global recognition. If he could give up the day job, which he hated, then Charlotte could live with him. That was the dream.

'Please don't hesitate to contact me if you have any concerns.' There was a note of finality in Miss Nichol's voice.

'Todd, do you have any questions?' Reggie was still trying to dictate terms. 'You haven't said anything.'

His smile held a hint of apology. 'I've been listening,' he answered smoothly, 'and I'm pleased Charlotte is doing so well. She told me how much she loves school ... and her teacher,' he added with undisguised warmth.

'That's lovely to hear.' Miss Nichol lowered her eyes and made a show of shuffling her papers. Her cheeks flushed pink.

'Thank you for all you're doing.' Todd stood and held out his hand. She took it. The feel of her soft skin made his body tingle.

'You're very welcome.'

***

Reggie and Todd parted company at the school gates. She wasn't best pleased with his 'lack of support' but she didn't seem happy about anything these days. He thought the constant pressure of a high-flying career was taking its toll on her but kept his opinion to himself. She wouldn't welcome his observations. He watched as she stalked to her red Mercedes and waved as she pulled away from the kerb. She didn't see; she'd already moved on.

These days, Todd couldn't imagine wanting to be with Reggie but that hadn't always been the case. When they met, she was sharp and sassy. Apart from the physical attraction, which flared instantly between them, she made him laugh. Her acerbic wit was softer then, humorous rather than cutting. He couldn't get enough of her and, it seemed, the feeling was mutual. He'd had his share of girlfriends and possessed the arrogance of knowing he was good-looking, sporty and intelligent, a potent combination he exploited fully. She knew it too; that had been his main attraction for her, he realised. He was 'in demand' from other female students and she lost no time in stamping her claim. They were foolish to get married so quickly, while they were still at university, but were blinded by infatuation and too full of self-belief to listen to concerns from anyone else.

Now, they saw each other infrequently; they both preferred it that way. Todd was her one failure and Reggie preferred not to be reminded of it. When he picked Charlotte up from her house, he usually saw the childminder. Sometimes, he was met by Nick, her partner; he was always affable enough and Todd knew Charlotte liked him. That was the main thing. Thinking of Charlotte brought a smile to his face. He wasn't at all surprised by her glowing school report. He'd expected nothing less. She was totally awesome and the centre of his world.

As he trudged towards his car, an old, dark green VW Golf, his mind wandered back to Charlotte's teacher, the stunning Miss Nichol. His reaction to her had knocked him sideways. He'd not felt like that since the early days with Reggie ... and not even then, he realised, looking back. It was a unique experience. And it wasn't just about her looks. There was something compelling about Miss Nichol, a connection drawing him in with the irresistible force of a magnet. He sensed an enigma lurking behind that smooth exterior, depths in which he longed to submerge himself. She was going to appear in his fantasies later that night. He'd peel off that prim, buttoned-up blouse she was wearing and watch as her skirt slid down her slim hips ... Todd swallowed hard and clamped down on his errant thoughts. Save them for later. He wanted to get some more research done in the hours before bedtime and maybe start drafting the ideas for his next novel into the start of a plan. Miss Nichol was not going to help with that.

He drove home and reheated the remains of a chicken curry he'd made the day before. While he ate, he scrolled through old news stories on his laptop. To give his books realism, he immersed himself in real-life, unsolved crime mysteries and noted down details of interest. As a lawyer, he'd met his share of wrongdoers so had some insight into the criminal mind. A few of his friends were police officers and they helped with procedural questions he had. But his imagination alone was not enough to come up with that killer story. Using elements from past cases might provide a winning formula – that was what he hoped, at any rate.

The plot of the next novel was going to centre on the mystery of a girl who'd gone missing and he'd googled several news articles so far, searching for that elusive hook into the narrative. There were many sad stories of people who'd never been found – runaways, people with mental health issues, unexplained disappearances. It didn't make for happy reading but he ploughed on dispassionately, focusing in on the peripheral details of each case, making random notes. By ten o'clock, his back was aching from being hunched over the screen, curry sauce lingered in a congealed mess on his plate and his half-drunk mug of tea had gone cold. Several pages of his notebook were satisfyingly covered with scrawl and his eyes were gritty with fatigue. Nothing he'd read had jumped out at him and the search for that nugget of an idea would have to continue tomorrow. He was philosophical about it. Writing a good book was hard work.

As he sat back from the latest news story, a girl who'd gone missing after going to work in London, his eyes wandered to a photo at the bottom of the text. It was a slightly blurred, black and white image of a young woman, her head turned away from the camera, her lips curved in a smile. He zoned in on the picture, studying it more closely. There was something familiar about her, something he recognised but couldn't put his finger on ...

It was late and he was tired. He switched off the computer and massaged his lower back as the screen turned black. It was probably nothing.

It was only later, as he lay in bed, eyes closed, allowing his thoughts free rein, that it came to him. The missing girl reminded him of Charlotte's teacher, Miss Nichol.

CHAPTER 5

Saskia
March, 2003

I snag a double seat to myself, deposit my coat and backpack on the adjacent grey cushioning and stare resolutely out of the window, actively discouraging anyone from asking me to move my stuff. Across the aisle from me, a family of four play their part in keeping my companion seat empty. One of the children, a red-cheeked boy of maybe seven or eight, is playing up. I guess, from the look of him and the harassed faces of his parents, he does that a lot and wonder why he isn't in school. The other child, a girl, about four years old, is nearly as bad. The two of them climb all over the seats, run up and down the carriage and have a fight which ends in the girl wailing, full screech, all before the train even starts moving. I don't mind. With them about, no-one is likely to notice me. The mum mutters an embarrassed apology vaguely in my direction; the dad is too busy bribing them with sweets and trying to avert further mayhem to spare me a second glance.

I shut my ears to the cacophony raging opposite and continue to stare out of the window as the train jolts forward. The bleak aspect of industrial warehousing eventually gives way to countryside, a blur of greys, greens and browns beneath a sullen sky. We rattle along and I try to pick out landmarks, anything to keep my mind focused on the present. I don't want to think of the future and, definitely not, the past.

That's proving difficult. The last time I'd been on a train was about six years ago, a family outing to the city to watch *The Lion King.* It was summertime and I'd worn the same pretty, cotton dress I'd worn to my cousin's wedding a month before. Dad sat opposite me, cracking jokes and making me and Mel, my sister, howl with laughter. Even Mum was smiling. It had been a perfect day – at least, until the journey home, when Mum had withdrawn into a cold rage and snapped at anything we said. She and Mel ended up rowing, a hushed flow of vitriol, while Dad and I, after futile attempts to smooth things over, reverted to uncomfortable silence. Once the memories start, it's impossible to stop more flooding in. It's three years now since Dad was killed in a car accident and our lives were plunged into turmoil. Mum went to pieces afterwards – 'understandable,' everyone said – but they assumed she'd recover. After a while, they stopped bringing casseroles, apple pies and words of comfort, thinking Mum would rally when she needed to. She didn't; not really. She'd always been volatile: sometimes, on her good days, she was a happy-go-lucky, carefree sprite who let us bunk off school and took us shopping; other times, she dissolved into a pool of sobbing despair. Then, none of us could reach her. The worst, though, was when she became a volcano of uncontrollable anger. Growing up, we'd always tiptoed around her, Mel and I, never knowing what to expect. Dad was the glue which held us together. When we were little, he would come home from work, cook tea, tidy the house and read us bedtime stories when Mum was having her 'bad' days. After he died, a head-on collision with a drunk driver, Mel and I had to pick up the slack. She's two years older than me. We look alike, people say; we both have long, brown hair, hazel eyes, high cheekbones and full lips. She's much prettier than me though, more rounded and soft-featured. My face is sharper, stringier, more serious.

There were moments when Mum *did* try, in the beginning. Encouraged by friends and neighbours, she bought groceries, washed clothes, cooked meals. Everyone said how well she was doing. But it didn't last. She started drinking and alcohol became her crutch. Pretty soon, she was only surfacing to go to the pub or the off licence around the corner. She barely ate and withdrew, bit by bit, deeper into her own world. I tipped bottles of cheap gin and vodka down the sink when I found them. She became sneakier and kept the bottles hidden in her room.

'It's her way of coping,' Mel said. 'Leave her to it.' It was alright for her. She had a boyfriend in tow by that point and was rarely at home. I can't say I blamed her but that left me alone to deal with everything. It was rough but I coped. I didn't tell a soul what my life was like, not even Kaz. I still felt a duty to protect Mum, like Dad would've done. It wasn't really her fault, I knew that. It was an illness. Things became even worse when Mel got in with a bad crowd and started skipping school. I was worried sick. Talking to her was hopeless – she was never going to listen to her kid sister – and I didn't know what to do.

Then, Mum brought Andrian home after a night at the pub. She was completely out of it and I cringed at the way she threw herself at him. It wasn't the first time she'd brought a man home since Dad died. There had been a succession of them, staying the night, leering at Mel and me as they headed off in the morning. This time was different though. Andrian was polite and respectful, both towards her and us. He asked for our help putting her to bed and left with a promise to call in and check on her the next day. We laughed after he'd gone. 'Yeah, right,' Mel sneered. First thing next morning, he knocked on the door, went upstairs to see Mum and, miraculously, brought her back downstairs with him 'to see us off to school'. It wasn't long before he moved in and took over shopping, cooking and cleaning duties. It was a weight off my shoulders. For a while, Mum seemed brighter and, more importantly as far as I was concerned, Mel ditched her lowlife friends and got back on track.

Andrian repeatedly asked Mum to marry him but she refused to consider it. For the life of me, I couldn't understand why. The man was charming, handsome, cared for her ... but she remained adamant. 'Once was enough,' was all she'd say. I could see Andrian was annoyed but he did his best to hide it. Each time she turned him down, he took her hand and murmured, 'I understand, my love, but you will have to forgive me when I refuse to take no for an answer.'

After the third refusal, though, things went downhill. Andrian started making excuses for Mum and we saw her less and less. The two of them rarely went out in the evening anymore and Andrian would disappear on his own. With increasing frequency, Mum refused to get up at all. Mel and I both tried to cajole her from her room but she turned away and pulled the covers over her head, shutting us out. At the time, I felt grateful that Andrian was looking after her, in spite of everything. I never realised the truth.

The train slowing shakes me from my reverie. Diss station. People crowd on the platform and, as we grind to a halt, I watch them peering into the carriages, searching for empty seats. Several make a beeline for my carriage but the little girl is wailing once more and most head straight through. A young couple are last on. They glance hopefully in the direction of the other passengers and then resign themselves to taking the seat in front of me. I brace myself to expect company by the next stop.

The train lurches forward and I find my eyes closing, lulled by the rhythmic rocking of its motion. In my mind, I see Andrian: tall, dark, early forties, coal-black eyes, a charming smile, always dressed in a t-shirt, jeans and a black, leather jacket. He arrived in Britain seven years ago. When I asked him why he'd left Bulgaria, the country of his birth, he answered, 'For a better life of course. Isn't that what we are all striving for, every day?' He spoke excellent English, albeit with a strong accent, and I admired him. I honestly couldn't see what he was doing, hanging about with my Mum, and asked Mel what she thought. She just shrugged. 'No accounting for taste. Maybe he likes having sex with unconscious women.'

'Ugh, that's horrible!' I shuddered. Mel liked to shock me. When she was fifteen, she revealed a stash of fruit-flavoured condoms she kept in her bag. 'Strawberry are the best,' she informed me.

I'd paid attention in Sex Education lessons but was only thirteen and pretty innocent when it came to sex. 'Why do they have flavours?' I asked. 'Why would it matter what they taste like?'

She winked and licked her lips. 'You think about it.'

It took a while and, when realisation dawned, my eyes widened in disgust. 'Ugh, that's gross!'

She just laughed. 'You're such a baby.'

Mel was always a flirt. She even batted her eyes at Andrian but he dealt with it with detached amusement. That, and everything else, meant I pretty much hero-worshipped him by then. 'He's a decent guy,' I said to Kaz when I finally told her about the addition to our household.

'Is he an illegal immigrant?' she asked.

'Of course not,' I responded in heated defence.

'Well, what does he do exactly?'

'He's a businessman.' In truth, I wasn't exactly clear about the nature of his business. He did tell me but I zoned out as he described different machinery components and their uses. Technical stuff was never my thing.

'Mmm. Sounds a bit fishy to me.'

'You're such a racist,' I declared hotly and turned my back on her, refusing to talk until she apologised at lunchtime. In my eyes, Andrian was our saviour and I wouldn't tolerate anything negative said about him.

After Mel completed her GSCEs, she stayed on at sixth form, but her heart wasn't in it and she suddenly announced that she wanted to go out to work. 'I hate school,' she said one night, a few months ago. 'There's no way I want to stay on and do boring A levels. Life is for living and I want to start. I don't want to stay around here a minute longer than I have to.'

Although I suspected it was coming, my heart plummeted at the thought of Mel leaving for good. 'Can't you get a job in Norwich?' I pleaded.

She regarded me with lofty scorn. 'Norwich doesn't have what I want. I'm going to London.'

'To do what?' I argued. 'Sleep on the streets?'

'Don't be daft. You're such a drama queen. I'll get a job before I go. Andrian has some contacts in London, don't you?' She turned to Andrian, eagerness shining in her eyes.

He nodded. 'A few,' he acknowledged. He gave her a slow smile. 'I think I know something which might be suitable.'

She responded by throwing herself into his arms. 'Oh thanks, Andrian. I knew I could count on you.'

'I'm not promising anything ...'

'I know, I know. Ooh, this is so exciting!' She danced around the dingy space which was our front room, pulling me to my feet and spinning me around. 'Isn't it great, Sass?'

Her enthusiasm was infectious and, stifling my own reservations, I grinned at her as she twirled and almost fell over a wooden side table. 'But what about me?' I wanted to say. 'Please don't leave me behind.' The words remained unspoken.

Andrian came through. A colleague of his was prepared to offer Mel an apprenticeship position as a PA, working for a small company called Veronik

Holdings. The employment package Andrian described seemed very generous and it seemed odd that they didn't want to interview her. It bothered me even more when a sneaky internet search at school found no results for a company called Veronik Holdings. I spoke to Andrian about my concerns.

'Ah, little mother hen.' Andrian smiled at me, an affectionate gleam in his eyes. 'It is good you look out for your sister but you need not to worry. All is taken care of. My recommendation is enough for Stan; we are like brothers.' He clenched his fist to his heart. 'He will expect Mel to work hard for her pay and, if she is not good enough, he will get rid of her. As for the computer thing ... pff!' He wrinkled his nose in disdain. 'Not everyone runs their business via the internet.'

'Yes but ...'

'Oh Sass, enough! I'm going and that's that. Why can't you be happy for me?' Mel exclaimed.

I gave up. 'I *am* happy for you.' I clasped my sister to me in a fierce hug. 'I really hope it all works out.'

'It will.' She pulled away with a confident smile. 'I'll make it work.'

That was two months ago. Three days later, she left home. I haven't heard from her since.

CHAPTER 6

Todd

It was four days before Todd returned to the report of the missing girl. On Friday night, he attended a retirement party for one of the partners at his law firm and the weekend, as usual, was spent with Charlotte – a trip to Banham Zoo on Saturday and swimming on the Sunday before delivering her back home in the evening. Alone once more, he watched a film, ate pizza and downed a few beers. His flat always felt quiet and empty after Charlotte had gone home, like the sparkle had fallen from his world.

By Monday night, though, he was motivated and keen to get back to his research. During the day, thoughts of the photo, and Miss Nichol, teased around the edges of his consciousness. They couldn't be the same person but he was intrigued nonetheless. He found the news story and his eyes travelled straight down to the picture at the bottom of the page. It was a grainy image of a young girl with long, dark hair and high cheekbones. It was frustrating that her head was turned slightly away but the hint of a mischievous smile playing on her lips was just visible. That mouth and the shape of the face were just as he remembered Miss Nichol. It was uncanny. The eyes too. But this woman was dark-haired. Otherwise, he could almost have thought it *was* her. He scrolled back and read the brief story with renewed interest.

The report was dated April 2nd, 2003, and bore the headline 'Norwich Girl Still Missing'. A seventeen-year-old girl had travelled to London, lured by the promise of opportunities in the big city. No surprise there. So many of the stories he'd read of missing people started in the same way. The girl had

34

received a job offer which turned out to be bogus. Police were still looking for a man of Eastern European descent, thought to be involved in her disappearance. There was further heartbreak. The girl's father had been killed in a road accident a few years earlier and the mother had later taken an overdose, leaving one remaining child, a fifteen-year-old girl. Todd leant back in his chair, touched by the weight of the family's tragedy. He wondered what had happened to the younger sister. How did anyone manage to cope with such devastation in their young life? The missing sister was never found or the story would not be there on this website of unsolved cases and he wondered anew what might have happened to her. The man who disappeared at the same time must have been involved. Sex trafficking, most likely. Not something he wanted to use in his novel. The idea of adopting an Eastern European as his antagonist had appeal, though. He scribbled notes, picturing a hard-faced, dark-haired man with cold eyes and a hawk-like nose. When he'd finished, he sat back and rubbed his eyes. Time to move on ... except the face of the girl in the photo tugged once more at his attention, just as Charlotte's teacher did. They weren't the same person ... they couldn't be ... and yet ...

Firmly, he flicked to the next story on the website. So many missing people out there. This research was tough, affecting him emotionally, pulling him all out of kilter. With a snort, he closed the website and leaned back into his chair. Perhaps, he should leave it. He had masses of notes; his time would be better spent going back through them and plotting the storyline for his next book. He was letting his imagination run away with him; it was time it was more gainfully employed.

***

The pub was heaving. It was Friday night and, as usual, Todd was out with his mates, Lee and Joe. He was wedged in a corner by the bar, drinking beer, celebrating the fact that he was a single man once more. His divorce had become final that morning. Lee, who'd been married for five years, was regarding him with a degree of envy, which bothered him. He really liked Lee's wife, Callie, a lively Geordie whom Lee had met when studying engineering at university in Newcastle, but there were tell-tale signs that the relationship was strained.

'This one will have to be my last,' Lee moaned, pulling a face as he indicated the pint glass sitting on the bar. 'I'm under orders. Home by eight. You don't know how lucky you are, mate. Free as a bird, able to come and go as you please.' He took a long swig of his beer and scowled. 'It's getting so I have to have special permission to be allowed out!'

'Come on, Lee. It's not that bad. Callie's a great girl,' Todd responded. 'And it must be tough for her at the moment, with the kids and everything.' They had three children aged seven and under and Callie had recently been made redundant from her job as a teaching assistant.

'Yeah, mate,' Joe chipped in. 'Things will get better when she finds another job. I know Liv said she was finding it pretty tough being at home with the kids all day.'

Lee snorted. 'Maybe.' He stared morosely at his friends. 'But I've spent every bloody evening this week in with her, watching the box. I bet Liv hasn't given you a time limit on your night out, Joe!'

'Well, no,' Joe replied, 'but, in fairness, she's out with work mates herself.'

'And they don't have kids yet,' Todd added.

'Take my advice, mate – don't!' Lee slammed his glass back down, causing liquid to spill over the sides and dribble onto the beer mat. 'Women change when they have kids. Look at Reggie!'

'I don't think that was anything to do with having Charlotte.' Todd smiled at his friend. 'Come on, mate. Cheer up.'

'Yeah, we're meant to be celebrating with Todd, not dragging him down with tales of our sad, married lives.' Joe's grin belied his words. He and Olivia had been married less than a year and were completely smitten with each other.

'Fair enough.' Lee grimaced and allowed his glance to sweep the throng squashed into the bar area. 'We should be looking for his next shag. The boy can't seem to manage on his own. Hey, clock that lot, the ones who've just come in.'

Todd shook his head. 'Not interested, I told you ... at least, not for that kind of thing ... not anymore.'

'You've gone soft, mate.' Lee was still looking in the direction of the doorway. 'I would if I had half a chance!'

'Not if they see you first,' Joe joked. He turned to view the women who had just entered and nodded. 'Not bad, I'll give you that, especially the blonde.'

'Trust you to pick the blonde,' Lee retorted. 'I'll take the dark one. That leaves you the one in the purple top.' He nudged Todd to look. 'Although, you lucky fucker, you get the choice of all three! I tell you, the sooner I get divorced the better.'

'You don't mean that,' Todd insisted, frowning as Lee downed the rest of his beer.

'Maybe ... maybe not. If things carry on as they are ...'

'Why don't you pick up some flowers on your way home?' Joe suggested, giving him a nudge. 'Guaranteed to warm up the chilliest of wives. A night of passion could be yours.'

'Yeah, right! Not with Teddy still sleeping in our bed!' Teddy was his youngest child.

Joe shrugged. 'Sorry mate. I've given it my best shot.' He grinned. 'Always works for me.'

'Yeah, well, you're a lucky sod and you haven't got kids. Things will change when you do,' Lee muttered darkly. 'Right, I'll be off. Better not be late. See you next week.'

Todd shook his head and turned back to his beer. 'Poor Lee,' he said to Joe. 'And poor Callie.'

'They'll get through it.' Joe was bored of the subject. 'Big game for the Blues tomorrow.'

The conversation turned to football and the current woes of Ipswich Town. Joe was a lifelong fan and season ticket holder.

'Oops, I'm so sorry!' Someone cannoned into Todd's arm just as he raised his glass. Beer splashed the front of his pale, blue shirt. 'I got pushed from behind. Oh no, you've spilled your drink. Let me get you another one.'

Joe smirked as Todd mopped the damp patch with a tissue. 'A way to get your attention,' he muttered under his breath. 'Make it work for you, mate.'

The woman's voice was low, melodious and strangely familiar. As Todd turned, he realised where he'd heard it before. 'Miss Nichol,' he said, gaping as the woman of his recent dreams materialised beside him.

'Oh.' She screwed up her face and then her brow cleared. 'You're Charlotte's dad. As I said, I'm really sorry about bumping into you like that. Let me get you another drink.'

'That's fine. It was just a drop.'

'Are you sure?' She regarded the wet splodge on his chest doubtfully and he took a deep breath. She was beautiful. Tonight, she was wearing jeans and a long, silky, midnight blue shirt, her blonde hair cascading in silken waves around her shoulders. He couldn't help noticing the curve of her breasts beneath the shirt and found himself becoming flustered.

'Look, let me get *you* a drink,' he said. 'You deserve it – doing such a great job with my daughter.'

Her face relaxed a little and she smiled, although her eyes remained wary. 'Thanks, but I'm getting a round in. I'm here with my friends.' She indicated two women chatting near the doorway. 'We were hoping to get a table but ...' She shrugged.

'Yeah, it's rammed in here tonight. No room to swing a cat. Not that I ever do, that is. Swing a cat, I mean.' What on earth was he saying? Where was the witty repartee for which he was renowned? Such lame conversation would hardly impress her! And, he realised, he did want to impress her. Very much.

She shot him an amused look. 'Glad to hear it! Well, it was nice seeing you again, Mr Matheson.'

She was turning away. He needed to do something quickly. 'Todd,' he said. 'My name's Todd.'

'OK, Todd.' She turned back and favoured him with a polite smile.

'Hey, Lily, can you get me the Bombay gin, not Gordons?' The dark-haired friend was calling across the room.

'OK.'

'Lily,' he repeated. 'That's a lovely name.' Just like you, he thought. He managed to avoid saying the words aloud.

'Mm.' She was clearly losing interest and the guy behind the bar was hovering, waiting for her order.

'Look,' he jumped in before he could change his mind. 'It's great seeing you out of school. I was wondering if you'd let me take you out for a drink sometime.'

Her expression hardened. 'Sorry, but I don't think so.'

'Oh, fair enough.' He tried to hide his disappointment. Doubtless, she was seeing someone already. Smiling ruefully, he said, 'I hope you don't mind me asking.'

'I don't date married men.'

'Oh but ...' His voice tailed off. She was already giving her order to the barman. He turned back to Joe who was checking his phone.

'Any luck, mate?' Joe's voice was quite loud and he could feel the woman behind him bristling. She'd heard; he could tell. He shot his friend an annoyed look and waited for her to complete her order so he could clear up her misapprehension.

'Listen,' he said, when the bartender moved away to fetch her drinks. God, his voice sounded desperate. 'Reggie and I, we're not married.'

She raised her eyebrows. 'Oh yes? Well, that makes it alright then.'

He missed the dry edge to her voice. 'Good. So, you'll let me take you out for a drink?'

'Sorry ... *mate*.' She shot him a look, eloquent with disapproval. 'But you're out of *luck*.'

The bartender was back with the drinks and she paid with the card she was holding ready in her hand. Her fingers were long, he noticed, and elegant.

'Look,' he said. 'We seem to have got off on the wrong foot. I'm Todd, newly divorced.' He held out his hand but she'd already picked up two of the glasses and was heading back to her friends. The remaining drink sat on the bar and he hesitated for only a second before picking it up and following her.

'Your drink,' he said as she spun back towards him.

'Thanks, Mr Matheson.' She took it and turned her back on him. Her friends regarded him curiously as he continued to stand there.

'Right, well, I'll see you around ... Lily.' He sloped back to the bar where Joe was watching with an amused expression.

'Bad luck, mate. Struck out there, didn't you? Still, the one in the purple top looked interested.'

He shrugged and picked up his beer. 'I knew her, that's all,' he said by way of explanation. 'I thought it would be nice to go out for a drink with her.'

'See, that's where you went wrong. A woman like that must be used to being taken to fancy restaurants. For my first date with Liv, I organised a champagne picnic. Women like the personal touch ... and you're out of touch. You need to up your game.'

'I'll bear your advice in mind,' Todd replied wryly.

'Trust me. Women love it.'

'OK. Now, can we change the subject?'

Over the next two hours, they drank more beer, swapped jokes on each other's phones and chatted about sport, money and cars, but Todd couldn't relax. The frustration of that conversation with Lily Nichol refused to abate. She'd got the wrong impression of him and that was irritating. More than that, he realised, it was a serious blow to the hopes and dreams he'd been secretly harbouring about her since they first met. While he plotted how to put things right, his glance flicked frequently across to where she stood by the door. He was so aware of her it was impossible to concentrate on anything else. An invisible thread of electricity fizzed between them and he sensed she felt it too, by the tense set of her shoulders and by the way she studiously avoided looking in his direction. Of course, he could just be kidding himself ...

She left before he could think of anything to rescue the situation. He clocked the exact moment she turned and his eyes locked briefly with hers. When he gave her an apologetic smile, she pretended not to notice, snatching up her bag and leading the way out of the pub. He turned back to Joe feeling utterly deflated.

'Sorry, mate. You really liked her, didn't you,' his friend said, following his gaze.

'Yeah. Oh well ...'

It wasn't to be. A guy had to be philosophical about these things. Knockbacks happen. But they weren't usually accompanied by such a bewildering sense of loss. That was a first for Todd and he knew Lily Nichol would fill his dreams for some time to come.

CHAPTER 7

Saskia
2003

10:56 a.m. Right on time, we arrive at Liverpool Street station. I'm in no rush to get off the train. I wait while other passengers scramble to their feet as it crawls to a standstill. A wave of trepidation leaves me reluctant to embark on the next phase of my mission. I'm terrified of what I might find. In my pocket, I have a scrap of paper with Mel's address: *White House, 143, Midmoor Road, London, SW19 4JD.* This is where Mel is staying – at least, that's what Andrian said. I believed him at the time; now, I'm not so sure.

With my backpack slung over my shoulder, I step off the train and cross the platform, my eyes scanning the row of shops beyond the barrier. I have no idea where Midmoor Road is, so I purchase a street map of London from a small kiosk. Then, I head for one of the cafes to study it over a cup of tea. I tease myself with the idea of a hot chocolate but baulk at the greater expense.

It's with some relief that I locate the road on the map, some way south west of Liverpool Street. I'd begun to wonder if it actually existed. My next step is to work out the easiest and cheapest route. That takes a while; it isn't something I've ever done before. I sip my sugary tea, poring over the map, oblivious to people bustling past. With the decision made – a short walk to Moorgate, take the Northern Line to Balham and then walk approximately one mile to Midmoor Road – I reach for biscuits from my bag to appease my growling stomach. The man on the adjacent table is devouring a toastie oozing with cheese. I'm sorely tempted to buy one myself but know I can't afford to waste my cash. Until I find Mel, my future is very uncertain.

I drain the last of the tea, now cold, and head for the station exit, map in hand. There are so many people, swarming like ants through the main concourse, and I feel small and insignificant amongst them. The streets too are busy and I thread my way along the pavement, often stopping to consult my map. I soon realise I should step to one side if I need to check my stride after a large man in a brown overcoat cannons into the back of me with a muttered expletive. 'Sorry,' I mumble although, technically, he had bumped into me. It's all very intimidating.

I find Moorgate station and buy a ticket at the desk there. I don't feel confident enough to use one of the machines. The attendant takes my money and pushes the ticket back without speaking or making eye contact. The brief interaction feels soulless.

The Northern line runs from platforms 7 and 8 which, I soon discover, are located in a deep-level section of the station. The southbound trains are running from Platform 8 and I can hear the rumbling of a train approaching as I head towards it. The seats are all taken and I take up a position where I can hold onto a rail. Looking at the map on the side of the train, I count eleven stops until I reach my destination. More people crowd onto the train when we reach Bank, and I'm crammed between a young girl in jeans reading a copy of *War & Peace* and a sweaty, middle aged man carrying a briefcase which repeatedly bumps my leg. After that, though, more passengers exit than embark and, by the time we reach Elephant & Castle, I'm able to sit down. Seven more stops.

My mind drifts once again to my sister. When she left, I didn't expect to hear from her straight away. She and I have always been close but less so in recent years. Since I acquired my phone, she only ever texted me when it was necessary and I knew she'd be too caught up in her new life to spare me a second thought. After a week, I sent her a text, just to say I hoped it was all going well. She didn't reply. More texts followed but I received none in return. At this point, I was pretty pissed off. 'Sod her,' I thought, 'if she can't even be arsed to send me a quick message.' Another week passed and I discussed it with Kaz.

'It's too easy to ignore a text,' she advised. 'Ring her. She's obviously busy but you're bound to catch her eventually.'

I tried, several times. The line was dead. Every time I tried. My irritation and annoyance morphed into a tiny nugget of concern. *Was she OK?*

I asked Andrian to help me contact her. He pulled a face and reached for his phone. 'I'm sure there is nothing to worry about little one,' he smiled. 'I will phone my friend Stan ... check all is well with your sister.' I watched anxiously as he held the phone to his ear and he gave me a wink of reassurance. Then, he returned the phone to his pocket. 'He is not answering. He is busy man. Please don't worry, Saskia. You know what your sister is like. She is fine, I'm sure.'

'Will you try again later, please Andrian?' I asked.

'Of course.' He picked up his leather jacket. 'Now I go out. Your mother is sleeping. I will see you tomorrow.'

The next evening, he said he'd spoken to Stan and that Mel was doing very well in her new job. Apparently, her phone was broken so she'd not been able to call. I was hugely reassured. That sounded like Mel. 'I'll write to her,' I said. 'Could you find out her address for me please?'

He sighed. 'Do you think she will bother to write back?'

'Probably not, but, if her phone is broken, she might've forgotten my number. I want to remind her of that and catch her up with news at home. It would make me feel better.'

He raised his eyebrows doubtfully but nodded. 'For you, I will find out where she lives.'

It took a couple of days and more nagging. As soon as I had the address, I rattled off a letter, trying hard to refrain from recriminations and asking lots of questions about her life in London. I even splashed out on a first-class stamp. Still, I heard nothing. Despite Andrian's explanation, I felt uneasy. But it was the phone call I overheard three days ago which catapulted my disquiet into panic overdrive ...

The tube train arrives at Balham. My stomach is knotting as I venture out onto the street. *Please let me find her.* I glance at my watch. 1:17 p.m. Plenty of time before it starts to get dark. I look around to get my bearings. The road is lined with tall buildings and cars stream past. I head east along Fernlea Road, checking my map constantly. I don't want to get lost. Emmanuel Road is next, followed by a left into Haverhill Road. I'm in a residential area now – terraces of red-bricked houses with white-framed, sash windows and parked cars. My heart skips as I turn right into Midmoor Road. On my left, the first house is number 26; to my right, number 28. I walk the length of the street until I reach Radbourne Road. The last house on the left is numbered 116 and on my right it's number 79. My chest constricts with the knowledge. There is no number 143. I fumble in my pocket for the piece of paper and check. *White House, 143, Midmoor Road, London, SW19 4JD.* The address I remembered is correct but doesn't exist. I turn around and walk back, nerveless fingers still clutching the map, my mind trying to numb out the dread.

I continue along into Haverhill Road where I'd noticed a guest house painted white. It isn't number 143 but there is a sign outside, advertising it as *White House Bed & Breakfast*. It's a possibility. Pausing uncertainly outside it, I check my map for the umpteenth time in the vain hope that I've missed something.

A woman with a small dog walks past and then stops. 'Can I help you, love?' she asks. She has spiky, pink hair and kind eyes.

I turn to face her. 'I'm looking for the White House, Midmoor Road but I can't seem to find it.'

'This is Haverhill Road, love.' She frowns. 'That's the only White House around here.' She gestures to the guest house. 'There isn't one on Midmoor Road. Are you sure the address is right?'

I hand her the piece of paper, hoping that somehow this woman will see something I've missed. She'll exclaim and say, 'Oh, *that* White House! It's just around the corner on the left,' or something like that. She doesn't. Instead, she gives me back the piece of paper and shakes her head. 'Sorry, love. Think you must have written the address down wrong. No such place.'

I smile back although I'm dying inside. 'You're probably right. Thank you anyway.'

She moves away and I shuffle forwards in the opposite direction. I have absolutely no idea what I'm going to do next. The air is growing colder and the sky is darkening. I need somewhere to stay. My steps slow as a plan begins to formulate in my mind. I stop and turn. I'll go back to the White House and ask if they have a vacancy. Hope suddenly blossoms in my chest.

Maybe Mel *is* staying there; it's the name of the road which is the mistake. That has to be it. I almost laugh out loud at my foolishness. Why hadn't I thought of that before?

I retrace my steps with renewed determination, refusing to let the lurking doubts creep back. I'm going to find my sister and warn her of the danger she might be in.

There are two steps leading up to the dark blue, front door and a bell to the right of it. A 'Vacancies' sign is hanging in the left-hand window so at least I'll be able to stay here overnight. The door is opened by a young woman with black dreadlocks and a wide smile. She notices my backpack and beckons me inside.

'Come in, come in.' She has a Caribbean accent. 'Are you looking for a room?' I nod. 'You've come to the right place.'

I step into a narrow hallway with a staircase opposite. Inside, it's warm and welcoming, with bright, vibrant, patterned wallpaper and a spotlessly clean, tiled floor. The woman leads me towards a small reception desk and opens a book. 'Name, please.'

'Saskia Potter.'

I search her face for a sign of recognition, waiting for her to look at me and say, 'Are you related to Mel Potter? She's staying with us too.'

She does no such thing. Instead, she asks me how many nights I plan to stay and tells me that the cost is £30 for a single room and £40 for a double.

'The single, please. Just one night.' I wriggle out of my backpack and find my purse.

'And will you be wanting an evening meal too? That will be another £5.'

The hallway is filled with the aroma of something spicy and my stomach rumbles at the thought.

'Yes please,' I say, handing over the cash. I clear my throat. 'I was wondering if my sister was staying here. Her name is Mel ... Mel Potter ... '

The woman looks at me curiously. 'No. I'm sorry. There's no-one else staying here at the moment and there's been no-one called Mel for as long as I can remember. Did she tell you she was staying here?'

'I thought so ... but I must've got it wrong. Sorry.'

'No problem, as long as you still want to stay?' At my nod of assent, she continues, 'Well, let's show you to your room. It's this way.'

I'm led up the stairs and through a door on the right. 'The guest rooms are this way. There are three. This is your room.' She unlocks the first door on the left and stands back to let me enter. It's much larger than I expected and then I realise that the bed is a double.'

'I only paid for a single ...'

'I know.' The woman smiles at my confusion. 'But, as I said, we have no-one else staying at the moment so you might as well have the nicest room. This one has its own shower room too.' She opens another door to show me. 'Although, if you want a bath, you'll have to use the bathroom. It's the next room on the left.'

'Thank you.' The woman's kindness touches my heart and I feel a little overwhelmed.

'You're welcome.' If she's noticed my fragile, emotional state, she doesn't let it show. 'It's a bit cold in here at the moment but I'll switch the radiator on and it'll soon warm up. You make yourself at home and feel free to come downstairs if you want some company. I'll be in the kitchen. There's only me here tonight. My husband works away during the week so it's nice to have someone to talk to. I'm Alisha, by the way.' She holds out her hand. 'Alisha Wainwright. Happy to meet you, Saskia Potter.'

'You too.' I shake her hand and manage a weak smile. 'Whatever you're cooking smells delicious. I'm starving.'

'Caribbean chicken stew,' Alisha grins. 'I hope you like your food hot and spicy. If not, I can make you something else.'

'The stew sounds great. Thank you,' I say again.

'No worries. Shout if you need anything.'

Alisha leaves and the room, drained of her presence, feels empty. She's humming to herself as she skips back down the stairs. I slump onto the bed with a loud sigh. The disappointment at my failure to find Mel here is crushing and a lump burns the back of my throat. I stand again in an effort to thwart the tide of emotion rolling in on me. A tea tray is perched on the chest of drawers and I fill the kettle from the tap in the shower room. Beside a small bowl of sugar, tea and coffee sachets, I discover a pack of two digestive biscuits, wrapped in cellophane, and I devour them before the kettle boils. The room is beautiful. The walls are painted white but hung with an array of colourful Jamaican prints. In the en-suite shower room, the towels are thick and fluffy. The room is slowly warming up and the hot, sugary tea helps to restore some of my natural optimism. I won't let myself think that something bad has happened to Mel. I can't. But, despite my best efforts to shut it out, the phone conversation I overheard three days ago worms its way back into mind ...

I'd left school early with a migraine and was lying on my bed, curtains drawn, eyes closed, when Andrian entered the house. He came upstairs and the door to his and Mum's bedroom opened. I heard him mutter something under his breath. It sounded like, 'Stupid slut,' but I couldn't be certain. His phone buzzed and he stood outside my bedroom door to answer.

'Dimitri ...' he said. He listened for a while before replying in Bulgarian. I could tell he was angry. One of the words he kept repeating sounded like 'police'. There was a pause and I heard the name 'Stan'. Another pause. He was waiting, presumably for Stan to come on the line. I lay like a statue, instinctively aware that he would be furious if he knew I was listening. Then he spoke, clearly and succinctly, in English. There was menace in his tone. 'Stan, if she's causing trouble, get rid of her ... no, I mean for good. I'll be down in a few days or so. Leave it until then ...' He lowered his voice and I strained to hear what he was saying. 'You know what to do. I'll sort things this end. It's time to move. The woman is no use to me and the younger sister is asking questions. I'll bring her with me.' His low chuckle and the mention of me made my heart freeze. 'Worth a fair bit, I'd say.'

He ended the call, cursing as he went downstairs. I remained motionless with shock, trying to process his words. *If she's causing trouble, get rid of her ...* Did he mean Mel? *The younger sister is asking questions. I'll bring her with me ... Worth a fair bit.* What did that mean? The urge to confront him was strong but I forced myself to stay in my room. He didn't know I'd overheard him. Best to keep it that way.

When I heard the front door slam, I sat up and reached for my phone to try Mel once more. More than ever, I needed to speak to her. But, of course, the line was dead. The migraine hammered at my temples and my bedroom walls whirled a dizzy dance. I sank back against the pillow, willing myself to feel better, trying to think what I should do ...

Every time I've mentally replayed that conversation since then, I've experienced the same nausea. The harsh voice and murderous intent were nothing like the Andrian I knew, the kind, charming, good-natured, affable man whom I adored. He'd become a different person. He *was* a different person; he'd been acting a part all the way along. Mel could be in danger. And me too. He was planning to take me with him to London. For what purpose? *Worth a fair bit.* I wouldn't let myself dwell on the implication behind his words.

Sometime that same night, I hatched my plan to travel to London to warn Mel. I had her address so I knew where to find her – or so I'd thought. My impulse was to go the very next day but I had no cash. It took two tense days before I was ready ... and here I am, no further forward. I feel exhausted at the hopelessness of it all. Lying back on the bed, I close my eyes, trying to decide what to do next ...

The next thing I know, someone is tapping at my door. 'Saskia?' It's Alisha.

With a start, I roll off the bed. 'Sorry, just coming.' A glance at my watch tells me it's almost 7:30 p.m. 'Sorry,' I say again as I open the door. 'I fell asleep.'

Alisha is looking worried. 'Oh, I'm so sorry for waking you,' she exclaims. 'I was just wondering about dinner ...'

'I'll be there in just a minute.'

'Great.' Alisha flashes me a smile. 'No rush. Come down when you're ready.'

I go in the shower room and splash water on my face. Looking in the mirror, I see that my skin is pasty and my make-up is smudged and blotchy. I look like a thirteen-year-old runaway. I wash it off and reapply some mascara and foundation, peering critically at my reflection. It's impossible to conceal the anxiety I feel and I now wish I hadn't chosen to eat with Alisha where I may have to face an interrogation. It'll be an ordeal I could've done without.

Giving myself a mental shake, I hurry downstairs. Alisha is hovering and leads me through to the dining room where two places are laid.

'I was going to eat with you but, if you'd prefer to eat alone ...'

'No, no, please do,' I reply instinctively, forgetting my wish from a moment ago.

'Good.' She looks pleased. 'Is water OK with your food? I do have wine ...' Again, she regards me doubtfully.

'Water's fine, thank you,' I respond. A jug is on the table and I pour myself a glass while she disappears into the kitchen. She returns with a basket of rolls and a dish of buttered rice. I help myself to a roll and slice it open. It is warm, freshly baked. A butter dish is on the table and I spread some on the roll before taking a bite. It's heavenly.

Alisha returns once more with two brimming plates. 'I thought you might be hungry. I certainly am,' she says as she sets the dishes down on the placemats.

We eat in silence to start with. The food is delicious and makes me feel so much better about everything. 'This is fantastic, Alisha. Thank you,' I say as I put my fork down and reach for my glass of water.

'Good. I'm glad you're enjoying it. It's nice to have someone to cook for.'

'Do you have many guests?'

'Not as many as I'd like. Things have been very slow since Christmas. I need to look into more advertising.'

We lapse once more into silence and I feel myself relax in Alisha's company. I'd been convinced I'd be subjected to questions as to why I was there. While I'd been in the shower room, I'd hurriedly prepared a cover story. I needn't have worried. In the end, it's me asking the questions. I discover that Alisha has been married for four years and has lived in London all her life. Her parents both come from Jamaica and she's hoping to holiday there later this year, visiting relatives. She works from home, proofreading technical manuals, as well as running the B & B. Her husband, Curtis, is a salesman for a national cleaning company and away, out on the road, for much of the working week.

'Did you manage to get in touch with your sister, find out where she is?' she asks suddenly.

'No.' I frown. 'Are there any other B & Bs in the area? It's so annoying. I'd hoped to catch up with her while I was in London but I must have written her address down wrong. She's not answering her phone either so I can't get hold of her that way.'

'There's one in Wandsworth and a couple in Clapham, to my knowledge, but there must be more. Are you sure she's staying in a B & B?'

'No. That's the trouble. I just had her address as The White House, Midmoor Road but that doesn't exist.'

Alisha begins to clear the plates and I stand to help her. 'No, no,' she protests. 'You shouldn't do that. You're a paying guest. Sit down and I'll fetch dessert.'

'I'd like to help,' I insist. 'You've been very kind and I'd like to repay the favour.'

We take all the dishes through to the small kitchen. Alisha pulls a cake from the oven, her expression apologetic. 'I'm afraid it's just a ginger cake,' she says, 'but it's good warm with some ice cream.'

'Sounds delicious,' I assure her. 'It's a real treat to have dessert.'

As we carry bowls through to the dining room, Alisha asks, 'Do you know where your sister works in London? That would be a way of finding her.'

I nod, filled with a rush of hope. I hadn't thought of that. 'Veronik Holdings. That's a great idea. The trouble is I don't have an address.'

'We could use the Yellow Pages,' she suggests. 'I'll have a look later.'

The cake is tasty and I feel fuller than I have in a very long while. Once again, I help Alisha clear the table but she refuses point blank to let me assist with washing up. 'If you did that, I'd have to give you a refund,' she argues. 'You go and sit down in the lounge. Help yourself to the TV or there are some magazines in there. I'll soon get this sorted.'

I do as she's directed. After my nap earlier, I feel wide awake and am itching to see if Veronik Holdings is listed in the Yellow Pages. While I wait for Alisha to join me, I flick through a copy of Good Housekeeping, which doesn't interest me at all, and then find, at the bottom of the pile, a tattered edition of Cosmopolitan from August 2002 with Sarah Michelle Geller on the cover. I'm soon engrossed in an article entitled '30 Seductive Lines to Use on a Guy'. I can't imagine myself using any of the suggestions on Darrell Parkinson but it's fun trying to picture his face if I did.

Alisha returns carrying three copies of the Yellow Pages. 'There you go,' she says, handing them over. 'Fingers crossed. I'll be back in a min.'

Eagerly, I discard the magazine and turn the pages of the first one. Nothing for Veronik Holdings. It's the 1999 edition so maybe it's too out of date. I find the most recent, from 2002. No Veronik Holdings. My spirits falling fast, I turn to the last one. It was printed in 1996 so I'm not holding out much hope. Sure enough, it isn't there.

'No luck?' Alisha can see the despondency on my face when she returns. I shake my head. 'I have a computer upstairs. I could try searching for you.'

'Thanks, but I tried that at school.' Damn. As soon as the words leave my lips, I know I've made a mistake. 'I mean at Sixth Form,' I bluster. 'I tried looking when I knew Mel was going to work for them.' I can feel the heat in my face and Alisha is studying me intently as I collect up the Yellow Pages. 'Thanks anyway. Actually, I think I'll go up now if you don't mind.'

'Not at all. What time would you like breakfast?'

'Er ... seven thirty?'

'Of course. I'll see you then. Sleep well.'

'Thanks Alisha.'

I trudge up the stairs. knowing sleep will be a long time coming and praying for a miracle to help me find my sister. The way things have been going, that's what I'm going to need.

'Mel, where are you?' I whisper into the darkness of my room. But I hear only the wind, hissing and moaning at my window. There are no answers to my question.

CHAPTER 8

Todd

Weeks passed. Work was boring, routine stuff but Todd came alive in the evenings, working on his novel. His next crime thriller was slowly taking shape. He'd given the victim a younger version of the face of the missing girl – the one who resembled Lily Nichol. After that embarrassing pub meeting, he'd not seen her at all so there had been no opportunity to set things between them on a more even keel. His pride refused to allow him to seek her out so the experience had festered, like an unhealed wound, making it impossible for him to drive the woman from his mind. In the end, he decided to go to the other extreme. He would turn her into a character, give her a secret life no-one knew anything about, and then kill her off. It seemed as good a way as any of exorcising her from his dreams. He was going to be ruthless about it ... except he hadn't completely decided whether or not she would die in the end. Despite everything his rational mind was telling him, he couldn't quite contemplate finishing her off completely.

It was Friday, past four o'clock and he was in the process of completing some paperwork on a business sale. The business belonged to an old school friend and he'd taken it on as a personal favour. He wished he hadn't. The sale had been complex and fraught with problems. When the phone rang on his desk, it was an additional irritation. Carly, on reception, should know better than to put calls through to him at this time of day on a Friday.

'Yes, Carly?' His tone was curt.

'I'm really sorry, Todd, but there's a Miss Nichol wanting to speak to you from Charlotte's school. Is it OK to put her through?'

'Of course.' His heart leapt. *Miss Nichol.* Clearly, the ridiculous crush he had on her was still alive and kicking, judging by the adrenalin racing through his body as he waited to hear her voice. Then, as he pondered the reason for her call, alarm seized his chest. *Had something happened to Charlotte?*

'Miss Nichol?'

'Yes, hello. I'm sorry to bother you at work.'

'That's OK. Is something wrong?' Ridiculous question. Of course, something was wrong! Why else would she be ringing?

'Not really ... Charlotte's fine ...' He exhaled loudly, relief flooding through him. 'I've been trying to ring your wife but she's been unavailable and I need to talk to you about something Charlotte disclosed today ...'

'Disclosed?' he asked, anxiety sharpening his tone.

'I wondered if you could come in to discuss it?'

'What, now?'

'If that's possible?'

'Of course, I'll come straight away.'

'Thank you.'

He put down the phone and grabbed his jacket. Charlotte had *disclosed* something. His mind scrambled at possibilities as he headed down to the car park and slid behind the wheel of his Golf. It had to be something serious: neglect, bullying ... *Oh God, please not something sexual.* Once that idea had taken hold, he couldn't shake it off and, by the time he arrived at the school entrance, he'd convinced himself that Reggie's partner, Nick, was a paedophile.

'Thank you for coming so quickly.' Lily Nichol ushered him into her classroom and shut the door behind her. 'Please take a seat.'

He swallowed his panic down and did as she directed, unsuccessfully trying to detect clues as to the nature of the problem from her face. Her demeanour was calm and professional. She'd given him a smile on his arrival, though. Surely it couldn't be anything serious?

She turned her hazel eyes towards him. 'I'm sorry to tell you this, Mr Matheson, but today Charlotte told me she's been taking things from other children in the class.'

'Taking things?' He hadn't imagined *that*. 'What? Surely you don't mean *stealing*?'

'Well ... yes ... although I'm sure Charlotte doesn't see it like that.'

He shook his head. 'There must be some mistake,' he argued. 'Charlotte would never steal anything. She knows it's wrong. She's so kind-hearted; she'd be more likely to give things away.'

Miss Nichol nodded in response. 'I know. It was a shock when she owned up.'

'She owned up?' He couldn't believe what he was hearing.

'Yes. Let me start at the beginning. We've had a number of personal items go missing – things which the children have brought in for different reasons. It started right at the beginning of the school year. The first was an apple. One child had bought in six apples on a paper plate for harvest. They were arranged – five around the outside and one in the middle – for our class display. The middle one went missing. We talked in class that it was wrong to take things, to steal, but we didn't want to make a big deal out of it. They're so young and we do have children coming into school who sometimes haven't had breakfast ...'

'I'm sure Charlotte always has breakfast ...' he protested hotly.

'Of course.' Her smile diffused his indignation. 'Anyway, after that, there were a number of things: a toy car from one child's collection; a stone which another child had painted; today, it was a signed copy of Michael Rosen's poems ... plus, I've noticed that small items from our class resources have also disappeared. As you can imagine, the parents of the children who have had things taken are angry. Today, once again, I told the children how serious it was and asked them, if they knew anything, to come and see me at breaktime.' She sighed and her eyes were full of sympathy. 'I'm afraid Charlotte stopped behind and told me she'd taken those things.'

Todd shook his head in disbelief. 'But that doesn't make any sense. Why?'

'Ah, well, that's where it all becomes a little unclear. She won't say. If she'd confessed to taking the items and then returned them, it would be easier to move on. We'd have informed you of the situation and tried to discover why she took them in the first place. Children do things like this for all sorts of reasons. As I said, they're very young. If they make mistakes, we always say that's OK and we try to put things right. But Charlotte told me she'd given the things to someone else so they couldn't be returned. She wouldn't tell me to whom she'd given them. And the parents want their children's belongings returned. I'm hoping you can help ...'

'Oh, I see ...' Todd didn't see at all but he thought he'd better say something reassuring. 'I'm sure we'll get to the bottom of this. Charlotte spends the weekend with me so I'll find out what's going on and speak to you first thing Monday morning. Her Mum and I are divorced,' he felt compelled to add.

'That would be great.' She stood to signal the conclusion of the meeting. 'Charlotte's a lovely girl. I'm sure, in her head, there's a perfectly reasonable explanation for all this.'

'I'm sure there must be,' he agreed. He stretched out his hand and registered the warmth of her skin against his. 'Thank you for letting me know.'

'Can I ask you to speak to her mum about it also?'

'Of course.' He gave her a confident smile. 'I'm sure, between us, we can clear up the mystery.'

He left the school feeling a whole lot better than he had when he'd driven there. Charlotte would tell him why she'd taken those things and he'd be able to explain everything to her teacher. Miss Nichol would be blown away by his sensitive and yet impressive handling of the situation and their relationship would develop from there ... He chuckled to himself. Maybe he was getting a little carried away. First things first, he would have a calm, reasonable, heart-to-heart with his daughter and find out what was going on.

***

'What do you mean, you took them because you wanted to? That's stealing, Charlotte! It's very serious. The school might have to tell the police.' Annoyance bubbled as his frustration grew. He'd been trying his best to be a cool dad but his daughter's obstinate refusal to tell him anything, beyond the fact that she'd taken the things and then given them away, was driving him crazy. Her pretty face was clenched in a mutinous expression, resistant to cajoling, pleading and now anger. They were sitting in a café eating chocolate ice-cream, her favourite, and he'd dangled the promise of swimming later when they'd 'got this school thing all sorted out' but she remained impervious to both bribery and threats. In hindsight, this was not the best place to broach the subject and he was all too aware of curious looks from other diners. Shovelling a spoonful of ice-cream into his mouth, he forced his shoulders to relax and clamped a lid on his irritation. Charlotte was so like him: dark, curly hair; brown eyes; the same stubborn set to her jaw when she didn't want to do something. He loved her unconditionally, would do anything for her, but, right at this moment, he wanted to shake the truth out of her.

'Never mind, sweetie. We'll talk about it later,' he ground out through gritted teeth. When we're alone, he thought. In the meantime, he needed to conjure up a fresh approach.

He still took her swimming, even though he was cross with her. She'd recently attained her 10m certificate from school and he couldn't wait to see her swim one whole width of the pool.

'Oh, I can swim further than that, Daddy!' she giggled and delighted in proving it to him, over and over.

Later, while he cooked fishfingers for their tea, he was still struggling to come up with a new plan of action when his attention was snagged by an animated film on the television. Charlotte was totally absorbed in the story which featured a family of puppies. Two of them were homed by a miserable, mean couple who kept them tethered outside and barely fed them. One day, they managed to escape. Roaming the streets, they were near to starving when the smell of sausages, cooling on a plate by an open window, attracted their attention.

'We can't just take them,' one of the puppies protested. 'That would be stealing.'

'Stuff that, I'm hungry,' said the other. He jumped through the window and wolfed down two of the sausages.

The other puppy scrambled through to join his brother. 'Oh, Barney, you shouldn't have done that!' he cried.

'What are you complaining about? I've left two for you.' Just at that moment, the window slammed behind them. The puppies were trapped.

'Quick, eat the sausages! We need to find a way out of here,' Barney urged. His brother, Buddy, shook his head. 'Oh well, suit yourself. I'll have them then.'

A shadow loomed behind them. 'Who's been eating my sausages?' a man's voice boomed. The puppies remained silent, shivering with fright. 'Answer me, or I'll beat you both!' the man shouted.

'It was me ...' Buddy raised a trembling paw.

It was a moment of revelation for Todd. Could that be it? Was his daughter protecting someone else? She knew stealing was wrong. It was so out of character. And there was this mysterious person, whom she refused to name, who now possessed all the stolen items. That could be the answer! But how was he going to get her to admit it?

They ate tea while they watched the end of the film together. As the credits rolled, Todd fetched two glasses of milk and put his arm around his daughter.

'Good film,' he said conversationally, 'but I didn't get why Buddy said he'd eaten the sausages when he hadn't.'

Charlotte shot him a look. She wasn't stupid, his daughter. She knew he was up to something. 'It's pretty obvious Daddy,' she replied.

He pretended to look puzzled. 'But he got punished and thrown out on the streets while Barney was kept. Poor, old Buddy was starving and his brother was fine. That doesn't seem fair.'

'Yes, but Barney rescued him in the end so it was OK,' Charlotte explained with the scornful patience of a five-year-old.

'I know ... but, to me, it doesn't seem right that Buddy was the one who had to suffer the consequences of Barney's actions.'

'No.' She thought about it. 'But he loved his brother and wanted to look after him.'

'If you were Buddy, would you do the same thing?'

'Uh huh.' She didn't need to think about it.

'But Buddy lied. It's not OK to lie.'

She bit her lip and turned her big, brown eyes to face him. 'But he couldn't tell the truth.'

'Why not?'

'Because his brother would've got into trouble.'

'I see ...' Todd nodded slowly. 'So, it's alright to lie if you're protecting someone else?'

'Yes.' She shot him a white-moustached grin. 'Can I have some more milk, please?'

'In a minute. I was just wondering who you were protecting when you told that lie about stealing things from school.'

Her face crumpled. 'I promised I wouldn't tell,' she whispered.

He took her in his arms and stroked her hair. 'It's OK, sweetheart. You don't need to tell me her name.'

'It wasn't a girl.' Her voice was muffled against his shoulder.

'A boy then.' Realisation struck him. 'Hey, was it your friend, Robbie?' She stiffened. *Bingo.* 'It's OK,' he soothed. 'You haven't told me. You haven't broken your promise.'

She remained in his arms, silent, thinking. Eventually, she murmured, 'What are you going to do?'

'Mm, that's a hard one. We'll have to have a think about that.'

She moved away from him, her eyes pleading. 'You could not say anything,' she said hopefully.

'I could ... but do you think that will help Robbie? Won't he just continue to take things and let you take the blame?' He allowed her to consider that for a few moments before continuing. 'Tell you what, I'll go and see Miss Nichol first thing on Monday morning. I'll tell her the truth but I won't mention Robbie's name. I think you need to tell *him* to give the things back, that he needs to think about how *he'd* feel if someone stole his toys.'

'He doesn't have any toys,' she said sadly. 'He's very poor, Daddy.'

'I see.' Oh heck, this whole situation was more complicated than he thought. 'That still doesn't make it OK for him to take things from other people.'

'If he gives the things back, he won't have anything to play with, Daddy.'

'Well, that's tough sweetheart but I don't know what we can do about that.'

'I know.' Her face cleared. 'I could give him some of mine. I've got loads of things.'

He hugged her tightly, his heart overwhelmed with love for his beautiful, generous, little girl. 'That's really kind of you, Charlotte. We'd better just check with Mummy first to make sure she's OK with whatever you decide to give him.' He was imagining the fallout should she give away some of Reggie's family heirlooms.

She pulled away once more. 'Can I have that milk now?'

'Of course.' He stood. 'Just one more thing. Why did you own up? You didn't need to, surely?'

'Well …' Her eyes became serious. 'Some of the kids had been saying it was Robbie. He'd been caught taking something once before. I was worried one of them would tell Miss Nichol and he'd be in big trouble. I think he's scared of his dad. He gets smacked when he does things wrong.'

'But, instead, you were the one who got into trouble.'

'Not really.' She said with airy confidence. 'I knew you'd be a bit upset but I thought you'd get over it.'

'But what about at school?'

She frowned. 'I knew Miss Nichol would be worried and she'd try to get me to talk about it. She wouldn't punish me or anything like that. And she wouldn't tell the other kids either. She knows I'm pretty good.'

Todd chuckled and gave her shoulders an affectionate squeeze. 'I think you're pretty good too.'

CHAPTER 9

Saskia
2003

I wake to the sound of stones rattling against a window and sit up, disorientated, alert to danger. It takes a few seconds to realise where I am and that the noise is hail, hammering against the glass pane. Not a good day to be out on the streets. My plan for today, concocted as I lay in bed the night before, is to find Veronik Holdings. I'm going to try the British Library and, if that fails, the Tourist Information Board. If the company exists, there must be an address for it somewhere. Another option – to find the nearest police station and report my sister missing – was discarded. Apart from an overheard phone conversation and a false address, I have no evidence that anything is amiss. And I'm worried they would return me home. The thought of facing Andrian in those circumstances makes me shudder. I wonder about Mum: how she's faring; whether she's found my note; even whether I should have brought her with me. Somehow, when I've found Mel, I'll try to get her some help. But I'm trying not to think too much about the future. The present is difficult enough.

I swing my legs out of bed and head for the shower room. Downstairs, I hear music and the occasional clatter of pans. If nothing else, I'm looking forward to breakfast. When I reach the dining room, my spirits lift at the smell of bacon. A jug of orange juice is waiting on the table, alongside a bowl of chopped fruit and a selection of mini cereal packets. I'm tipping cornflakes into a ceramic bowl painted with poppies when Alisha appears, carrying a small jug of milk. She smiles when she sees me.

'Good morning, Saskia. I wish I could say it's a beautiful morning but ...' She grimaces and gestures to the deluge which continues outside. 'Just help yourself to whatever you'd like. I'll bring a pot of tea and I'm cooking you a full English breakfast.'

'That's great. Thank you,' I smile in return. There's something about Alisha's warmth and positive energy which boosts my confidence. Today is going to be a good day. By the time I've demolished my cereal and a plate of sausage, bacon, egg, mushrooms and beans, accompanied by two rounds of toast, I'm feeling set up for the challenges ahead. Over breakfast, I study my street map of London and plan a route to the British Library. Then, I check with Alisha that I can spend another night here. It's an extravagance I can't really afford but, that way, I can leave my heavy backpack in my room and be assured of somewhere to sleep tonight. My buoyant mood doesn't last long.

'Going anywhere nice today?' Alisha asks as I reach the bottom of the stairs on my way out.

I hesitate. No reason not to tell her. As I share my intentions, I'm aware she's regarding me dubiously. 'The Library? I'm not sure that'll help you much. There must be a way we can find out where that company is ... I'll phone my friend, Marianne. She might know.'

I sit and wait, restlessly watching rain stream down the misted window pane, trying to stay positive. *Today, I'll find my sister.* Even as I say the words in my head, anxiety claws at my stomach. I chew on my bottom lip, my fingers drumming the table strewn with magazines beside me. *What if I can't find her? What will I do then?*

My troubling thoughts are interrupted by Alisha's return. 'Marianne says your company should be listed at Companies House,' she tells me.

'Where's that?' I ask, eager to head there straight away.

'I'm not sure ... but we may be able to find the information online. Come through to my office and we'll have a look.'

She leads me back through the dining room to a small sitting room beyond it. In one corner, there's an old, wooden desk with a computer on its surface. She sits in front of it and taps the keys. The screen whirrs into life and we wait in silence for it to be ready. It seems to take forever. When the home screen has finished loading, Alisha clicks on the Internet Explorer icon.

'Apparently, there's a website,' she says, scrolling down and clicking on the link. 'Maybe we can search online and you won't even need to go there.' There's another pause. 'Sorry,' she says. 'It's an old computer and it's very slow.'

'Please don't worry. It's really kind of you to help me,' I reply.

'Here we are. Yes, we *can* search for a company. What was the name again?'

'Veronik Holdings.' I spell out the name and she types it in. Once again, we wait.

'Here we go.' The page appears and she takes her time going down the list, allowing me to read each one. There are several derivations of the name Veronik, like Veronica and Veronika, but not one is called Veronik Holdings. 'Perhaps the name is slightly wrong,' she suggests. 'It might be best to go through all the possibilities and investigate them a bit more. Some do have London addresses and could be the company you're looking for. Can I leave you to it? I'll just be in the kitchen. Help yourself to paper and a pen.'

'Of course. Thank you.' She leaves and I take the seat in front of the computer. After more than an hour searching through, I have just two possible addresses: one is for Varonic Holdings, a construction company based in Queen Victoria Street; the other is for Veronica H. Limited, an import company with an address in Gray's Inn Road. Varonic Holdings is the closest fit to the name but Veronica H. Limited is also a potential match. I recall Andrian saying something vague about an import/export business. Neither company, though, fills me with the sense that they're the right one. My hopes are slipping away, like grains of sand through an egg timer, and my despair grows. I'll check them out though, just to be sure, and extract the street map from my coat pocket. Queen Victoria Street is located in central London with Cannon Street the nearest tube station. Gray's Inn Road is further west.

I find Alisha in the kitchen, humming along to the radio, and tell her where I'm going. 'Good luck,' she smiles. 'I'll keep my fingers crossed for you.'

'Thanks,' I say and, zipping up my coat, I head out into the rain.

***

Varonic Holdings proves to be the office address of a large construction company. The girl manning the reception desk is helpful and sympathetic but adamant that no-one by the name of Mel Potter works for the company.

'I've only been here eighteen months though. Would she have been here before that?'

I shake my head. Another dead end.

Pinning all my faith on my next port of call, I battle my way back through driving rain to the tube station. On the way, a woman in front of me swings around and catches me full on the face with her umbrella. The shock of it takes my breath away.

'Ooh, sorry love.' Her voice can barely be heard above the noise of traffic and the incessant thrashing of water against hard surfaces.

'It's OK,' I mumble, my eyes stinging at the impact. I feel like bursting into tears. Instead, I continue resolutely on to Gray's Inn Road and to the address on my piece of paper.

Another disappointment. Veronica H. Limited no longer exists. I walk the length of the road and back again but the business is nowhere to be found. The premises for the address I have are empty; a sign hangs in the window saying 'To Let'; the door is locked. Mel clearly doesn't work here.

I return to the White House late afternoon, drenched to the skin and no further forward. With a heavy heart, I let myself in using the key I've been given. I can hear Alisha singing in the kitchen and scurry up the stairs before she can intercept me. I don't feel like discussing my day and I long for a hot bath. Once I'm in my room, I peel off my clothes. My coat has provided no protection from the weather; I'm wet through, even my underwear. I hang everything up around the room, wondering how I'm going to get it all dry before I leave in the morning. Leave ... where am I going to go? I daren't return home but I can't afford to stay where I am. A youth hostel? Try to get a job? I'll have to earn some money if I'm going to keep searching. There are too many decisions to make and I feel weary with the weight of it all.

It takes me ages to get into the bath, the hot water stinging my chilled flesh, but at last I sink my shoulders beneath the surface and savour the bliss. I lie there for a long time, my mind closed to the choices I've yet to make ...

A tap at the door brings me back to full consciousness. 'Yes?' I call.

'Are you OK, Saskia? Is there anything you need? Any wet clothes you want drying? You must have got yourself soaked out there today.'

I smile at Alisha's thoughtfulness. 'Thanks. You're right – my clothes are drenched. I was wondering how to get them dry.'

'Just bring them down when you're ready. I've got a tumble drier. All mod cons here.'

'Thank you.'

One problem solved; if only the others were so easily fixed. While I get dressed, I debate asking Alisha for advice. At first, I throw out the idea. That would be crazy. How can I think of sharing all this with a stranger? But I feel I'm suffocating beneath the burden of it all. She's shown me nothing but kindness and, instinctively, I trust her. I allow the possibility to dangle before me. The opportunity to offload some responsibility is tempting. I gather up my soggy clothes and head downstairs, still undecided.

'The kettle's just boiled. Would you like some tea?' she asks, taking the bundle of wet things from my arms.

'Yes, thanks. This is really kind of you,' I reply.

'All part of the service.'

I sit down on a rocking chair covered in a vibrant, yellow and orange, woollen blanket. I'd like to make my own tea but I don't know where things are kept so I wait, feeling guilty for causing Alisha extra work. She returns and is soon handing me a steaming mug, three sugars, just how I like it. On the hob, another fragrant stew bubbles and she gives it a stir.

'That smells fantastic,' I say. My insides feel hollow. I haven't eaten since breakfast.

She grins. 'It's lovely to have someone to cook for. Now, how did you get on today? Did you find Vero ... was it Veronik, that company? I'm assuming you haven't managed to track your sister down or you'd be looking a bit happier than you are now.'

'No to both,' I say. There's a pause and I sip my tea, conscious of Alisha's eyes upon me.

'I'm sorry to hear that.' She turns away and begins getting ingredients from a cupboard. I feel she wants to say more but doesn't want to appear nosy. 'Does that mean you'll be staying longer?'

I wish I could but I know I can't afford it. 'No.' I give her a sad smile. 'I'll miss your cooking, that's for sure ... and your company.'

She nods. I watch as she pours flour and suet into a bowl and sprinkles the mixture with different spices from a rack. She adds water from a jug and kneads everything together. 'Help yourself to more tea. There's some in the pot and sugar and milk are right there,' she says as she works. I refill my mug and sit back down.

She finishes making dumplings, tips them into the stew and washes her hands. Then, she turns to face me once more. 'Look, tell me to mind my own business ...' she begins and I brace myself for her inevitable questions. 'But I need to know that you're OK. Do your family know you're here, Saskia?'

'It's just my mum.' I think of the letter I left her and wonder again if she's even read it. 'It's complicated.'

Alisha frowns. 'Have you had an argument, run away from home?' she asks.

'No, it's not like that ...' She looks so concerned that I feel my defences crumble. 'It's a long story.'

'I'm a good listener, if you want to talk.'

I tell her everything. She's right – she *is* a good listener. I speak of Dad and his accident, Mum's depression and, latterly, her alcohol and drug dependency. I tell her about Andrian, the way he helped Mel get a job, Mel's silence since leaving, the overheard conversation. Once I start talking, it's like I can't stop until I've got everything out. And she doesn't interrupt; she just listens, her kind face absorbing my troubles.

'How old are you, Saskia?' she asks, when I'm finished at last.

I think briefly about lying. The truth is going to be problematic. 'Fifteen,' I say, reluctantly.

'Oh, you poor thing!' She leans into me, stretching an arm around my shoulders and giving me a squeeze. 'That's an awful lot for a fifteen-year-old to deal with. What are you planning to do?'

I tell her of my half-formed thoughts of staying in London and getting a job. She shakes her head. 'That's not going to solve anything,' she says firmly. 'If Mel is in trouble, you're going to need help finding her.'

'You mustn't tell anyone!' I exclaim. 'They'll send me back.'

'Look, Saskia ...' She takes hold of my hand. 'From what you've told me, your sister could be in danger. I think she needs to be found as soon as possible. You're going to have to tell the police.'

I jerk my hand away. 'No.' I know what that means. Social Services will be called too. I'll be taken back. They'll speak to Mum and Andrian. 'I don't want to tell the police. Anyway, I've got no proof. They won't listen. It'll just cause more trouble.'

'Saskia, this could be really serious. For your sister's sake, you can't risk not telling them.'

Her response is not what I want to hear. I was hoping she'd reassure me – tell me my fears were groundless. The fact that she's taken what I've said so seriously makes me feel sick. She sees that I'm weakening and presses home her point. 'Mel's life could be at stake. Whatever the consequences, you can't ignore that fact.'

I say nothing. My stomach is churning. She's right. I review the past hours and wonder what on earth I was thinking. Mel may be in danger and I've done nothing to help. I should've gone to the police straight away. Instead, I was thinking of myself – the danger I could be in. And what about Mum? I've abandoned her ... left her with Andrian whom I no longer trust. I'm a selfish idiot! My face crumples and Alisha puts her arms around me.

'You've been very brave, Saskia,' she murmurs, 'but you need to call the police. You can't help your sister on your own.'

'Alright,' I whisper.

CHAPTER 10

Todd

The luminous, unclouded May sky matched Todd's spirits as he drove his daughter to school, twenty minutes earlier than normal. It was rare for him to feel so cheerful on a Monday. The weekly journey was habitually a gloomy one; he wouldn't see his daughter for another five days and a soul-destroying week, untangling legal problems, loomed ahead. Today, though, there was a spring in his step as he ushered Charlotte towards the classroom.

Miss Nichol was waiting, hair pulled back in a ponytail, dressed in green leggings and a floaty, floral top. At the sight of her, Todd's pulse quickened and his mouth felt parchment dry. She greeted Charlotte with a wide smile and gave her a small task to do in the class 'shop' to keep her occupied at the other end of the room. Both adults watched while Charlotte hung her coat on her peg before disappearing behind the shop canopy.

Turning to appraise him with cool, hazel eyes, Miss Nichol invited him to sit. In return, he flashed her his best, boyish grin, the look, he'd been told, which melted girls' hearts, and watched for the thawing in her demeanour. There was none.

'Did you manage to find anything out?' she asked, clearly impatient to be rid of him.

'Yes.' He schooled his face into something more serious. 'I did. She didn't want to tell me at first but, eventually, she admitted that she hadn't taken anything at all. She was trying to protect someone else. She wouldn't tell me who that person was,' he added, careful to avoid any gender clues, 'but I guessed. She made me promise not to tell you. I'm sorry.' He smiled an apology and stared into her eyes, awaiting her response. This was the moment he'd been anticipating with relish. She was bound to be impressed by his success.

If she was, she hid it well. 'I thought it must be something like that ... and don't worry, I won't try to beat a name out of you.' She gave him a wry smile and he glowed at the twinkle he saw in her eyes. 'I can guess too. You can leave it with me.' She leaned forward to stand.

'Oh, another thing ...' Todd rushed to prolong their interaction and she settled back down. 'Charlotte did agree to talk to the person. She was confident she could persuade whoever it was to return the stolen goods. You see, she felt sorry for this person. She's going to give him some of her own toys instead,' he added with a burst of pride. 'Oh damn.' He frowned as he realised what he'd revealed. 'I was trying to avoid saying he or him. I guess I wouldn't last long under interrogation.'

Her face filled with humour. 'Yes, that was pretty hopeless,' she agreed. 'Your daughter is a much tougher proposition. You did well to get her to talk at all. You're obviously very close.'

His heart filled with warmth at her implied praise. 'We are ... and yes, you're right. Look,' he rushed on before she could dismiss him, 'I'm sorry about that night a few months back.' He saw her stiffen and cursed himself inwardly for mentioning it. Too late to go back now. 'Anyway, I didn't mean to make you feel uncomfortable. And I would, genuinely, like to take you out for a drink sometime ...' His voice trailed off as she gave him a tight, professional smile and stood.

'Thanks for taking the time to come in, Mr Matheson.'

'Right.' Now he felt awkward. 'I'll be off then. I'll just say goodbye to Charlotte.'

She nodded and turned to her computer, where she was setting up something on a large interactive whiteboard. He found his daughter counting out pretend money.

'Can you buy something from me, Daddy?' she asked. 'I'm the shopkeeper.'

'Sorry, sweetheart. I've got to go to work.' He gave her a hug. 'I've told Miss Nichol what you told me and she's going to sort things out. Have a wonderful week.'

She nodded calmly. 'I will. You too, Daddy.'

As he was leaving, he turned to call goodbye to Miss Nichol but now she was crouched inside a large cupboard with her back to him. He left feeling ridiculously dejected. Clearly, she wasn't remotely interested in him. Her loss, he told himself. He wouldn't ask her again.

***

His bad mood lasted the whole week. By the weekend, he was prepared to admit to himself that the woman had really got under his skin. Giving up on her wasn't an option. Instead, he planned a different charm offensive, a slow burn approach.

To start, he called his ex-wife and offered to pick Charlotte up on Fridays after school. This involved taking her back to Reggie's to pack her weekend bag and meant he had to change his night out with the lads but, otherwise, the new arrangement had lots of advantages. Firstly, it meant he got to spend an extra night with Charlotte; secondly, he was in Reggie's good books as she didn't have to pay a childminder for that afternoon and evening; thirdly, he was able to see Miss Nichol. He also found excuses to pop in and see her on a Monday morning. She seemed to tolerate these regular visits as he was careful to talk to her only about Charlotte. And it was working. He definitely felt that she was warming to him. There was humour in her eyes when she asked, 'What is it *this* time?' He'd half expected her to tell the receptionist to refuse him entry but she didn't and their relationship, he liked to think, was slowly but surely blossoming.

One morning, she raised her eyebrows at the sight of Charlotte carrying some flowers. 'They're for you ... from Charlotte,' he grinned. 'Because you're such a lovely teacher.'

'Thank you, Charlotte.' She graciously accepted the flowers. 'Can you go and sort out the shape boxes for me, please? I noticed that the 2D and 3D shapes have got muddled up.' Charlotte skipped off happily and Miss Nichol turned to face Todd.

'Thank you for the flowers,' she said with a smile, 'but this has got to stop. People are starting to talk.'

He gave her an innocent look. 'What about?'

She sighed and laid the flowers on her desk. 'Look, Mr Matheson, I know what you're doing.'

'And what's that?'

She blushed. For the first time, she appeared self-conscious around him and his heart leapt. 'You know ... all this attention ... inventing reasons to show up here on a Monday ... now flowers ... you need to stop. As I said, people are noticing.' Her cheeks were now suffused with colour.

'So? You don't strike me as the sort of person who'd worry too much about what people thought.'

'I don't ... look, this is awkward ...'

'Would it be less awkward if I asked you out ... made it official?' There, he'd gone and asked her again. So much for playing it cool!

She turned exasperated eyes upon him and pushed a loose strand of hair from her face. 'No. I can't. I mean, it wouldn't be appropriate.'

'Why not?'

'Look Mr Matheson, I'm Charlotte's teacher. It would be unprofessional to start a relationship with you, if that's what you're suggesting.'

She looked vulnerable and he ached to take her in his arms. 'Is that the only thing that's standing in the way?' he asked gently.

She frowned. 'Maybe ...' she whispered. Silence stretched between them, throbbing with tension. 'Look, I ...'

'Tell you what, how about we make a deal?' he interrupted. 'I'll agree to stop pestering you on Mondays and you agree to an evening out with me when the summer holiday starts and you're no longer Charlotte's teacher.'

She smiled. 'I guess I could agree to that. At least I'll be able to get on with things again. Do you realise that Monday morning is the worst possible time for a parent to interrupt a teacher?'

'Sorry,' he chuckled, his whole insides dancing with jubilation. 'It won't happen again. You'll probably miss my visits – you won't know what to do with all the spare time!'

'I wouldn't bet on it,' she said drily. 'Thanks again for the flowers.'

He sang along to the radio all the drive to his workplace that morning. At the top of his voice. The end of term was only seven weeks away. He couldn't wait ...

CHAPTER 11

Saskia
2003

Things happen quickly. Alisha calls the local police station and, after fifteen minutes, someone calls her back. They want us to go there and make a statement but Alisha asks them to come to us. 'She's only fifteen ...' I hear her say. 'She'd be more comfortable in surroundings she knows.' She grins as she puts down the phone, aware that I've overheard. 'Well, I'm hungry and I don't want my stew and dumplings going to waste.'

The food is delicious but I struggle to eat. My nerves are frayed like old sacking as I await the shrill of the doorbell. I push meat around my plate in an effort to fool Alisha. I don't.

'I'm an idiot,' she says, leaping to her feet. 'You won't want to eat when you're sick with worry. I'll put it in the oven for you to keep it warm. Maybe, you'll fancy it later.'

I nod gratefully and allow my plate to be taken from me. Outside, it is still raining and I listen to the gushing of a gutter overflowing. Alisha eats in silence. We're both taut with expectation and jump when the doorbell does ring. My stomach plunges. It's a moment of no return. I hear voices in the hallway and then they appear, two people, a man and a woman, dressed in suits, not uniforms. Alisha introduces them but their names don't register. I stare at their faces, my heart thumping. The man is older, grey-haired with a face like a kind uncle; the woman has sharp, brown eyes and regards me with chilly detachment. Instinctively, I focus on the man.

They ask me so many questions. I tell them all about Mel and the circumstances surrounding her disappearance. I feel embarrassed as I tell them how I've tried to look for her. Beneath their scrutiny, my actions seem pathetic. They become more animated and exchange glances as soon as I mention Andrian's name. Their interrogation changes direction and they want to know everything about him, his associates, names, men I've seen him with. My responses are hopelessly vague; I actually know so little about him. All I can tell them is that someone called Stan was in charge of Veronik Holdings and that Andrian mentioned the name Dimitri when I overheard him that time on the phone. I think of Mum and realise she might be able to tell them more from their nights out together. The officers listen and the woman writes in a notebook. They tell me nothing, not even when I ask them what they know about him. As they leave, they tell me they'll do all they can to find Mel. Their smiles of reassurance don't reach their eyes.

I remain in the kitchen, trying to process what I've learnt from the interview, while Alisha follows them out. They didn't seem surprised at what I'd told them. Guilt constricts my chest. I should've spoken to them sooner about Mel, when I wasn't able to contact her. If something bad has happened to her, I'm to blame.

Alisha returns and finds me pinching back tears. She sits beside me and pats my arm. The gesture is too much and a strangled sob escapes from my throat. 'Oh, Saskia, you poor thing!' she exclaims and folds me to her. Once the tears have started, I can't seem to stop them. I shudder and shake as I cling to her, like a lifeline. She croons, strokes my hair, but she doesn't tell me everything's going to be fine. She can't.

Eventually, I pull away, spent, empty, soggy as a used tissue. 'Sorry,' I mumble.

'Don't be daft.'

I force myself to lift my head, to meet her kind, brown eyes. 'What's going to happen now?' I ask.

'For the time being, you're going to stay here. The police agree you can't go home at the moment. They're going to talk to your Mum and let her know you're safe. When they find Andrian, they'll take him in for questioning. That's all they would tell me.'

I stare at her, knowing I can't pay for a third night. 'I don't have enough money ...' I begin.

'Hush.' She rests her hand on mine. 'Don't worry about that. We can sort it out later.'

We sit for a while. She offers me the food she has kept warm. It smells tempting and I manage to swallow a few mouthfuls. While I eat, she tries to distract me with chat about some of her early cooking disasters. I pretend to listen but my thoughts are elsewhere. *What has Mel got herself embroiled in? Drugs? Sex trafficking? Is she already dead?*

I lay down my fork and start to frame an apology but Alisha is one step ahead and interrupts. 'You look dead on your feet. Do you want to get an early night?' I nod with gratitude and escape to my room.

Alone, in the darkness, I undress and slip beneath the covers, squeezing my eyes shut, willing sleep to claim me. I concentrate on the rhythms of the rain peppering the window, the staccato rattle of machine gun bullets. Fears persist, insidious, encroaching upon every corner of my mind. despite my efforts to shut them out. Dad's face swims into focus, just as it did when I was little and fretting about something. His voice is soothing. 'Hush now, little Sassy. It'll all work out. You'll see.' I can almost feel his gentle hand caressing my hair. How I long to be that child again – the one who believed his words and could cocoon herself in his fairy tales! Annoyed with myself, I shut him out too, unable to take comfort in platitudes, all too aware that, in real life, things *rarely* work out.

***

When I wake, the rain has stopped and I lay for a moment as realisation dawns. *Mel.* I throw back the covers. 7:33. Somehow, I've managed to sleep but nothing has changed. My sister is missing. Downstairs, the radio is playing an upbeat song and Alisha is clattering in the kitchen. The steady drone of traffic rumbles outside. How can life go on as normal? I want to shout at the world to stop ... to do something ... to find her. Instead, I take a deep breath and try to control my rising panic. She *has* to be OK ... she just *has* to. On automatic pilot, I dress in jeans and a sweatshirt and drag a brush through my hair. In the mirror, the face staring back at me is eerily white with black smudges under the eyes, remnants of yesterday's eyeliner. It seems a lifetime ago – yesterday morning – when I was still pretending to be a grown up, when I thought Mel's disappearance was just a lack of communication, when I didn't *really* believe, deep down, that anything could be wrong. I spit on a tissue and wipe the black splodges off. No more pretence.

Alisha meets me at the kitchen door and gives me a wide smile. 'There you are! Perfect timing. I've just made pancakes. Would you like to eat in the dining room or shall we slum it here in the kitchen?' Her breezy manner cannot disguise the concern I see brimming in her eyes.

I force a smile. 'Here is fine.' I sit on the same seat as yesterday, when the police came. The memory jabs afresh and the thought of pancakes makes me feel sick. Alisha places a mug of tea in front of me and I take a sip. Its sweet warmth calms me and I take another.

'Are you hungry?' Alisha's question is tentative. She is wary around me, anxious to please, trying her best to make things better. Her kindness is almost unbearable and I want to cry. Instead, I force myself to nod.

'A little,' I lie. 'A pancake would be lovely, thank you.'

I see her shoulders relax and her smile loosen into something more natural. She slides two plates onto the table and fetches the pancakes and a plate of crispy bacon from the oven. 'I like bacon and maple syrup with mine,' she says, 'but there's sugar and lemon if you'd prefer.'

I opt for the latter and force myself to take a bite. Like the tea, it makes me feel better and I realise I am hungry. I concentrate on eating. The pancake disappears surprisingly quickly and I take another. I sense Alisha's approval but she makes no comment and we eat in silence.

'Those were pretty amazing pancakes,' I say at last as I lay down my fork.

She nods and pats her stomach. 'I always eat too many. That's why I don't make them very often.' She starts clearing plates and I get up to help. 'It should be fine today,' she says conversationally. 'How about a walk? I could do with working off some of those breakfast calories. Or we could head up to the city? See some of the sights while you're here?'

I mull it over, touched by her suggestions – attempts to keep me from brooding, no doubt. The alternative is to sit here all day, waiting for news.

Distraction would be better but the thought of heading into the crowds lacks appeal. Also, I'm unwilling to stray too far ... just in case.

'I'll have my phone with me and the police have my number,' Alisha says, reading my mind. 'There's no need to hang around here all day waiting for them to call.'

I nod. 'A walk sounds good,' I say. 'I could use some fresh air.'

She looks pleased. 'Good choice. Tell you what, I'll pack us up a picnic and we'll walk up to the park. It's beautiful this time of year.'

I think about arguing, insisting that I don't want her to go to any trouble, but instead I smile. It's so exhausting making decisions. It feels good to have someone looking after me. 'Lovely,' I agree.

***

It is a beautiful day. The spring sunshine, tentative at first but gradually gaining in strength, bathes the London streets in a golden glow. Alisha chatters all the while, determined to prevent me from wallowing in my thoughts. I try to concentrate on what she's saying but, like yesterday, my eyes are darting everywhere, scanning faces, searching for my sister. She could be living on just the next street. I have to keep believing that's a possibility.

It takes us about forty minutes to walk to our destination. It would have been less but Alisha seems to know everyone we meet on the way. Each time, she introduces me as her friend, Saskia, and asks after their friends and family. The fixed smile I adopt makes my face ache. While I wait, I observe the genuine affection with which others greet her. She radiates joy and that light is reflected back at her in the eyes of the people she meets. I think once more how lucky I am to have ended up at her B & B.

I'm carrying a blanket and some of our picnic lunch in my backpack. Alisha is similarly laden but that's where the resemblance between us ends. I'm wearing a faded pink T-shirt and jeans; she looks spectacular in a large, floppy hat, a multi-coloured, long-sleeved top and bright yellow, baggy trousers. Her arms are toned and her skin is smooth, like polished walnut. Beside her vibrancy, I feel dull and washed-out.

We reach the place she calls the park – Tooting Bec Common. It's not what I was expecting. For some reason, I'd anticipated a small, enclosed green space with formal flower beds. Instead, it's a large, rambling, open area of grass and trees.

'There's a café, tennis courts, sports pitches and even a lido,' Alisha announces, 'but this is the part I like best.' She gestures around us at the people out enjoying the better weather, many of whom are accompanied by dogs. 'I'd love to have a dog,' she sighs as we continue along the path. 'I always wanted one growing up. One day ... when Curtis and I manage to get a place in the country.'

'Is that the dream – to move out of London?' I ask, curious to know more of her story.

She nods. 'We're city folk and we love the place but we both want to live away from the crowds. When we were nineteen, we spent a holiday hiking around the Yorkshire moors and that was it. We were hooked. Every year now, we book a cottage somewhere rural and explore the area, you know, checking out places where we might want to live. We're saving every penny we can in the meantime and hoping that the B & B really takes off.'

After we have walked the path skirting the perimeter, she stops and puts down her backpack on a bench under a large oak. 'Let's have our picnic here,' she says. 'The grass is still too wet to sit on.'

We drape the blanket over the bench and unpack the goodies Alisha has managed to rustle up for our picnic – fluffy, white rolls packed with curried chicken, pineapple chunks and packets of crisps.

'Have you and Curtis been together long?' I ask.

'Since we were sixteen.' She grins. 'We met at a fair queuing for the dodgems. I was with a friend and so was he. We got chatting and then they kept bumping us with their dodgem. That was it; love at first sight.' She laughs. 'Actually, I fancied his friend to start with but I've never told *him* that. You're sworn to secrecy!'

I smile and think of Darrell Parkinson. School seems a million miles away. Kaz has texted several times to ask how I am and I've kept up the pretence of being in bed with flu. I wonder again if Mum has found my letter. Probably not. She hasn't tried to phone me but I'm not surprised. Most likely, she's remained oblivious to everything. Worry stabs me suddenly; if Andrian is planning on disappearing, there'll be no-one to looking after Mum.

'Are you OK, Saskia?' Alisha lightly taps my hand and I start.

'Yes, fine.' My response is automatic and I shake myself back to my surroundings. 'Sorry, I was miles away.' I smile and take another piece of pineapple although I don't really want it. The silence drags between us and I feel I need to add something more. 'I was just thinking about my mum.'

Alisha nods slowly, weighing her words before she speaks. 'You know, there *is* help out there, both for you and your mum. You just need to ask for it.'

I don't reply. After the police visit, I suspect the decision will be taken from me. If Mel isn't found, I'll be taken into care. *Don't think about it. Stay positive.* I picture an alternative scenario, one borrowed from a time before Andrian came onto the scene, when it was just me, Mel and Mum. We'll manage when this is all over. And it *will* soon be over, I pray fervently; it has to be.

'Seriously, Saskia. It sounds like your mum is in urgent need of medical care,' Alisha persists, breaking into my wishful thoughts. She reaches across to squeeze my hand. Her fingers are warm and strong. 'There's nothing to be ashamed of.'

The concern and sympathy I hear in her voice makes me want to cry all over again. Her words prick my conscience. Am I being selfish? Possibly ... probably. I didn't realise ...

The ringing of Alisha's phone jolts us both into a state of alertness. She looks at the screen before standing with a muffled, 'Sorry,' and turning away to answer it. I busy myself tidying away the leftover picnic. She's moved out of earshot so I can't hear what she's saying.

When she returns, her face is serious. 'That was the police. They're coming to the house to update us. I said we'd be back in half an hour.'

My heart leaps and I clamber to my feet. As I shake the rug, I ask, 'Do they have any news? Have they found Mel?' My voice is husky with hope.

'They didn't say – just that they were going to give us an update.'

'Oh.' My shoulders droop. Surely, they would've said if they'd located her. The next thought fills me with dread; they wouldn't say over the phone if they'd found her body ... 'No!' I whisper under my breath. My feet start moving of their own volition ... striding out ... almost running ...

'Saskia, wait!' Alisha runs to catch up with me. 'There's no need to sprint. We've got time.' Her eyes lock with mine. 'The police gave me no indication that it was bad news. I expect they want to tell us what they've discovered so far and, possibly, to ask a few more questions. Try not to worry.'

I acknowledge her words by continuing at a more reasonable walking pace, focusing on putting one foot in front of the other, trying to ignore the fear throbbing through every nerve-ending. We don't speak until we are back in Alisha's kitchen. 'I'll put the kettle on,' she says.

I sit once more at her table and drum my fingernails on its surface. It'll be good news, I tell myself, over and over. It has to be.

Although I'm expecting it, the doorbell brings a fresh lurch of adrenalin. I remain where I am, taut with tension, while Alisha hurries to the front door. Once again, there is the brief hum of hushed voices in the hallway before they enter. It's the same two officers, same suits, different shirts. My eyes dart to their faces, searching for clues as to what will unfold. They are serious, sombre. The man avoids eye contact; the woman looks straight at me and bites her lip. I draw in a steadying breath, preparing for bad news. My nails dig into the palms of my hands. Chairs are scraped across the tiles and they sit. The wait is unbearable.

The man clears his throat and Alisha breaks the silence by offering them both a cup of tea. I exhale a shuddering whoosh of air and he looks at me for the first time as he shakes his head at Alisha. I see pity there and can contain myself no longer.

'It's Mel, isn't it? Is she dead?' My voice is a shriek of high-pitched panic.

'No, no ...' For an instant, the man's shoulders relax and I feel my own body collapsing with relief.

'Oh ... I thought she must be dead ... the way you came in and all ...' I'm babbling. 'Have you found her though? What's happened? Is something wrong?' My questions tumble into one another.

'We haven't yet managed to find your sister,' says the woman. She looks across at the man and then continues. 'But we do have some news. This morning, a team of police officers travelled to Norwich to your home to interview your mother ...' A brief hesitation. 'I have to inform you that they found her dead. I'm very sorry.'

I gasp with shock and stare at the woman. That can't be right. My mum? There's a surreal stillness in the room as I look at one face and then the next. The same tragedy is written there; the same sympathy shines in their eyes.

'Oh Saskia, I'm so terribly sorry. That's awful! What happened?' Alisha takes two strides to stand beside me and I feel her hand on my shoulder.

'It's too early to say.' The man responds to her question. 'The indications are that she may have taken an overdose but a forensic team are at the scene and there will need to be an autopsy. We'll know more when those reports are completed.'

'Oh no!' I sob and sink my face into my hands. This is my fault. I wasn't there to look after her. An overdose!

'We are also investigating the possibility that she was murdered.' The woman's voice breaks into my consciousness.

'Murdered?' I echo. 'Who? Andrian?'

She shakes her head. 'As we said, it's too soon to say. We found no sign of the man you call Andrian at the property but there are some details of your mum's death which cannot be immediately explained.'

'What?' I ask.

The man intervenes. 'I'm afraid that's all we can tell you at the moment. In the meantime, I need to take details of where you will be staying. Do you have other relatives who could look after you?'

'No.' I don't need to think about it. Mum was estranged from her family. I've never met them. Dad had a much older sister, married with two grown-up children. The last time I saw any of them was at his funeral and, before that, at my cousin's wedding, six years ago. I wouldn't begin to know how to contact them.

'She can stay here,' Alisha says and the hand on my shoulder tightens its grip. 'I'll look after her.'

The woman stands and the man follows suit. 'She's only fifteen,' she murmurs to Alisha, as if I can't hear her. 'Still a minor. We'll have to let Social Services know.' In a more upbeat voice, she says to me, 'The search for your sister is continuing. We're doing all we can. As soon as we have any news, we'll let you know.' The tone lowers once more, 'Again, we are very sorry for your loss.'

And that's it. They leave. Such a short time they were here. Barely five minutes. Just long enough to shatter my world. I wait for grief to take hold. When Dad died, I couldn't stop crying. Now I just feel numb. It's too much. I can't take it in.

Alisha moves to sit beside me. 'I really am so sorry, Saskia,' she says. 'Your poor mum ... you poor girl ...' I hear tears in her voice and she rises swiftly. 'I'll make tea. Lots of sugar for the shock.'

My phone pings. A text. *Is it Mel?* With urgency borne of desperation, I pull the phone from my pocket and scan the screen. It's from a number I don't know. Then, I read the words and gasp. The phone lands with a clatter on the table.

Alisha turns. 'What is it? What's happened?'

I can't speak. I gesture at the phone. Alisha picks it up and reads the words aloud.

You stupid brat. You ruin everything with your meddling. I pay you back no matter how long it takes. I find you. I kill you. Like your precious sister. You destroy my life. I destroy yours.

It wasn't signed.

'Oh honey,' Alisha exclaims. 'This is sick. Who would send you something like this?'

'Andrian,' I reply.

CHAPTER 12

Lily

I can see the playground from my window, filling up with children, parents and carers. My eyes seek out Todd Matheson, despite my resolve to remain indifferent. Most Mondays, I catch a glimpse of him outside but he no longer makes a habit of showing up in my classroom. That's a mixed blessing. It used to be a huge distraction, not least because I was on tenterhooks until he arrived, but this is worse. He's like a magnet for attention: tall, impossibly attractive, laughing and joking with the parents standing nearby. Women gravitate towards him, fluttering like moths. As I watch, stunning single mum, Ashley Tobin, sashays to his side and places a proprietorial hand on his arm. I turn away abruptly as I see her batting her eyelashes at him. The invitation in her eyes is a neon light, even from where I'm standing. Irritated with myself, I tidy the book corner and wait for the children to start coming in. Honestly, anyone would think I was jealous!

Another glance through the glass. Todd has gone and I see children retrieving backpacks and heading towards the building. Another school day begins.

***

It is mid-morning when my radar picks up raised voices coming down the corridor. I edge away from the small group of children sorting shapes on the carpet to see what's happening. A hard-faced man is striding towards us, fists clenched. My heart lurches. This isn't good. It's Mr Hathersett, the father of five-year-old Tommy in my class.

'I'm sorry, Miss Nichol but Mr Hathersett insisted on seeing you now. I told him you were teaching.' Faith Jung, the unflappable school secretary, looks hot and bothered. And worried. I see panic in the fixed stare ... in the clenched teeth ... in the way she is, even now, trying to head him off, get in his way. 'He slipped in when another parent was leaving.' She manages to dart in front of him, blocking his path to the classroom.

He pushes her roughly aside. That's when full blown alarm sets in.

'Miss Thorpe, would you mind taking the children outside for a little play? They deserve it after all their hard work this morning.' My voice is 'teacher' calm as I begin steering the children nearest me towards our outdoor area.

My young teaching assistant looks up in surprise. 'The whole class?' she questions. 'Now?'

'Straight away. No, don't worry about your coats.' I begin ushering children towards the outside door.

Jess Thorpe's eyes widen behind the pink frames of her glasses and she leaps to her feet. 'Let's go and play a game of chase on the field.' Thank goodness. She's got the message and is going to move them from harm's way.

'Not you, Tommy,' the man growls, grabbing his child by the arm. 'You're coming with me.'

The boy yelps but I bite my lip. I need to get the rest of the class away from the scene first. Fortunately, they are only too eager to comply and there's a rush for the door. Jess sweeps up two girls playing shops with baskets of fruit and the door shuts behind them. I lock it and pocket the key.

'Out of my way.'

'Mr Hathersett ...' I keep my tone friendly as I walk over to where Faith is now standing, once more braced in the doorway, blocking his exit. 'I wonder if I might have a word?'

He turns, slightly confused. 'Ain't got nothing to talk about. I'm taking my boy and that's that. Now get out of my way.' His face is red, boiling with pent-up aggression. Faith maintains her stance, grim and determined. The boy, Tommy, white-faced and quivering, wriggles in his father's grasp. All three of us are aware of Kevin Hathersett's history of violence and the restraining order currently in place to keep him away from his wife and son.

'Mr Hathersett,' I soothe, 'why don't you come and sit down? Perhaps you'd like to see some of Tommy's work. He did some lovely writing this morning, didn't you Tommy? Let me just fetch his book.'

'Stay where you are,' he barks. 'I don't wanna look at no book. I just want my son. Move, bitch, or *I'll* move you.' The bunched fists are no idle threat.

I take a deep breath. My hands are trembling and I thrust them in my pockets. 'Please Mr Hathersett, just listen for a moment. If you take Tommy now, you'll be in breach of the court order. You'll go to prison. Please think about that.'

'I won't,' he sneers. 'They won't find us.' He grabs Faith by the arm and wrenches her away from the doorway. At the same time, Tommy squirms free and scuttles towards me, his face a mask of terror. He grabs my cardigan and hides, cowering, behind me.

'You little bugger ...' Snarling, his father spins and strides in our direction. That's when he pulls a switchblade from his back pocket and points it in my direction. 'Hand him over, or else ...'

I back towards my desk, keeping the child behind me. Sunlight dances on the knife in a series of warning flashes. My heart pounds a painful tattoo in my chest. Licking dry lips, I beg, 'Please be reasonable, Mr Hathersett. Put the knife down. This is bound to end badly.'

'Badly for you, you mean.' Snaking his free arm around me, he lunges for the boy, knocking a vase of flowers off my desk. With a squeal, Tommy twists away and sprints between the tables. His father sees where he's headed and positions himself between the door and his son. 'Tommy, you come here this minute or I'll beat the living daylights out of you.' Warily, they eye each other, waiting to see who is going to make the first move. 'Come on, lad.' His voice is wheedling now as he advances. 'We're going on an adventure, you and I. We'll have lots of fun.' The terrified boy remains silent, edging away, trying to put distance between him and his father.

While his attention is fixed on his son, I creep behind my desk and pull open my cupboard door. My bag lies on the floor, just inside. Keeping my eyes straight ahead, I lean in and rummage until my fingers close around cold metal. My can of mace spray. Grabbing it, I move swiftly to the doorway. 'Go. Call the police,' I whisper to Faith.

'They should already be on their way. I told Jane to call as I tried to stop him coming in. I'm not leaving you alone,' she hisses back.

We watch helplessly, eyes on the knife, as Mr Hathersett backs his son into a corner and then pounces. Tommy squeals in pain as, arms pinned behind his back, he's marched towards us.

'Mr Hathersett, I can't let you take Tommy,' I say firmly.

He points the blade at me. 'You can't stop me,' he snarls. As he moves within arm's length, I dodge to one side, whip the can of mace from behind my back and blast him full in the face. 'Aargh.' He screams and releases Tommy, his free hand clutching at his eyes. 'You bitch!' He flails wildly, lashing out at me, the knife slicing wickedly through the air, but I've darted away and am now racing for the outer door. 'This way, Tommy,' I call, pulling the key from my pocket and manoeuvring the lock. Faith has fled the other way, leaving the man stumbling towards us, clawing at his face and swearing loudly. 'Quickly!' The terrified child remains statue still, frozen with shock. I leap towards him, drag his rigid body through and lean my body weight against the door whilst I attempt to jiggle the key into the lock. My fingers won't work properly and I lose perilous seconds with my fumbling. Just as the man's face looms at the glass, the key turns. I hear his bellowing rage and thumps on the door behind me, but I don't look back. Instead, I scoop Tommy into my arms. 'Don't worry,' I murmur as I stagger across the outdoor play area and onto the school field. 'Daddy's not badly hurt. I just needed to stop him from taking you.' He clings to me. Even when I finally stop at the gate of the main playground and dare to look around, he won't let me put him down. I cuddle him as I scour the field, watching for a pursuer. The locked door won't necessarily stop him. He could smash the glass.

'Lily!' The male voice behind me makes me jump. Michael Winterbottom, the headteacher, is pushing the gate open and ushering us through. 'Are you alright?'

'We're fine, aren't we Tommy?' The child buries his head in my shoulder and doesn't respond.

'The police are here,' he mouths. 'They're with him now. Best if we wait here until ...' He mimes putting handcuffs on his wrist. It takes several attempts before I grasp his meaning. At another time, I would've found his charade hilarious. As it is, reality is setting in and I grip the boy as hard as he's holding me.

'Come and sit down.' Michael is regarding me with concern. 'You look a bit pale. Tommy, why don't you let Miss Nichol put you down. We won't let anything happen, I promise.'

His response is to snuggle even closer. I carry him to a bench and sink wearily onto the hard surface. 'How about we give your mummy a call in a little while?' I murmur and feel him nod. Poor little mite. Who knows what's going on inside his head? I stare at the exposed, vulnerable nape of his neck and ache for him, for all he's been through, both today and previously. His hair is cut short and I can see where the brown skin becomes paler beyond his polo shirt. I wish there was something I could do to keep him safe. Not for the first time, I feel overwhelmed by a sense of helplessness.

'Are you alright, Miss Nichol?' Michael repeats.

I swallow the painful lump in my throat and blink back the tears threatening to surface. 'Fine,' I croak. 'Honestly.' I try to smile but suspect it's more of a grimace. Looking around, I wonder where the rest of my class are. 'I assume Miss Thorpe has Honeybee class under control?'

He gives a wry smile. 'I'm not sure we can say that exactly but they're safely in the library. She walked them all round to the office to make sure we knew what was happening. By that time, Mrs Smith had called the police and had just told me what was going on. I was about to head down to your room when Mrs Jung appeared and told me you had ... er, incapacitated ... our intruder. Then, the police turned up and headed straight there. I came out to find you and Tommy. Looks like your quick thinking saved the day.' He gives my arm a gentle squeeze.

I say nothing. The adrenalin firing through me minutes before has ebbed away, leaving me exhausted and embarrassingly weepy. Yes, the worst has been averted for now but, try as I might, I can't picture a fairy tale, happy ending. Tommy's dad might have been arrested; he might be charged and convicted. That doesn't mean wife and son will be free of him. Morosely, I keep my arms around the boy on my lap, wishing I had the power to protect him. There is so much evil in the world. My actions today might bring some respite but they won't solve the problem in the long term. Once his father is released, the danger for Tommy will be ever-present. No real escape. I know it. I live it.

***

The aftermath seems never-ending. Tommy's mum turns up, wearing dark glasses and an air of dramatic excitement. I notice she's changed out of the onesie she was wearing when she dropped her son off that morning and is now in full make-up. 'My poor boy,' she screeches as she prises him off me. 'What am I going to do? That man will never let us go. We'll never be free of him.'

He shudders and turns back to me. I drop to my knees beside him. 'Don't worry, Tommy. The police are talking to your dad. They'll make sure you and your mum are safe.'

'You don't know Kev Hathersett,' the woman in question says scornfully as she digs her bright, red nails into her son's shoulders and pulls him back into her embrace. 'The court order was a fat lot of good. That man is a sackload of shit and I walked right into it.' She looks down at the pink slingbacks she's wearing as if to see it caked on her heels.

'Hmph.' Michael Winterbottom clears his throat. 'I know you're upset, Mrs Hathersett ...' he begins.

'Upset?' Her voice is shrill. 'I'm a lot more than just upset. My only child was almost snatched from me! I thought he'd be safe at school.' She turns accusing eyes upon him.

'Yes, well ...' he murmurs weakly.

I watch and listen as Sonya Hathersett rails at the world about her misfortune. Whilst I feel sympathy for her, my heart bleeds for her son. He is suffering through no fault of his own. How many children there are in hopeless situations ... in danger ... through the actions of adults! Eventually, Sonya and Tommy are driven away by two police officers and things start to return to normal. Children skip out onto the field, enjoying the summer sunshine. It's lunchtime. Not for me, though. Instead, two more police officers interview me at length. The fact that I had a can of mace in my bag is a tricky issue. What was I doing with something like that in an unlocked school cupboard? Why did I have it in the first place? I tell them I'd been recently accosted by a man trying to steal my bag late at night. I'd been on my way to my car after seeing some friends. Yes, I was alone at the time. No,

I didn't know the man and I hadn't reported it. Why not? Because I hadn't been hurt and I didn't want the fuss. It was dark; I wouldn't have been able to identify him. It spooked me, though. Since then, I carried some mace with me ... just in case. I didn't intend to bring it to school; I'd just forgotten it was there. Yes, until I needed it today. Yes, I supposed that was quick thinking. The officers regard me with suspicion but let my lies go without further comment. My statement is read back to me and I sign it.

After they leave, Michael Winterbottom tells me to go home. 'You've been through a lot today,' he says kindly. 'Go and run yourself a nice, hot bath and have a glass of wine. Can I call anyone to make sure you have some TLC?'

I shake my head. 'I'm not going home, Michael, but thank you for suggesting it. I'll be better off here, getting back to normal. And I need to see the children in my class. Show them that all's well.'

'If you're sure ...'

'I am.'

I regret that decision later in the day, when a woman from the local press arrives. Michael gives her a brief statement but she isn't satisfied with that. She wants to speak to me. Somehow, it seems, she already knows most of the facts. I have a horrible suspicion that Tommy's mum has contacted them. Probably for her fifteen minutes of fame. And money, of course.

I can't help my cynicism. It's part of my self-protection strategy. I'm careful, wary of trusting people. That's why I'm guarded with Todd Matheson. I like him – a lot – and I know he likes me. My stomach does this funny flip flop thing every time I see him and I feel myself getting hot and bothered. That hasn't happened to me before. He's divorced and soon I'll no longer be teaching his daughter so there's no real reason not to get to know him better. But I haven't come this far without being cautious. I'm not going to change now.

I find out about the news reporter from Faith Jung who appears, flushed and a little breathless, in my classroom, beckoning me out into the corridor. 'The Press are here,' she whispers. Her eyes are wide with excitement. Now the danger is passed, she's enjoying all the drama. 'They want to talk to you and me about what happened.'

I scowl. There's no way I want media attention, even if it is just the local paper. 'Surely Michael will give them a statement. I don't think it's advisable for anyone else to talk to them; there could be a safeguarding issue. Also, it might compromise a police prosecution.' Faith looks crestfallen at my reaction, forcing me to relent a little. 'If Michael says it's fine, then you could speak to them but please keep my name out of it. And be very careful about what you say.'

'It's a woman from the *East Anglia Chronicle*. And it's too late. She already knows our names. She says she's going to print the story anyway with the information she's got.'

'How on earth did she get hold of it?' Tetchiness born of anxiety sharpens my voice and I realise I'm taking my irritation out unfairly on Faith. 'Sorry,' I add. 'I know it's not your fault.' And I'm pretty sure I know the answer. Damn Sonya Hathersett! 'Look, I can't leave my class. Why don't you talk to the reporter alone? Just tell her we removed the children from harm's way and managed to stop a parent from unlawfully taking a child. End of story.'

'But what about the spray?' she asks.

'What about it?'

'Can't I say anything about that? You were amazing, Lily. You should be nominated for a bravery award.'

'Absolutely not. Please don't mention the mace spray.' I'm horrified at her suggestion. 'Anyway, *you* were the brave one, barring his way – not once, but twice! Tell them that.'

'Oh but ...' I can see she's torn.

'Look, Faith, I've got to go.' Right on cue there's a crash from inside the classroom. 'You can handle it.' I return to the class to find my teaching assistant on her hands and knees, surrounded by a small group of children. 'Are you alright, Miss Thorpe?' I help her to her feet.

'Yes, fine. I tripped over. No harm done.' Her face is beetroot red and I usher the children away to give her a moment to recover.

'Miss Thorpe wasn't looking where she was going,' Ella Harris informs me sagely. 'She tripped over the Lego box. She's always telling us to look where we're going but *she* didn't. That's why she had an accident.'

'Thank you, Ella. Now you know why it's good advice.' I tell all the children to start tidying away their activities and check on poor Jess whose dignity is hurt but, thankfully, nothing else. Part of my brain, however, continues to fret about the arrival of a press reporter. All my adult life, I've sought to retain a low profile and publicity of this nature could be dangerous. I can only pray it won't come to anything.

By the end of the school day, I'm exhausted and make a rare, early exit. A letter has already gone out to parents, making light of the incident earlier and reassuring them that none of the children were in any danger. That's because the paper was going to print something, I realise. Otherwise, the less said the better. A few parents wanted to talk to me about it and I downplayed the whole incident, managing to calm their concerns. The rest were happy to gossip and speculate in the playground.

I reach my car when a woman springs at me from behind a tree, clicking a camera in my face. Too late, I throw up an arm to shield myself. 'What's going on?' I exclaim.

'Suzi Hunter, East Anglia Chronicle,' she says coolly, gimlet grey eyes scrutinising every detail of my reaction. 'You're quite the heroine, Miss Nichol. Can you spare me a few minutes of your time?'

'No.' I take a step forward as she does the same, effectively barring my way. 'Look, I've nothing to add. I'm tired and I want to go home. And please don't use that picture you took.'

'Just tell me what was in your mind as you sprayed mace at the intruder?'

'Nothing was in my mind. I was just trying to stop a pupil from being taken from my classroom. Now, please let me pass.' Reluctantly, she steps aside and I pull open my car door.

'Are you afraid of publicity, Miss Nichol?' she asks as I slide behind the wheel. 'Do you have something to hide?' I stare at her, momentarily lost for words. 'Can you tell me why you were carrying a can of mace in the first place?' She presses home her advantage, thin, red lips curved in a predatory smile.

'I have nothing against the press. I just don't think it's appropriate to create a news drama over something like this. There's a little boy involved and the publicity will be bad for the school,' I retort.

'I'm afraid I disagree. As I said before, you're a heroine. You single-handedly prevented an abduction of a pupil at your school. That's the kind of news people like to read, and it only reflects your school in a good light.'

'I was just doing my job.'

'Thank you, Miss Nichols. That's a great quote. Have a good evening.'

I slam the door shut and then open my window. 'Don't print that picture,' I call after her. She raises an arm and waves but doesn't turn around. 'Bugger,' I mutter under my breath as I start the engine. I'd put money on a photo of my face appearing with the report. I just hope it isn't going to cause a problem.

***

It's in the paper two days later with the headline 'Just doing my job!' Underneath, in slightly smaller letters, are the words, 'Brave teacher thwarts abductor'. The photo taken by Suzi Hunter is there but it's a side profile, slightly blurry, and my long hair screens much of my face. I'm reasonably confident that I can't be identified from it. Another bonus is that the incident hasn't made the front page. It's a fairly low-key report, sketchy on details. The school is named, as are the Head, Faith Jung and I, but parent and child are not. Also, there's no mention of the mace spray – just that a man with a knife forced entry into a classroom of five-year-olds and attempted to remove his own child. 'A cool Miss Nichol first instructed a teaching assistant to take the other children outside. Then, she bravely stood her ground, refusing to let the man take her pupil. She managed to disarm him and removed the child from the room. The police have arrested the assailant and he remains in custody.' There are then some quotes from Michael Winterbottom and Faith Jung, including the line, 'She's a heroine.' I put the paper aside and exhale with relief. It could have been better, from my point of view, but it could also have been much worse.

There's a lot of ribbing in the staffroom about my 'heroine' status and Michael has brought in cakes in my honour. Dave Parker snidely suggests the staff had better be careful not to upset me from now on or I might zap them with spray too.

'Good idea, Dave,' I smile sweetly. 'Watch your back next time you offload extra duties on to me.' As a member of the senior management team, he has responsibility for timetabling and it's a known fact that he and his cronies always get off lightly when the duty roster is published.

'We'll have to call you *Macy* from now on,' he sneers, his piggy eyes gleaming with annoyance. 'There's a rule against bringing harmful substances into school. You're lucky the police aren't prosecuting *you*.'

I shrug dismissively. 'I'd forgotten I had it. It was a lucky mistake, I guess.'

'Is it still in your bag?' He isn't going to let it drop.

'Of course not. I told you I hadn't meant to bring it to work. It just happened to be in my bag.' I don't add that, this morning, I've left it locked in my car.

'Give it a rest, Dave. Have another cake. You need sweetening up.' Sarah Peters, the Year 5 teacher, thrusts a plate towards him. 'And leave our heroine alone. I'm proud of her. In fact, I'm thinking of getting something like that to keep in my bag. You never know when you might need it. There are so many slimeballs about.' She gives me a sly wink.

'Exactly. Thanks for bringing cakes, Michael.' I stand, not enjoying all the attention and keen to return to my classroom.

'My pleasure.'

He might be a hopeless headteacher who allows the likes of Dave Parker run rings around him, but Michael Winterbottom is a pretty nice guy, I decide, as I stride down the corridor, my mood buoyant with relief. The weight of worry from the last two days has lifted. I'm confident now that the whole thing will soon blow over, a momentary hiatus in my carefully constructed, calm and orderly life.

'Crisis averted,' I tell myself, blissfully unaware of what lay ahead.

CHAPTER 13

Saskia
2003

The wind sighs and moans as I step out of the car. We've had warmer days recently but today is heavy with slate clouds, and gusts whip my hair across my face. My mum's funeral. Flanked by Jane and Vicki, social workers with whom I've spent a fair amount of time these past weeks, I watch the coffin lifted from the hearse and carried into the crematorium. I know there is a police presence today, for my protection, but I can't see anyone in uniform outside the squat, grey building. And there's no sign of Andrian.

Not that I expect there to be. The police think he's long gone. After I received the threat, they took my phone but there were no further messages and the number from which the text originated no longer existed. Andrian had vanished. Frustratingly, I've been told very little. My liaison officer, Kate, can't answer my questions about what has happened to Mel. No one knows. She has vanished too. When I ask Kate for news of Andrian, she becomes cagey and speaks to me as if I'm six. 'We know he's a very bad man and officers from the Met in London are doing all they can to find him, but they fear he may have returned to Bulgaria with some of the other men involved.'

'Involved in what?'

She looks even more uncomfortable. 'I can't really say. We know that they kept some girls imprisoned at a house in London and that they may also have been shipping girls out of the UK. It's possible that your sister is safe and well, abroad, somewhere.'

Sex traffickers. I'm not stupid. Based upon what I overheard from Andrian on that fateful afternoon and the claim of her death in the text, I fear Mel may have been killed. But, deep down inside, even though there seems little hope, I refuse to believe it.

Over the last few months, I've cried myself dry and today I feel nothing as I'm urged forward to my seat in the front row of the crematorium. I catch glimpses of faces I recognise as I pass, people I knew in Thorpe St Andrew. It seems weird seeing them now, in these circumstances. Stony-faced, I sit through the ritual of saying goodbye to my mum. I was told the coroner recorded an open verdict on her death. The cause was a massive drug overdose and may have been accidental but I know the police suspect Andrian's involvement. Kate only divulged that piece of information because I was blaming myself for leaving her alone, but it actually made it worse. If I'd reported my fears to the police straight away, maybe she'd still be alive. The guilt is hard to bear, a canker eating me from within. In the end, I've had no choice but to shut it out, lock down my emotions, try to exist without letting myself feel anything.

The night I found out about Mum, I stayed with Alisha Wainwright but they took me away the following day to a place called Happytrees House. It's a home for kids who have nowhere else to go. Ridiculous name. I assume someone thought it would help make the kids who end up there feel comfortable. It just made me angry.

While I was there, there were twelve of us, aged seven to fifteen, with a team of adults, always at least four on duty. There was a lot of screaming and shouting. We were locked in our rooms at night, 'for our own safety.' I kept my head down. I wasn't going to be there long and had no interest in getting to know any of them.

There was one girl, only eight years old, called Stacey. She was the most troubled of them all: violent, aggressive, always pinching other kids' stuff. Even the staff were wary of her and kept their distance. I didn't blame them. If they went too close, she'd lash out. I saw her wallop a woman called Joan with a plate of spaghetti bolognaise she called 'disgusting'. She spent a lot of her days having 'time out' in a locked room, padded so she couldn't hurt herself. One day, she took my hairbrush. I found her in the communal dayroom, running it through her short, straggly, brown hair, gloating at me in triumph.

'Oh good, you've found my brush,' I said mildly. It was the first time I'd spoken to her.

'S'mine.' Glaring, she tucked it behind her so I could no longer see it.

'No, it isn't but it's fine if you want to borrow it,' I smiled. Despite my resolution to remain untouched by the people here, something about this tiny girl wormed at my heart. She scowled. When she took stuff, the other kids responded aggressively, resulting in a fight, or they told one of the adults. She always denied taking whatever she was accused of and never gave it back. I guess she took comfort in her victories. I wasn't following the trend and she was unsure how to react. 'Leave it in my room when you've finished with it.'

'S'mine,' she shouted as I left the room but I didn't respond.

The brush wasn't returned. Instead, she upped the ante, taking a succession of things – a pen, a magazine I was reading, even one of my T-shirts. I found her wearing it, ridiculous in the oversized, worn, red top with a picture of Snoopy on the front, and the sight made me laugh out loud. That made her cross.

'What you laughin' at?' she demanded, wrapping her thin arms across her body.

'Sorry. It looks better on you than me. It was a bit small for me. You can keep it if you like.'

'Can I?' Something leapt in her eyes, a light quickly extinguished.

'Sure. I have a few other things I've outgrown. You can have those too. Do you want to come and see?'

I watched her struggle with indecision, stubbornness warring with acquisitiveness. The latter won. 'OK.'

She followed me docilely to my room and watched as I dug out another old T-shirt and a pale green hoodie with a hole in the sleeve. 'Here, you can have these.' I tossed them across the bed and she hugged them to her, staring at me with wide eyes. It made me wonder how often she'd been given things. 'It's polite to say thank you when someone gives you a present.' She clamped her lips mutinously together and I shrugged. 'Suit yourself.' I turned my back on her and picked up another magazine, an old one I'd found in the dayroom.

'Thanks,' I heard her mumble. I smiled and looked around but she'd fled.

That small step forward with Stacey gave me an idea but it took several days before I could bring myself to action it. I had a dress, the one I'd worn the day we went, as a family, to London on the train six years earlier. It was pale yellow cotton, embroidered with large, white daisies. Sentimentally, I'd kept it, hidden in my cupboard – a reminder of happier times when I still had my dad ... my whole family. Tears formed as I held it to my chest, remembering. *Stop it! No use being soppy.* I smoothed it out and laid it carefully on my bed. Then, I went in search of Stacey.

She was overjoyed and her excitement thrilled me. 'Can I try it on?' she asked as she twirled around my room, clutching it to her.

'Of course.' I watched as she pulled it over the thin, cotton top and jeans she was already wearing.

'It fits!' She preened in front of the small mirror on my wall, standing further back to get a better view.

'It suits you.' I grinned. 'You look lovely in it.'

'And I can keep it?' Hope gleamed in her grey eyes.

'Yes.'

She smiled at me shyly. It was the first time I'd seen her smile properly – a genuine upward curve of her lips as opposed to the maniacal grin she affected when she was upsetting someone. 'Thanks.' She shot out of the door, no doubt to go back to her room to squirrel it away, leaving me with a warm glow. That glow burned even brighter when later, after tea, I returned to my room. There, lying on my bed, were the hairbrush, pen, magazine and all the other things she'd previously taken from me.

It was Stacey who got me thinking about my own future. She made me realise how much I enjoy helping others. When I leave school, I've decided, I want a career where I can do just that. In particular, I want to help children. I wish I could do more for Stacey and hope she'll be OK now I've left Happytrees for good. Already, it seems like a lifetime ago.

I blink away my thoughts as the coffin disappears from view. I can't say goodbye, can't bear to think about my mum's body turning to ash. Instead, I picture Mel, laughing at me as she teases me about boys. She has to be alive.

Surely, I'd know if she was dead? I was told that the police made several arrests – men of Eastern European descent – when they discovered four young girls imprisoned in a house in Brixton. They think Mel was there but she wasn't amongst the seven. *Get rid of her ... no, I mean permanently.* Those words haunt me and, for the first time today, I fight back tears. The police have failed to find Andrian. That's why they're here today, in case he shows up, and why I'm facing a future with a new identity.

The service is done. I check my watch. Less than twenty minutes. Poor Mum. As I'm gently nudged to my feet, I look up and realise that the crematorium is packed. There are even people standing at the back. Mum would've been pleased with that at least. Quickly, I look down again. I don't want to see pity in people's eyes. With Jane and Vicki shielding me, I walk outside into the blustery air.

'Sass?' It's Kaz. She's wearing a smart, black dress. Her mum and dad are with her but hang back as she approaches. 'Sass ... I'm so sorry ... what's happened is just terrible. I feel so bad for you.'

I try to smile. 'Thanks, Kaz.' I sense Jane and Vicki watching. Their presence irritates and I grab Kaz's arm, leading her away. 'Give me a few minutes,' I say to my guardians.

Jane frowns. 'Fine. Just remember what we told you.'

She's referring to the decision to leave my old life and my name behind. I must tell no-one, they said. For my own protection. Do they think I'm stupid?

I ignore her and lead Kaz away from the groups of people, now chattering, relieved the ordeal is over and they can return to their own lives. When we can't be overheard, I turn to face her. Her pretty face is scrunched with concern and I'm flooded with sadness. How can I bear to leave my best friend?

'What's going to happen to you?' she asks. 'Where will you live?'

'Foster parents,' I shrug as if it's no big deal. 'Not around here.'

My response shocks her. 'You're kidding! That's *awful*. You can live with us. Mum and Dad won't mind. We've plenty of room. I'll ask them now.'

I reach out an arm to stay her. 'That's kind but I can't. It's already decided.'

'But you *can't* move away from here,' she wails. 'It's your home. And what about me?'

'I'm sorry, Kaz. There's stuff I can't tell you right now but I've got to go. I promise I'll keep in touch ... somehow.' She just stares at me in horror. 'It'll be OK. You'll be fine ... I'll be fine.'

'That sucks!' Her face crumples.

I put my arm around her. She turns and pulls me into her embrace, gripping me tightly, as Jane scurries towards us. 'We have to go,' she says. I disentangle myself from my best friend and step away.

'Fine.' I give an apologetic wave to those who have gathered closer, sensing my departure, wanting to offer me their condolences, and stride towards the car in which I will travel to my new life. As I slide into the rear seat, I keep my face averted, my head held high. My eyelids prickle with grief and I dig my nails into the palm of my hand, the pain a welcome distraction, as we drive away.

CHAPTER 14

Todd

The end of term arrived and Todd wasted no time in reminding Lily of the pact they'd made. For their first date, they agreed to meet at The Fox, the pub where he'd bumped into her before, the occasion he'd prefer to forget. He hoped it wasn't a bad omen but it was her suggestion. 'Just a drink,' she said. 'I'll meet you there.'

He baulked at that. 'But I wanted to take you out for dinner somewhere nice,' he protested, mindful of Joe's previous advice.

'That sounds too serious. We're just going out as *friends*, remember?'

He remembered no such thing but thought it would be wise to quit while he was ahead. It was a start. He could be patient.

The evening was warm and balmy, a night for lovers. She arrived wearing her hair loose, a silky, golden cloud around her shoulders, and was dressed casually in a fitted, aquamarine top, jeans and sandals. Seeing her, his heart thumped a crazy rhythm, making coherent thought almost impossible. With effort, he hid his crippling rush of desire and managed to greet her without embarrassing himself too much. *Relax*, his mind commanded, as he stood at the bar ordering a beer and a glass of white wine. *Don't mess up.*

They carried the drinks outside where a soundtrack of chat and laughter filled the air. It was busy and the clientele included several twosomes: some young, some older, a few holding hands, others deep in conversation and one couple not looking at each other at all, their complete attention focused on their individual phones. Todd thought how sad that was. It was as if they had no interest in each other. He couldn't imagine ever preferring the company of a screen to Lily.

They managed to snag a spot in the furthest corner of the garden and sat on a bench, side by side. She was close enough for her fragrance, sensual and slightly musky, to tease his senses but far enough away to avoid any accidental contact. For the first time in his life when out on a date, his palms felt sticky and his mind flustered. In contrast, Lily seemed composed and at ease as she settled herself and planted her bag on the bench between them. When she raised her glass, he clinked his against it. 'To us,' he smiled, looking deep into her eyes.

She arched her brows. 'To becoming friends,' she quipped in response.

He grinned. There was definitely a spark between them, despite her protests. He felt it in the frissons of tension humming between them, like invisible pulses of sexual energy. His spirits rocketed and the old confidence resurfaced. When she asked him about his life, he relaxed into tales from his childhood and some of the scrapes he'd got into with his older brother, Jamie. He recounted the time when he and Jamie had got into trouble for nicking a six-foot, inflatable clown from outside a toy shop. They'd only done it for a bet and hadn't realised there was a CCTV camera which had recorded their antics.

'A giant clown?' she chuckled. 'With a big, red nose?'

'Yep. It was bigger than we were. It was windy that night and we had a hell of a job hanging on to it.'

'What? The nose?'

'Ha, ha, no ... the clown.'

'What on earth did you do with it?'

'Squashed it into Dad's shed in the back garden. We were planning on taking it back the next day, after we'd shown it to Neil Foster and won the bet. Instead, the police turned up. Luckily, they saw the *funny* side ...' he grinned, 'and we got off with a warning.'

'Told you off for *clowning* around?' Her eyes sparkled as she awaited his response.

He laughed, dredging his brain for a comeback. 'Exactly ... I thought that was a kind *jester*.'

'Weak,' she groaned.

'Sorry.' His expression was unrepentant and he launched into a series of stories, tried and tested, guaranteed to make her laugh. He told her all about his family: his mum and dad, who lived in Skegness and had just celebrated forty years of marriage; his sister, Grace, married with two kids and still bossing him around; and his partner-in-crime, Jamie, currently working in Dubai.

'Sounds like you're a very close family,' she said.

'We are but I'm guilty of not seeing them as often as I'd like. I guess it's easy to take them for granted.' He shrugged. 'As you teachers might say, could do better. How about you? Tell me about your family.'

She reached for her drink. 'Not much to say. We're not like your family.' When he pressed her further, she told him she had parents living in Kent and that she too had an older brother, Simon, a recently-married graphic designer living in Canterbury. Each nugget of information had to be prised out of her with a question; she seemed reluctant to offer it willingly. He noted her reticence and steered the conversation instead to her work, about which she was passionate.

'I love teaching.' Her face shone as she spoke. 'It's exhausting, often frustrating, but always rewarding. The kids are great.'

'All of them?' he queried. Charlotte liked to tell him about the 'naughty' children in her class.

'All of them. Some are more challenging than others; they're not all model pupils like your Charlotte. But each child is special. Often, the difficult kids have a lot going on in their lives which we know nothing about. You wouldn't believe some of the things they have to contend with at home.'

'I can imagine,' he murmured. 'That's what makes you such a good teacher – the fact that you care about the kids.'

'Thank you.' In the half light of dusk, he saw her cheeks flush pink. 'Tell me about your work.'

He pulled a face. 'I wish I enjoyed it as much as you love yours.' Briefly, he sketched details of his job, making her laugh at his description of some of the characters in his office. And later, as darkness wrapped itself around them, he opened up about his passion for writing and the books he'd published himself.

'That's amazing. I'll have to look them up. I love a good crime novel,' she said.

'Please don't feel you have to,' he protested.

'Not at all. I want to.' She glanced at her watch. 'I guess it's time to make a move.' The beer garden was now deserted and staff were circulating, collecting empty glasses.

'Yes. I guess we'd better,' he agreed, reluctant to move.

They bid each other a polite farewell and she left, as she came, under her own steam. But she *did* agree to see him again *and* gave him her phone number. The evening had been a success and he returned home a happy man, confident in his ability to break down her barriers in the weeks to come.

***

It took a while. He remained patient, courting her with every ounce of self-control in his possession, wary of frightening her off. She was cool, determined to stay 'just friends' even while the flame growing between them intensified. There was a part of her which she kept closed off, difficult to pin down. The mystery appealed to the writer in him. He wanted to unlock her secrets, show her that she could trust him. Getting to know her was certainly a challenge. On one date, after a particularly evasive answer to one of his questions, he asked if there were any dead bodies in her closet.

'Yes.' She snatched her hand from his. 'The bodies of nosy men who refuse to respect a girl's privacy.' At her defensiveness, he backed down but it made him wonder. She was definitely hiding something. He couldn't begin to imagine what it might be but it had to have something to do with her family and her childhood. Any curiosity he displayed about those aspects of her life made her prickly

She insisted upon regular updates as to the progress of his latest novel which was taking him longer than usual to write. Meanwhile, she'd read his first two books – in a flatteringly short space of time – and said how much she'd enjoyed them. Spurred by her enthusiasm, he was happy to give her the gist of the plot.

One night, after a meal in a country pub a few miles north of Bury St Edmunds, he told her how he'd based the missing girl in his book on the real-life tragedy of a young woman who'd disappeared several years earlier. 'It was strange,' he mused with a smile. 'I'd just met you at parents' evening and then went home to do some research. There was this photo of a girl who looked the spitting image of you. That's when I knew you'd got under my skin – when I was seeing you in photos of other women.'

'Oh.' She lapsed into silence and he frowned, wondering what he'd said wrong. The expression on her face reminded him of a cornered doe. He took a sip of his beer while he contemplated what to say next, anxious to prevent further withdrawal. 'What was the girl's name?' she asked eventually, twisting her hair between her fingers and refusing to meet his gaze.

'I can't remember now ... it's a while since I looked at the story. Does it matter? I could find out.'

'No, no, not at all. I just wondered. It seems very sad – a story of a missing girl.'

'It was. That story got to me. Probably because the girl looked so much like you.' He grinned at her but she was still looking down, her fingers now playing with a cotton hanging loose on her shirt. 'I remember the girl had gone to London for a job and was never seen again. The story was even more tragic than that. The dad had already been killed in an accident and there was something else, something awful, but I can't remember what it was.' He dug deep into the recesses of his memory but nothing surfaced. 'There was a younger sister too.' He screwed up his face, thinking. 'She had an unusual name.'

When he looked across, her face was drained of colour, deathly white. 'Let's change the subject.' She exhaled and stood, avoiding his gaze. 'It's too sad a story for such a beautiful evening. I'll go and fetch us another drink.' He noticed the tremor in her hand as she reached for his glass.

'Are you OK, Lily?' he asked.

'Of course.' She smiled weakly. 'Same again?'

He nodded and watched as she disappeared, like a wraith, around the corner. That was odd. Did she know something about the story? How could he ask her? He couldn't, he quickly decided, not without upsetting her. Best to let her tell him things in her own time.

She was gone a while and he was beginning to worry that she'd disappeared too. That's how insecure he felt around her. But, when she returned, she'd recovered her composure. Whatever had disturbed her, she'd got over it and the tension had disappeared. Todd relaxed too and his tone became more teasing, the mystery over the missing girl soon forgotten. She didn't object when he draped a casual arm around her shoulders and, for the first time, when he flirted with her, she responded, her beautiful eyes dancing with a seductive sparkle. Emboldened, at the end of the evening, he took her in his arms and kissed her, gently at first, but then with the pent-up passion of months of waiting. Her lips tasted of strawberries from the Pimms she'd been drinking and parted at his touch; her body felt soft and pliant against his. He held her tightly and she pulled him even closer, her hands tangling in his hair, her hips pressing against his.

'Oh God,' he murmured huskily, relaxing his hold. 'I've been waiting so long. You're incredible.' He waited for her inevitable withdrawal, cradling her tenderly against his chest, hardly daring to breathe lest he spoil the moment.

Instead, she raised her lips once more to his ...

CHAPTER 15

Saskia
2004

'See you later.' I wave goodbye to my friends on the bus. My new friends. From my new school. Not that we're close. Not like me and Kaz were. Anyway, with GCSEs fast approaching, I'm spending most of my free time revising. My education is my future and I'm not going to mess it up. There's little spare time for a social life and that suits me just fine.

I've been lucky. My foster parents are great and I now live in a gorgeous house. I even have my own bathroom! Sometimes, I have to pinch myself. Mel would love it. Her dreams for the future always included a big house with an en-suite bathroom.

I miss my sister, more than I can say. My counsellor tells me I'm doing very well – whatever that means – but that's because I don't have a choice. I have to get on with my life but that doesn't stop me thinking of her every day. In my head, she's very much alive but I know the police think she's dead. The men involved in the Veronik trafficking ring have all been tried and convicted. The trial was reported in the papers. My foster parents tried to shield me from all the news while it was ongoing but I read every word written about it. I wanted to know. In the press though, there was no mention of Andrian and certainly nothing about Mel. It was like neither of them ever existed.

I have a new identity. No-one here, apart from my foster parents, knows who I am, not even their son, who's away at university. He seems OK – a bit geekish but nice enough. After I received that threatening text from Andrian, everyone involved in my case thought it best for me to have a fresh start. That was fine by me. At the time, I was too numb to care and just went along with their suggestion. And once it had happened, there was no going back, so it was up to me to make the best of it. At least, I feel reassured that Andrian can't find me ... as long as my identity remains a secret. With my new life around me like a security blanket, I've done my best to shut out the bad stuff. Mind you, I'm still jumpy and fearful that people will discover who I am – that girl in the papers whose family are all gone. It's made me a bit standoffish but I don't want anyone getting too close. I'm friendly enough, and enjoy a laugh with the kids here, but that's as far as it goes. It's called being careful.

The afternoon is warm and I'm carrying my blazer. Spring sunshine filters through the trees, dappling the pavement. As I walk along the leafy avenue towards my new home, I fish in my bag for my phone, the one no-one knows I have. There's only one number saved and I ring it. No answer. I don't expect there to be. I let it ring just three times and hang up. It's our code, mine and Kaz's. If she hears it and it's safe to call me back, she will. This is the best time to phone her. She should be at home by now, alone, upstairs in her room. I keep the phone in my hand and wait, leaning up against a tree. I think it's a cherry. It's a mass of pink blossom. As I'm studying the flowers, the phone vibrates in my hand. Kaz.

'Hi,' she says. I've trained her not to say my name, just in case.

'Hi, how was your day?'

'Same old. I'm freaking out about exams though. How about you?'

'Fine. Same.'

We chat for a few minutes. Mostly, she does the talking, telling me all about people from school and what's been happening. I can only tell her general stuff. She doesn't know where I am or anything important about my new life and I'm cautious about revealing anything which might give her a clue. Not that I don't trust her. I do. But I have these horrible nightmares about Andrian getting hold of her, asking her about me. Best for us both if she knows nothing. Probably stupid, I know. I often wonder if I'm being paranoid. *Better safe than sorry.* Something Dad used to say a lot. Guess it's rubbed off. Not that it helped him.

'Look, I *do* need to tell you something.' Her voice has become hesitant and my senses fire up to full alert. There's a long pause.

'Yes ...' I say to encourage her.

'Well, it's awkward. You might be a bit upset.' Instinctively, I know what she's going to say before she voices the actual words. My throat burns with mounting dismay. 'It's just ... Darrell and I have got pretty close recently ... after you left and, well ... he asked me out yesterday. And I said yes. I hope that's OK?' Her concern for me, and for my reaction, resonates across the distance between us. For a moment, I can't bring myself to speak. Anger, jealousy and bitterness flare in my chest. Darrell Parkinson is mine. That's what I want to say. Keep your thieving hands off him. You're supposed to be my friend. 'I'm sorry, Sass. I know how much you liked him. And he liked you too. But you're not here and ... well ... I've grown to like him too ... a lot.' Those last words were barely a whisper.

'Don't say my name,' I snap, grateful for the chance not to answer her question.

'Oh, sorry.'

The rage dissipates, leaving me feeling raw and empty. I swallow the lump in my throat and take a deep breath. 'It's fine, Kaz ... whatever.' The careless words reveal my hurt and she renews her apologies.

'Oh, you *are* upset. I knew you would be. Look, I'll tell him I've changed my mind,' she says and my objections melt away.

'Don't be daft.' My voice is gruff but it's the best I can do. 'You and Darrell, hey? Who'd have thought it! I hope it works out for you both.'

'Are you sure?' I hear her relief.

'Of course. Actually, I was going to tell you about this boy in my maths class. He looks just like Justin Timberlake. And I think he may like me too ...'

'Ooh, JT? That knocks Darrell out of the park -inson!' She laughs a little too hard at the lame joke. 'Exciting! I'll look forward to hearing how things develop.'

'Mm, well, I'd better go.' I'm eager to end the call but I force the words out. 'I hope you and Darrell have a good time.'

'Oh, thank you. That means so much. Love you.'

'You too.'

I hit the red button with unnecessary force. *Dammit.* Kaz and Darrell. The sense of loss, of what might have been, is overwhelming and bitter tears trickle down my cheeks. I wipe them roughly away. I've no room for self-pity. I'm a survivor. I owe it to my family to look forward, not back.

Thrusting the phone into the zipped section of my bag, I head home.

CHAPTER 16

Todd

Things developed quickly from that first kiss. Both Todd and Lily were only too keen to make up for months of frustrated passion. They couldn't get enough of each other. It wasn't long before she was regularly staying over at his place during the week and they were officially a couple. They met up with friends and were invited to social events together. Todd worried how Charlotte might react to his new relationship and refrained from seeing Lily at the weekends when his daughter was staying. Eventually though, the time came when he braced himself to sit down with his daughter and break the news. He needn't have worried.

'Oh, I already knew that!' she said scornfully. 'Lucy saw you with her, walking in the park, holding hands. She told me.'

'Oh,' he replied, slightly flummoxed. Lucy Adams was one of Charlotte's school friends.

'I knew you liked her anyway. That's why you kept finding excuses to go and see her on Monday mornings while I was still in her class.'

'Oh,' he said again. 'And ... er ... how do you feel about that? About us seeing each other?'

'Good. I like Miss Nichol.' She turned back to the book she was reading, before looking up once more, puzzle lines crinkling her forehead. 'There *is* one thing though, Daddy ...'

'What's that?'

'Will I still have to call her Miss Nichol?'

He laughed. 'You will when you're at school. I guess you'll have to ask her what she'd prefer out of school.'

'She won't want me to call her Mummy, will she?' Her face scrunched into a frown. 'I've already got a Mummy.'

'You have.' He ruffled her hair. 'No. I'm pretty sure it'll be fine for you to call her Lily.'

With that hurdle negotiated, the three of them often spent weekends together – biking, having picnics, eating pizza, watching films, always laughing. Todd couldn't remember a time when he'd felt happier. Life was good. More than good. Of course, he still wanted a literary agent and a big-name publishing deal. Those ambitions burned as brightly as ever, especially now his novel was nearing completion. He'd written the first draft, edited it and sent it out to beta readers. Early responses were positive but, despite Lily's pleas, he wouldn't let her read it.

'I want it to be perfect, the best it can be, before you see it,' he said when she asked him again, one evening, when they were alone.

'But I already know some of the plot,' she wheedled. 'I just want to know what secrets Jenna was hiding and if there's a happy ending for her.'

Jenna was the name he'd given the missing girl in his book. As a teenager, she'd disappeared, one May evening, after leaving a friend's house on her bike at around 6 p.m. The bike was found lying in a ditch, a few miles from the route she should have taken. Despite a massive police search, she was never found. Then, on the anniversary of her disappearance, her parents received a postcard from her, in her writing, with a cryptic message they were unable to decipher. The police investigation gained new life as a consequence but petered out again when no further evidence emerged. Every year, another postcard would arrive and the investigative cycle would be repeated. All to no avail. Distraught and frustrated, Jenna's parents hired private investigator, Andy Schofield, a cynical, ruthless ex-police officer and the main character in Todd's novels. It was when he started digging that Jenna's secrets began to emerge ...

'You won't have to wait too much longer. I'm just making sure you stick around,' he teased. 'And anyway, if I tell you everything now, you won't want to buy the book.'

She pouted. 'You're so mean. I bought the other two. Don't I get the third free?'

'Play your cards right ...' He wiggled his eyebrows suggestively. 'We could probably work something out.' He pulled her to him and kissed her, effectively silencing further protests.

'That's your answer for everything,' she murmured.

'It's a damn good answer,' he mumbled, sliding his hands beneath her top and teasing the sides of her breasts.

'Mm,' came her response. Her own hands were already busy working the button free on his jeans.

It was always like that with the two of them – an instant flare of physical attraction, ignited with as little as a single glance. Much as Todd enjoyed his daughter's company, he treasured these times when he and Lily were alone, when they could discover more about each other and he could peel off her layers, both literally and figuratively. The first was as wonderful as in his dreams; the lightest touch was enough to spark passion which consumed them both. The second, getting to know more of the person behind those defensive walls, was much trickier. She shared so little of herself and he didn't like to probe. When he was alone, he speculated about what might have happened to make her so reticent. He wondered about an abusive ex-boyfriend but, when he tentatively broached the subject of past relationships, she was casually dismissive.

'There's been no one special,' she informed him with a shrug. 'As you know, I'm very picky about the men I see, so they've been few and far between.' She smiled then, and leaned over to kiss him gently on his lips, 'I knew there was someone like you out there. I wasn't going to settle for anything less.' She only had to do something like that to make him forget those little niggles bothering him.

There were things about her life which she clearly didn't want him to know. In particular, she was very evasive about her childhood and her family. He'd asked when she was going to take him home to meet her mum and dad. She said it wasn't a big deal, that they weren't that close.

'You're not ashamed of me, are you?' he joked.

'Don't be daft,' she replied and changed the subject.

When he first asked her to move in with him – she stayed over most nights anyway – she said it was too soon. Fair enough. Over subsequent weeks, he repeated his invitation, again and again, but her response didn't change. Eventually, he gave up, accepting that he needed to give it a lot more time. Pushing would only drive her away.

But disappointment began to fester in the back of his mind. Why was she so reluctant to make a commitment to him? He wanted to marry her – maybe, have children together – but he didn't dare broach the subject when she wasn't prepared to sell her flat and move in with him. He hadn't even told her yet that he loved her. She made it clear she wanted to take their relationship at her own pace and that was fine by him. After the delayed start, he accepted that things had accelerated so rapidly between them that she wanted to exercise some caution. He was a bit overwhelmed with it all himself. She wasn't ready and he was happy to wait for as long as it took.

Except, seeds of worry began to grow. Was she *ever* going to commit to him fully? What could he do to help her take that leap of faith? When she continued to safeguard her innermost thoughts and feelings from him, he could see no clear path to the promise of a future together, try as he might. As weeks became months, and their passion showed no signs of dimming, he should've felt reassured. Their relationship couldn't be stronger. Except, deep down, he knew he wanted more ... more than she was willing to give. And further agonising doubts followed. They leapt, unwelcome intruders, into his consciousness, refusing to be dismissed, despite all his efforts to ignore them. Could it be that she didn't see her future with him and Charlotte at all? Was this merely a transient interlude for her, one from which she was planning to move on? He didn't believe it and yet the worry persisted, especially at night-time when sleep eluded him. Then, he would stare into the darkness, listening to the gentle breathing of her slumber, seized with terror that, one day, he'd wake up ... and she'd be gone.

CHAPTER 17

Saskia
2010

'You've got an interview next week? That's brilliant! Fingers crossed. I'm sure you'll smash it.' Gemma, a friend from secondary school, beams at me as we sit opposite each other in a coffee shop in Canterbury, enjoying a long-awaited catch-up.

My smile is less confident. 'I hope so. I'm excited about it. Nervous though.'

'It'll be fine. They'll love you.'

'It's at the school where I did my final placement so they do know me already.'

'Even better. I bet it's just a formality.' Crumbs flake from her mouth as she tries to eat her pastry and talk at the same time. 'You work so hard, Sam. You deserve this.'

'Thanks, Gem.' Talk of the upcoming interview sends my nerves fluttering and I'm keen to change the subject. 'How's your work going?'

She stuffs in the remaining morsel and launches into tales of her life as a junior marketing executive, working in a busy office in Canterbury. It sounds like her work colleagues are a fun crowd and she loves her job. Her face glows as she chats, a smile playing about her lips as she recounts some of the stunts they pull.

'Last week, we had one of those team building sessions, paintballing in the woods. I was on Rob's team.' Rob is a guy she's fancied since she started there, eight months ago. 'It was a riot. Especially when we were up against the Heiffer. Can you imagine? What an opportunity for revenge!'

I giggle. 'What happened?' The Heiffer is a senior marketing executive named Diane Heiffenberg, so nicknamed because she treats everyone, in Gemma's words, like 'cowshit'. She's the only person I've ever heard my friend complain about.

'You should have seen her! She turned up in full combat gear, while the rest of us were just in jeans, and kept interrupting the guys giving us instructions. She'd been before so she wanted to show off. Anyway, Rob and I made a pact to target her and then the whole team joined in. She was completely spattered in paint, head to toe, by the end of the day. Far more than the rest of us. Best bit, though, was when she tripped and fell head first into the mud. It was quite dry in the woods, with all this nice weather we've been having, but she managed to find a lovely, boggy patch to topple into. I only wish I'd had my phone handy to take a pic. She went in face first, arse in the air. You should've heard the fuss! Rob and I were killing ourselves laughing.'

I smile and take a sip of my coffee. 'I assume she didn't hurt herself?'

'No, just her dignity. She likes to dish out crap so it was good for her to get a taste of it! Perfect karma.'

It's great to catch up with Gemma. I haven't seen her for a while. After sixth form, my teaching degree kept me in Canterbury, at the university there, while she headed to Sheffield for a course in marketing. Since she got this job, back in the city, we've met up a few times but it's been difficult to manage more. I was busy with my final teaching placement and let her down on more than one occasion. Now I'm finished, it's time to make amends. I've also organised catch-ups with Kerry and Matt, my other school mates, later in the week. All three of them were good to me when I first moved to Kent – made an effort to get to know me, despite my prickliness. They're part of the reason I feel happy in this skin, in this life. My foster family are the other reason. From the outset, they've been nothing but kind, accepting and, most of all, loving. I couldn't help but fall in love with them too. At first, I resisted it, troubled by my conscience at what I felt was a betrayal of my real family.

But not anymore. As Leonardo da Vinci said, 'Life without love is no life at all,' and I remind myself of that when I'm feeling guilty about moving on. And my family would've wanted me to be happy. I can accept that now.

Every day I think of Mel and wonder where she is. I refuse to believe that she's dead. Instead, I have a theory that she vanished, like that magician we saw all those years ago when we were kids, and will return one day when I'm least expecting it. I may be kidding myself but the illusion helps.

Gemma looks at her watch and sighs. 'I'd better be getting back to work. I'll just pop to the loo first.' While she's gone, I scan the other groups in the room. The small coffee shop is busy for a Wednesday lunchtime and the cramped space is filled with the loud hum of conversation and clatter of china. There's a varied clientele: some deeply engaged in conversation; some sitting on their own, reading or checking phones; families; tourists; couples; a slice of society taking a quick break from work or shopping or sightseeing. It feels good to sit amongst them, enjoying time out, taking a breath from the petty struggles of the day.

The bell on the door behind me jingles and I feel the shift of air on the back of my neck as more customers enter. They walk past me and head for the counter. The woman is slim and elegant, dark hair in a chignon, long legs shapely in high heels. She exudes the kind of sophisticated glamour of the beautiful and rich. Her companion is a man, tall, fit and athletic, dark hair peppered with grey, wearing an olive jacket and black jeans. A handsome couple. I watch idly over the rim of my coffee mug. Business colleagues, maybe? No, he rests his hand possessively on her waist as they stand at the counter. It's a strong hand, lightly tanned. They're a couple. I start to weave a romantic fantasy about them. It's a thing I do.

The woman turns to speak to him. I see her lips moving, red and glossy, her skin flawless. She's older than I first thought. Probably late thirties or early forties. As she turns back to speak to the assistant, the man spins around. He's checking the room for a spare table. *Good luck with that.* Then, I catch my breath and drag my eyes to his face once more. I see the irritation in the harsh planes of his countenance as he realises there will be nowhere to sit and his lips curl as he mutters something to the woman. She shrugs and waves an imperious hand at the girl behind the counter. They're leaving. I can't tear my eyes away, although I know I should. I stare, transfixed, horror building, as they head towards the door. The woman sees me looking and gives a polite smile. The man notices too. His hooded eyes lock with mine and I see him start, his step faltering slightly as recognition hits. Too late, I avert my head. My heart is doing a frenzied dance in my chest and I can barely breathe. I even smell his cologne as he brushes past, a heady, musky scent. It's him ... Andrian.

He stops and turns back. 'You go on. I won't be a minute,' he says to the woman, his voice clipped with that Eastern European accent. I feel his approach as he returns to stand beside me. 'Well, well,' he mutters, his voice low. 'After all this time. Little Saskia.' He says my name like a caress but his fingers take an iron grip of my arm. I refuse to acknowledge him. 'How wonderful to see you again. Mind if I sit down?' He doesn't wait for a reply; instead, he slides into Gemma's vacant seat, his teeth exposed in a wolfish smile.

I say nothing. I'm thinking hard. Mostly about escaping but I know I can't. I'm trapped. He's sitting between me and the door. I want to scream at the other people in the coffee shop, tell them what this man has done, insist that someone restrains him while I call the police. But I do nothing except stare at his face, waiting to see what he will do. My body is paralysed with fear.

'How long is it since I've dreamt of catching up with you ... fulfilling that promise I made ... is it six ... no, seven years?' I remain silent, willing the nightmare to end. 'Still, what do you English say ... better late than never?'

I can't speak. It's like I'm a child again – powerless, unable to do anything but submit to his will. I detest this man with the whole of my being and yet I sit, mute and motionless.

'Are you alright, Sam?' Gemma has returned, curious at the unexpected interaction between this stranger and me.

I see he's annoyed at the interruption but he grants her his most charming smile. 'Sam ...' he emphasises the name, 'is an acquaintance from way back. Sam ... Potter?'

'No, it's Smith,' Gemma leaps in before I can stop her.

'Of course, that's right. Sam *Smith*. How could I have forgotten! Well, Sam, I'll make sure we keep in touch ... now I've found you again. I'll look forward to it.' He stands and, like a perfect gentleman, helps Gemma into her seat. As he leaves, he stoops to whisper in my ear, his fingers clamped like a vice on my shoulder. 'I *always* keep my promises.'

'Weird guy.' Gemma raises her eyebrows at me as Andrian disappears through the door and out of sight.

'Yes.'

She sees my closed expression and shrugs. 'I guess I'd better make a move.' She gathers up her things and leans in to give me a hug when I don't move. 'You enjoy your leisure while you still can. Good luck with the interview. Let me know how it goes.'

'Will do.'

When she's gone, I reach for my phone with trembling fingers. I daren't leave the safety of the coffee shop. Andrian might be out there still, waiting for me. The threat in his voice was unmistakeable. I'll ring Kate – Kate Bell, the police liaison officer who supported me when Mel vanished and Mum died. She'll tell me what to do. Better yet, she'll send someone to come and get me.

But Kate doesn't pick up and a recording tells me to leave a message. I don't. I wait a few minutes and try again. Still no reply. Now what? The waitress is looking pointedly at my empty coffee cup and I order another to buy time. I need to think of a plan but my mind seems stupefied and all I can see is him. His eyes glittering with triumph, mock my futile efforts to shut him out.

I eke out the coffee over the next thirty minutes and try Kate three more times, without success. The waitress hovers once more and I bite my lip. 'Excuse me,' I ask. 'But is there a back way out of here I can use?'

She frowns. 'Staff only.'

'Do you think you could show me? My ex-boyfriend is outside and I'm trying to avoid him. Please?'

She hesitates. 'We're not supposed to ...'

'Please,' I say again. 'I'm a bit scared of him to be honest.'

She glances over her shoulder at the counter and sighs. 'Alright, but come now, quickly.'

We head in the direction of the toilets and then through a door leading to the kitchen. 'Through there,' she mutters, pointing. 'There's a door at the far side. It's unlocked.'

'Thank you.' I say over my shoulder but she's already bustling in the other direction. When I reach the door, I inch it open and peer out. It leads into a back alley, full of overflowing waste bins. No people. I creep out and sneak past the back of other shops along the street. When I reach the end and see pedestrians walking, I don't hesitate. I leap in amongst them, walking quickly, keeping my head lowered. At any moment, I expect to feel Andrian's grasp on my arm, pulling me back, but it doesn't happen. Still, I daren't look behind; he may be tracking me, watching to see where I live. I reach a bus stop and leap onto the bus just pulling in. I've no idea where it's heading; the need to escape is all-consuming. As soon as I've done it, I panic. If he is following, he'll get on behind me. I'll be trapped.

It's a single decker and I slip to the back. Only then do I glance behind. No sign of a tall, dark Bulgarian in an olive jacket. As the bus pulls away, I heave a sigh of relief. For the moment, I feel safe ... but I know it won't last.

CHAPTER 18

Todd

Things were looking up. Lily had agreed to go on holiday with him and Charlotte over the Easter break. Before she could change her mind, Todd booked a cottage in the Cotswolds. It was an area he'd visited often when he was a child and he had fond memories of pretty villages, honey coloured, stone walls and rolling hills. An internet site for the area promised farm and wildlife parks, steam railways and child-friendly museums – plenty to keep Charlotte amused. The place he booked also had access to a swimming pool for days when they just wanted to hang out and chill. It was going to be perfect.

He couldn't help hoping, when they were relaxed, away from the hustle and pace of day-to-day life, that she'd open up to him a little more. There had been another incident, just that morning. She was in the shower when her phone rang. It was lying on the bed beside him and he glanced across at the screen to see who it was. The caller ID displayed the initials KB, not anyone he knew. When she came out of the shower, he told her about the call.

'Who is KB?' he asked.

She was annoyed. 'Have you been looking at my phone?'

'Hey!' He held up his hands. 'It was right there. When it rang, I couldn't help seeing the screen.'

'OK. Sorry.' She smiled then, and wrapped her arms around him. 'I'm just cranky because you didn't join me in the shower.'

'I'm sure I can make up for it,' he grinned, pulling the towel away from her body. He never had learnt the identity of KB.

***

That evening, when she returned home from work, he could see straight away that something was wrong. She charged into his house, wild-eyed, as twitchy as a young doe, and locked the door behind her.

'If anyone rings the doorbell, don't answer it!' she gasped.

'What's happened?' He stepped forward to take her in his arms but she ducked around him.

'Not here. In the kitchen,' she whispered over her shoulder.

Her anxiety was contagious and he felt his heart leap. 'Lily, what's going on?' he asked again.

'The press,' she muttered, throwing down her bag and sinking onto a stool. 'They want to talk to me.

He wasn't sure what he'd been expecting but it wasn't that. 'The press? News reporters?' She nodded. 'But why?'

She sighed. 'Do you remember that incident at school last summer ... when a parent tried to abduct his son from my class?'

'Yes.' He'd heard the gossip on the playground and knew Lily had been involved. There had been a letter from the school about it too, playing the whole thing down and saying the children had been in no danger. It had taken place before they started going out, when he was trying to stay away from her. He dredged his memory for further details but nothing sprang to mind. 'I didn't really know what had happened,' he said. 'I think at the time it seemed a lot of fuss about nothing.'

Her shoulders sagged. 'Exactly. Well, the case has now come to court and the papers – the national papers – have got hold of it. There was a story in *The Gazette* today. Reporters have been at the school and, apparently, they're staking out my flat. A neighbour phoned the school to warn me. At the moment, they don't know I'm here. Sarah smuggled me out in the back of her car, covered with a blanket. But I don't know how long that'll last. If they turn up, you've got to convince them I'm not here.'

He was bewildered. 'But why are they going to all this trouble to speak to you? I don't understand.'

Wearily, she told him exactly what had happened. He listened with growing astonishment. 'God, Lily, that's incredible. I'm not surprised they're calling you a heroine.'

She shrugged. 'Anyone would've done the same. I couldn't let him take Tommy. The poor, little boy was terrified. It was my job to protect him.'

'Yes, I see that, but *mace* spray?'

'Yeah, well ... it was just something I kept in my bag. Just in case ... you know.'

He shook his head, flabbergasted at what she was telling him. 'You shouldn't have put yourself in danger like that.'

She gave him a look. 'Tell that to Kevin Hathersett! I didn't exactly have a choice.'

'God, you could've been killed!' The realisation dropped into the pit of his stomach, a cold, hard ball of fear and he grabbed her hand. 'Lily, please don't take risks like that in the future.'

'I'm not intending to,' she said, her voice dry.

He smiled. 'Let me get you a drink. It sounds like you could use one.' Pulling a bottle of wine from the fridge, another thought struck him. 'So ... why don't you want to talk to the press about it? From what you've told me, they're only going to have good things to say about you.' He poured her a glass of chilled Sauvignon Blanc.

'Thank you,' she mumbled as he handed it to her. Her face was closed off, creased in an obstinate refusal to tell him more, the expression she wore all too often.

He tried again. 'Seriously, Lily, surely it would be best to get it over with. Talk to them and then they'll leave you alone.'

She snorted at that. 'As if it were that simple! You think they'll be satisfied with a few brief words? Then they'll all go home?'

'Well, they will eventually. But if you say nothing, it's like you have something to hide ...' Her sharp intake of breath made him pause. When she said nothing, he ploughed on. 'Look ... I've had a little experience with dealing with the press. It comes with the job. In the past, when clients were being harassed by reporters, we've released a statement. Your school could do that. But I also think that a brief interview – giving the press your side of the story – is your best option to get them off your back. Speak to your headteacher and ask him to take advice from the local authority about what you should do. We can try to keep the whole thing as low-key as possible. If you do nothing, chances are the press will hound you until they get what they want.'

She squeezed her eyes shut. 'I just want it all to go away,' she murmured.

'I know.' He wanted to comfort her but wasn't sure how best to go about it. If only he knew what she was so afraid of ...

***

The next day the story was on the front pages of several newspapers. Lily took Todd's advice. A statement was issued from the school and she gave an interview to one of the tabloids in return for a donation to the NSPCC. Todd watched over her anxiously and she was subdued but otherwise calm. Reporters moved on to something else and their lives returned to normal. There were just a few days until the end of term and, in Todd's opinion, it couldn't come fast enough. They'd both welcome a break away from all the stress and drama.

Later that night, something disturbed him from his sleep. Beside him, the space in the bed was empty. He called out but there was no response. All the lights were off and Lily wasn't in the bathroom or getting some water. Puzzled and slightly concerned, he pulled on shorts and a T-shirt and went downstairs. There was no sign of her. Mild worry turned to full-blown fear. Hadn't he always thought this might happen? Hadn't he fretted that she might, one day, disappear, like the girl in his novel?

Having searched the house, he noticed her coat was missing and opened the back door. 'Lily,' he called, 'Are you out here?'

'Yes. Over here, on the grass.' Relief rippled through him, as he squinted into the darkness, dissolving the knots of tension in his neck. *She hadn't gone.* After a few moments, when his eyes adjusted, he spotted a dark shape. She was wrapped in her coat, lying on a rug, staring upwards.

'What are you doing out there?'

'Looking at the stars,' she replied calmly, as if it were a perfectly rational occupation for the middle of the night.

He wanted to shout, tell her how worried he'd been. Instead, he grabbed his coat and hat, thrust his bare feet into his boots and walked over to her. 'Is there room for me on that rug?' he asked. In response, she shuffled over and he lay down beside her. 'What made you come out here?' He kept his tone light, mildly curious.

'I couldn't sleep.' she replied. 'And it's a beautiful night for stars. No cloud.'

He nodded, even though she couldn't see him. 'Can you identify them?'

'Some. The easy ones. Venus. The Plough. Orion's Belt.' She pointed her arm to show him. 'There have been a few satellites coming over too.' She chuckled. 'I like to give the stars my own names. Look, you see that one over there ... small but very bright ... that has to be Charlotte. And that one, next to it, I've named Michael Winterbottom.'

'Why?' He was intrigued that the headteacher of Lily's school merited a star.

'Oh, well, if I tell you, you've got to promise not to tell another living soul.'

'I promise.'

'You see it's a bit pale and feeble-looking.' She giggled. 'That's Michael Winterbottom.'

'And those two over there, really close together, looking as if they're fused together ...' he joined in the game, '... that's you and me at the moment.' He squeezed her tighter. 'Hey, have you found one to fit Dave Parker?' She'd told him a bit about the work colleague who was a constant thorn in her side.

She uttered a short laugh. '*He* doesn't deserve a star.' After a moment, she added, 'Nope, he definitely isn't up there. Sadly, he was so up himself, he imploded years ago.'

He burst into laughter, loving this strange moment of closeness with her. 'When I was a boy,' he said. 'I used to spend hours out at night, looking at the stars through my telescope. It wasn't a very good one though. I couldn't see much more with it than I could see without it. Still, I liked to fancy myself as a bit of a stargazer.'

'Which ones do you know?' she asked.

'Not much more than you. My favourite is Canis Major.' He pointed to show her. 'You can pick it out if you look for Sirius, that really bright star over there.' He traced his finger in the air. 'The head is diagonally above it; along there is the line of its back; there are the legs and there's the tail.'

'I see it,' she said.

'And over there is Cassiopeia – five stars making a W.'

'Oh yes, it really does look like a W. That's an easy one to remember.'

'Did you know ...' he was on a roll now, '... that the Plough is also known as the Big Dipper? It's part of the Ursa Major constellation. If you imagine a line connecting the front stars of the Big Dipper and continue along that line upwards, the first bright star you come to is Polaris, the North Star.'

She turned to face him. 'I hadn't realised you were an astronomer. If I had, I'd have invited you to join me out here sooner.'

'Lucky I came anyway.'

A comfortable silence grew between them. In the distance, he could hear the hum of occasional traffic along the A14. She snuggled closer and shivered.

'You're getting cold,' he said.

'I know. I've been out here a while.'

'Anything bothering you?' he asked lightly.

He felt her shrug. 'Not really. Just life, I guess. I was lying out here thinking how small and insignificant we are compared to all of this.' She stretched her arms out to the sky. 'Nothing on Earth lasts. I was thinking about us and how soon we will all be over.'

He tightened his grip on her. 'I'm not going anywhere.'

She carried on as if he hadn't spoken. 'And then I was thinking about the stars – how beautiful they are. But even *they* don't last forever. Eventually, they burn themselves out. Everything changes.' Her voice was sad, wistful, redolent with regret.

Sudden fear clutched at his heart. 'Lily ...' His voice throbbed with emotion. 'Are you trying to tell me that you've got a serious illness, that you're going to die?'

'No! What on earth makes you think that?' She squeezed his arm. 'I'm perfectly fine. Sorry, I didn't mean to scare you. I guess I'm just being a bit maudlin. I get like that sometimes. Even when I'm happy, I worry that things will go wrong.'

He exhaled loudly, his breath puffing clouds into the cold air. 'There are no guarantees about anything,' he acknowledged slowly, choosing his words with care. 'But, if you're talking about you and me ... as I said, I'm not going anywhere. I'll always be here for you, Lily.'

Her sigh resonated with an emotion he didn't recognise. 'I know.' She shuffled to a sitting position. 'We'd better go in. It's late and we've both got to get up for work.' They stood and she picked up the rug.

'Lily,' he said again, his heart clenching at the sight of her hunched shoulders. 'I promise you. I'm not going anywhere. I love you.'

She reached for his hand. 'I know. Me too.'

There. They'd both said the words. Joy rushed through him. He wanted to dance naked on the grass and shout it to the world ... but she was already heading inside. It was only later, when she was safely sleeping beside him and he replayed the moment in his head, that he realised she hadn't actually told him she loved him. *Me too.* It wasn't quite the same. And she *hadn't* promised to stay with him, as he had to her.

Two days later, just before the start of the Easter break and their holiday in the Cotswolds, she was gone.

CHAPTER 19

Saskia
2010

Seeing Andrian again has changed everything. I want to scream my anger and frustration aloud. I like my life as it is. Things are coming together. I've worked hard for my degree and my dream of teaching is at my fingertips. I want to pretend I haven't seen him – forget it happened.

But he'll find me. The menace in his words was clear. 'I always keep my promises.' I'd believed him all those years ago when he'd vowed my fate would be the same as Mel's. As years passed, my fear had diminished; my confidence had grown. It was an empty threat. He wouldn't find me and why would he bother looking?

But now he knows my name. Still, I try to convince myself it will be OK. Samantha Smith is a pretty common name. He doesn't know where I live ... or anything else about me ... as long as I'm careful ...

Maybe he had been looking for me. Perhaps our meeting hadn't been a coincidence. He might have been in Canterbury because he knew I lived there.

The debate warring in my head lasts for the rest of the day and long into the night. I can't face food and go to bed early, feigning stomach cramps. Sleep is elusive and I toss and turn, imagining footsteps outside my window and the shadow of a man looming over me.

The next morning, I phone Kate Bell's number and, this time, I'm redirected to a different line. It takes her a few moments to remember who

I am. She's no longer working as a police liaison officer, she tells me, but is now a detective inspector, still based in Norfolk. As I start to tell her what happened yesterday, resurgent panic makes my words rushed and jumbled.

'Calm down,' she says in her no-nonsense way. 'Take a deep breath and tell me exactly what happened.'

I follow her instructions. When I finish speaking, she is reassuring. 'It sounds like it was a complete accident, him bumping into you like that. I'm surprised he's come back to the UK. At least now we have an idea of his whereabouts. I'll get an alert put out for him with his description. With any luck, we'll be able to pick him up. You're sure it was him?'

'Yes. He spoke to me.'

'Tell me exactly what he said.'

I repeat his words and there's silence. Eventually, she asks, 'Did you feel he was threatening you?'

'Yes.' Wasn't it obvious?

'And he now knows your new name?'

'Yes.' The admission brings a fresh wave of despair.

'Look, leave it with me. I'll phone Kent police and see if they can organise some protection for you. Nothing heavy. A car driving by your house at night, that kind of thing. Just until they pick him up.' Another pause. 'I wonder how long he's been back in the country?' she muses. 'The last I heard, it was thought he'd gone back to Bulgaria. I'll check and see if there are any updates on his case. Of course, it all happened a while ago ... I wonder if any of his associates, the ones who were convicted, have been released yet? That could explain his presence back here ... Anyway, I'll get on to it and call you back when I have something to report. I'm sure they'll soon pick him up. Stay vigilant,' she adds. 'Dial 999 if you see him again or anything suspicious.'

I throw the phone on the bed and cover my face with my hands, overwhelmed by a sense of hopelessness. My fears have not been placated by Kate's assurances. The thought of a police car driving by the house every so often does not make me feel any safer. Nor do I share Kate's confidence that the police will 'soon pick him up'. Andrian knows I called the police back in 2003, leading to the break-up of his operation and the arrest of his accomplices. He'll assume I'll call the police again, now I've seen him, and keep his head down. Disappear for a while. Wait for his chance to pounce.

And the police won't be there watching over me indefinitely. It's a problem with no easy solution. If I do nothing, he'll track me down. If I run, I'll leave behind the life I want, the people I love. I'm so caught up in my dilemma that a knock at my bedroom door makes me jump.

'Sam, how are you feeling, darling? I've brought up a tray. Do you think you could manage some tea and toast?' It's my foster mum, standing outside my door, waiting for me to say it's OK to come in. My heart swells with love for her. Since I've lived here, she's always knocked, respected my privacy, never entered my room uninvited.

'Great, thanks,' I call and the door opens. 'You didn't need to do this. I'm fine.' Guilt at lying about the stomach cramps the night before stings my conscience.

She places the tray on my bedside table and smiles. 'I know ... but you know how I like to spoil you. I'm glad you're feeling better, darling. Have you remembered that Hugo and I are out for lunch today with John and Wendy? It's a long drive so we'll be leaving shortly.'

'That's right,' I smile back. 'Have a lovely time and don't let him eat prawns.'

She chuckles. 'I don't think he'll do that again in a hurry – not after ending up in hospital the last time! Now, are you sure you're feeling better? You're not just saying that so you don't upset our plans. We can always postpone the lunch.'

I swallow, touched, as always, by her care and concern. 'Don't be daft. I'm fine. You go ahead and have a lovely day.'

'As long as you're sure. We'll be back by six, I should think, but I'll text when we leave. There's plenty of food in the fridge and some pies in the freezer, if you fancy something like that.' She blows me a kiss and heads out of the door, leaving me feeling blessed ... and incredibly sad.

I know what I'm going to do. Leaning across the bed, I shift the tray in front of me and take a sip of tea. There are two slices of freshly-made, brown toast, some butter and homemade marmalade but I'm not hungry. I wait until I hear the car start up in the drive. Then, picking up my phone, I call Kaz. It rings three times and I hang up, like I always do. Almost immediately, she rings back.

'Hi. What's up?' She sounds breathless, as if she's been running.

I tell her. Over the years, I'd divulged my reasons for moving away and starting afresh. I'd confided nothing of my life here in Kent but she knew all about Andrian. 'Kaz, I want to ask you a favour. You know that cottage your mum and dad have in Brancaster? Is anyone using it at the moment?'

She's puzzled by the question. 'I don't think so. I'd have to check. Why?'

I take a breath. 'I wondered if I might borrow it for a while. Come and stay. I'd feel happier lying low, just until Andrian is caught. Hopefully, it won't be for long.'

'I'm sure you can, if it's free. They did rent it out as a holiday let for a while but I think they stopped. Got fed up of it never being free when they wanted to use it for an impromptu weekend away. Ooh,' she added, suddenly excited, 'I could take a few days off ... come and stay with you there. It would be so great to see you.'

'You too.' Her enthusiasm is infectious and makes me realise how much I miss her. 'I'd love that.'

'I'll check straight away and get back to you.' She rings off and I leap into action. I have a lot to do if I'm to be gone while the coast is clear. As I'm searching for suitcases, still in my pyjamas, Kaz phones to tell me the cottage is free for as long as I need it. She offers to pick me up from Norwich train station and drive me there herself. I thank her and say I'll text an arrival time when I've checked timetables. After I've showered and packed my cases, I ring Kate Bell again.

She answers abruptly. 'Have you seen him?'

'No.' I tell her what I'm planning – that I'm going away for a few days. 'I'll feel safer that way. So, I won't need any protection.'

'OK. We'll probably continue with the surveillance of your home anyway in case he shows up there.' She tells me that she's spoken to her counterparts in the Kent force and a description of Andrian has been circulated. 'Also, we've put out that old artist's impression of him. Unfortunately, we don't have a photograph ... we never did. You're one of the few people who would be able to identify him,' she adds. I remember. In 2003, I'd spent some while with a man who had tried to construct a likeness of Andrian. It never really looked like him but I was unable to pinpoint exactly what was wrong with it.

'All the more reason to lie low,' I respond. I promise to keep in touch and she says she'll call with any updates.

Then, I write a note. It's a struggle; I can't tell the truth. That would cause even more worry. After several miserable attempts, I make up something which is pretty inadequate but will have to do:

Finishing uni, getting my degree, applying for jobs ... it's all been a bit overwhelming. I need a break to recharge my batteries. Please understand. Don't try to find me. I'll be in touch.

Love you lots,

Sam xx

How can they understand? They're going to be so hurt. I pray the police manage to arrest Andrian quickly so I can soon return. Picking up my phone, I ring for a taxi. 'Ten minutes,' the operator informs me. I give him the address and lug the cases downstairs. The wait is the worst part – it gives me time to fret. Regrets engulf my thoughts: the interview for my dream job; the plans with friends which I'll have to cancel; the holiday my parents have invited me on ... *Am I doing the right thing?*

A silver car pulls up outside, the name of the taxi company printed along its side. It's a temporary solution, I tell myself firmly. A necessary precaution. It won't be for long. Grimly, I step outside and march to the waiting vehicle. The driver, a short, swarthy man, takes my cases from me and loads them into the boot while I fasten my seatbelt. Then, he starts the engine, makes a desultory comment about the weather and we drive away.

NOW

CHAPTER 20

Todd

The envelope lay stark white on the grey desk, his name in black ink on the front – Lily's distinctive, neat writing. He knew what it meant. For a few seconds, he stared at it, trying to convince himself, despite the certainty, that there was nothing to worry about. There had to be a logical explanation. This wasn't the end ... *was it*? It couldn't be ... yet ... And where was *Charlotte*? Reluctance turned to urgency and sent him scrambling to open the crisp, white envelope with trembling fingers. Where was his daughter? Had Lily taken Charlotte with her? Inside the envelope was a single sheet of paper, folded in half. He flattened it out and read:

Dear Todd,

Charlotte is at Lucy Adams' house having tea. I said you'd pick her up at 7:30.

I'm sorry but I can't do this anymore. It was fun while it lasted but I don't think we're right for each other. If I stay longer, trying to make it work, Charlotte will be hurt when I leave and neither of us wants that. Have a good time in the Cotswolds, just the two of you. By the time you get back, you'll have forgotten all about me. I'm going away for a bit. Please don't try to find me.

Todd, you are wonderful. Any woman would be honoured to have you by their side. I will always treasure our time together. Sorry for the cliché but you are not to blame – it's me.

I'm so sorry.

Lily.

He read it through quickly – shocked, disbelieving and yet, deep down, not entirely surprised. Then, more slowly, he read it again, trying to pick out clues behind the stark words. *Not right for each other?* Sod that! He grabbed his phone and called her. This time there was no ringtone. Just empty, unhelpful silence. He jabbed out a text.

Please come home. I love you. We can sort this out xx

Where had she gone? He started to make a mental list of places: her flat ... her parents in Kent ... one of her friends? None of his ideas seemed likely; she'd know those were the first places he'd look. But maybe this was a test ... perhaps she really wanted to be found, despite the note. The past week had been an emotional rollercoaster for her with all that stuff with the press. It wouldn't be a total surprise if she'd had some kind of breakdown. Nothing else really made sense. And she had been tetchy the night before, which was completely out of character. A glance at his watch told him it was 6:30 p.m. There was a bit of time before he needed to collect Charlotte. He might as well try the friends he'd met; one of them might know something or be able to point him in the right direction. First, he called Sarah, a colleague from work and probably Lily's closest friend. She seemed surprised by his call and said she hadn't seen Lily since the finish of the school day, which also marked the end of the spring term.

'She was in a rush to get off so hasn't come out for a drink with the rest of us,' she said. He could hear the babble of voices and laughter in the background. 'She was looking forward to getting away with you and Charlotte. There's nothing wrong, is there?' The sudden note of concern in her voice convinced him that she knew nothing more.

'No, no ...' He tried to keep his voice bluff and jolly. 'Just a miscommunication between us, that's all. Expect it's my fault. And I can't get through to her on the phone at the moment. Is Jess with you?'

'Yep, sure is.' She was another work friend. He could cross her off his list. 'Anyway, have a wonderful break away, won't you?'

'Will do. Thanks, Sarah.'

Next, he tried Suzi, a friend Lily had met at her Pilates class. She didn't pick up and he didn't leave a message. He didn't want to alarm her. Quashing his misery, he grabbed his car keys and headed out of the door. He just had time to visit Lily's flat before he fetched his daughter. Maybe, he'd catch up with her there. At that moment, his phone pinged and his heart leapt. *A message. Lily.* Eagerly, he yanked it from his pocket.

Message failed to send.

On automatic pilot, he drove to where Lily lived on the other side of town. It was a red-bricked, three storey Victorian building which had been converted into three separate apartments. Lily lived on the ground floor. She'd never given him a key; he hadn't needed one. They always stayed at his place. He pressed the buzzer and waited. Nothing. After a minute or so, he tried again. When there was no response, he tried the buzzer for the first floor and racked his brain for the name of the guy who lived there.

'Who is it?' A disembodied voice sounded before he could think of it.

'Hi. I'm looking for Lily.'

'Ground floor,' the voice replied and disconnected. *Damn.* Todd rang the buzzer again and the voice returned. 'Now what?'

'Lily's not answering and I wondered if you might know where she is?'

A slight pause. 'Sorry mate. I can't help you with that.'

'OK, thanks. Sorry for bothering you.' He tried the buzzer for third floor but there was no response from that either. Despondently, he returned to his car and slumped into the driver's seat. What more could he do? He checked the clock on the dashboard and realised it was almost half past seven. He'd better fetch his daughter ... and think about what he was going to tell her. A wave of anger washed over him. How could Lily do this – just walk away without any kind of discussion? He and Charlotte didn't deserve that. Well, two could play at that game. He threw his phone on the front seat and started the engine. She didn't want to be found? So be it. He wouldn't bother looking.

***

Charlotte cried when he told her that Lily wouldn't be going on holiday with them. It broke Todd's heart.

'She's had to go away for a while, baby,' he told her, 'so she can't come with us.'

'But why?' his daughter wailed, turning tear-filled, brown eyes to him as they packed her suitcase.

'I'm not too sure.' What could he say? 'I think maybe she doesn't want to hang out with Daddy anymore.' It killed him to say the words aloud but he couldn't lie to her. There was silence as Charlotte absorbed this information.

He busied himself folding various pairs of jeans, shorts and T-shirts into her case.

'Is it because I made a fuss about the fish?' She was referring to an incident during the week when, over-tired and over-wrought, she'd thrown a rare tantrum about eating the fish pie Lily had made. Her voice sounded small and unsure; it pierced his chest.

'No, baby! Definitely not! It's nothing to do with you. It's me.' The words from Lily's note taunted him as he scooped her into his arms.

'Daddy, she *is* coming back, isn't she?'

He hugged her tighter and sat down on her bed. 'I don't know,' he admitted, fighting back his own pain. 'I can't tell you that because, to tell you the truth, I just don't know.'

She wept again at that, loud, noisy sobs of heartbreak. 'Won't we see her again, Daddy?'

Fresh anger bubbled anew in his chest. How careless of Lily, how selfish, to treat his daughter like this! 'Look at me, Charlotte.' She raised her tear-streaked face from his chest. 'I promise you that we are going to have a wonderful holiday, just the two of us. Whatever happens, you'll always have me … and Mummy. Now, let's get this packing finished and get you off to bed. Don't want you to be tired and grumpy for our holiday.'

Charlotte's tears stopped eventually and, once she was asleep, he cracked open a beer. He couldn't face the lasagne sitting in the fridge. He'd shove it in the freezer where he could forget about it – and Lily. There was still his own packing to complete and that's when he received another shock. All of her things were gone. He should have expected it really but it was another punch to his gut to see the clothes she kept at his – all her toiletries, everything of hers – vanished. He stared at the empty spaces, a lump choking his throat, his rage at her dissolving in a mire of emotion. What was he going to do without her? Getting a grip on himself, he pulled his case out from under the bed. He'd do the same as he'd always done, the same as he'd done before she came into his life. And, first of all, he and Charlotte were going to have a brilliant holiday.

He packed, showered and lay in bed, staring wide-eyed into the blackness. Sleep was going to be all but impossible but he'd planned an early start in the morning. They had a long drive ahead and the first weekend of the Easter break was going to mean busy roads. Restlessly, he turned and slid his hands under his pillow, as he always did. There was something there. It felt like paper. He switched on his bedside lamp to find the small scrap clutched in his fist. There were just four words:

Remember I loved you.

He switched the light back off and lay for a while imagining her voice saying the words. She'd never actually said them to him. 'Me too,' she'd replied when he whispered them to her. How he'd longed to hear her say them! And now, here they were, written down, in the past tense.

Still holding the paper in his hand, he wept.

***

The weather held fine and was unseasonably warm for their time in the Cotswolds. It was lovely to spend two whole weeks with his daughter; she was such a joy to be with. He had to admit, it wasn't the most exciting holiday destination for a five-year-old but she seemed to delight in everything. With her small hand in his, he could almost believe that all was right with the world.

It wasn't though. Neither of them mentioned Lily but she loomed large in Todd's thoughts, especially at night when Charlotte was fast asleep. For the first week away, he resisted any urge to contact her. He owed it to Charlotte, and himself, to let her go. She'd already hurt them both and he wasn't going to let it happen again. As they settled into the second week though, that urge to know what had happened to cause her sudden departure grew stronger. That would be the only reason for trying to find her, he reasoned. He and Lily were finished whatever. But he was kidding himself. The simple truth was that he missed her. By the second Tuesday, he was ready to forgive her almost anything, if she'd just return to him. That night, he gave in and tried her mobile number once more, only to find the number was disconnected. She'd obviously meant it; she really didn't want to be found.

Agonising over her reasons for leaving kept him awake, long into the night. For a while, he tormented himself with the idea that the words in the note spoke true; she'd gone off him; it wasn't working. Was he deluding himself in thinking they were crazy about each other? Maybe. He'd made all the running in the beginning, after all. But then, once they'd kissed that first time, he could've sworn she wanted him as much as he desired her. There had been no signs, nothing to hint, that she was losing interest. No – he didn't believe the reason she gave in her note; the scrap of paper he'd found under his pillow belied it. Why would she do that if she didn't care about him? There was something else – something to do with her past and that caginess she always exhibited when he'd tried to discuss it. It *had* to be that. She was hiding something. And the recent publicity had totally freaked her out. He was sure that had something to do with it too. But what? And *where* was she?

He lay wide-eyed in the king-size bed thinking hard. There had to be something she'd let slip, some way of finding her. Now he'd made that subconscious decision to look for her, adrenalin pulsed through his body, making sleep impossible. He picked up his phone again and started making notes:

- *Parents living in Kent; where?*
- *Dad retired surgeon*
- *older brother Simon in Canterbury; graphic designer; not close*
- *teaching degree at Kent University*
- *Moved to Suffolk for teaching job. Why? Why not Kent?*

That was it. He threw down his phone once more and lay back against the cool pillow. That was all he had to go on. Her aversion to all forms of social media had been a standing joke between them.

'Why would anyone want to broadcast details of their life all over the internet?' she retorted when he'd called her a dinosaur. 'Anyway, as a teacher, I have to maintain a professional persona, even outside school. It wouldn't be OK to post pictures of me out partying and drinking too much, like so many people do, would it?'

'You never drink too much!' he'd chuckled. 'But I take your point.' He tended to avoid social media as well, most of the time, but he was signed up to Facebook and Twitter and occasionally enjoyed scrolling through, mostly to see what his mates were up to. If she'd had an account, he would have been able to check out all her contacts, but that was a non-starter. Doubtless, the main character of his novels, super sleuth Andy Schofield, would discover her whereabouts without too much difficulty. If only he could use his mindset! The thought made him smile. It's easy to fathom a mystery when your thoughts and actions are governed by a writer who knows all the answers!

Anyway, he had a starting point – find her parents or her brother. The brother might be the best bet. That's where he had most information. Simon Nichol; graphic designer; Canterbury. He'd start searching when he got home. Hopefully, Simon didn't share his sister's dislike of social media.

Charlotte mentioned Lily for the first time on the return journey. After two dry weeks, the heavens had opened and rain hammered against the windscreen, making driving slow and difficult. He'd allowed Charlotte to have her tablet to watch videos so he could concentrate. By the time they'd reached Cambridge and were on the home straight along the A14 to Bury St Edmunds, he had a blinding headache and was feeling decidedly irritable, swearing under his breath at other drivers when they got too close behind him or cut him up.

'Are we nearly there, Daddy?' Charlotte had put down her tablet and was fidgeting in her car seat.

'Not long now.' He frowned. 'Do you need the toilet or can you wait until we get home?'

'I can wait.' There was a pause. 'Will Lily be there when we get home?'

'I don't think so, sweetheart.' The sight of her forlorn face in his rear-view mirror tugged at his heartstrings.

'I miss her, Daddy.'

He exhaled, a long, slow breath. 'Me too, poppet … me too.'

'Can we find her please, Daddy – ask her to come home?'

He nodded. 'We can try.'

***

He'd hoped to see her at school when he dropped Charlotte off that first Monday back after the Easter break but the Reception class were being greeted by a teacher he'd never seen before. There was no sign of Lily. When he asked for her at the school office, Faith Jung told him that Miss Nichol was on a leave of absence. Further questions were met with a frosty stare. 'I'm afraid I can't help you, Mr Matheson.'

That evening, after work, he googled *Simon Nichol graphic designer*. There were 440,000 results. He started going through them but soon realised the hopelessness of the task. Then, he tried LinkedIn. Several people were listed with that name so he created an account for himself, to make contact with any possible suspects. His heart sank as he went through the list. The only one who worked in graphic design was spelt Nicholl. Having checked the profiles of all, he invited three to connect. He didn't hold a lot of hope that any of them would prove to be Lily's brother.

The same frustrations were encountered on Facebook and Twitter. There was no-one he thought might be a match. Next, he googled graphic design companies based in Canterbury. There were fifteen listed. He clicked on each one in turn, looking for a mention of Simon Nichol. Nothing. He decided to be more specific in his search, this time typing the name of each company and adding *Simon Nichol, Canterbury*. Once again, there was no match but three of the companies mentioned directors or staff named Simon. He made a note of their numbers and resolved to phone them during the working day. It was a long shot but it was possible the siblings had different surnames; that might explain the lack of closeness between them. He briefly pondered searching for Lily's parents but realised he didn't even know their first names. Still, what the heck! He tried *Nichol surgeon Canterbury* in Google and laughed when it returned 671,000 results. He scrolled through the first three pages before giving up. More information was needed to narrow the search.

For a while, he sat staring into space. His mind wandered to their first meeting and the coincidence of the missing girl in his research. That report was worth another look. She'd been a bit freaked out when he mentioned it. Maybe there *was* more to the similarity in looks between Lily and the missing girl than he'd thought. He pulled up the website and scrolled until he found what he was looking for.

Norwich Girl Still Missing

Police are still searching the whereabouts of Melanie Potter, 17, of Thorpe St Andrew who disappeared after travelling to London to take up a bogus job offer.

Friends say that Miss Potter was excited about working for Veronik Holdings and left home on January 10th. No one has seen her since.

A police spokesperson said that investigations regarding her disappearance and Veronik Holdings continue. They want to hear from

anyone with information about a Bulgarian man named Andrian Petrov who had been living at the family home.

Neighbours were shocked to learn also of the tragic death of her mother, Nerissa Potter, 41 who died from an overdose shortly after her daughter went missing. They say that Mrs Potter had struggled to cope since the tragic death of her husband, Sean, 3 years earlier, after a head-on collision with a drunk driver. It is thought that the remaining daughter, Saskia, 15, is being looked after by family.

The mum had died from an overdose – that was the bit of the tragedy he'd forgotten when he was telling Lily. He noted down all the names and pertinent details and then sat for a while, staring into space, thinking hard. His two buddies in the police force might be able to help. He made another note to contact them and then shut down his laptop.

His head felt scrambled and he needed some fresh air. After changing into running gear for the first time in months, he headed out onto the streets. The evening was cool and dusk was creeping in. There was minimal traffic and he soon settled into a comfortable rhythm. He enjoyed running and used to try to get out as much as possible after a day spent sitting at a desk. It felt good to get back into his stride.

Tonight, he decided to head towards the town rather than take a more rural route. It was as he turned past the Greene King brewery that he first noticed the low hum of an engine behind him. He glanced over his shoulder and spotted a dark blue van pulling in alongside the kerb. There had been a similar vehicle parked down the street as he'd left his house, with perhaps a man in the driver's seat but he couldn't be certain. The head had been lowered and angled away from him. Waiting for someone or something, he'd thought at the time. Watching for the coast to be clear before slipping inside one of the houses ... or waiting for a lover to nip into the passenger seat, before driving off somewhere for illicit sex.

Sweat dripped down his face and his breathing became laboured as he pounded on. He was out of shape. Slowing to a walk, he resolved to get back to regular running. This five-mile circuit used to take him thirty-two minutes. A glance at his watch told him he was way off that pace. Once more, he broke into a run, wishing he'd chosen a shorter route. As he headed into the final mile, he heard the same engine noise again, a distinctive, rattling drone, but, when he turned, he could only see a pair of headlights, a long way back. It had grown too dark to see if they belonged to the blue van. Unease skittered down his spine and, despite the protests of his body, he quickened his pace. Was someone following him? The thought was ridiculous but that was what it felt like. By the time he reached his home street, his lungs were burning. There was an empty space where the van had been parked earlier and all was quiet. He walked the last hundred metres, allowing his hammering heart to slow to a more comfortable rate. There were no headlights swinging in behind him. As he unlocked his front door and stepped inside his house, he chided himself for his over-active imagination.

By the time he'd showered and watched an hour of television to help him wind down, he'd forgotten all about the van. It was only when he went upstairs to his bedroom, which overlooked the street, that he remembered. Pulling the curtain to one side, he scanned the cars parked beneath the street lights – just in case. There was no van. Shaking his head at himself, he let the curtain drop and went to bed.

***

'Hi, is that Simon Danes?' Todd was on his third call to graphic designers in Canterbury. The other two were non-starters and this one would be too but he had to try. He could imagine his friends telling him his behaviour was desperate; he agreed. Still, here he was, making the call anyway.'

'Speaking.' The man's voice was pleasant, well-modulated.

'Hi Simon. My name is Todd Matheson. I was wondering if you'd heard anything from Lily?'

'Lily?'

'Yes, Lily Nichol. Isn't she your sister?'

There was a pause, followed by a snort. 'Not unless she's changed her name! I don't know anyone called Lily Nichol. Sorry.'

'But you *do* have a sister?' *What was wrong with him? Let it go.* For some reason, he couldn't. He had to be sure.

Another snort. 'Sort of. I haven't seen her for … ten years. Not since she finished university.'

'University?' Todd latched on to the word. 'Did she do a teaching degree?' There was a slight, indrawn breath.

'She did as a matter of fact,' Simon admitted. 'Look. What's this about? Why do you think this Lily is my sister? Is this some kind of cruel hoax?'

'Wait. Please don't hang up!' He was clutching at straws but what if he was on to something? 'Is your dad a surgeon?' Silence. Todd held his breath as he waited.

'Look, who are you?' Simon now sounded suspicious. Who could blame him?

'Todd Matheson. I'm looking for a woman called Lily Nichol and I have reason to believe she might be your sister.'

'What makes you think that?'

'She told me she had an older brother named Simon who lived in Canterbury and worked as a graphic designer. You're married but you don't yet have children. Your dad is a surgeon.' There was another long silence.

'Why are you calling me? Has something happened to her?' Todd detected anxiety in the question. Hope burgeoned in his chest. Could he really have found Lily's brother?

'No, well, not exactly,' he replied. 'She's disappeared. She left me a note ending things between us and I don't really know why. I'm trying to find her.'

A grunt of derision. 'You and me both. I guess it's possible. Your Lily could be my sister but I haven't seen her for a very long time. She might be using a different name. I wouldn't know. Again, it's possible. My sister just upped and left ten years ago. She left a note too.'

Ten years ago. That was when Lily moved to Suffolk. 'Can we meet?' Todd felt the excitement he'd been holding back bubble to the surface. This really *could* be a lead.

'Maybe ...' The man's voice was cautious and then he sighed. 'I guess we could but I'm pretty tied up here at the moment. Work has been manic.'

'I'll come to you,' he said eagerly. 'I'll drive down after work. Leave off early. I could be with you ...' He did a rough calculation of the journey time in his head, '... by around six thirty. Would that be alright?'

The man laughed. 'Hell, you're keen! Sure ... why not? Come to the house.' He gave Todd the address. 'I'll see you later.'

Todd ended the call with a sense of elation. Maybe ... just maybe ... he was going to find some answers.

CHAPTER 21

Lily

The wind is bracing as I stride along the beach beneath the wide, blue sky, immersing myself in the rhythm of the waves rolling in. Every day is different; the sea offers up a fresh selection of fare on the sand and greedy gulls squawk and squabble as they scour for tasty morsels. Two fishermen sit, within calling distance of each other, on three-legged perches at the water's edge. They are a comforting constant in my daily walks and I look forward to seeing them – here, every morning, without fail, regardless of the weather. Sometimes, I stand and watch for a while, waiting to see if they catch anything.

I don't remember seeing them ten years ago when I was last here. Kaz was with me for some of that time. I recall we talked and walked for miles, engrossed in ever-changing discussions about my future. The days away from my home in Canterbury drifted into weeks. While fury and despair at my plight grew in equal measure, I waited for news of Andrian's arrest. But nothing came of the police alert and, whilst I was assured that he remained on their 'wanted' list, Kate Bell admitted that, unless they got lucky, Andrian wouldn't be found. Once again, he'd disappeared off the face of the planet. Kate wondered if my sighting of him had scared him off. 'You bumping into each other probably spooked him as much as you. It exposed him once more. He knows you can ID him. I reckon he's scarpered. Let's hope it's for good,' she told me. I'm not sure if she was just trying to reassure me or if she genuinely believed that. I wasn't convinced. He might well have been lying low for a while – that would make sense – but I had no doubt that he fully intended what he'd promised. Kate hadn't been there to witness the intent in his eyes or the ruthless twist of his lips as he uttered his threat. I believed him with all my heart; it was the one, stone-cold certainty in my life. I couldn't go back.

In the end, having resigned myself to staying away for good, I dyed my hair blonde, called myself Lily Nichol and got a teaching job at a small, village school in Suffolk. I told Kaz I was leaving my haven in Brancaster but refused to tell her anything else, for both our sakes. Once again, I was completely alone, cast adrift like a piece of flotsam and, until Andrian was safely behind bars, I was determined it should stay that way. This time, I wouldn't make the mistake of allowing *anyone* to get too close. The pain of losing them wasn't worth it.

I missed the job interview in Canterbury, of course, and my delay in applying for other teaching jobs meant that I missed the crop of vacancies to start in September, at the beginning of the school year. Eventually, I managed to secure a temporary, maternity cover contract although obtaining it brought its own set of difficulties. The name Samantha Smith had to go on the job application form – for references and proof of my teaching qualification – but I didn't dare continue using it. That presented a problem. Once I'd been offered the post, I solved it by attending a confidential meeting with the Head and Chair of Governors of the school where I asked for permission to be known as Lily Nichol. To persuade them, I fabricated a violent, abusive ex-partner who posed a danger to my safety. I was in the process of changing my name officially anyway and they were sympathetic to my request. When the paperwork came through, I became Lily Nichol for real and, as far as I'm aware, no-one else at the school was any the wiser. When that temporary contract ended, I applied for, and was offered, the job at my current school.

It all sounds easy but it wasn't. It had been so hard to walk away from my life a second time. Every day, I thought about my foster family and wondered how they were. They were so kind to me and, from the outset, treated me like a daughter and sister. I mourned their loss. But I never risked going back. I couldn't. It wasn't just me I was worried about. I'd never forgive myself if

Andrian threatened or hurt them in any way. Over the years, I kept in touch with birthday cards and stuff like that but I was always careful not to let slip any indication of my whereabouts. I don't know if they tried to find me. Probably not. I expect they felt betrayed and the cards went straight in the bin.

Over the intervening years, I stuck to my decision and found I could live happily by myself. My job fulfilled me; it was all I needed. I had friends but no-one too close. Occasionally, I dated – men who made me laugh and were fun to be around – but my heart remained entanglement-free. Until Todd. I knew he threatened everything as soon as I met him. That was why I fought so hard to keep him at a distance. But the man's persistence knew no bounds and, the more I got to know him, the tougher it became to continue my resistance. My body thrummed with awareness every time he came near. At night, he filled my dreams. Yes, in the end, I gave in ... but I had a plan. It seems laughable now, looking back. I thought seeing him would help me to get him out of my system. My heart thought otherwise. I fell totally and completely in love. It was impossible to think I could live without him but still I held back from making the commitment I knew he wanted – we both wanted. How could I make a future with him whilst Andrian was still out there? There were times when I nearly told him everything. I knew what he'd say. He'd refuse to believe that the threat was serious; he'd tell me that, together, we could face anything. It was so tempting to let him sweep my fears away and believe in that happy-ever-after.

And then, I saw that photograph. I'd found Andrian, now masquerading as a legitimate businessman called Nick Georgiev. It was my chance to get him put away for good. But, even then, I hesitated. If Andrian had a new life with a new identity, perhaps he'd given up on looking for me. Telling the police was a risk. There was the chance that Andrian would elude capture once again and my safety would be compromised. In the end, there was only one decision I *could* make. I owed it to my mum and my sister to put my trust in the police; with any luck, I would be free of him once and for all.

My fantasy was short-lived. The police could find no proof that Nick Georgiev was Andrian. They thought I was mistaken. In my mind, there was no doubt but my accusation was not enough. They needed evidence and there was none. Case closed. I could've kicked myself. I should've known that, if

Andrian was parading himself so publicly, he'd covered his tracks. He *knew* his real identity could not be discovered. Only I know he's Andrian Petrov: the man responsible for my sister's disappearance; the man likely to have caused my mum's death; the man behind the sex trafficking ring and many other crimes. And he would be aware that I was the person who tipped off the police. It could be no-one else. I was still the splinter festering in his side and he would redouble his efforts to find me. Now, it wasn't just revenge or unfinished business; I had the power to compromise his future. He'd have to eradicate that threat.

And then, at the worst possible time, I found my name and face plastered all over the national newspapers. When the story of Kev Hathersett's failed attempt to abduct his son from school was first reported, it had been a low-key mention in the local press. For months afterwards, there had been nothing more and I'd convinced myself the danger was passed. But I hadn't realised that the advent of the trial would breathe new life into the whole episode. The old report had been rehashed and, unfortunately for me, one of the national papers got hold of it. Public interest gained momentum and the story exploded. With my picture and the story of my 'heroism' being so high profile, I had to act ... quickly. I couldn't risk staying where he could find me ... and Todd and Charlotte. My blood turned to ice at the thought.

By now, they will have returned from their holiday in the Cotswolds. My disappearance will have upset their plans but I think they will have gone without me. Todd would never let Charlotte down by cancelling the holiday she was anticipating with such excitement. The guilt I feel about how much I've hurt them twists like a corkscrew in my heart the more I think about it. I miss them ... so very much. The pain I experienced before, when I left my foster family, is nothing compared to the utter desolation I feel this time around. I've ached to call Todd so many times. I want to tell him to wait for me ... that I didn't mean what I said in that awful note. But I can't. The stakes are too high. I picture Andrian's cruel face and renew my resolve. Every day I've been here, I've raged against the injustice of it. Andrian has carved out a successful life for himself while I'm back in Brancaster, alone, trapped in a terrible loop, forever running from the past.

I still haven't figured out what I'm going to do next. Apart from dyeing my hair back to its original dark colour, I feel I've achieved nothing. I know

I need to find a way out of this and claim back my life but the path ahead is clouded in fog. I'd hoped Kate Bell might be able to help me but her advice was to go home. 'You're overreacting,' she told me. 'Andrian Petrov *isn't* Georgiev. He's long gone. You need to get on with living your life. You're letting your obsession with that man ruin your future. Let it go.'

I wish I could follow her counsel but I know she's wrong. Andrian *will* be coming for me and it's up to me to find the proof which will convict him before that happens. As yet, I haven't worked out what to do but something will come to me. That's the one thought I'm grasping like a lifeline. I refuse to be a victim any longer. I *am* going to end it, one way or another ...

CHAPTER 22

Todd

The drive to Canterbury took longer than he thought. There were tailbacks on the M25 and he queued for over an hour. Traffic flowed more freely once he was on the other side of the Dartford tunnel and he parked outside Simon's house at almost seven o'clock, having rung ahead to say he was running late. It was a modest, brick, semi-detached building built in the 1970s style of others along the street, on the outskirts of the city. Todd was thankful there was room for his Golf in the small driveway as cars were parked on both sides of the road. Switching off his engine, he took a deep breath and shook his shoulders, feeling stiff after the long drive. He wasn't looking forward to the return journey later that night. Hopefully, it would be worth it.

A tall, gangly man appeared in the doorway. Todd's smile was rueful as he crossed the driveway to shake his hand. 'Sorry I'm late. The M25 was a nightmare. Todd Matheson.'

The man's grip was firm and his face welcoming. 'Simon Danes. I can imagine. Come in.'

Todd followed him into a narrow hallway and through into a much larger, open-plan room with a kitchen at one end. A tiny, dark-haired woman wearing oven gloves was transferring an earthenware pot into the oven.

'Take a seat.' Simon gestured to a stool by the kitchen island. 'This is my wife, Manuela.'

She smiled in greeting and spoke with a Spanish accent. 'Pleased to meet you. May I fetch you a drink?'

'Thanks, some water would be great. I'm parched.' He gave her a grateful smile before turning back to Simon. 'Thanks so much for agreeing to see me.'

'Not at all. I'm intrigued,' Simon said, crossing over to the fridge and peering inside. 'Cold beers in here. Are you sure I can't tempt you?'

Todd pulled a face. 'Better not. I've got a long drive home.'

'Right. I'll leave you to it.' Manuela pulled off the oven gloves, gave Todd another shy smile as she handed him a glass of water, and directed a fierce look at her husband. 'Food will be thirty minutes.'

'OK.' Simon waited before Manuela had left the room before he gave Todd a complicit grin. 'Manuela is passionate about cooking. It's her Spanish blood. I can get away with being late for everything else but never for her food.'

Todd smiled politely and sipped at his water. 'I'd better make this quick then.' He studied the man who had settled on a stool opposite, looking for similarities with Lily. Simon's face yielded none. His eyes were widely spaced and bright blue; his jaw was square and nose slightly hooked, eagle-like, giving his whole face an angular feel. Nothing like Lily's exquisite features. Todd's apprehension grew. In the preceding hours, in the car, he'd replayed the phone conversation with Simon several times in his head and come to the conclusion that he was acting like a lunatic. Instead of haring down to Kent, he should've at least double-checked that his Lily and Simon's sister were the same person. He'd been desperate and illogical. Chances were, he'd show a photo of Lily and Simon would shake his head. Complete waste of a journey.

Steeling himself, he opened his one picture of Lily on his mobile and passed it across the granite work surface. It was slightly blurry. She'd just looked up, the beginnings of a frown on her face. Simon studied it for an agonisingly long time. Finally, he looked up at Todd. 'I think it *could* be her,' he said. 'Do you have any more photos?'

Todd exhaled in a rush, a combination of relief and elation coursing through him. 'No. That's the only one. She hated having her photo taken.

Pathological about it. Refused point blank. I caught her unawares with that one and she told me I had to delete it. I'm glad I didn't.'

Simon nodded slowly. 'That sounds like her too. Hang on a minute.' He disappeared, returning a few moments later with a green, leather-bound book. 'Family photo album,' he explained. 'There's only one in here of Sam. That's my sister – Samantha Smith.' He looked up at Todd and gave a wry smile. 'It's a long story. Anyway, here it is. Take a look and see what you think.' He showed him a double-page spread of family photographs and pointed to the one in the top right-hand corner. 'There she is.'

Todd studied the picture, ignoring the older man and woman also in the photograph and focusing in on the teenage girl. Her head was partly turned away from the camera but his heart leapt. It *was* her; he was sure of it. In the photo, her hair was cropped and dark. It suited her. She looked like a very young Audrey Hepburn. Avidly, he drank in every detail. She was thin, less curvy, dressed in shorts and a baggy T-shirt and looking towards the other woman in the picture. She hadn't realised the photo was being taken, he thought. Her stance was relaxed and she was smiling – a wide smile which lit up her face. Carefully, he absorbed the rest of the photo. It was clearly a family occasion. There were presents on a table and the older woman was holding flowers. She was smartly dressed and elegant. There was warmth between them. He saw it in her eyes, in the tender way she was looking towards the girl. The man was grey-haired, slightly balding and dressed in an open-necked shirt. His right hand was resting lightly on the woman's shoulder. All three looked as if they were sharing a special moment. It was a lovely picture.

Excitement shone in his eyes when he eventually tore himself away from the album. 'That's definitely Lily,' he said.

'Oh my God. I'll need to call my mum. She was distraught when Sam vanished from our lives. But first, tell me all about her, everything you know.'

Todd did. He started at the beginning, the meeting with Charlotte's teacher, continued with his attempts to break down Lily's defences, their subsequent relationship and, finally, to his discovery of the note two and a half weeks ago. By the time he'd finished, Manuela had returned. Todd looked at her apologetically. 'I'm sorry. I've still got some questions to ask you, Simon, but I realise your food is ready. Would you mind if I returned in about an hour?'

'Not at all but I have a much better plan.' It was Manuela who replied. 'Why don't you stay and eat with us? There's plenty. Then, you can continue your chat – as long as you don't mind me listening.'

'That's very kind but ...'

'Good plan,' Simon interrupted. 'Nobody ... but nobody ... should ever turn down the chance to sample Manuela's cooking.' He grinned at his wife.

'Absolutely.' She beamed back at him. 'Now that's decided, Simon, can you get out the cutlery? I'll dish up. It's chorizo and bean stew with home-baked bread.'

'It smells delicious.' The aroma in the kitchen was mouth-wateringly good and Todd suddenly felt ravenous. 'If you're sure.'

While they ate, Simon continued to ask Todd about Lily, having filled Manuela in on the gist of the conversation thus far. 'What did she tell you about us?'

Todd shrugged. 'Very little.' He decided to be completely frank and said, 'She told me you weren't close.'

'That's not true,' Simon spluttered, laying down his cutlery and staring in disbelief. 'Why would she say something like that? We were very close. Of course, she wasn't with us that long ...'

'What do you mean?'

Simon sighed. 'I told you it was a long story. I was an only child. My parents tried and tried for another but my mum miscarried four times – all girls. It wasn't to be. They were brilliant parents and I had a wonderful childhood. Dad was an orthopaedic surgeon; he's now retired. Mum was a nurse. She gave up her hospital job when I was small but, later on, went back as a part-time, community nurse. I was at university when they first decided to try fostering. It knocked me for six. They'd just, more or less, got rid of me; Dad was thinking of retirement; I'd pictured them going on cruises, seeing the world, that sort of thing. Instead, they wanted to commit themselves to looking after children. I couldn't understand it and, I have to confess, tried to talk them out of it. They're pretty stubborn though and they'd made their minds up. Anyway, Sam was fifteen when she came to live with them. I didn't know her background. My parents knew more but they didn't speak of it and neither did she. I asked them but Mum said she couldn't tell me. She only said that Sam had been through a lot of trauma and needed lots of love to help her heal. One time, I did try to ask Sam about it. She'd been with us a few years by then. I was back living at home and we grew pretty close – at least, I thought we did. So, I asked if she wanted to tell me about her past. She instantly clammed up. It was like she was frightened to talk. I just told her that if she ever wanted to discuss anything, I was there for her.'

'It's interesting that you think she was scared of something from her past. I got that same vibe,' Todd mused.

'Yeah, well, she never did talk about it and I didn't ask again so ...' Simon shrugged, '... it remains a mystery. Anyway, she was a bright kid. Despite everything, she got good GSCEs and A levels and stayed here in Canterbury to do a teaching degree. I remember her as self-contained but warm-hearted. She adored my parents.' He smiled. 'She had a wicked sense of humour too. Always took the piss out of me, I recall. At the time, I was a bit of a geek ...' Manuela snorted and he laughed. 'OK, I still am ... I was always into computers and design. To be honest, I suffered from social anxiety, especially around girls, and it was easier to hide behind a screen than go out and face my fears. Anyway, she got that and she helped me. Young as she was, she insisted on dragging me out with her and her friends. She was a tigress, very protective of me, and it worked. I grew in self-confidence and realised girls weren't so scary after all ... at least, until I met Manuela! She terrified me!'

His wife raised her eyebrows. 'That's because you know who's boss.' She waggled her fork at him. 'And don't you forget it.'

'Yes dear,' Simon replied submissively. 'I probably wouldn't have met Manuela if it hadn't been for Sam.' There was a pause. 'Come to think of it ... she's got a lot to answer for!'

'Very funny,' his wife retorted.

Todd smiled distractedly. He wanted to hear more about Sam. 'You said she just disappeared. When was that?'

Simon rubbed his chin. '2010. She'd finished her degree but wasn't around for the graduation ceremony. Left a note for my parents saying she needed a break ... or something like that. And that was it. They haven't seen her since. She always remembered our birthdays, Christmas, my parents' anniversary, things like that. Sent cards ... so we knew she was OK. We just didn't know where she was. The cards had postmarks from all over the country. The last time I heard from her, it was our wedding day. Again, it was just a card with a personal message. She must've been keeping tabs on us all the time.'

'Did anything happen leading up to her disappearance?' Todd asked. 'Did she change in any way? Did something happen to make her run?'

'No idea.' Simon pulled a face. 'I wish I knew. My mum blamed herself. I know she'd been trying to persuade Sam to go on holiday with her and Dad and Sam wasn't sure. More than that ...' he shrugged again. 'You'd have to talk to my mum. Actually, I really ought to ring her – let her know about you. I'm sure she and Dad will want to talk to you. Will you excuse me for a moment?' He left the table, leaving Todd alone with Manuela.

There was an awkward silence which Todd filled with more compliments about the food. She brushed them aside and gave him a searching look. 'Tell me about Sam,' she said. 'Simon has often talked about her but she's always seemed such a mysterious figure. I'm intrigued to hear your take on her.'

He gave a wry smile. 'Like Simon, I'm biased. Apart from my daughter, she's the best person I know. We were really happy together but I always knew there was stuff she wasn't telling me. I figured she'd been hurt in the past and she didn't want to talk about it.' He grimaced. 'I guess I hoped that, eventually, she'd trust me enough to share all her secrets. Not that I particularly wanted to know; I just hoped she'd be able to move on.'

She nodded. 'That's what Simon always said. There was a part of her she kept closed off from her family, even though she clearly loved them and they adored her. I know Vanessa – that's Simon's mum – was terribly hurt when Sam left but she's always defended her. She says Sam would've had a good reason.' She pulled a face. 'I don't think I would've been quite so understanding in the circumstances.'

'That's because you didn't know her.' Simon strode into the room and sat at the table. 'My mum is beside herself with excitement. She and Dad would really like to meet you but they're out at some charity thing tonight. I know it's a lot to ask but would you be able to stay in Canterbury until tomorrow?'

Todd mulled it over. Simon had hinted that his parents had more information about Lily's background and he really wanted to discover what they knew. He could phone the office in the morning and say that something had come up. His appointments could be postponed. There was nothing to stop him. 'I guess I could. Can you suggest somewhere to stay tonight?'

'Brilliant. Thank you so much. There's a good guesthouse just down the road from here. I'll ring and see if they have any vacancies.'

'Don't be silly!' Manuela shot her husband a look. 'Todd can stay here. We have a spare room. As long as you don't mind sharing it with all our clutter. It's full of stuff that won't fit anywhere else.'

'No, no,' Todd exclaimed. 'I don't want to put you to any more trouble. You've been very kind ... feeding me and everything.'

'Not at all,' Simon interrupted. 'Manuela's right. We have a spare room. Sorry I didn't think of it straight away ... probably because it doesn't look much like a bedroom at the moment.'

'That's settled then.' Manuela stood and gave both men a grin. 'You two can clear up while I get the room ready.'

'Well ... if you're sure ...'

'Positive. I'll leave you to it.' She swept from the room and Simon chuckled. 'You see what my life is like! I never stand a chance when Manuela makes up her mind about something.'

'She's very kind. You both are.'

'Not at all. I'm so pleased you managed to track me down. It's the least we can do.'

***

Vanessa and Hugo Danes had aged from the smiling figures in the photograph Todd had seen the previous evening. They were clearly recognisable but their faces were thinner, more wrinkled and their bodies more stooped.

'Come in, come in.' Vanessa greeted him warmly and ushered him inside where Hugo was standing, ready to grasp his hand. 'It's so good of you to put yourself out like this. Can I get you tea ... coffee?'

'Coffee would be lovely. Thank you.'

Hugo led him into a spacious living room with wide, glass doors which afforded an impressive view of an immaculate lawn and borders resplendent with colour. 'Please take a seat.'

'What a wonderful garden.' Todd didn't know much about horticulture but his host grabbed the opening with alacrity, launching into a detailed account of problems they'd encountered in the garden that spring.

'Slugs are the bane of my life at the moment. Still, it's all worth it,' he was saying as Vanessa appeared with a tray of mugs and biscuits.

'Darling, I hope you're not boring our guest! I used to be the gardener of the family but since Hugo retired, he's become obsessed.'

'Not at all. Thank you.' Todd accepted his mug and waited until Vanessa was seated. So many questions were buzzing in his brain. Where to start? 'I believe I may know your foster daughter, Samantha,' he began.

'Not foster daughter ... our *daughter*,' Vanessa corrected. 'We've always thought of her as that anyway ... as soon as she came to live with us. I know she wasn't officially ours but ... anyway ...' Her voice tailed off. 'Sorry, I'm rambling. Please, go on.'

Todd smiled. 'I know her as Lily – Lily Nichol. I've known her for about eighteen months and we've been together for around eight months. I thought we were in love. Then, just over two weeks ago, she vanished. There was a note telling me that our relationship wasn't working and I wasn't to try to find her. I know it's possible she felt that way but I don't believe that's the reason she left. The more I think about it, the more it doesn't add up. If she wanted to end our relationship, she just had to tell me. She didn't have to disappear altogether. She's even left her job.'

'As a teacher?' Vanessa asked.

'Yes. That's how I met her. She was my daughter's teacher.'

'Oh, I am glad.' Vanessa was nodding. 'I'm so pleased she got her teaching job. She was passionate about it when she was training. Since she left, we've had no idea at all where she was and what she was doing. At least she's doing something she loves ... or she was.' She frowned. 'I agree with you that things don't add up. It was the same when she disappeared from our lives. I've always had my theory ... I don't know if you're interested in hearing it?'

'Definitely. Is it something linked to her past? Do you know anything about that?' He intercepted a look between husband and wife. 'I promise I won't betray any confidences.'

'We didn't know everything about her. We were given a little information but we've never shared it with a living soul,' Vanessa said. 'Not even Simon. If she was going to learn to trust us, we felt we needed to do our utmost to respect her privacy. I can tell you what we told our son. She'd been through a lot of trauma and tragedy. I wouldn't feel right about saying any more.'

Todd exhaled in frustration. 'But I wouldn't breathe a word ...'

'No. We can't tell you more about her past. It wouldn't be right,' Hugo insisted.

'Fair enough.' Todd fixed his smile back in place. 'Tell me about your theory,' he said to Vanessa.

'She was frightened,' she replied. 'She must've been. I think she's on the run. And she has a different name, you say. Why would she change it? I believe something happened a long time ago ... something beyond the basic facts we were told by her case workers. When she left us, she said she was finding things a bit overwhelming and needed some time and space. I believed that for a while but not when she never came back. We knew she was OK because she sent us birthday cards and suchlike. But we were close. Why wouldn't she let us know where she was? We weren't the type of people who would try to stifle her in any way. Like you, I felt her disappearance made no sense. There had to be another reason, one she couldn't tell us. And it must have been a big reason. Before she left, she was excited about her future. She even had an interview for a teaching job lined up. I know how much she wanted it. Something *must* have happened to scare her away. I admit, all these years, I've been worried sick about her. It's driven me mad, especially when a birthday or anniversary is coming up and I'm wondering if this is going to be the occasion when we don't receive something from her. I pray that time never comes ... otherwise I'll be left thinking that her past has finally caught up with her ... that she's no longer alive.'

Her final words were muffled by a choked sob and Hugo leaned across to squeeze her arm. 'There, there, dear, don't upset yourself. That hasn't happened and let's pray it never does. I'm hoping this young man will help us find our girl.' He looked expectantly across at their guest. Todd was silent.

Vanessa's words carried the ring of truth. Whenever he'd mentioned her past, Lily had not simply been evasive ... there had also been fear, quickly concealed, but there nonetheless. 'I'm afraid my wife and I have a difference of opinion on this,' Hugo continued with an apologetic glance toward Vanessa. 'I think she reads too many psychological thrillers. The truth is likely to be much simpler. She has attachment issues, possibly caused by post-traumatic stress disorder. When she gets too close to someone, she starts to panic that she'll get hurt all over again and she runs away.'

Vanessa was already shaking her head. 'No. As I've told you before, that doesn't explain the cards she sends. Why is she persisting in maintaining the relationship if that's what she's running away from?'

'My dear, PTSD is a very complicated condition. It can manifest itself in all sorts of ways. Anyway, those are our theories. What's yours?' He swivelled bright, blue eyes to focus on Todd.

'Honestly, I don't know. Without knowing what happened to her before she came to you, I'm afraid I'm in the dark.' Todd was feeling slightly deflated. He'd hoped this morning he was going to discover something which would help him find Lily. So far, that was looking unlikely. 'It *really* would help if you could tell me ...'

'No chance, young man,' Hugo said in a voice which brooked no further discussion. 'Please don't ask us again.'

'Can you tell us about her life as Lily? I'm dying to know more about the young woman she's become.' Vanessa's eyes, as she smiled at Todd, pleaded with him to accept the situation.

Todd relented. He couldn't blame them for their loyalty to Lily, however frustrating he found it. As he answered questions about her life, her career, her friends, he relaxed. It felt good to relive some of those memories. He told them about the incident at her school when she was hailed a heroine. Hugo's face was alight with pride and Vanessa's eyes were moist.

'Oh, that sounds like Sam!' she exclaimed, clasping her gnarled hands together. 'She would always stand up for anyone who needed help. Do you remember, Hugo, that time she was out with Simon and some youths started picking on him, trying to muscle in on her? They thought they were a couple, you see,' she explained to Todd. 'She gave them what for! Those boys soon left them alone. Simon told us all about it afterwards. She never said a word.

That was Sam. She always put others first. That's why I think there *must* have been a good reason for her to leave like she did. She would *never* have hurt us if it was in her power to do otherwise.' Flags of colour bloomed on her cheeks as her speech grew more passionate. 'Sorry,' she said, her poise returning as she picked up her coffee cup. 'I'm repeating myself.'

Todd smiled, picturing a young Lily seeing off a gang of youths. He could imagine it. She wasn't the type to shrink from protecting the weak or confronting injustice. 'I completely agree,' he said to Vanessa. 'Lily is a strong, brave woman ... but I'm with you; I think there's some secret in her past ... something that scares her ... and that's why she runs away.' His mind was suddenly assailed with the memory of her face, drained of colour. When was that? What had he said to spook her? He hadn't thought much of it at the time. If only he could remember when it was ...

He realised the Danes were both looking at him strangely. 'Sorry,' he said, 'I was just remembering this one time when she reacted strangely. It was something I said ...' Images flicked from one to the next like a sideshow in his head. Different pictures of the two of them together. And, then, there it was ... the time he told her about the research for his novel and the report he'd found about a missing girl who looked like her. Was that it? Was that her secret? The possibility blossomed in his consciousness to full, technicolour reality. That would explain why she looked different in Simon's photo and had a different name. If, when she first went to live with the Danes, she was officially 'missing', it would be reasonable to assume she'd go to extreme lengths to stay hidden. He studied the curious faces staring at him and took a deep breath. 'I've just thought of something. I may well be whistling in the wind but I wondered if you would be kind enough to hear me out.' He plunged on. 'I'm a crime writer. Before I start a novel, I do some research and base my plots around true-life stories. I like to think it gives them a gritty realism. Anyway,' he continued, 'I told Lily about a story I read shortly after I'd first met her. It was about a girl who'd gone missing after moving to London to take up a non-existent job. It was weird because the missing girl looked just like Lily. When I told her that, she looked as if she was going to faint. She made an excuse, went off on her own for a bit and, by the time she came back, she was fine. I didn't think anything more about it at the time but, given her disappearance ...' He paused and looked across at Vanessa. Her mouth had dropped open and she was avoiding his gaze. *Interesting.* Encouraged, he ploughed on. 'It was a tragic story because, after the daughter disappeared, the mother was found dead of an overdose. The dad had died in a car accident a few years earlier. That just left a younger sister ...' He waited. The colour in Vanessa's face had been washed away; Hugo was squirming uncomfortably in his chair. 'Is it her?' he asked. 'Is Lily ... Samantha ... the girl who disappeared?'

The tension in the room was now palpable. Vanessa was regarding him with dismay but said nothing. It was left to her husband to answer his question. 'No,' he said. 'It isn't her ...'

Todd shook his head. He didn't believe him. Everything about their body language told him he was right. 'I'm afraid I don't ...'

Hugo raised a hand to stop him. 'Let me finish,' he said gruffly. 'It isn't her. Sam is the younger sister.'

CHAPTER 23

Lily

Last time I went into hiding, the loneliness wasn't as bad. This time around, I feel it like a dead weight around my neck, dragging me down, sapping my energy and my spirit. Every day, I torment myself with thoughts of Todd and Charlotte. What will they be doing? Is Todd already seeing someone else? Have they both moved on? I know Charlotte will be back at school, working hard, playing with friends. That's where I should be right now – in my classroom, surrounded by children – miles away from this pretty cottage with wooden floors brightened by patterned rugs, and seascapes by local artists on the pale, grey walls.

Michael, my headteacher, was great when I called, without warning, just before the end of the Easter holiday, saying I needed a leave of absence. He knew how distressed I'd been by the media attention over the Hathersett incident and was dismayed when I told him why. I didn't tell him the truth exactly. Instead, I resurrected the abusive ex-boyfriend I'd used before, someone who'd previously made threats about what would happen if he found me. I admitted to Michael that I'd changed my name almost ten years ago to escape and how fearful I was that the recent publicity would allow him to find me again. It was close to the truth but I still felt bad, especially when he was so understanding.

'Take as much time as you need,' he said after listening to my garbled explanation. 'Is there anything I can do? Have you told the police?'

'I have and thanks Michael, but this isn't something you can help me with. I really appreciate your support, though.'

'Think nothing of it. Your safety and well-being are the most important things, Lily. We can manage without you. But keep in touch. I hope you soon get your ... situation resolved.'

'So do I. Thanks so much, Michael.'

Thinking about that conversation, and Michael's kindness, reminds me of lying out on the grass with Todd, naming the stars. I remember being a little rude about my headteacher. 'Pale and uninteresting,' I called him, or words to that effect. I want to take it back – tell Todd that Michael Winterbottom is a good man, reliable and dependable, there when you need him. I sigh, a tide of sadness rolling in. Will I ever see either Michael or Todd again?

Today, the weather outside is as bleak as I feel – dull, grey drizzle washing the colour out of the day. I wonder if the fishermen are still out by the sea, flicking their wrists and firing bait into the water with the dexterity of orchestral conductors. I expect they are; a drop of rain wouldn't stop such hardy, single-minded souls. Their resilience puts me to shame, I think. It's time to shake off the shackles of self-pity and make some decisions. There are no perfect solutions to my problems and I've already spent too long agonising over what I should do. Now, I need to get on with it.

My most immediate issue is finding somewhere else to stay. When I phoned Kaz for help over two weeks ago, she explained that the cottage would only be free for three weeks. It had been booked up by holidaymakers, on and off, until September. My time is almost up. I'd been holding tight, praying something would turn up or that, somehow, I could return home. Neither has happened and I have to start looking. I check online but find nothing in Brancaster itself. The thought of moving locations doesn't appeal; the small seaside resort has become a comfortable bolthole. I feel safe here. Picking up the free local newspaper posted through the door yesterday, I turn to the classified ads. I'm skimming through 'houses to let' when my phone rings. It's Kaz.

'Good news!' she says before I can say anything. 'You don't have to move out. You can stay put.'

'What, here? But ... how come?'

'I didn't want to say anything before now in case it fell through. Mum and Dad have been in the process of buying the place next door as an additional holiday let. The whole thing has been dragging on and on but Dad's been pestering his solicitor and worked his magic. To cut a long story short, they now own next door and have been down to check it out.'

'I didn't see them!'

'No. They said they didn't want to put you at any risk by making contact. They send their love, by the way. Basically, next door was used as a holiday let before and they bought it fully kitted out. The cleaners have been and it's ready to go. It's bigger than the one you're in so they contacted the people who'd made bookings and asked if they minded transferring. All of them were more than happy so you're fine to stay where you are ... for as long as you need.'

I feel overwhelmed by such generosity. 'I can't let them do that,' I protested. 'They should be letting out both properties.'

'Please don't worry about it, Sass. They're only too happy to help. You know how much they love you.'

Her words bring tears to my eyes. 'Please thank them for me,' I say, my voice choked with emotion. 'But I do need to start paying rent while I'm here.' She starts to argue and we haggle for a few moments before she caves.

'Fine. Whatever you want. At least you don't have to worry about finding a new place.'

'That's such a relief, I can't tell you.' I pace about the room, energised with renewed positivity. My first problem is resolved; it seems like a good omen for broaching the second. 'While you're on Kaz, is there any way you can source me the name and number of a reliable private investigator? I need someone completely discreet who can dig into Nick Georgiev's past and find something the police have missed – something which proves he really *is* Andrian Petrov.'

There's a brief silence while she mulls it over. 'A private investigator! I like it. What gave you that idea?'

'Todd's novels.' Over the past two weeks, I've talked endlessly of Todd in our phone chats. She's probably sick to death of hearing me mooning over him. 'His main character is a guy called Andy Schofield. He's an investigator who manages to solve crimes when the police can't.'

'Sounds like just what you need!'

'That's what I thought. I've been researching investigators who work around here. I've found a few but it's impossible to know how good they are. Andrian is a dangerous guy and I need someone who knows what he's doing … or what *she's* doing. No reason why it couldn't be a woman.'

'Mm, I see what you mean. I guess most investigators are hired to spy on unfaithful husbands and wives. Well, leave it with me. I'll see what I can come up with.'

'Thanks, Kaz.'

I cast my phone aside and sit back, feeling pleased with myself. There, I've done it. The idea I'd been mulling over the last few days has been put into action. Now I just have to hope Kaz – or possibly, her dad, who seems to know everyone – can come up with a name.

Peering out of the window, I see it's still raining but I grab my coat anyway. No reason not to go out for a walk. 'A drop of rain never hurt anyone.' That was something Dad used to say when Mel and I complained about having to watch the local team play football with him on Saturday afternoons, whatever the weather. Today, the memory makes me smile. He was right. Humming an upbeat tune to myself, I head outside and towards the beach. If I get a move on, the fishermen will still be there …

CHAPTER 24

Todd

The information Todd learnt from Vanessa and Hugo Danes was enlightening but, ultimately, left him no further forward. He still had no idea where to look for Lily. Upon returning home, he spent hours scouring the internet for information linked to that original news report but found nothing useful. It was as if Saskia Potter, as well as her older sister, had been of no more interest to the newspaper-buying public. That couldn't be true, he thought. There must be people from her past who knew her, who wanted to know what happened to her. And someone out there must know why it was necessary for Saskia to change her name when she was fostered. He'd rung both of his two mates in the police force to see if they could dig up any information for him but they were unable, or unwilling, to help.

'More than my job is worth. Sorry, bud,' the first had said.

The other was part of a team working a big murder case and was run off his feet. 'Try me again in a few weeks. Maybe, we'll have cracked this by then.'

So much for that. Todd pulled a wry face as he recalled how he'd written scenes in his novels where Andy Schofield called upon police associates for assistance. It seemed that strategy didn't work so easily in the real world.

Vanessa Danes had phoned a few times when she'd thought of other snippets of information from Samantha's past. She'd been going through the paperwork regarding the fostering process and had remembered a conversation she'd had with one of the social workers. The woman – she couldn't remember her name – had stressed the importance of confidentiality with regard to Samantha. Vanessa had never learnt her foster daughter's real name and had been told details of her case history only so that she could help the teenager recover from her trauma. There was a child protection order in place preventing any disclosure of her personal details.

'At the time, I didn't think anything of it,' she told Todd. 'I just accepted it as normal. It was our first time fostering so we took everything the professionals said as gospel. I remember asking if Sam would want to maintain contact with friends from her old school. The response was a definite 'no' which didn't make sense to me. Why did she have to sever all ties to her past? It seemed a bit extreme but, as I said, I just accepted it all. The question didn't arise while Sam was living with us. She never mentioned a soul from her life before and I didn't dare rock the boat. We were living on eggshells at the beginning. But then, we got to know her. She settled in at school down here and made new friends. She was a sociable person – she even managed to prise our Simon out from under his shell. I can't believe that she didn't have lots of friends before. Why didn't she want any contact with them? It wasn't as if she'd done anything wrong. Anyhow, I'd put all this out of my mind until you came. Then, I got to thinking about it again and … well … I'm *convinced* she goes on the run to protect her identity. There's someone out there or something she's afraid of. I'm scared for her, Todd.'

He suppressed his own fears and tried to reassure Vanessa. He'd find her; he'd think of something; yes, he'd keep in touch. Words were easy. After the call, he sat for a long time, apprehension wringing his insides to mush. What if she *was* in trouble? What if, in trying to find her, he was putting her in danger? With a jolt, he remembered the blue van from a few nights ago. At the time, he'd suspected it might be tailing him. Did that have anything to do with Lily's disappearance? Probably not. He hadn't noticed it since … but, in all honesty, he'd forgotten about it. Now, the memory, in conjunction with Vanessa's fears, sent spears of worry spiking his chest. If Lily was in danger, he *had* to try to find her, to help her … but he needed to take care he wasn't leading someone else to her.

That night, he returned to the news report once more. The name, *Andrian Petrov*, loomed large on the page. Who was he? Why did he disappear too? Did the police ever find him? Was he involved in Melanie Potter's disappearance? Already, he'd tried googling him and spent a while going through the search results. He didn't expect to find anything useful and he didn't. He'd pictured the man many times; after all, he was the inspiration for the villain in his latest novel. The thought did nothing to reassure. The man called Andropov, in his book, was a murderous sadist.

Frustration churned as he finished reading. He was wasting his time; there was nothing useful in the report. And yet ... as he reached to change the screen, his eyes lingered on the first line. *Melanie Potter, 17, of Thorpe St Andrew.* The place where they lived. What if he went there? It was a long shot, almost worth dismissing altogether, except he had nothing else. He puffed out the breath he hadn't realised he'd been holding and reached for his keyboard. *Thorpe St Andrew.* He typed in the name, picturing it as a tiny village, the sort of place where everyone knew everyone else, a goldmine of useful information. Unfortunately, this wasn't the case. It was described as a small town and suburb of Norwich, situated approximately two miles east of the city centre. He clicked on the website for the local high school and searched its archives for photos dating from the time Lily might have attended there. There were none. Next, he tried *Saskia Potter Thorpe St Andrew.* Again, nothing, except for a story about a Harry Potter actor being a former student at the school. He tried Facebook and, from there, found a link to the Thorpe St Andrew website. That had a history section but it yielded nothing useful and there were no links for historic news stories. There was a local directory and he clicked on the accommodation section. It was decided. He'd take a couple of days off the following week and nose around. Surely, if he asked enough people, he'd find someone who knew of the Potter tragedy seventeen years earlier? There *must* be someone out there she trusted – someone who knew where she was ...

***

Almost six weeks passed before Todd was able to take his trip to Thorpe St Andrew. The firm of solicitors for whom he worked, Braithwaite & Hart, became embroiled in a tricky insolvency case and the partners refused his request for leave point blank.

'We need you on this,' Nathan Hart told him. 'Find a solution acceptable to all parties and you can take as much time off as you like.'

'I might hold you to that,' he replied, resigned to his fate. He was considered the firm's expert when it came to insolvency matters.

'And show young Miss Knight the ropes too, would you. She'll benefit from the experience.'

Todd groaned inwardly and shot a pointed look at the senior partner. Pale blue eyes remained guileless but Todd wouldn't mind betting Nathan Hart knew exactly what he was doing. Abigail Knight was relatively new to the company – young, bright, attractive and full of confidence. She'd made it clear from the outset that she was interested in him and that made him uncomfortable, not least because other colleagues had noticed and teased him about it. Since his divorce, there had been many unsuccessful match-making attempts by his peers at work and this might well constitute another. None of them knew anything about his relationship with Lily. Instinctively, he thought she'd prefer it that way and anyway, there was no-one at work with whom he socialised. Most of his colleagues were older and married. It was easier not to mention it.

Todd sighed. 'Of course,' he said. 'It'll be good to have another brain working on this one.'

'Excellent. I know we can count on you to sort it out.'

Dismissed, he returned to his office to find a stack of box files awaiting him. Brilliant. This was going to take even longer than he'd first thought. He looked up at the light knock on his door. 'Come in.'

'It's only me. I hear we're going to be working together. I can't wait.' Abigail Knight's perfect white teeth flashed him a coy smile. 'I hope you don't mind.'

'Of course not. Come and take a seat. Looks like we've a lot to get through.' He watched as she closed the door behind her. Her long, dark hair was neatly coiled in a bun on the nape of her neck and she looked a picture of efficiency in her buttoned-up blouse and figure-hugging skirt. Green eyes framed with long lashes gleamed with eager anticipation as she slid into the chair opposite.

'Good job I'm a fast worker.' She gave him a cheeky wink and licked her red lips.

'Yes ... well ...' He launched into the details of the case, as had just been told to him, feeling an irritation he was careful to conceal. Her demeanour, as she listened, felt slightly predatory; she was the cat to his mouse and he wasn't sure how best to deal with it. The thought almost made him laugh out loud. God, what a wuss! Who'd have envisaged he'd ever think such a thing? Before Lily, he'd have enjoyed a little harmless flirting. What was to stop him now? Lily *had* left him, after all ...

'Earth to Todd.' Abigail's teasing voice pulled him from his thoughts. 'You were talking about a possible merger with the Rowling Corporation?'

'Yes ... sorry ...' He looked up from the papers in front of him. 'I was just considering something ... anyway, it's not important.'

'I hope I'm not distracting you.' Her face was a picture of innocence as she wriggled in her chair, her breasts straining against the fabric of her blouse.

'Not at all,' he replied smoothly, his attention back on work. Yes, she was great to look at and available but she didn't interest him. Too obvious. Not his type. And she wasn't Lily.

***

The working days settled into a comfortable pattern, often extending late into the night. Abi had a sharp brain and came up with several creative ways of moving forward when they hit a stumbling block on the case. She was hardworking and didn't complain about the long hours. On the contrary, he was often ready to call it a day when she would suggest grabbing a takeaway and continuing. He was fine with that. The more they worked, the sooner they'd be finished and he'd be able to resume his search for Lily. He'd heard nothing from her and he didn't expect to but it was Charlotte's birthday in a few weeks. In his heart, he was hoping she'd send a card, as she did for the Danes family, something which would let him know she was alright.

Abi constantly surprised him. He hadn't expected to enjoy working with her but he did. She made him laugh with her wry observations on office politics and they'd fallen into an easy friendship. If she wondered at his single status and his continued resistance to her charms, she never mentioned it. He couldn't help noticing, though, that she took every opportunity to get close to him. Sometimes, she would peer over his shoulder, letting her chest nestle against him, her perfume assailing his senses. In those situations, his traitorous body would respond; he prayed she didn't notice.

Her attention was flattering though – a balm to his bruised ego. A couple of times, he'd found himself on the verge of telling Abi about Lily. He just wanted to talk about her, to breathe substance into his thoughts of her. But he never did; he was worried Abi would tell him to get over her. His theory that Lily was on the run from danger could be his way of rationalising her behaviour to suit his own feelings. As time went by, he wondered if maybe Hugo Danes was right. Lily's tragic past could have left her with relationship issues; the person she was running from could be him. Always, he squashed those concerns. He wouldn't believe it. But there was only one way to find out for sure and that meant finding her. He'd seen a blue van twice more; once parked further along his street and once behind him, when he and Abi were driving out to meet the client. It gave him that same uneasy twinge but he couldn't be positive that each time it was the same vehicle. There were lots of vans out there. Chances were that both occasions were coincidences.

With Abi's help, Todd managed to bring the tricky insolvency case to a successful conclusion. The client was delighted and Nathan Hart regarded them both with smug satisfaction as he told them so.

'I knew you two would be a good pairing and I was right,' he declared with the air of a priest bestowing his blessing on a happy couple. 'I have a treat for you. As a thank you, the client has invited you both to the Suffolk Show Ball, as his guests. Yes ...' He held up a hand when Todd tried to interrupt, '... I know I promised you a few days off, Todd, and you shall have them, but the Ball is tomorrow night so I'm sure you can wait until after then. I don't have to remind you, I know, that this represents an excellent PR opportunity for the company. It's not something which can be turned down.'

'Definitely not.' Abi was alight with enthusiasm. 'I'm sure we'll remember that, Mr Hart.'

'Good.' Nathan's voice held a note of finality. 'It's at Trinity Park in Ipswich. I'm happy for you to book rooms somewhere on the company expense account. You deserve a good night out.'

Was that a twinkle in his eye? Todd suspected so. He sighed. It would appear churlish to refuse. 'Thanks Nathan,' he said. 'I'm sure we'll enjoy it.'

'You can count on it,' Abi grinned.

***

Todd sat drinking champagne, smiling at the elderly lady on his left and tugging irritably at the collar of his dress shirt. His companions were pleasant enough and his host, a portly, bald man with no neck who reminded him of Winston Churchill, couldn't do enough for him. Jim Johnson-Smyth was hugely grateful to him and Abi for saving his company from bankruptcy and was spending money like water to celebrate. At this rate, the rescue package was going to need bolstering, Todd thought cynically. Personally, he was already wearied by the fake bonhomie and networking but Abi was in her element. She glittered and sparkled in a red, low-cut dress, happy to take centre stage. Todd found himself subjected to several envious stares as they made their entrance, Abi holding his arm and teetering beside him on impossibly high heels. A photographer from the press intercepted them with a request for a picture and Abi squeezed close, positioning herself so that his arm naturally curved around her slim waist. From that point on, people took them to be a couple and Todd felt it would be ungentlemanly to Abi to protest to the contrary, especially as she appeared only too happy to continue the fiction, constantly touching his hand or his arm and adopting a teasing tone of affection towards him. It was going to be a long night.

When the band struck up, Abi dragged him onto the dance floor, wiggling her hips and encouraging him to spin her around. As the song finished, he prepared to make his escape but she detained him. 'I love this one,' she murmured as the beat slowed. 'Dance with me.' She slid into his arms, pressing her body into his and resting her head on his shoulder. Todd sighed and pulled her nearer, shutting his eyes and relishing the closeness of a beautiful woman. He could almost imagine he was dancing with Lily ...

'Hey, you two, get a room!' Jim Johnson-Smyth's booming voice cut across the dance floor as he swept past them with his wife. Todd's eyes jolted open and he released his grip but Abi pulled him back towards her.

'Good idea!' She winked at Jim and then gave Todd a look smouldering with desire. 'I'm happy with that suggestion if you are ...'

'I ... erm ... I think maybe I've had a little too much champagne.' He cleared his throat. 'Look, Abi ...'

'Just think about it.' She blew him a kiss and sashayed from the dance floor.

As he returned to his table, his thoughts were jumbled. The past weeks had been leading up to this and he was confused by the way his resolve was crumbling. Abi was a beautiful woman who wanted to have sex with him. Was that so terrible? It wouldn't mean anything. To distract himself, he spent the next half hour inviting the other women around the table to dance. Duty done, he strolled outside to get some air. It was a beautiful, starry evening and he quickly located familiar constellations. The last time he'd gazed at the stars, he'd been with Lily. His heart ached at the memory. He could hear her voice, wistful and sad, as if she was right there with him.

'I was thinking about the stars − how beautiful they are. But even they don't last forever. Eventually, they burn themselves out. Everything changes.'

Her words were etched on his brain like a brand. Yes, he thought, things change ... but he wouldn't. Not while there was still hope. He would remain constant.

Much later, after a taxi ride back to their hotel, Todd walked Abi to her hotel room.

'Are you coming in?' The invitation was paired with a sultry look of promise.

He shook his head and bent to kiss her lightly on her cheek. 'Night Abi. Thank you for a lovely evening.'

She sighed and shrugged her slim shoulders. 'It could've been so much better. Night Todd.' Pulling a face, she stepped into the room and closed the door behind her, leaving him to weave a slightly unsteady path to his own room, alone.

CHAPTER 25

Lily

Weeks have passed and it feels like I'm no further forward in my search to find a private investigator. After I first asked her to find someone, Kaz rang within a couple of days to give me a name. She'd asked a close friend who'd used an investigator to check out the credentials of some potential business partners. The investigator he used, a man called Lenny Burroughs, had impressed him sufficiently to be given a resounding endorsement. Apparently, the guy was a computer genius and would leave no trail. 'If you use him,' Kaz told me, 'Nick Georgiev won't have any idea he's being investigated.' Lenny Burroughs sounded too good to be true. Excited, and a little nervous, I rang his number. It went to voicemail and I left a message, asking him to ring me. He called back that same evening but it wasn't good news. He was fully booked for the next three months and unable to take anything on until September. Despondent, I rang Kaz.

'Oh, I'm so sorry,' she said. 'I should've checked his availability before I gave you his name. Then, you wouldn't have had your hopes dashed like that.'

'It's not your fault, Kaz. It's just one of those things. I rang on the off-chance that your friend had recommended any other investigators.'

'He didn't.' She sighed. 'Look, leave it with me. I'll keep asking around. I'll try Dad too. He might know of someone.'

'You won't mention anything about me, will you?' I asked anxiously.

'Of course not! You should know me better than to ask that!' she retorted.

'I know. Sorry. Silly question.'

'I'll forgive you. And I'm sorry the computer guy didn't work out. Don't worry. We'll find someone amazing ... as good as Andy Skoda.'

'Schofield,' I chuckled.

'Yes, him. Someone like that. I'm on it.' With that, she ended the call, leaving me smiling. Her optimism was contagious and I felt a lot better.

But that was almost six weeks ago. Since then, Kaz had rung several times to provide updates but finding someone reliable who could start on my case in the very near future was proving difficult. 'I know it's tough but you just have to be patient,' she said.

'At this rate, it'll be September and Lenny Burroughs after all!' I bit back in frustration. Immediately, I felt guilty. It wasn't her fault. I really didn't deserve her help. 'Sorry, Kaz. Don't listen to me. I'm being grumpy and ungrateful.'

'It's understandable. I know it's tough, being in limbo at the moment, like you are.'

She's right. It *is* tough. Sometimes, I've taken the bus to various places further along the coast, just for a change of scene. Those trips out feel like a real treat but also have a downside. I so miss having someone to share them with. It's times like those when my longing for Todd becomes a physical ache. Then ... and the night times.

To give myself something else to do, I've taken up gardening, albeit on a very small scale. The flower beds bordering the decking in the tiny back garden were becoming overgrown and looked a lot better after I'd weeded them. Spurred on by the improvement I'd wrought, I bought some pots and filled them with geraniums and fuchsias. The resulting bursts of colour cheer me when I'm feeling low. And watering and dead-heading are soothing jobs which help provide structure to my day. They give me something to do beyond walking and reading.

I do love the small cottage where I'm staying. It nestles on a quiet street about half a mile from the beach, mostly shielded from view by tall shrubs, and reasonably secluded. There are other houses nearby, including the nearest, which is now owned by Kaz's parents, but most of them are holiday lets. I haven't been bothered by anyone since I've been here. Even next door is currently empty. There was a family staying there last week and I'd enjoyed the anonymous companionship of small children, playing and arguing on the other side of the hedge. But now, that too is churchyard silent.

My current existence is unutterably lonely. I pray I won't have to endure it beyond September. That would take me into a new school year. Whilst Michael Winterbottom has been a model of patience and support, it wouldn't be fair to ask him to keep my job open beyond the summer. I'd have to tender my resignation ... let him find someone to replace me. It doesn't bear thinking about. Something needs to happen before then.

***

After lunch, I stroll into the village. I've realised that Charlotte's birthday is coming up and I haven't yet bought her a card or a present. I'll ask Kaz to organise the postage for me so Charlotte doesn't receive a package postmarked Brancaster. I should've thought of it last week when I saw her. On that occasion, we met in a café – any chance to get out of the cottage – when she took a detour on her way to visit a client. She suggested she may be able stop by again sometime in the next week. I'm trying not to look forward to it too much in case it doesn't happen. My friend is now thirty-four weeks pregnant with her first baby so there's always a chance she won't feel up to making the trip.

I take a roundabout route and stop at a telephone box to make a call. I know I'm paranoid but, when I first came to Brancaster, I left my mobile phone locked in my flat and bought a new one. The only person from my past who knows that number is Kaz and I'm trying to keep it that way. I dial the number I've memorised and wait. Jamie works nights so this should be a good time to ring him. He lives in the flat above mine.

'Hello.' His voice sounds sleepy.

'Oh, sorry Jamie. It's Lily. Did I wake you?'

'No, no. Hi Lily. How are you?'

'Fine thanks. Is everything OK back home?' I'd left Jamie my key so he could keep an eye on my flat and retrieve my post. He'd also promised to let me know if anyone came poking around. The first time I called him, he told me of Todd's visit, which sent my emotions shooting all over the place. Stupid! I didn't want Todd looking for me but I'm ridiculously pleased to know that he was.

'Everything's cool. Nothing to report. Oh, your plants were looking a bit sick so I've been watering them.'

'Oh, thank you! You're a star.'

'No problem. Any idea when you're coming back?'

'Not yet. Look, Jamie, I've got to go, but thank you so much for all you're doing. I really appreciate it.'

'My pleasure. Bye, Lily.'

I hang up the phone and step back onto the pavement. There are a few more people milling around than when I first came here eight weeks ago but I don't mind that. I feel safer in the company of others, less conspicuous. Although it's early June, it's much cooler today than of late and the sky is charcoal, threatening rain. Most holiday makers are avoiding the beach and some are browsing the high-quality gift shops instead.

It doesn't take me long to find a gift for Charlotte – a beautiful writing set with notelets, pretty pens and paper, all decorated with pictures of puppies. I know she'll love it, although Todd may not thank me. She's been crazing him recently for a puppy of her own and this will fire her enthusiasm even more. Poor Todd. It isn't practical for him to get a puppy at the moment, but it's not easy telling that to Charlotte! Present and card selected, I purchase the items and head back, just as it starts to rain, fat drops which herald the deluge to come. I have an umbrella with me but it proves useless in the face of the wind whipping across from the sea and, by the time I get back to the cottage, I'm drenched. Flinging myself inside and closing the door behind me, I'm peeling off my outer layers when my phone rings. Kaz. I'll ring her back later.

Naked except for my underwear, I scurry upstairs and turn on the shower. The hot jets of water feel wonderful against my chilled skin and I stay there for some while. By the time, I'm out, dry, dressed and back downstairs, I find I've missed two more calls from Kaz. It must be urgent ... could the baby be making an early appearance?

'Hi Kaz,' I say when she instantly picks up. 'Are you OK? Is there any news?'

'Yes,' she replies. 'I've been trying to ring you. I've found a private investigator, someone who specialises in crime-related jobs. He sounds just what you want.'

After so many weeks of waiting, that wasn't what I'd been expecting at all. 'That's brilliant!' I exclaim. 'Is he able to start straight away?'

'Yes.' Her voice sounds smug. 'He wants a face-to-face meeting with you. Tomorrow.'

CHAPTER 26

Todd

At just after eleven o'clock on Monday morning, Todd reached the Bed & Breakfast accommodation he'd booked in Thorpe St Andrew. Charlotte had stayed the weekend, as usual, so he'd had to put off his travels until then. She'd been subdued and he was a little anxious about her. When he'd asked if anything was the matter, she'd shrugged, 'not really,' like a teenager. Having checked that everything was fine at school and at her mum's, he'd not pressed her further for fear she'd ask him about Lily. He couldn't bear facing her disappointment.

It was a windy morning. Clouds scudded across oases of blue and there was a chill in the air. His satnav told him he'd reached his destination and he pulled into the gravel driveway of a detached, forlorn-looking building set back from the road. A faded sign announced optimistically 'Sunnyside Lodge Bed & Breakfast Accommodation'. On the internet, when he'd booked it, the façade looked bright and welcoming. The photograph must have been taken in the spring with daffodils and tulips providing vibrant colour. Now, the garden was overgrown and cream paint flaked from the window frames. Not a great start. Grabbing his bag, he headed for the front door where a notice informed him to ring the bell. He pressed but heard nothing. As he waited, he turned back to face the road. There was a dark blue van parked near the entrance to the drive, its engine still running. His heart lurched in his chest. *Was it the same one?* He hadn't noticed it on the journey, or when he pulled in, and he had been checking his rear-view mirror with vigilant regularity.

He spun around again, alerted by the sound of a key turning in a lock. The door opened and a wizened, old lady peered suspiciously up at him. She reminded him of an overripe tomato –round, wearing a bright, red apron, but shrunken and shrivelled.

'Mr Matheson?' she croaked.

'That's me.'

She frowned. 'I was expecting somebody older. Oh well, you'd better come in.' She led the way through a high-ceilinged hallway to a small room which served as an office. A computer sat on an antique desk and the woman's fingers flew over the keyboard with surprising speed. 'Right. You're in the Maverick Suite – up the stairs and on your left.' She handed him a key. 'Breakfast is served between eight and ten, not a minute later. I don't do evening meals anymore but there's a Harvester just up the road.'

'Um ... I'm not sure if there's been a mistake but I didn't book a suite.'

She gave him a toothy grin. 'All our rooms are called suites. It was my Harvey's idea. Thought it made them sound posh. I named them after my favourite TV programmes. Maverick was my favourite. James Garner ... now he ...' she sniggered, '... he used to send me all of a quiver. The other rooms are Dallas, Dynasty and Kojak. I wanted to call one Mash but Harvey wouldn't allow it. He said it didn't sound classy enough. He's dead ... Harvey ...' she continued without missing a beat, '... died nearly six years ago now. It's not the same without him but what else would I do? So, I'm here all on my own ... but don't you go getting any ideas.' She giggled girlishly and waggled a finger at him. 'I'm too old for the likes of you.' He smiled and picked up his bag. 'What's a young man like you doing in Thorpe anyway? I don't usually have guests your sort of age. They prefer those soulless chain hotels in the city.' She gave a dismissive snort. 'No accounting for taste.'

Her question caught him unawares and he hesitated, not sure what to say. As she watched his face, her watery eyes surprisingly sharp, he wondered why not tell her the truth – start his nosing around straight away? She'd lived there a while; she may have known the Potter family. He gave her his most charming smile. 'I'm trying to find some information about a family who lived around here. They were called Potter. It was a tragic case. The father was killed in a car accident and then, a few years later, the eldest daughter disappeared. She went to London for a job and was never seen again. Then, the mum died of an overdose and that just left the youngest daughter.'

She listened, her face growing suspicious. 'Are you one of those reporter people?' she asked. 'Stirring up muck, trying to cause trouble?'

'No, nothing like that. I'm actually a writer, trying to do some research for a book.' The half-truth tumbled out of its own volition.

'What, a real-life type of book?'

'No, I write fiction, crime thrillers. You may have heard of me ... Todd Matheson.'

She hadn't, obviously, but was suitably impressed. 'Ooh, a famous author,' she gushed. 'Are you going to put me in your next book? I could be a Miss Marple type character. Constance Cleverly. See, my name would be perfect!'

'It's a good name,' he agreed, before turning the conversation back to his original question. 'Do you remember the Potter family?'

She thought for a moment, nodding gravely. 'I didn't know the family but I do remember the story – terrible, it was. I don't recall the details. It was a while ago.'

'Yes, it was. 2003 to be precise.'

She sucked in her cheeks and shook her head. 'My memory's not as good as it used to be. I do remember it being in the news. I think the family lived in Vincent's Road but I may be wrong. I seem to remember Mr Patel ... he ran the shop ... jumped-up, little man he was ... so full of himself ... anyway, he was interviewed ... couldn't wait to get on TV, that one ... jumping on the back of other folks' misery ... but there, he's dead now.'

'Vincent's Road, you said?'

She nodded. 'I think so. Patel's is on that street. I believe it's a Co-op now.'

'That's a really good start. Thank you, Mrs Cleverly.'

'Oh, call me Connie. Mrs Cleverly makes me sound old.'

He grinned at that. 'OK. Thanks, Connie.'

The stairs were carpeted in threadbare, gold and brown swirls but his room was surprisingly modern, with crisp, white linen on the double bed and a tiled, en-suite shower room. He made himself a coffee from the assembled sachets on a tray and ate two shortbread biscuits. His room overlooked the front drive and the road beyond it. The dark blue van he'd noticed earlier had moved and was now parked further along. He stood watching it for a few minutes, increasingly convinced that he was being followed. It was pretty unbelievable and he wanted to reject his suspicion out of hand – put it down to the fanciful imagination of a crime writer. But the presence of that blue van also corroborated his concerns for Lily. Was someone else out there trying to find her? Were they using him to do so? Just as he was debating the wisdom of confronting the driver, the van pulled away and disappeared from view. It could have been making deliveries in the area ... but he was going to take extra care from now on.

He logged on to the Wi-Fi and used his phone to locate Vincent's Road. Now, he had a starting point. With renewed hope, and feeling somewhat detective-ish himself, he headed back down the stairs and out to his car. Someone out there would be able to tell him more about the family. He just needed to find the right person.

***

He found Vincent's Road but continued on by and pulled into an industrial estate further along. There, he sat for a while, watching and waiting, but saw no vehicles acting suspiciously. Locking his car, he headed back on foot, periodically checking over his shoulder. No-one appeared to be paying him any attention. A newsagent's shop sat on the corner of Vincent's Road and was the first place he tried. A young girl was chewing gum behind the counter and, in the absence of customers, was flicking through a magazine. Todd's query about a family called Potter, who lived in the street in 2003, sparked nothing but disinterest.

'Sorry. No idea who you're talking about. I'm new around here. And anyway, I was just a baby then.'

'Is there anyone else in the shop who might remember the family?' Todd looked hopefully over her shoulder towards the closed door behind. 'The manager? The owner?'

'Nah. That's my dad and he's new around here too. Took over this place last year. Sorry.'

That encounter set the tone for the afternoon. Methodically, Todd traipsed along either side of the street, ringing doorbells, knocking on doors. At many places, no-one was home. From the majority of the rest, he received a hostile reception. Most thought he was selling something or were too busy to listen to what he had to say. Some had moved there only recently. One elderly gentleman, Steven, beamed at him and ushered him inside, thinking he was there to mend the TV. He insisted on making a cup of tea, even when Todd explained he wasn't the repairman. With Steven watching expectantly, Todd played with the TV controls. The screen was blank when he switched it on but he soon realised it was on the wrong input setting. By pressing the correct button on the remote, the screen burst into life and Steven was delighted. He was just protesting that such a simple fix didn't require payment when the television engineer turned up. An altercation ensued when the man demanded his callout fee. Steven was adamant that Todd was the real TV repairman and this was an imposter, trying to trick him out of his money. In the end, Todd gave the guy twenty quid out of his own pocket and he went away mollified. He then spent over an hour chatting to Steven about the Potter case. One minute, Steven would be nodding and saying he remembered the story and the next he'd forgotten what they were talking about. It reminded Todd of his grandad who'd suffered from dementia in his later years. He ended up listening to Steven's stories of his childhood growing up during the war – fascinating, but not how he'd intended to spend his time. In the end, though, that was the most fruitful part of his day. At least, someone had benefitted from his visit.

By late afternoon, as he headed back to the B & B, he was feeling much less optimistic about his quest. Finding Lily seemed hopelessly out of reach. This trip could be a complete waste of time. As he pulled into the driveway of Sunnyside Lodge, he noted the absence of the blue van. He'd been watchful throughout the afternoon and was as confident as he could be that no-one had followed him. Again, he wondered if he was letting his imagination run away with him. Blue vans were pretty common, after all.

Connie was waiting for him. She shot into the hallway, slightly flushed and clearly agitated, as he used his key to open the front door. 'Oh, Todd, I'm so sorry. Have you been out looking for that family on Vincent's Road?' At his nod, she moaned, 'Oh dear ... dearie me ... what a fool I am.' In her anguish, she patted floury hands on the red apron and puffs of flour dust fluffed into the air around her.

'What are you sorry for?'

'Oh, I'm such an idiot. After you'd left, I remembered it wasn't *Vincent's* Road at all. I was getting confused. Mr Patel owned the shop on *Langley* Street on the Notley estate, not the one that's now a Co-op. I wanted to tell you but didn't have your phone number. I didn't know what to do. I don't drive, you see, or I'd have tried to find you. And, nowadays, it's really too far for me to walk.'

Her face was flooded with worry and Todd masked the frustration he was feeling. 'No problem.' He gave her a reassuring smile. 'I'll try Langley Street tomorrow. I didn't have any joy today.'

'Of course, you didn't and it's *all* my fault,' she wailed. 'Anyway, what's done is done. I know I said I didn't provide evening meals but I've made a steak and kidney pie and I wondered if you'd like to join me, as my guest. I wouldn't expect any payment and it'll be a whole lot better than anything you'll get down the road, if I do say so myself.' Her head twitched from side to side, reminding him of an anxious mother hen.

'That would be lovely. Thank you,' he said politely.

'Oh good,' she beamed. 'Well, it'll be ready at seven. I'll lay the table in the dining room.' She scurried off and he made his way up the stairs to his room. Looking on the bright side, he now had a plan of action for tomorrow so the day hadn't been a complete write-off. He glanced out of his bedroom window, subconsciously looking for the dark blue van. It wasn't there. Yawning, he rolled the last bit of tension from his shoulders and headed for the shower.

CHAPTER 27

Lily

I wake brimming with a sense of anticipation. Today, I'm meeting the private investigator Kaz has lined up for me. Leaping out of bed, I check the sky from my bedroom window. Overcast – a hint of sunshine teasing at the edge of a mass of grey. It seems a good omen. Our assignation will take place at a café in Brancaster Staithe, which is within walking distance, so I'm relieved to see it isn't raining.

The man I'm meeting is called Howard Jones. Since Kaz told me that, I can't think of him without picturing the eighties pop star singing *What is Love?* I find myself randomly launching into the song at odd moments. It helps calm my nerves.

I set out after breakfast and a cup of strong coffee. I have an hour to get there by the appointed time so I can enjoy a leisurely walk. Dressed in jeans, a t-shirt, a light waterproof jacket and walking boots, I take the path across the marshes, enjoying their untamed beauty. Much of the route comprises a raised boardwalk which provides dry and easy walking. I see several birds skimming the surface of the reeds and wish I knew what they were. When I reach Brancaster Staithe, I pass a car park, already half-full and with a van by its entrance. A billboard stands beside it, advertising drinks and seafood. Cockles are the 'special' of the day. The thought makes my stomach queasy. I smile at the man behind the counter and continue on.

I know Brancaster Staithe is a small fishing port in the middle of the saltwater marshes but it seems miles from the sea itself. Watery inlets weave between the reeds, and boats out-number people. I turn off the coastal path and head inland where I know the café is situated. I checked one of the walking guides in the cottage last night and again this morning before I left. I'm also carrying a map zipped up in my jacket pocket as an extra precaution. It wouldn't do to take a wrong turn and arrive too late to meet Howard Jones.

At a few minutes before the appointed time, I enter the café and look around. A man in his forties is sitting in one corner, a mug in front of him and a copy of *Horse and Hound* lying on the table. It's him. He looks up expectantly as the bell on the door tinkles and I walk across to his table. 'Howard Jones?' I ask.

He rises and offers his hand. I notice he is medium height with broad shoulders and slightly tubby around the middle. He's wearing a plain, blue shirt and the buttons are straining to stay intact. 'The very same.'

'Lily Nichol.' I sit opposite him and smile. 'Horse and Hound?' I query.

He shrugs. 'My daughter is into horses.' He has a kind face with calm, blue eyes. My radar says he's a nice bloke. Whether or not he'll be up for the task, though, is anyone's guess. 'So ... how can I be of assistance?'

I tell him the unvarnished truth. I have to trust him. If he's any good, I'm sure he'll check out whatever I tell him anyway. First, I outline the task – to dig into the background of the man who committed crimes against my family in 2003. I try to keep my voice void of emotion as I fill in the details, starting at the beginning: Andrian's relationship with Mum; my sister and her disappearance; the overheard phone conversation; my trip to London; the discovery of my mum's body; the threatening text Andrian sent me; the police investigation and subsequent arrest of men involved in sex trafficking. Continuing the story chronologically, I describe my new life in Kent and the encounter with Andrian in 2010. I explain how his repeated threat sent me into hiding once more, this time in Suffolk. Finally, I describe recent events and my fear that the publicity I'd received would enable Andrian to find me. I reach into my pocket and extract the article about Nick Georgiev which I'd printed out. He listens with a neutral expression as I allege that Georgiev and Andrian are one and the same. When I'm finished, he asks sensible questions. How do I know Andrian was involved in that sex trafficking ring?

Why am I so sure Georgiev is him? What do the police think? I answer, pausing only when a waitress brings my order of coffee. Scepticism lurks in his eyes when I reveal that the police think Georgiev is genuine and I become impassioned, trying to convince him otherwise.

When I fall silent, he puffs his cheeks and exhales in a low whistle. 'It's quite a story. I'll do a bit of digging and see what I can find out, if that's what you want. I have to warn you though, if the police have checked out his background and he's come up clean, I'm unlikely to find anything.'

'Look, I don't know how he's done it but he's fooled the police. I'm hoping he won't fool you too.'

He raises his eyebrows at that and smiles. 'OK. You've convinced me. I'll see what I can find out.' I agree to pay his fee for making initial enquiries and he keys my mobile number into his phone. He then texts his bank details and says he'll make a start as soon as he's received payment. I promise to transfer money later that day. It's an eye-watering sum and will take a chunk out of my already depleted savings. I hope it won't be money wasted.

As he stands to leave, I catch hold of his arm. 'Be careful,' I say. 'Don't underestimate Andrian.'

He gives me a reassuring grin. 'I won't,' he replies. 'Don't let this body fool you.' He pats his tummy. 'I know how to take care of myself. I'll be in touch.'

With mixed feelings, I watch him amble out through the door and onto the street. Despite his assurances, I'm not convinced he'll be much help. I guess I'd been expecting a man along the lines of ex-SAS Andy Schofield and he was far from that. But appearances can be deceptive and I berate myself for jumping to conclusions. I'd warned Howard against underestimating Andrian and here I was – possibly guilty of underestimating him. Despite his genial, cuddly demeanour, there was no reason why Howard Jones, private investigator, shouldn't possess a razor-sharp intellect, Machiavellian cunning and deadly, physical skills. Time would tell.

CHAPTER 28

Todd

The following day was grey with light drizzle but Todd, fuelled by an impressive, full English breakfast, felt fired up and ready to go. Connie was an excellent cook. Dinner the previous evening had also been delicious and she clearly relished having company. Hours had passed with surprising speed as she chattered about her life with Harvey and told funny stories about some of their guests.

'We had one gentleman who came down to breakfast in his bathrobe.' She leaned across the table. 'When he sat down, he undid the tie around his middle and ... well ...' Her voice dropped to a whisper. 'He wasn't wearing *anything* underneath. I didn't know where to look. It quite put me off my own breakfast. I mean, who can enjoy biting into a sausage when you've seen *that*?' She chortled, her face flushed and full of mischief. Earlier, she'd fetched one of Harvey's bottles of red wine and it now stood empty. 'We've had lots of famous people staying here you know.'

'Really?'

'Oh yes ... Pierce Brosnan, Julia Roberts and that bloke from Watchdog. All incognito, of course. Harvey said it wasn't them but I know better. I'd recognise Pierce's voice anywhere, although I was a bit surprised by the ginger hair and beard. He was *so* charming. It was definitely him ... and Julia. She looked just like she did in Notting Hill, just a bit older and plumper ... and very picky about her bacon, I remember. I loved that film. I'm hoping that one day Hugh Grant may choose to stay here. It keeps me going ... that thought.'

Todd chuckled and finished the dregs of his wine. He felt more relaxed than he'd done for weeks. Definitely, he'd have to bring Lily here ... when he found her.

'You'd *never* believe the things guests leave behind,' Connie continued. 'It makes me blush to tell you some of them ... I mean ... handcuffs, whips ... even a ball and chain! What some people get up to behind closed doors! Harvey kept all the ... items ... in case the guests asked for them to be returned. They never did. Too embarrassed, I expect. I think, between you and me, that Harvey had a few of his own ideas about how to use them but I told him what he could do with his handcuffs! I ask you ... at our time of life!'

'Harvey sounds like quite a man.'

'He was.' Connie's eyes misted. 'I miss him terribly. Anyway, he'd have been very impressed that we have a famous author staying. He loved books.'

'Mm.' Todd tried to recall if he'd said he was well-known. Probably not, but he felt uncomfortable with the misconception, especially now he'd got to know Connie. 'I'm afraid I'm not famous by any stretch of the imagination.'

'Oh, that doesn't matter.' She swept away his protests. 'You're not famous *yet*. I'll be able to tell guests that I knew you *before* you became a best-seller. Harvey would have loved talking to you and been so interested in the books you've written. Tell me about them.'

The rest of the evening was thus spent and, afterwards, Todd slept surprisingly well. Feeling refreshed and, having given Connie his mobile number, just in case, he marched down the drive. Today, despite the dampness in the air and the black clouds overhead, he'd decided to walk. Notley Road and Langley Street were barely half a mile from Sunnyside Lodge and, after all the food he'd consumed, he felt he could use the exercise. He looked left as he turned out of the gateway and his heart jolted in shock. The dark blue van was parked a hundred metres further along the street. He stopped and stared but couldn't make out if anyone was inside. He was too far away. Stiffening his spine, he changed direction and headed towards it. That's what Andy Schofield would do. Investigate.

He was still over fifty metres away when a man dressed in a black jacket and jeans emerged from the driver's side and strode briskly away from him. He looked to be in his twenties, with very short dark hair. Keeping his head lowered and hands thrust deep in his pockets, the man turned left down the first side street. Todd broke into a jog, past the van, until he reached the same street. The man had vanished. 'Dammit!' he muttered, although a part of him was a little relieved. He might be channelling Andy Schofield's mindset but he knew that a green belt in judo, attained at the age of eleven, would hardly cut it if more physical skills were required. With a final glance down the street, he turned back. When he reached the vehicle, he stopped to peer inside through the windows. It was empty. Not a surprise. He pulled out his phone and took a photo of the number plate before walking on, deep in thought. Andy Schofield was sceptical of coincidences and so was he. It was time to accept that the man *was* following him. He stopped to take another look behind him but the path was empty. Quickening his pace, he turned left at a T-junction and then first right. Notley Road. Terraced houses lined the street and he picked his way around cars parked up on the pavement. He checked his phone and walked on until he came to Langley Street. This was it. Another glance behind him but there was no sign of the man in the black jacket. Time to start knocking on doors.

He'd been along one side of the street with no success and was heading back when his luck changed. A young woman opened the door to him and listened, her head tilted in concentration, to his spiel. She remembered the story of a girl going missing but didn't know the Potter family as she'd only moved to the street from elsewhere in the city after the event.

'It was in all the papers,' she said, 'but it was a long time ago. You ought to talk to Mavis Little, three doors down. She's lived here since the Dark Ages. She's ancient but she's still pretty sharp. And she'd love to gossip about it. She could talk for England.'

Thanking her, Todd moved straight along to the house she'd indicated and rang the doorbell. Nothing happened. He rang it again. Still nothing. He would've given up had it not been for the woman's recommendation, and the fact that he could detect the strains of a television gameshow. Stepping away from the door, he peered through a window. The room was dark but he could just make out the figure of a woman asleep in an armchair. Feeling a bit guilty, he rapped sharply on the window until the woman stirred. Then, he tried the bell once more. This time, the door opened to reveal a tiny woman with straggly, grey hair leaning on a walking stick.

'Hello,' he smiled. 'My name's Todd Matheson and I'm a writer. I'm doing some research for my latest book and it concerns the Potter family who used to live in this street some years before.' Whereas most people greeted that with, 'Don't know them mate,' or 'Sorry. Only just moved in,' or slammed the door in his face, she regarded him curiously, her filmy eyes assessing.

'Oh, yes?' The words were rasped with the wheeziness of an asthmatic.

'I wondered if you might be able to help me with some of the details from the time when the eldest daughter, Melanie, went missing. It was in 2003.'

She scowled at him then. 'Why do you want to know about that?'

That threw him. 'Er, I think I said ... I'm a writer ...'

'Yes, yes,' she interrupted. 'I know what you said but I wasn't born yesterday. Are you a reporter? If so, you'll pay good money for what I know. You want to drag up old dirt, you can pay for it!'

'Of course, I can pay you for information, if you have some to give, but I'm not a reporter. I'm a crime novelist.'

Her eyes narrowed. 'Sorry, young man, but I don't believe you. Why would a novelist be knocking on people's doors?' He started in surprise. 'Yes ... I saw you earlier, going along the other side of the street and bothering folk. I wondered what you were up to so I nipped across and asked Ted Jennings opposite. He told me what you were doing. He knew the family too but he didn't trust you, he said. And I don't trust you either.'

She was about to shut the door but Todd held out his hand. 'No, wait. I do write crime novels and I did find out about the family when I was doing some research for my latest book but you're right ... that isn't the whole story. Look, can I come in? I promise that I mean no harm to anyone. In fact, it's completely the opposite. If you let me in, I'll tell you the whole story.'

'Mm ...' She was wavering and he forced himself to be patient. 'Alright. I'll let my natural nosiness get the better of me. It's one way of passing the time, I suppose. You can come in and I'll listen to what you have to say. You'd better not try any funny business, though, or I'll give you what for.' She waved her stick as a threat and he grinned in his best, non-threatening way.

'I give you my word.'

He followed her into a small sitting room and waited while she switched the television off. 'Sit down,' she ordered, her voice still tetchy. 'And tell me what's really got you interested in the Potters.'

He started with the news report and the resemblance between the missing girl and Lily, his daughter's teacher. 'As I got to know Lily, I didn't think anything more about it. We fell in love ... and then she disappeared.' He could tell Mavis was hooked by the way she leaned towards him, straining to hear every word. 'I've been trying to find her but I didn't have much to go on.' He recounted how he'd found Simon, Hugo and Vanessa Danes and his discovery that their foster daughter, Samantha Smith, and his Lily were one and the same. 'Eventually, after speaking to Mrs Danes, it emerged that Samantha Smith was originally Saskia Potter who lived around here all those years ago.'

'Saskia.' Mavis Little exhaled the word on a gasp. 'After all this time ...'

'Yes.' Todd waited. Her eyes had filled with tears and, for a moment, she seemed lost in her own reverie.

Eventually, she spoke again, her face drooping with sadness. 'I always wondered what had happened to her. They were such a lovely family but then Sean was killed – he was her father – and things fell apart. Nerissa, the mum, had always been fragile and she pretty much clocked out altogether. Drink, mostly, but drugs too. Those poor girls. I felt particularly sorry for Saskia. She was a sweet, little thing.' She frowned. 'Nerissa got herself a new man – some eastern European chap. I can't remember his name. He was no good though. He disappeared about the same time as the sister. The police were looking for him, I know that much, but nothing ever came of it. Nerissa died of an overdose and Saskia vanished. We saw her at Nerissa's funeral but then she was whisked away. No one around here knew what had happened to her or where she'd gone. Poor little mite.'

Todd nodded. 'I think she was happy with the Danes family. But then, after graduating from university, she just upped and left. They haven't seen her since. And she turned up in Suffolk with yet another name.'

'That's very strange.' Mavis' animosity had completely dissipated. 'She's like some kind of vanishing act. I wonder why she does that?'

'Yes. I'm worried that she's in some sort of danger. There seems to be some catalyst which sends her into hiding but I'm at a loss to know what it is.' He shrugged. 'I just wonder if it's linked to something which happened here in 2003.'

'So *that's* why you're here.' Mavis raised watery eyes to his. 'You may be right but I don't know any more than you. I wish I could help.'

He thought for a bit. 'Can you remember anything about Saskia – anything at all – from that time? Her friends? Anyone she may have confided in?'

Mavis stroked her chin as she deliberated. 'I don't think so. The girls came around here for tea now and again but they didn't want to talk about life at home. Who could blame them? I'd ask about school and that kind of thing. I don't remember them mentioning their friends.'

Todd stood up, swallowing his disappointment with a smile. 'Well, thanks very much for your help. Perhaps I could leave you my mobile number, in case you think of anything?'

'Wait a minute. There is something. She had a Saturday job at the hairdresser round the corner, *Just a Snip*. I know because I get my hair done there. It's still there, still run by the same woman, Helen Batty. Batty by name and batty by nature.' She cackled at her joke. 'She might know something.'

'Brilliant.' Todd handed her his business card. 'Thank you. That's great. You've been very helpful.'

She peered at the card and frowned. 'Wait a minute. It says here you're a solicitor.' Accusation crept into her eyes. 'You said you were a writer.'

He sighed, eager now to find *Just a Snip* but resigned to giving her an explanation. 'I am. Solicitor by day and writer by night. One day, hopefully, I'll be successful enough to write full-time but, until then, the other job pays the bills.'

She wasn't convinced. 'What books have you written then?'

He listed the titles and then pulled out another card and a pen. 'Look, here's my author website.' He scrawled the name on the card and handed it to her. 'You can check me out. I promise I haven't lied to you.'

'Alright,' she mumbled, looking slightly mollified. 'Good luck with your search. If you find Saskia, tell her ...' she paused, '... tell her we all think of her, those of us still left on the street.'

'I will.'

Mavis gave him directions to *Just a Snip* and he set out. The air outside felt cool after the stuffy warmth of the house and he paused to zip up his jacket. As he did so, the hairs on the back of his neck began to tingle. He spun around, eyes darting from right to left, scanning the neighbourhood. No man in a black jacket. There was a young woman with short, dark hair, talking on her phone, further down the street. She was leaning against a lamp post, her eyes staring right at him, but she quickly looked away when she saw he'd noticed. Was she watching him? Had she taken over from the guy?

Todd walked on briskly, ignoring the itch to look behind, and took a circuitous route, darting into shops he passed and hiding behind displays, checking to see if the woman was following. After the third shop, and seeing no sign of her, he decided that he must have been mistaken. Either that or he'd lost her. With a sigh of relief, he continued on his way.

Just a Snip was situated about a quarter of a mile away on the edge of the estate. It formed part of a small, tired group of shops which included a grocery store, a newsagent and a betting shop. The façade looked old and worn and the pink paint of the lettering was faded and peeling. A sign in the door said 'Open' and, as he walked in, a bell chimed.

'Be right with you,' a woman's voice called. There was no-one in the room. He stood patiently, taking in the scene. Three hair driers lined one wall alongside a patched, leather-look sofa. Opposite was a sink and a row of mirrors facing adjustable chairs. Posters of models sporting various hairstyles adorned the grey walls. 'Ooh, hello.' A middle-aged woman with spiky, bright pink hair appeared from the back of the room. 'And what can I do for you, love?'

'I'm looking for Helen Batty,' Todd replied.

The smile slipped just a fraction. 'What's it concerning?'

'Mavis Little suggested I speak to her ... to you?' She gave a slight nod. 'I'm looking for someone who used to work here a while ago. Back then, she was called Saskia Potter.'

'Oh yes, Saskia, bless her. Poor kid.' Her face softened momentarily before hardening once more as she looked him up and down. 'What's she to you?'

Todd hesitated. He didn't really want to tell this woman any more than he had to. Mavis Little had forced his hand but, if Lily was in hiding somewhere, possibly in fear for her life, broadcasting his search to all and sundry could be unwise. He decided to revert to his 'author research' story.

'You're an *author*?' Helen's body language relaxed. 'What kind of books do you write? You should write *my* life story,' she continued without giving him a chance to answer. 'That would make a book and a half!' She chuckled. 'Trouble is, no-one would believe it!' Her grey eyes glinted with mischief. 'But I don't suppose you write that kind of book.'

'Not unless it's crime thriller material,' he grinned.

'Mm, probably not ...' she winked, 'but there'd be lots of sex!'

He laughed. 'Look, can I buy you a cup of coffee or something? I'm trying to get some background on the Potter family and I'd be very interested in anything you could tell me.'

'That's the best offer I've had today.' She checked her watch. 'Well, it *is* lunchtime ... and I've no appointments for another hour ...'

'Lunch it is.'

'Done. Just let me lock up. There's a good café just around the corner. The owner's a friend of mine. She'll be glad of the business. Things have been a bit quiet for her recently.' She grabbed a purple, linen jacket and locked the door behind her. 'And it won't do my reputation any harm to be seen out with a good-looking, young chap.'

By the time they reached *Sue's Café*, he'd discovered she was single, had four daughters and seven granddaughters. 'Not a boy amongst them,' she declared. 'We're a family of girls. A force to be reckoned with when we all get together. Right, here we are.'

She pushed the door open and they were greeted by an exclamation from behind the counter. 'Well, well, look what the cat's dragged in!' Arched eyebrows gestured towards Todd. 'Good to see your taste has improved.' The woman was small and squat, with short, ginger hair and plump chins which wobbled when she laughed.

'This is ... Vincent.' Helen linked her arm with his and pulled him close. 'Vin, this is my jealous mate, Sue.'

'Pleased to meet you, Sue.' Todd held out his hand and gave her his lopsided smile.

'Ooh, be still my beating heart,' she simpered as she grasped it. 'This is a turn up, Helen Batty. I'll want details later. Please ... take a seat.'

The café was deserted and Todd chose a seat by the window, looking out. The tables were all covered with white cloths and adorned with small vases of flowers. 'This is very nice,' he said.

'I know. Poor Sue does her best but it's hard to compete with the big chains. Kids these days only seem to want that plastic, mass-produced rubbish. There are lots of businesses in Thorpe and, once upon a time, this café did a roaring trade. Sign of the times, I suppose.' She lowered her voice. 'Sorry about the introduction. I suddenly realised I didn't know your name! I'm hardly going to convince Sue that you're my toy boy if I had to ask you in front of her.'

Todd chuckled again. He liked this woman. 'No problem. Vincent's fine.'

'On the spot like that, I couldn't think of the names of any authors so I went for a painter.'

'Vincent Van Gogh? I'm flattered ... although both my ears are intact.'

'Nah ... Vincent Johns ... he lives opposite ... he's a painter ... and decorator.' She giggled as she picked up the menu. 'I'm starving. Think I'll have a veggie burger. Sue makes them herself and they're ...' She made a loud smacking sound with her lips.

Sue reappeared and Todd ordered a cheese and ham toastie and a mug of coffee. While they waited for their food, he asked Helen about Saskia.

'She was such a lovely kid – hard-working, eager to please. I was sad to lose her, especially in those circumstances. I often wondered what happened to her.' Helen sighed. 'We never heard anything about the missing sister either. I guess her body was never found. Terrible it was. No wonder poor Nerissa took an overdose.'

'Did you know the man who'd been living with them ... Andrian Petrov?'

She shook her head. 'A few folk around here met him. He and Nerissa used to go in *The Black Horse* quite a bit back then. But no-one knew anything about him. He kept himself to himself. Scarpered after Melanie disappeared.

The word was he was an illegal immigrant and wanted to marry Nerissa so he didn't get deported.' She shrugged. 'Probably trying to stay one step ahead of the authorities. Who can blame him? People liked him though. Thought he was a nice chap. Nerissa went to pieces after her husband was killed and she seemed better for a while, so they said. Saskia never said anything about him and I never asked.'

'What about the sister, Melanie? Did you know her?'

'Not really. Met her a few times. A good kid, by all accounts. Saskia looked up to her. I think they were pretty close. They looked very similar too. Beautiful girls. Lovely bone structure. Saskia was thinner, more serious, but they were both stunning. I think Mel was quite a heartbreaker.'

'What about Saskia? Did she have a boyfriend?' The thought sent spikes of jealousy shooting through him.

Helen thought for a bit. 'I don't think so.' She shook her head. 'I remember Kaz used to tease her about Darrell Parkinson but I don't think they ever went out together. She didn't seem that interested in boys – not like the young girls who work for me now. They think about nothing else!'

'Kaz?'

'Mm ...' She paused as Sue slid a plate in front of her. 'Thanks love ... that looks fab-u-lous.' She picked up her burger and took a large bite. 'Mm ... I'm in heaven. Now, what was I saying? Oh yes ... Kaz ...' She frowned. 'Now, what was her surname? Haven't thought about her in years. She was Saskia's best friend and often turned up at the shop, waiting for Sass to finish her shift. Nice girl. Posh. Not from around here. Her family used to live in that really nice house on the corner of Colfield Avenue. Might still be there for all I know. Clarkson!' she announced triumphantly. 'That was her name ... Kaz Clarkson. I knew it'd come to me. Anyway, Sass used to spend a lot of time at Kaz's house. She thought the world of her ... and her mum and dad.'

Todd picked up his sandwich, his mind speculating. 'Do you think they'd have kept in touch after she moved away?'

Helen shrugged. 'You'd have thought so ... but who knows? No-one from around here ever heard a word from her and I didn't see Kaz after that. Maybe Saskia wanted a fresh start. Difficult to say.'

Not much to go on. Still, it was a lead. He wasn't going to give up hope just yet. 'What was the name and address of that house again – the parents' house?'

'I think it's just called The Rectory. That's what it used to be. It's near the church on the corner of Colfield Avenue, set back from the road behind some trees. I went there once, a long time ago, for a children's Christmas party organised by the church. I always dreamed of living there one day. It was a damned sight different from the two up, two down I was brought up in. Sass and I used to talk about the house sometimes between clients. Talking of which ... I probably ought to be getting back. Thanks for the lunch.'

'You're welcome. I guess I'd better pay in cash if we don't want to blow your story.'

'Oh yes.' Helen pulled a face. 'I didn't think of that! Do you have enough?'

'Hopefully.' Todd checked his wallet. 'All good.' He paid the bill and added a generous tip.

'Come back soon,' Sue called as they made to leave. 'Helen, I'll be calling you later.'

'Let's hope I'm not too busy to answer,' she replied airily, linking her arm once more with Todd's. 'Come on, lover.'

As they turned left to head back to Helen's salon, Todd glanced back down the street. 'Hold on a sec,' he murmured, disentangling his arm from hers. The woman with short, dark hair he'd seen earlier – the one with the mobile phone – was sitting in a bus shelter, phone still in hand, facing his way. As he stared in her direction, she turned casually and sauntered off in the opposite direction. Surely twice couldn't be coincidence? Darts of adrenalin sent his heart thudding against his chest. He wanted to charge after her, confront her, but was conscious of Helen beside him. 'Did you see that woman?' he asked her. 'Do you recognise her?'

She squinted at the retreating form. 'Yeah, I think she's MI6.' She chuckled. 'Just kidding. I didn't recognise her ... but she *may* be from around these parts. Hang on a minute ...' Mistrust grew in her face. 'What's going on Vincent? What is it you're not telling me?'

'What do you mean?' he hedged. He took her arm again and steered her along the street. 'Nothing. I just noticed her earlier, that's all.' He kept his tone light.

'Hmph. I'm not an idiot.' Her heels on the pavement rang loud in the ensuing silence. 'You should've seen your face when you asked about that woman! Come to think of it, you asked far too many questions about Saskia for an author doing some random research. Are you really an author at all?'

'I really am.'

She bristled and the death grip on his arm tightened. 'I don't believe you,' she said flatly. 'Are you police?' She gasped and stopped abruptly. 'Has something happened to her?'

'No to both questions.' He turned his head to scan the street behind but the woman had vanished. 'I *am* a writer ... but I'm also Saskia's friend. She might be in some trouble and I'm trying to help her.' He sensed her body relax a little.

'Then why didn't you say so?'

'If I'd known you were Thorpe St Andrew's answer to Miss Marple, I probably would have. Look, it's complicated. I know that's not much of an answer but ...'

'You want me to trust you, is that it?'

'Yes.'

He heard her sigh. 'That's the trouble with me ... I've always been a sucker for a good-looking bloke.'

'Thank you, Helen.' They walked on to *Just a Snip*. 'You've been very helpful. If I find Saskia, I'll bring her to see you. That's a promise.' He withdrew his arm.

'I suppose that will have to do.' She huffed and took a step towards the door before turning. 'Fancy a quick snog before you go? Just for the neighbours, you understand. I have my reputation to think of.'

He grinned and gathered her in his arms, squeezing her gently, intending to give her a light peck on the cheek. She had other ideas and ducked her head to plant her lips on his.

'Whoops. Hold on a sec.' She whisked a tissue from her bag and dabbed around his mouth. 'There, that's better. See you soon, lover boy.'

'Can't wait.' He smiled to himself as he saw the net curtains in the window of the house next door twitching, and headed back along the street. As he walked, he spun around at regular intervals, checking for anyone lurking behind him. There was no-one as far as he could see but his disquiet refused to abate. The sense that he was being watched and followed had solidified into something more certain. To be on the safe side, he repeated the evasive manoeuvres he'd used earlier and made impulsive stops at a bike repair shop and a bank. Reassured, he continued his journey, reasonably sure that no-one was tailing him.

The Rectory in Colfield Avenue was an impressive, grey stone building, surrounded by sweeping, verdant lawns and colourful flower borders. Large, leaded windows with duck-shell blue frames watched like benign sentinels as Todd crunched up the curved, gravel driveway. His fingers were crossed that the Clarksons remained in residence. If Kaz and Saskia were close as girls, there was a chance she might know something which would help him find her. But first, he had to find Kaz.

A slim, blonde woman in her late fifties opened the door almost immediately. 'You've just caught me,' she announced, her voice clipped with the accent of privilege, her smile warm and welcoming. 'I was just on my way out. Are you the man who's come to look at the boiler?' She regarded Todd doubtfully.

'No, sorry. I'm looking for Mrs Clarkson.'

'Speaking.'

A good start. 'Great.' He gave her his lopsided smile. 'Pleased to meet you. My name's Todd Matheson. I was wondering if I might be able to have a word with Kaz?'

She looked taken aback. 'Kaz doesn't live here ... not for years. She's married. Expecting her first baby.' Her face softened at the prospect. 'May I ask what it's concerning?'

'I'm looking for an old friend of hers. Back from schooldays. Saskia Potter.'

There was no disguising the flash of panic. He recognised it on her face even as she shut it down, as quick and unexpected as the shattering of a lightbulb. Her eyes hardened and she pressed her lips together in a moue of wariness. 'I'm afraid I can't help you,' she said. Her voice, so warm a few seconds before, was tinged with frost. She was hiding something.

'I'm a friend. I'm worried about Saskia.' He held out his hands, imploring her to believe him.

Her face sagged a little. 'I'm sorry. I can't help you.' She went to shut the door.

'No ... wait!' Todd called. 'Please!'

She hesitated and, for a moment, he thought she was going to relent. He caught a final glimpse of her face, creased with worry, and then the door was closed, firmly, behind her. He stood there, taken aback. pondering what to do next. Mrs Clarkson was not an actress. He'd taken her by surprise and her reaction had proved she knew something about Saskia. There was a secret there, behind the beautiful, stone façade. Nothing for it; he'd try again. Just as he raised his hand to press the doorbell, the door opened and Mrs Clarkson stepped out, now wearing a navy jacket and carrying a matching handbag.

'I'm going out,' she snapped, sweeping past him and heading for a small silver Toyota parked in front of the garage. 'I suggest you leave.'

'Mrs Clarkson ... please.' He scurried after her. 'Wait. I really need to talk to you ... to explain ...'

She spun on her heel, her eyes flinty. 'Mr Matheson, I've told you I can't help you and I've asked you to leave. I suggest you do so or I'll have to call the police.'

'But I love her ...' he blurted out, desperate to forestall her. 'I love Saskia ... except I know her as Lily but ...'

'I don't know what you're talking about. Please go.' She extracted her phone from her bag and gave him a purposeful look.

'OK.' He held up his hands in a gesture of defeat. 'I'm going but please ... if you know where she is ... can you ask her to contact me ... let me know she's alright?'

He turned without waiting for a reply and, shoulders slumped, sloped back down the drive and out onto the street.

CHAPTER 29

Lily

Every time my phone rings, I wonder if it's Howard Jones with news. So far, he's rung just once and that was to tell me he'd received my payment and would be making a start on my case. It's only been forty-eight hours since then and, realistically, I shouldn't expect to hear anything *that* quickly, but still ... When I feel the phone vibrate in my pocket, my heart leaps. It could be him.

It isn't. 'Hi Kaz,' I say, feigning cheeriness.

'Any news from your super sleuth yet?' she asks.

'Not yet. Any news on the baby front?'

'Nope, she's not planning on coming anytime soon. I had a midwife check-up yesterday. Everything's fine.'

'She?' I query. 'Is the baby a girl?'

'No, just me thinking it's a girl and calling her 'she'. Next week, I'll probably be convinced it's a boy. You know what I'm like. As long as she's healthy ... or he is. Anyway, enough about me and the bump. I was going to drive over to see you this afternoon, if you're free ...'

Her words give me a much-needed boost. 'Hold on, I'll just have to check my diary.' I leave a brief pause. 'Yes, that would be fine. I think I can squeeze you in.' I giggle. 'Oh, Kaz, I can't wait! Are you sure you should be driving?'

She laughs. 'Don't be daft. It's a baby I'm having, not an elephant! I can still just about fit behind the wheel. Should be there around half two. I'll only be able to stay for an hour or so but I have some news which might interest you.'

'Really?' I'm intrigued. 'What?'

'I'll tell you when I see you.'

***

I rush to greet her as she struggles out of her car. 'You look amazing!' I say as I wrap my arms around her.

'I know.' She grimaces. 'Radiant ... blooming ... everyone says so.' She leans into her car and drags out a bag. 'Here, I've brought you some magazines.'

'Thanks.' I take the bag from her and peer inside. 'That's kind ... although you *do* know we have magazines and books in Norfolk too?'

She chuckles. 'I know but I didn't want to turn up empty-handed. I would've brought wine but ...' She gestures towards her swollen body, '...it's not much fun watching other people drink. Call me selfish!'

'OK *Selfish*, how are you feeling?' I lace my arm in hers and steer her into the cottage.

'Absolutely fine. Just bloody uncomfortable. It's hard work being the size of a house.'

I smile. 'I can imagine.' After I've made mugs of tea, we take them outside to enjoy the afternoon sunshine. 'So ... what's your news?' I've managed to restrain myself from asking until she's comfortably seated on the decking.

'Oh that, it's just something about your man, Todd.'

I almost drop my mug. 'Todd?' I gasp. 'Is he alright?'

'Yes. At least, he was yesterday when he called by my parents' house, asking for me.'

'You? But why? How?' I'm poleaxed by her revelation. I don't know what to think.

She hunches her shoulders. 'No idea how he got there. He turned up out of the blue. Mum was freaked out.'

'Did she tell him anything?'

'Course not! He asked for me and then, when she asked what he wanted, he mentioned you. He's looking for you. Somehow, he knows we're friends.' She frowns. 'It must mean he knows about your past. You must have let something slip.'

'I didn't!' I retort. My head is spinning. In a flash, I remember that time when he mentioned the newspaper photo of a missing girl who looked like me. It was an old report about Mel. Somehow, he must've realised the connection. It had to be that. But how would he know about Kaz?

She's sipping at her tea, looking thoughtful. 'Anyway, Mum gave him short shrift and he left. But he wanted you to know that he's searching for you. Asked her to pass on a message. "Please tell her to call me," he said.' She rolls her eyes. 'Sounds like he's as crazy about you as you are about him.'

My chest swells with love for him. He hasn't given up on me; despite everything, he's trying to find me. I ache to phone him ... ask him to come here ... even if it's just for a little while ... but I can't. I crush my errant emotions and change the subject. If Kaz notices my flushed cheeks, she doesn't say anything. Instead, we chat about baby stuff for a while, before moving on to Howard Jones and my impressions.

'Well ...' I have to be honest. 'He wasn't quite what I was expecting.' She raises her eyebrows so I continue. 'He was older than I thought he would be ... and a bit podgy.'

'Ah,' she nods sagely. 'You were picturing someone like Jack Reacher?'

'A bit.' I confess, wrinkling my nose.

'Well, Dad said he came recommended. One of his business pals was having trouble with another company. There was some kind of scam involved. Anyway, Howard got it sorted so he must be OK.'

'I hope so.'

She leaves shortly after that and my thoughts eagerly return to Todd. The fact that he cares enough to search for me fills me with elation. As I cook myself some pasta, I dance around the kitchen, singing along to the radio and wiggling, Beyonce style, to *Single Ladies*. The song ends and my hips slow. As I stir my sauce, I begin to consider all the implications of Kaz's news.

Number one and most important: he *must* really love me. I don't really want to think about anything else. I want to wallow in what I feel about him and my longing to hold him close. For a few blissful seconds, I imagine him in the kitchen with me; I'm wrapped in his arms, my back to him, and he kisses the nape of my neck. I turn and lift my face to his, my arms locking around his neck. Our lips touch, teasing at first and then with increasing urgency and I slide my hands under his shirt, feeling the smooth hardness of his body ... I blink my eyes open as I hear the pasta boil over. *Damn.* I mop up the starchy water and move on to other, less welcome thoughts.

Number two: if he's traced me to the Clarksons, he knows about my past. That I'm Saskia Potter, sister of a girl who went missing. I picture him, once more, telling me about that news article he found when he was researching his book. If he knew the truth then, I wonder why he didn't say anything. Perhaps, he was giving me time, waiting until I was ready to tell him. Another wave of tenderness washes over me. I don't deserve him.

Number three fills me with anxiety: I moved away because I didn't want him or Charlotte in the way of any danger. Even though I'm thrilled that he's looking for me, I can't allow him to find me. I know Kaz's mum told him nothing but perhaps it's time to move from here. It would be best if *no-one* knew my location. Emptiness settles in my chest at the prospect.

Number four brings full-blown panic: if Todd has got that close, in his search for me, then it's possible that Andrian has too! He might be on his way here right now. I look out of the window, heart thudding, almost expecting him to materialise in front of me. Quickly, I close the curtains. I might not be safe here. Even worse, Kaz and her family might be in danger. I picture him with Kaz, threatening her to get the information he wants. *Oh God.* Feeling a bit frantic, I ring her and tell her what I'm thinking.

She's just got home. 'Calm down, Sass. You've no reason to think that.' Her voice sharpens. 'Have you seen anything suspicious?'

'No.'

'I'll keep my eye out but I'm sure there's nothing to worry about. No-one except me and Mum know where you are and we're not telling anyone. You're safe there.'

'I'm sure you're right,' I sigh, 'but I'm thinking about moving on somewhere else anyway. I hate that you have the responsibility of keeping my whereabouts a secret. I think it would be safer if you didn't know where I am.'

A brief silence. 'Don't you trust me?' She sounds hurt.

'Of course, I do. With my life. But I don't want to put *your* life at risk. It's better for you if you know nothing.' Another pause. 'Kaz, are you still there?'

'Yes ... just thinking about what you're saying. I don't agree but it's up to you, Sass. If you feel more comfortable moving on, then that's fine with me. Pop the key in the secret place when you leave. And make sure you let me know you're OK. I still expect phone calls.'

'I will ... and Kaz, thanks for everything. I love you.'

'Love you too. I'll send up a prayer to the gods of justice that Howard Jones comes good ... that this is all over soon and you can come out of hiding ... once and for all.'

'Me too.' I end the call, close to tears.

***

By the morning, after an undisturbed night, I'm changing my mind about moving on. My emotions were all over the place last night and I was freaking out for no good reason. Kaz is right. No need to panic. Apart from the Clarksons, no-one knows where I am. Todd doesn't; why should Andrian? I'm not entirely convinced by this rationale but I'm also reluctant to leave.

The early morning sun is warm and soothing and I take my coffee out onto the decking, where the garden is sheltered from the cool breeze. On the way, I pull out a local newspaper from the bag of magazines Kaz brought with her. It's a Suffolk edition and a wave of homesickness hits me. I smile as I skim through the pages, catching up on snippets of life from the county I now consider my home. Kaz is a complete star and I wonder how I'm going to make all this up to her. She totally deserves her current happiness. I know she loves her job, as a freelance editor and proof-reader of technical journals, and her home in Southwold, which she shares with her husband, Tom. I haven't met him but she's shown me pictures and glows when she talks about him. Just like I do when I wax lyrical about Todd.

I turn over a page, still thinking of Todd, and there he is, in full colour, grinning at the camera, totally gorgeous in a dinner jacket and bow tie. He takes my breath away and I drink in the sight of him, all my senses tingling. Dragging my eyes from his face, my gaze sweeps across the entire photograph. His left arm is around a stunning woman in a scarlet dress. I stare at that arm, at the fingers closing possessively around that ridiculously slim waist, and my joy turns to dismay. *He's with someone else.* I can't bear to look but I have to know everything. The caption beneath the photograph announces: Abigail Knight and Todd Matheson. *Oh God!* Here I am mooning over him and he's out romancing some raven-haired, green-eyed beauty! I scan the page, searching for more pictures of him, but there are none. just lots of photographs of other attendees at the Suffolk Show Ball. Well, that didn't take him long. Of their own volition, my eyes return to Todd and his companion and self-pity stabs my heart. So much for pining like a lovesick teenager – he's moved on. *But if he has, why is he trying so hard to discover your whereabouts?* A small voice of hope persists, refusing to believe the worst. *Probably just to tie up loose ends, like he does in his novels.* No, I can't bring myself to believe that. There has to be a rational explanation. I spend the next ten minutes trying to find one which convinces me. *He's attending a social function on behalf of work; the woman could be a work colleague; she's just a friend; he needed a plus one.* Except, I tell myself ruthlessly, he's never mentioned her. Jealousy sears my soul as I notice the way their bodies are leaning into each other. I want to scream. Instead, I throw the paper down in disgust. Best to forget Todd Matheson once and for all. It's time to move on.

CHAPTER 30

Todd

Todd returned home, thinking he'd made progress in his quest to find Lily: he'd made contact with someone who knew something, who might have passed his message on to her; and he'd hoped she would call. As the days crawled by, that sense of anticipation slowly crumbled, bit by bit. His phone remained stubbornly silent.

The first few evenings back home were spent on his computer, searching for information about Kaz Clarkson. He looked for a social media profile, something which might reveal her married name. No such luck. Not for the first time, he wished he was a computer whizz or knew someone who was. That's what Andy Schofield would do. He'd call someone who could miraculously access the data he needed. If only real life was that easy! It crossed his mind that he could pay someone to find out for him but that thought made him uncomfortable. It was one thing for him to look for Lily; a stranger was a different story.

The first weekend after his return, he toyed with the idea of going to see Mrs Clarkson again. It would have meant taking Charlotte with him, though, and he decided against it. His little girl seemed to have recovered from the trauma of Lily's disappearance and he didn't want to do anything which reminded her. Currently, she was beside herself with excitement at the prospect of being a bridesmaid at the upcoming marriage of her mum and partner, Nick. He'd heard endlessly of dress fittings, who was going to be there and how Reggie had fallen out with her sister over her refusal to invite any children to the celebrations except Charlotte. They were both fiery. He could imagine the eruption when that bomb was dropped. An invitation had been delivered through his own letterbox but he had declined. It was just easier for everyone for him not to be there and he sensed Reggie was relieved when he told her. They were all moving on. If only he could too ...

He *had* tried. He'd been out with his mates, Lee and Joe. They'd met Lily, of course, and were aware that she'd left him. Determined to cheer him up, they dragged him to a football game. He allowed them to bully him into going, fed up with the prison of his obsession, and, for a few hours, managed to shut Lily from his mind. The banter was what he needed and he threw himself into the mix with grim determination. He thought he put up a pretty good show but, when they bid each other goodnight, he saw pity in his friends' eyes and in the back slaps which went on for too long.

'It'll get better, mate,' Lee murmured with an arm around his shoulder. 'Trust me. I know what it's like.'

In a fit of pique at Lily, when she failed to ring him, he also took Abi out to dinner. It was a mistake. For a few hours, he indulged his masculine ego, flirting and appreciating her efforts to charm him. He'd set out intending to let things between them take their natural course but, as she wrapped her arms around him and pressed her mouth against his, he found he couldn't go through with it. He liked Abi and knew he wasn't being fair, using her like that. Once again, he felt a real jerk when he pushed her away with an embarrassed apology but she was philosophical about it.

'You're not ready,' she whispered, a wry expression on her beautiful face. 'Let me know when you are.'

In the long, dark hours, when sleep eluded him, he wondered why he couldn't just let Lily go. There had been none of this angst when he and Reggie had split and they'd been married for ten years. It wasn't just the pain of losing her, he decided. It was the not knowing, the 'what if' which kept him dangling like a carp on a hook. What if she was in danger? What if she still loved him? His mind twisted through a labyrinth of alternating hope and despair. What if, when he found her, she'd met someone else? What if he never found her? That was the crunch. That would be the most unbearable thing – never knowing. He had to try, risk everything, just to know the truth.

Over the past week, he'd seen nothing to make him think he was still being watched. It made him wonder if he'd imagined things in Thorpe St Andrew. Back in the mundanity of his daily routine, the whole idea of being followed seemed increasingly far-fetched. He maintained his vigilance but nothing remotely suspicious happened to upset the monotony of his days. Nothing happened at all – that was the problem. He'd reached a dead end. Mrs Clarkson knew something. Maybe she even knew where Lily was. She was his only lead but she wasn't talking. How could he convince her to tell him what she was hiding? Andy Schofield would somehow trick her out of the information with his sharp wit and invincible charm. That's how he would write it in a novel. As he lay in bed, he played out different scenarios in his head. Andy would have invented a pretext to get himself invited into her home. He wouldn't have mentioned Saskia at all. Over a cup of tea, he would have admired the wedding photos.

'Is that you?'

'Oh no, that's my daughter, Kaz.'

'She's very beautiful. That's why I thought it was you.'

No, that was too strong. Mentally, he deleted the last sentence.

'She obviously takes after you.'

Better. Less creepy.

Mrs Clarkson smiled over the delicate porcelain. 'You're too kind.'

'Not at all. Who's the lucky chap?'

'Her husband? That's Mark Storey. He's a heart surgeon. Lovely man.'

And just like that, he'd know Kaz's married name. Todd sighed and rolled over. It was so much easier when you wrote the script. Something like that *could* work but Mrs Clarkson now knew him. Perhaps, he could get someone else to try ... Lee might be persuaded. He was always up for anything. Maybe it *was* time he drafted in some help.

***

Lee spluttered over his pint. 'You want me to do *what?*'

'Trick yourself into a woman's house and find out information about the family – in particular, the daughter's married name and where she lives,' Todd answered calmly, like it was the sanest thing in the world.

'But why?'

Todd shrugged. 'For a bet. Twenty quid if you pull it off.'

'You've got to be joking, mate. I'd probably get arrested, knowing my luck.'

'OK. Fifty quid.'

'Not doing it. My days of pulling crazy stunts are over.' He took a sip of his beer. 'What the heck possessed you to think of something like that?'

Todd thought for a moment. Had Lee been keen to give his mad scheme a go, he would have told him the truth, at least, in part. As it was, he still felt that the fewer people who knew Lily's story the better. She wouldn't thank him for broadcasting details about her past. She hadn't even told him! Instead, he said, 'I was thinking of using that idea in my book but I wasn't sure it would work. I just thought it might be fun to try.'

Lee snorted. 'Well, *you* try it then! What's the guy in your book – Andy What's 'is name – trying to find out exactly?'

'Schofield. He's trying to find someone but he only knows her first name and maiden name, not her married name.'

Lee screwed up his face, trying to make sense of it all. 'Well ...' Another swig. 'All sounds a bit daft, mate, if you ask me. Why wouldn't he just sign up to one of those databases that tell you all that stuff? My sister has been investigating our family tree and, so far, she's gone as far back as the 1850s. She's using one of those sites that advertise on TV – I can't remember the name. You have to pay a bit but you can see copies of birth and marriage certificates, that sort of stuff. Can't think why she'd go to all the bother but our Julie is interested in things like that. Every time she phones now, it's to tell me about another ancestor she's managed to discover. Apparently, my great-great-great-great grandad was a miner from Yorkshire ...'

Todd's attention had wandered. He was cursing his stupidity. Why hadn't he thought of that?

'Don't churches keep records of marriages, as well?' Lee was still talking. 'If you know where the wedding took place, you could ask to see the record.'

'Great ideas, mate.' Todd slapped him on the back. 'That deserves another drink. Although I am a bit disappointed by your reluctance to go undercover. It would've been a laugh.'

'For you maybe. I bet you'd have staged the whole thing as a set up. There would've been hidden cameras and I'd have found myself trending on

Twitter. Yep, I knew it!' he exclaimed at Todd's feigned grin. 'You dog! For that, you *can* buy me another pint.'

For the next few hours, Todd hid his impatience to return home and became a listening ear for his friend. Since his wife, Callie had thrown him out of the family home, Lee had fallen into a state of depression. Prior to the split, he'd bemoaned his married status but single life brought him no joy. He missed his children and, most of all, he now realised how much he loved his wife.

'I was a complete moron,' he said sadly. 'No wonder she'd had enough. She was having to cope with the kids and I was out drinking, every night, by the end. When I *was* at home, all we did was row. It was pretty awful. Most of it was my fault.'

'Having three kids so quickly was bound to put pressure on your marriage. Don't beat yourself up, Lee. These things happen.'

'But what can I do?' he wailed, staring morosely into his beer as if searching for the answer there. 'She went out on a date last week. Annabel told me.' Annabel was his oldest daughter. 'The thought of her out with another guy is a knife in my guts. What am I going to do, Todd?'

'Have *you* tried asking her out, you know, for a proper date? The works. Dinner. A film. Whatever she most likes doing.'

'She wouldn't come,' he said flatly.

'How do you know? Try it. You might be surprised.'

Lee twisted his glass between his hands. 'I suppose I *could* pretend I wanted to talk about the kids ...'

'No! Absolutely not! You need to get the romance back between the two of you. Make it clear that it's a date, that you love her and want to spend time with her. When she says yes ...' He held up a hand when Lee tried to argue. 'And I bet she *will* say yes – as long as you ask her right – then make sure she feels really special. Take her flowers. Let her know how you feel.' He gave a short, self-deprecating laugh. 'Not that I have any right to be giving you relationship advice. My track record is hardly something to aspire to!'

'No, no, mate, this is good. Now, how do you think I should ask her? What should I say?'

The conversation continued while they finished their drinks. At just after ten o'clock, they parted company, both feeling happier. Todd strode home, eager to try out one of the websites Lee had suggested. *Kaz* Clarkson. Not for the first time, he wondered what Kaz was short for. Caroline? Cassandra? Hoping that the search engine wouldn't prove too specific, he switched on his computer and signed up for a free trial. Despondency soon began creeping in. This was a site aimed at building a family tree. He'd already given his name with his payment details and it wasn't Clarkson. When he began inventing information about his family, to include that name, the site crashed and he had to start over. After trying again, with no luck, he changed his search and googled *UK marriage certificate online.* The top result was the site to which he'd already signed up and he clicked on it. The screen asked for details he knew and he typed Kaz Clarkson in the name boxes and Thorpe St Andrew, Norfolk in the location section. No results.

After countless more attempts, he was on the cusp of giving up. His eyes were gritty with tiredness and a glance at his watch told him it was past midnight. The name Kaz was causing a problem. He'd tried different versions of her name – Catherine, Karen, Caroline – and, with ever-growing frustration, scrolled through the results, checking and discarding them, one by one. Having run out of ideas, he googled *Kaz is short for what name?* Lots, apparently. Having met Mrs Clarkson, he couldn't see her naming her daughter Kazimir or Kassia. Then, his eyes lit upon the name Kathryn. He hadn't considered alternative spellings of that name. Resolving to make this his final attempt for the night, he typed it in.

The computer screen refreshed, revealing seven possible matches, and he worked through them starting at the top. Kathryn Jennings and Stuart Clarkson. Surnames the wrong way around. The second was possible. Kathryn Clarkson married Elijah Ntobe at King's Community Church, Norwich in 2005. Mentally, he calculated her age. If it was Kaz, she'd have only been sixteen or seventeen when she married, assuming she was a similar age to Saskia. He jotted it down, nonetheless. This was the best he'd had so far. The next two were easily discarded. Yawning, he moved on to number five and shot up in his seat, blinking at the data in front of him. On Saturday 12th August, 2017, Kathryn Anne Clarkson was married to Thomas Foley-Watts at Thorpe St Andrew Parish Church. Could this be the breakthrough he'd been waiting for? Had he actually found Kaz? Swiftly, he flicked to the section for information about births. If this Kathryn Anne Clarkson was Saskia's school friend, she would most likely have been in the same school year and therefore born in 1987 or 1988. Holding his breath, he typed her name and 1987. No results. He tried 1988. This time, his search yielded one match. He clicked on the link and found himself looking at a copy of the birth certificate. This Kathryn was born in Bristol on April 13th, 1988 to John and Margaret, nee Cole. The occupation of the father was listed as company director. It was a definite possibility that Kathryn Anne Foley-Watts could be Saskia's Kaz.

The clock on his computer screen told him it was now 00:47 a.m. and he could barely keep his eyes open. Reluctantly, he hit the shut-down button and stretched his back. Tomorrow would be soon enough.

CHAPTER 31

Lily

After a week of days spent vacillating and sleepless nights, I'm still residing at the cottage in Brancaster but, the longer I stay here, the more uneasy I become. At night, the creaking of old joists sets my heart racing. *Andrian is coming. That was him on the stairs.* Several times, I've tiptoed from my bed and stood, listening at the door, before switching on all the lights and creeping downstairs to check rooms which stand empty of intruders and doors which remain locked. A few days ago, I found a solid piece of driftwood on the beach and now keep it by my bed, within easy reach. Just in case. For my peace of mind, if nothing else, I should move on.

Despondently, I pick up my phone to check accommodation listings. This cottage has been my haven; I don't want to leave. *Is it necessary?* If only I knew the answer. My heart says no, but my head is not so sure and I'm weary of my night-time paranoia. *Can I trust my heart?* Probably not, but I don't know. The same goes for my feelings about Todd. That newspaper photograph awakened all my old doubts and insecurities. Even though Kaz has given me proof that Todd is going to great lengths to find me, which should convince me that the photo means nothing, I can't help fearing the worst. The weeks of enforced solitude are turning me into a neurotic mess. I honestly don't know what to think anymore.

My gaze drifts to the window and the garden beyond. Today, the sky looks freshly washed and, as I watch, a pretty, long-tailed tit settles on the birdfeeder which I put up a few weeks ago. The call of the outdoors lures me, tempting me to postpone the decision yet again. *Why not? It can't hurt.* Relieved, I put my phone in my pocket. A walk will help me mull things over. Pulling on my trainers and a hoodie for protection against the bracing sea breeze, I head towards the beach. It's become an integral part of my hermit existence. I love that invigorating feeling of striding out along its sandy expanse, leaving my print in its damp surface. There are a few people out – walking dogs, running or, like me, taking a morning stroll and enjoying the sunshine. The fishermen are there, in their usual spot, and I wonder how much they've caught this morning. A black Labrador bounds up to me with his ball, realises that I'm not his owner and races away. The wind is cool and whips colour into my cheeks. It really is beautiful here, so open and vast. The rhythmic lapping of the waves against the shore is comforting and I head closer to the water, all the time scouring the ground to see what has been washed up. Lots of seaweed and shells, all different shapes and sizes. I pick up my favourites, discarding them as I find better ones. It's something I always do. At the end of my walk, I'll keep only the very best one and leave the rest for others to discover. Absorbed in my task, I'm oblivious to everything and everyone else. Despite my good intentions earlier, I can't bring myself to think about the decision awaiting me.

My phone vibrates in my pocket, breaking my concentration and pulling me back to the real world. It's Howard Jones. He's called a couple of times during the week, but only to ask some additional questions. I hope, this time, he will have some information for me. I could seriously use some good news. Eagerly, I answer the call and hunch against the wind, trying to exclude the outside noise.

'Hello Lily,' he says. 'Just calling to give you an update. I've made a bit of progress and think I may be on to something. It's too soon to give you any details but I now believe that Nick Georgiev *may* be an imposter.'

'Really? You believe me?' My excitement leaps like a flame.

'I do. That's not to say I think he's Andrian Petrov ... just that some of my enquiries have raised a few question marks about Georgiev. That's all really. I should have more in a day or so.'

'That's brilliant!' My mind is racing, trying to think of sensible questions to ask, wanting to know more.

'I'm keeping eyes on Georgiev, tracking his movements,' Howard continues. 'It helps to know his daily routine.'

'Where is he now?' My eyes widen as I realise what this information could mean.

'At his office in Chelmsford.'

'Can you let me know immediately if you think he's heading my way, to Norfolk?' I ask.

'Of course. I'm aware of your situation. That's another reason for keeping an eye on him – for your protection.'

'Oh!' I hadn't thought he might be looking out for me. 'Thank you.'

'I'll be in touch.'

I put the phone back in my pocket, giddy with a mix of relief and optimism. Howard's suggestion that Georgiev is not who he claims to be is such a leap forward! For the first time since I engaged the services of a private investigator, I feel positive about the outcome. And I can stop panicking that Andrian knows where I am and is coming after me. Howard Jones has my back. For the moment, I can stay in Brancaster.

Smiling to myself, I take a look at my watch. 10:30 a.m. The time has flown by. At school, it will be break time and children will be spilling noisily out onto the playgrounds. I hope my class has someone lovely teaching them. They're such great kids. I'm assuaged with a pang of guilt as I think of the impact my sudden absence may have had on some of my more vulnerable pupils. Michael promised to look out for them though. My headteacher has been a total rock and I'll be forever grateful.

I turn and head back towards the cottage. The beach is filling up as the wind eases and the sun's rays intensify. It promises to be a beautiful day. I pull off my hoodie and tie it around my waist, relishing the warmth of the sun on my bare arms. On impulse, I kick off my trainers and dip my toes in the cool water. Squeals and giggles from the past wash over me – Mel and I racing into the sea, vying to be first, shrieking at the icy shock. We used to love going to the beach. Memories of the two of us dragging Dad with us into the waves bring a lump to my throat. Happy times. Mum would never go near the water. She used to lie on a blanket, behind a windbreak, reading a book, while the three of us cavorted in the sea or played ball on the sand. Then, ravenous, we would pile into the picnic: sandwiches, crisps, pork pies, cake from the bakery, fizzy drinks for a special treat. Those days hold a special place in my heart. How I wish I could click my fingers, like a magician, and take myself back there, just for a while, so I could truly appreciate the joy of it all. At the time, as a child, I was always looking forward ... never staying long enough in the moment to value its worth. Life had seemed so easy then. Now, memories of those times are bittersweet – infinitely more precious because the lights in them have been extinguished.

But, for the first time since my sister disappeared, optimism for the future trickles into my soul. With the help of Howard Jones, I may soon have answers to my questions about Mel, and my mum. Andrian Petrov may finally get what he deserves. And, at long last, I may have a chance to emerge from the shadows of a past enslaved by fear ...

CHAPTER 32

Todd

Friday – usually Todd's favourite day of the week but, today, the hours in the office seemed interminable. Bogged down in the construction of a legal agreement bespoke to the two parties involved, Todd glanced at his watch and calculated the time he had to get it done. It would be tight. Picking Charlotte up at the usual time of 5:30 p.m. meant that he couldn't stay late at the office. The pressure made his temples throb and, more than ever, he longed to quit his job. If he never had to read or write another contract, he would be happy.

By midday, his head was pounding and he needed fresh air. Paracetamol too. Coffee. And a sandwich. Decision made, he strode out of the office and along to the deli around the corner. While he stood in the queue, he switched his mobile phone back on and checked for messages. A voicemail from Lee asking him to call. Yesterday, his friend had texted to say he had a date with his estranged wife, Callie, that night. Crossing his fingers that it had gone well, Todd stepped out of the queue and onto the street to ring him back.

'Hey, mate. How are you doing?' Lee's voice sounded chirpy. A good sign.

'Fine. How about you? How did it go last night?'

'Pretty good. The flowers were a nice touch – thanks for that idea – and she was impressed with the choice of venue. We went to that little Italian place down St John's Street, Mamma Mia. It was really good.'

'Great. Did you tell her how you feel about her?'

'I did. You'd have been proud of me, mate.'

'And?'

Lee sighed. 'She didn't say she loved me back if that's what you're wondering. I don't know ... she listened ... she told me why she'd felt I had to leave ... agreed with me when I said I'd been a moron ...' A wry chuckle. 'She said she wasn't sure how she felt about things and that she'd have to think about it. I'm going over to spend some time with the kids tomorrow and I'm planning to suggest we all have a family day out on Sunday. Do you think that's a good idea?'

'Definitely. I'd say that's very positive. Don't push her. Just be your normal, fun self, the man she fell in love with, and make sure you all have a great time.'

'Thanks, mate. I know there's a long way to go but it's a good start. At least, we're speaking to each other!' He laughed. 'I appreciate your help.'

'No problem. Hope it all goes well. I'm rooting for you.'

'Cheers.' The line went dead and Todd returned to the queue, still smiling. His friend's news had lifted his spirits and his thoughts turned to his own quest. The next step was to find an address for Kathryn Foley-Watts, aka Kaz. Judging by Mrs Clarkson's reaction to his visit, he was on to something. First step, find Kaz; the second, persuade her to reveal Lily's hiding place ... if she knew it. That was his plan. Sounded easy, but he was all too aware that it wouldn't be. When he reached the front of the queue, he ordered an Americano coffee and a cheese and pickle sandwich. Much as he would've liked to sit at one of the tables outside, he took his lunch back to the office. The quicker he got back to work, the sooner he'd be finished.

By 5:30 p.m. the knotty contracts had been completed, Charlotte was strapped in her seat in the back of his car and his headache had lifted. The weekend could officially begin.

'How was your week, sweetheart?' he asked his daughter.

'OK.'

He frowned. Usually, she talked non-stop on the journey to his house but today she'd been quieter. Again, he wondered if it had anything to do with Lily.

'Is anything wrong, Charlotte? You don't seem your normal, sunny self.'

She sighed, 'Not really.'

Something was up. He decided to leave it for now. The car wasn't the best place for a heart-to-heart. He'd tackle it later. Instead, he chatted about his plans to take her back to Banham Zoo the following day. They'd been once before and she'd loved it. Today, though, her enthusiasm for even that seemed very low key. There was definitely a problem.

'Tell me what's up.' A direct approach was best and he confronted her across the table as she sipped at a glass of milk. She shrugged and didn't reply. 'You can tell me, sweetheart. Maybe I can help. Is it something at school?' She shook her head. 'Something at home?' This time, she hesitated and twisted her mouth before shrugging. At home then. Not Lily. He relaxed and gave her his friendliest smile. 'Whatever it is, sweetheart, I can only help you if you tell me.'

She frowned and carefully set her milk down on the table. 'I *like* my school.' The words were emitted in an explosion of fury. 'I don't want to leave.'

That confused him. 'Why would you have to leave your school?' he asked.

Her face darkened into a scowl. 'Mummy said so.'

Cogs started clicking in his brain and he had a horrible feeling he knew where this conversation was heading. 'Why does Mummy want you to go to a different school?'

'She says I'm old enough now to go to boarding school but I don't want to go. I like my school.'

'Oh, baby ...' He held out his arms and she ran into his embrace. Trying to keep his voice calm and to hide the anger simmering inside him, he stroked her dark curls. 'I'll speak to Mummy. I'm sure we can sort it out. Tell you what, I'll phone her now. Why don't you go and watch some TV?'

When she was on the sofa watching Blue Peter on iPlayer, he stalked into the kitchen and rang Reggie's mobile.

'What's wrong?' She answered on the second ring.

'There's nothing wrong ... that is, Charlotte's fine. She's here with me.' He hated that she always managed to put him on the back foot.

'Why are you calling then?' she snapped. 'I'm at work.'

'Charlotte's upset. She's under the impression that she might be going to boarding school.'

'Oh.' There was a pause and he could sense her irritation. 'I don't have time to discuss this now.'

'We haven't discussed it at all and yet our daughter has been told.' He could feel the heat rising in his tone and struggled to keep his anger in check. 'As I said, she's pretty upset.'

'I'm sorry about that but it's for her own good. Pilar has handed in her notice and Nick and I thought that boarding school would be a good solution. We're both really busy at work and barely see her as it is. That's pretty lonely for a young girl.'

His rage finally bubbled over. Pilar was Charlotte's childminder. 'I see. You want to pack Charlotte off to boarding school as a convenience because you're losing your childcare arrangements!'

'You're being dramatic and I really don't have time for this,' she replied coolly. 'Charlotte will soon get used to it.'

'No, she won't. If you're finding it difficult to look after our daughter, she can come and live with me. That way, she can stay at her current school where she's happy and thriving and you won't need to worry about her.' There – he'd said it.

There was a pause and then a sigh. 'Look, Todd, I'll think about it. Things are tricky at the moment, what with work and the wedding. It's been difficult to give Charlotte the time she needs. Maybe it *would* be easier if she lived with you for a bit ... just until things settle down. Pilar is working until the end of this month so we've got three weeks to think on it. I know Charlotte doesn't want to change schools but, personally, I do think that private education, at some point in the future, will afford her better opportunities. But I agree she's still very young for boarding school. It was just that Nick thought ...'

'I don't give a damn what Nick thinks. Charlotte is *our* daughter, not his.' He took a deep breath. 'Anyway, as long as we can agree that boarding school is off the agenda, we'll work something out. I know you want what's best for her, Reggie.'

'Of course. Now I really *do* have to go.'

'Bye,' he said but the line was already dead. He stared at his phone, replaying the conversation. Could he manage to look after Charlotte? On his own? Why not? He'd committed himself now and felt only excitement at the prospect. He'd wanted to wait until his writing was successful enough for him to give up the day job but that could be years ... if ever. Somehow, he would manage. His office was pro flexible working. He could do it. Grinning like an idiot, he joined Charlotte on the sofa. She looked at him expectantly.

'What did Mummy say?'

'She agreed that you were happy where you are and that it would be a shame for you to change schools. All sorted.'

Her face broke into a beaming smile and she squealed with delight. 'Thanks, Daddy. You're the best.'

Her joy brought a lump to his throat. 'No. You're the best,' he murmured as he ruffled her hair. 'I'm starving. Shall we go out for tea?'

'Nah, let's get pizza. And can we watch a movie together?'

'Sounds good to me,' he replied.

***

Much later, when Charlotte was asleep in bed, Todd turned to the task of finding an address for Kathryn Foley-Watts. It was an unusual name and his hopes for success were high. A google search immediately returned a useful result – a website, offering freelance editing and proofreading services in the east of England. That could belong to the correct Kathryn Foley-Watts. Eagerly, he read through her resumé, the different services in which she specialised and the testimonials. All impressive but yielding no clues to her precise location. The contact page provided an email link. He started to compose an email and then deleted it. Unless he sent it from a fake address, she would recognise his name and ignore it. The thought of setting up a fake email account and tricking her into meeting him sat uncomfortably with him. Far better to see if he could find her address and visit in person. Maybe, Lily would actually be there, staying with her friend. He didn't want to do anything which could alert her in advance and scare her into running once more. For the first time, he felt that he was hot on her trail and he didn't want to jeopardise things.

He turned to social media and quickly discovered an account in the name of Kaz Foley-Watts on Facebook. Surely, that was her? But there was no profile picture and her account was private so, unless she accepted a friend request from him, he couldn't access her posts. Another dead end. He thought for a bit and then tried a google search for Thomas Foley-Watts, her husband. The top result was a link to a company named Beach View Holiday Cottages based in Southwold. Thomas Foley-Watts was named as the managing director. He clicked on the link but soon realised that was only useful if he wanted to book a holiday cottage. Still, he was building a profile of the couple and felt he was closing in. There was a possibility they lived in Southwold or reasonably nearby. What he needed was a telephone/address book for the area. He decided to make himself a coffee while he deliberated his next move. As he scooped a generous spoonful of instant granules into a mug, it occurred to him that this information may be available online. Who used a telephone book these days? Taking his coffee back to his desk, he googled it and, hey presto, there it was – a link to an online BT phonebook. In the 'search' box, he typed the name Foley-Watts and tried Southwold as the location. He pressed enter and received one result: Mr and Mrs T. Foley-Watts with a phone number and an address of The Beeches, Howes Lane, Southwold. He'd done it; he'd found Kaz.

CHAPTER 33

Lily

For the past two nights, my sleep has been deep and dreamless and I'm feeling re-energised. Since my conversation with Howard Jones two days ago, I've embraced an aura of calm. Things are set in motion and I'm in control; this time, I'm the one determining the course of events – not Andrian. The sense of empowerment feels good.

Another beautiful morning; another walk along the beach. It's busy today. Holiday-makers are already out in force, determined to make the most of the predicted sunshine. I skirt wide, giving ample room to the windbreaks and beach towels, smiling at other walkers doing the same. My route is leisurely; I've nothing to rush for and I walk further than usual.

I pause and take a deep breath, inhaling the moist, salty air, before turning back. The day stretches ahead of me, a blank canvas of possibilities. Instead of fretting about my enforced isolation, I'm trying to see this period of leisure as an opportunity. Carpe diem – seize the day. Yesterday, I took a leaf out of Todd's book and began writing a memoir. What happened to me is a story which should be told but, as yet, I haven't got very far. I spent most of the afternoon sitting out on the decking with a pen and notebook, jotting down a few ideas, brief sketches of my childhood when there were still the four of us in the family. Somehow, I can't bring myself to think about later ... Dad's accident ... when Mel disappeared ... Perhaps soon, when I know Andrian has been brought to justice.

More memories accompany my return along the beach and I catalogue them in my head, hoping I'll be able to remember them when I have my notebook in front of me. I consider stopping to list them on my phone but I'm keen to get back. The sun is burning the skin on my arms and my throat feels parched. As I reach the edge of the beach where it meets the shingle path, I sense eyes watching me. Curious, I look around. Scattered groups of people are all busy doing their own thing, taking no notice of me. Something's not right though. I feel it, a creeping chill rising along my spine to the back of my neck. Despite the sunshine, I shiver. Slowly, I turn my head to scan the entire expanse of sand. Suddenly, I see him – a young guy, standing a little way away, oddly dressed in a heavy, leather jacket, staring right at me. As I meet his gaze, we make eye contact in that fleeting, awkward way of strangers catching each other watching. I stand, motionless, frozen in the tension of the moment. Then, we both look away and, when I risk another peek, he's heading back up the beach, holding a phone to his ear. It isn't Andrian – that had been my first thought when I saw that tall, dark, jacketed figure – but it spooked me nonetheless.

As I head back to the cottage, I rationalise away my immediate instinct that the man wished me harm. It was nothing; he was probably just checking me out. But, something about the intensity of his scrutiny continues to bother me and I can't shake off a feeling of impending threat. I keep looking over my shoulder to check he's not following. Although I don't see him, I sense he's still there. Even back at the cottage, my edginess remains. My sanctuary no longer seems impenetrable but as fragile as glass, on the brink of shattering. As I drink iced water, I berate myself for letting the guy on the beach upset me. It was nothing; I'm stronger than that. But I cannot recapture my earlier optimism. All my life, ever since Mel vanished, I've been waiting for the knife to fall. I'm sick of it, bone-weary of the ever-present worry. One way or another, I want it over.

***

As if in answer to my unspoken prayer, Howard Jones rings later that day. 'It's still early in the investigation and I don't want you to get your hopes up too much ...' Despite his opening note of caution, my mood soars as I hear the 'but' coming. 'But I really *do* think I might be on to something.'

'And?'

'I told you I was a bit of a dark horse. I could see you were a bit sceptical when you met me but you shouldn't judge a book by its cover. I *am* good at what I do.' He sounds smug, making the most of his moment of glory. There's a pause while he waits for me to agree with him. When I say nothing, he continues, 'Anyway, as I told you when I last rang, I've been doing some digging. I've managed to find an ex-employee of Turner Packaging, someone who left under a bit of a cloud. I tend to find people like that make useful sources of information and so it proved.' There's a pause.

'Yes?' My voice sounds breathless.

'It turns out that this chap has an axe to grind against Nick Georgiev. Reckons he's a real dodgy character. He'd never heard of the name Andrian Petrov but he's put me onto someone who might well know more. I'm meeting him later.'

'Oh.' After his build-up, I'm left feeling disappointed. To me, it doesn't sound like he's any further forward.

'This guy, the one I'm meeting later, used to be Nick Georgiev's right-hand man. I'm hopeful he might know a bit more about his past. The police are right. His background checks out. Rock solid. But, interestingly, the man known as Nikolas Georgiev was always a loner. Came to Britain in 1972 at the age of six with his mother who died in 1990. No information on his father or any other family. Bright boy. Got a job in a factory but worked hard and was promoted. Various jobs. Proved he had a real talent for marketing. Then, in 2010, he met and married Sophie Turner whose dad was Chairman of Turner Packaging. Not a whiff of anything illegal.'

'Oh.' Now, I'm feeling totally deflated. Could I have been mistaken in thinking it was him? Did Andrian Petrov have a double? I voice those thoughts to Howard Jones and he chuckles. 'My thoughts exactly. I have to admit that, when I found all that information, I thought you were barking up the wrong tree.' His cliches are beginning to grate and I listen impatiently, wishing he would get to the point. 'But then I found Vic Greenaway – the disgruntled, ex-employee – and he gave me pause to wonder. Everything I've discovered about Nikolas Georgiev is that the man is as straight as a die: clean-living, hard worker, a genuinely nice guy. Anyway, according to Vic Greenaway, the current Nick Georgiev isn't like that at all. He's charming and charismatic but totally ruthless – gets rid of anyone who gets in his way. Apparently, he's not above using threats or blackmail. He's also a real ladies' man. Since his marriage, it's well-known that he's had a string of affairs. Now, those two men, the past Nick Georgiev and the present, don't sound like the same person at all, do they?' He pauses to allow time for that to sink in, expecting a reply. I feel excitement building at his words but I'm waiting for more and say nothing. After a lull, he answers his own question. 'Well, that's what I began to suspect at any rate. And, with a bit more digging, I discovered something else. When I checked Nick Georgiev out with his previous employers – all of whom had only good things to say about him, incidentally – a couple of them mentioned rumours that he was gay. They were surprised, to say the least, to learn he'd got married. Now, that doesn't sound like the present Nick Georgiev who, according to my new friend Vic, cheats on his wife with young girls. What do *you* think?' He presented the last question with a flourish, like pulling a rabbit from a hat.

'What exactly are you telling me?' I want to hear what *he* thinks.

'I've given it a great deal of thought and have reached the conclusion that, maybe, at some point before 2010, probably in 2009, Andrian Petrov became Nick Georgiev.'

'But how? What happened to the real one – Nikolas?'

'Who knows? He must be dead but how that happened is anyone's guess. Obviously, if I'm right, his body was never found. My theory is this: Petrov becomes aware of Georgiev and their remarkable similarity in appearance; Petrov gets rid of him and takes on his identity. It would have been an opportunity for him to assume legitimate status. In 2009, Georgiev was working as a sales and marketing manager for a company called Tompkins Engineering and suddenly went off sick. He handed in his notice while he was still off. The MD was pretty upset by the manner of his departure, when I spoke to him, and kept saying it was out of character. Then, a few months later, he popped up working for another company in a different part of the country. That could have been the time when Petrov became Georgiev.'

'Oh my God!' I exhale in a rush. His theory makes sense. 'That's fantastic – well, not for the original Nick Georgiev, of course ...' My mind is whirring like a dynamo. 'But how are you going to prove it?'

'Give me time.' I can hear the smile in his voice. 'As I said, I'm meeting this other guy later this evening. Hopefully, I'll find out something useful then.'

'OK ... well, thank you ... so much. Can you let me know?'

'Naturally. We'll speak afterwards.'

'Thanks. Be careful,' I add as an afterthought.

'Always.' He ends the call and I fling myself on a sofa, digesting the information I've been given, trying to curb the elation pulsing through me. Howard is right; it's too soon to get over-excited. Everything he said, as yet, remains hypothetical. Cold, hard proof will be needed and that may well prove difficult, if not impossible to acquire. Nevertheless, it's a huge step forward. I'm teeming with respect for my investigator and self-reproach for my original lack of faith in him. Better than anyone, I should know how deceptive appearances can be.

***

I spend the evening on tenterhooks, waiting for a call. To distract myself, I find a book from the shelf in the cottage. I've already read many from the assortment of old paperbacks and I take my time browsing before selecting a crime thriller. It's by a well-known author whose books I've enjoyed in the past. I settle in a comfortable armchair, surrounded by cushions, and begin to read.

By ten o'clock, I'm growing twitchy. I make a coffee, determined to stay awake until after the phone call. The darkness outside exposes my nerves and tugs at the vulnerabilities I fight to keep hidden. For the second time, I check I've locked all the doors. The man I saw earlier down on the beach returns to haunt my thoughts. He looked so out of place, dressed as he was, and he was watching me for sure. Could he have been one of Andrian's men? No, I *won't* let myself think that; it would mean Andrian knew where I was ... Restlessly, I return to the novel and persevere but it fails to keep my attention and, eventually, I discard it altogether.

By eleven o'clock, I'm pacing the cottage, phone in hand, debating whether or not to call Howard Jones. I don't want to do anything which might compromise him but I need to know what's happened. My emotions alternate between concern for his safety and irritation that he might have forgotten to ring me. By quarter past, I can stand it no longer. I locate his number in my contact list, press *call* and wait for it to start ringing. It doesn't; the line is dead. I try again with the same result. That's why he hasn't called; his phone is out of charge. I pace a bit more, before deciding I may as well go to bed. He'll ring in the morning, offering profuse apologies for his failure to call me as promised. If he has good news, I'll forgive him. I try to squash a persistent niggle of worry for him. He told me he could look after himself ... but, as I undress, fears resurface, like bubbles of air from an underwater swimmer. Different scenarios unfold in my head, culminating in a surprise appearance from Andrian himself at the meeting ... *Andrian holding a gun ... Andrian threatening Howard and insisting he reveal my whereabouts ...*

Damn the coffee and the crime thriller – both poor choices, given my state of mind. Annoyed with myself for letting my imagination run away with me, I burrow into the bedcovers, knowing sleep will be a long time coming.

A car stops outside the cottage. I sit up, listening, senses on full alert. Nothing happens. The car must be still there. Panic roils in my stomach and I hardly dare breathe. Then, I hear the click of a car door, opened quietly, and the squeak of the gate.

Someone is coming ...

CHAPTER 34

Todd

Charlotte chattered non-stop on the way to Southwold, excited to be going to the beach on a sunny Sunday morning. Todd tried to concentrate on what she was saying but other questions were too big a distraction. *What if Kaz doesn't know anything; what if Lily's there but won't see me; what if I see her and she tells me, face to face, it's over between us; what if I'm too late?*

'Daddy, you're not listening,' his daughter wailed.

'What? Sorry, sweetheart, tell me again ...'

As promised, he'd taken Charlotte to the zoo on Saturday and it had been a joy to see her trouble-free and laughing once more. But he couldn't relax. Now he knew where Kaz lived, his stomach churned with tension and anticipation. Combining the trip with a visit to the beach seemed like a good compromise and saved him from having to wait until Monday evening.

Once again, his daughter's squeal interrupted his thoughts. 'I can see the sea ... look Daddy ... over there!'

He smiled. 'I see it.' The water shimmered slate grey against the azure blue of the sky. 'It looks freezing.'

She giggled. 'I don't care. You will come in with me, won't you Daddy?'

'Mm.' The satnav directed him to turn left and he switched his focus to following the route. He'd told Charlotte they had to make a stop-off before the beach but that it wouldn't take too long. Another left turn and a slow drive along a narrow lane which seemed to go on forever. They passed two large houses before the satnav announced they had reached their destination outside the third. Todd stopped the car and turned to smile at Charlotte. 'We're here.'

The house was a large, red-bricked, modern building forming an L-shape with a brick-weave drive. A green Toyota Prius was parked in front of a separate double garage. Charlotte had already undone her seat belt and was scrambling out of the car. 'Hurry up, Daddy,' she ordered.

He followed her to a front door framed by jaunty, pink clematis. Large pots of multi-coloured geraniums and petunias lined the front wall. Todd pressed the bell and stood back to wait. Holding Charlotte's hand helped him feel rooted and in control.

The door was opened by a heavily pregnant, young woman regarding him with suspicion. 'Can I help you?' Her voice was polite but cool, her mouth unsmiling.

'I'm looking for Kaz Foley-Watts.' Todd only realised how hard he was gripping his daughter's hand when she pulled it away.

'Are you having a baby?' Charlotte asked, staring at the woman's large bump, encased in a long, bright orange top.

'Yes, but not yet.' The woman's lips curved for the first time as she looked down at the small girl. The smile disappeared as she transferred her attention back to Todd. 'I'm Kaz,' she said. Her gaze travelled to the lane beyond him. 'What do you want?'

'My name is Todd Matheson and this is my daughter, Charlotte. We're good friends of Lily Nichol and I'm really hoping you can tell me where she is.'

His words provoked a flicker of recognition, swiftly replaced by a blank look. 'I don't know who you're talking about.' Her voice was flat. 'Sorry, I can't help you.'

'No, wait, please,' he implored as she started to close the door. 'I know you're Saskia Potter's best friend; Saskia is Lily Nichol; I want to help her.' His words tumbled out in a rush. 'Please.'

'Please,' Charlotte echoed solemnly. 'I want Lily to come back.'

Todd glimpsed momentary indecision in Kaz's eyes and pressed home his advantage. 'Look, can we come in for a few minutes?'

'Oh, alright,' Kaz capitulated with a sigh. 'But I can't tell you anything.' She opened the door wider to let them in and they took their shoes off before following her through to a spacious, open-plan kitchen and living area.

'You have a lovely home,' Todd said as Kaz reached for the kettle.

'Thank you. I only have decaff coffee,' she said. 'The real stuff is too much of a temptation. Would you like some?'

'Thanks.'

'What would you like, Charlotte?' Again, she smiled, warmth emanating from her like a halo, when she addressed the child. 'I have squash, juice or water.'

'Water please,' Charlotte replied.

Todd helped her onto one of the stools around the island in the centre of the large space. 'Thank you. That's very kind.' He flashed her his warmest smile as she placed the water on the gleaming, black, marble surface.

'So ...' Kaz set down two mugs of coffee and manoeuvred her bulk onto a stool. 'I'm listening.'

He took a breath. Where to start? Somehow, he needed to get this woman onside. But there were things he didn't want to say in front of his daughter. He should've thought of that. Shooting her an anxious glance, he said, 'Charlotte, honey, do you want to watch something on my phone?' At her nod, he found a video she liked watching and handed the phone over. To Kaz, he said, 'Can we talk privately?' She raised her eyebrows as if to ask whose choice it was to bring a child. 'Please?' he added. Without a word, she stood and led the way, carrying her coffee, to the adjoining dining room. Settling on a window seat, she eyed him warily.

He took a seat across from her and smiled again, trying to reassure her. 'Thank you. I really appreciate this.' She didn't respond and his face assumed a serious expression as he considered how best to start. With Kaz offering no encouragement, he looked away from her, staring at his coffee mug as he spoke. 'You had a friend called Saskia Potter. When you were both about fifteen, some terrible things happened. Saskia's sister, Melanie, went to London to work and was never seen again. Her mum took an overdose. Saskia was taken into care and placed with a foster family. For reasons unknown to me, she changed her name and became Samantha Smith. She went to university and qualified as a teacher. Things were looking up for her. But then she vanished. No warning. She left a note and maintained regular contact with her foster family but they had no idea where she was, what she was doing or why she'd left. They've not seen her since. Again, she changed her name, this time becoming Lily Nichol, right up until three months ago. That's when, yet again, she disappeared. This time, I was the one who received the note.' He stopped. It was difficult to say these things to a stranger. When he looked up, Kaz's eyes were fixed on his face. The compassion he saw there spurred him on. 'We were in love ... very happy together. It made no sense. Before that happened, we'd been talking about her moving in with me. Charlotte was distraught and I ... well, I was too.' He gave her a wry smile. 'I couldn't accept that she didn't love me anymore; there *had* to be another reason. So, I've been trying to find her. Anyway, to cut a long story short, the search led me to Kaz Clarkson.' Another smile. Kaz was still watching him. Her tension was visible in the taut line of her shoulders, the stiff set of her jaw and in the tight grip she had on her coffee mug as it sat in front of her, as yet untasted. 'I found your parents' address and met your mother. She got rid of me sharpish, even threatened to call the police. It was a bit of an over-reaction and I couldn't help thinking that she was hiding something. So, then I tracked you down ... and here I am.'

There was silence. Kaz took the first sip of her coffee and he did the same, waiting for her response. At last, eyes averted, she said, 'I still can't help you. I'm sorry.'

'Do you know where she is?'

His direct question caught her by surprise and she bit her lip. 'I'm sorry, I can't help you,' she repeated.

'So, you *do* know.'

He was rewarded with a fierce glare. 'I didn't say that.'

'No, but you didn't deny it.'

She banged her mug down. 'Look, Todd, I can't tell you where she is. Is that clear enough for you?'

'But I'm really worried she could be in danger. Look, I don't know all the ins and outs – not yet – but I do know she's afraid of something ... or someone ... She can't keep living her life like this. I want to help.'

The anger left her, as quickly as it had appeared, and she sighed once more. 'You and me both,' she murmured. Silence stretched between them. Todd waited, hardly daring to breathe.

'Can we go to the beach now?' Charlotte had appeared and was looking at him with baleful, brown eyes.

'In just a minute, poppet.' He looked at Kaz, his eyes entreating her to relent.

She stood. 'I believe you, Todd,' she said quietly. 'I wish I could help you but I'm afraid I can't. I will try to get word to Lily and tell her that you're looking for her ... what you've said ... but it's up to her. That's the best I can do. Sorry.' She waddled back to the kitchen, heading towards the front door. There seemed to be no option but to follow. He'd given it his best shot but, even if she wanted to help, she was bound by a promise to her friend. She wasn't going to tell him where Lily was and he had to respect that.

As he reached the hallway, he noticed a pile of papers lying on a side table. They were fliers, advertising a holiday let in Brancaster. He peered closer. The north Norfolk coast would be a good place to take Charlotte in the summer. There was a photograph of a pretty brick house, painted pale blue, called Fisherman's Cottage. He took one of the sheets.

'This looks nice,' he looked up to smile at Kaz. 'I'll think about booking. I did take a look at your husband's website when I was trying to find you and that got me thinking about holidays.'

Her face was waxy white and her eyes wide as she stared at the paper in his hand. 'That one's fully booked at the moment,' she muttered, a strangled note to her voice. 'Check out the website again. There'll be something better there.' She cleared her throat and reached to snatch the paper from him but he evaded her grasp, folded it and put it in his pocket. 'The door is this way.' She was glaring at him now.

'Right.' He gave her an apologetic look and slipped on his trainers. 'Thanks very much for your time ... and the drinks. Please tell Lily we miss her and we want her home.'

They left and, having checked Charlotte was safely strapped in the car, Todd slipped into the driver's seat, thinking hard. That was weird. Kaz's reaction, when she saw him looking at the flier, must mean something. She looked horrified. Why? Did it have something to do with Lily? Hope surged within him. It was a long shot but worth following up. He patted his trouser pocket, feeling the slight rustle of the paper. A trip to Brancaster to check out the cottage would be his next priority. And even if that proved to be a dead end, he felt that the visit to Kaz hadn't been a wasted journey. He'd definitely managed to engage her sympathies – at least, right up until that final encounter. Despite what she said, he thought she *did* know where to find Lily. With luck, she might persuade her to call him. Whistling softly, he started the engine and, with Charlotte's exhortations in his ear, they headed for Southwold beach.

CHAPTER 35

Lily

My heart thunders in my chest at the crunch of gravel beneath my window. *Someone's coming!* It can't be Kaz; she would've rung first. *Howard Jones?* With trembling fingers, I grasp my phone. No messages. No missed calls. A rap at the door. I sit, frozen with fear, picturing Andrian standing on the step, waiting to pounce when I appear. *Everything is locked. Stay put. Pretend I'm not here.*

Another knock on the front door, louder this time. I want to peer out of the window, see who it is, but dare not. If it's Andrian, I'm lost.

The silence envelopes me, thick and tangible. It stretches into what seems like minutes but must be only seconds. Then, more footsteps – this time, going round to the back of the cottage. Another knock. Each time, it sends my pulse skittering. I grip the edge of the duvet, shivering despite the warmth of the bed. *A weapon. Something to defend myself.* My eyes cast wildly in the darkness until I remember the piece of driftwood. I reach down to retrieve it from the floor.

'Sass.' A low hiss, barely discernible and then again, a bit louder. 'Sass!'

Was it a woman's voice? I release my grip on the driftwood, scramble out of bed and, cautiously, crack open the window, peering into the darkness. It has to be Kaz. No-one else knows I'm here. 'Kaz, is that you?' I whisper. There's no reply. Whoever it is has disappeared. I scurry downstairs, feet bare, in my shorts and T-shirt pyjamas. In the hallway, I come to a standstill, wary once more. As I watch, the letter flap in the front door is pushed open and a face is pressed against the opening.

'Sass, if you're in there, open the bloody door for Christ's sake!'

I gasp and stare, mesmerised, as the flap drops and shudders against its metal surround. Blood roars in my ears. *It can't be!* I won't allow myself to consider it ... and yet ...

With a yelp, I snap out of my stupor and lurch towards the door. My fingers tremble, slipping and sliding, as I turn the key in the lock and draw back the bolt. A hard lump of hope clogs my throat and, feeling breathlessly dizzy, I throw open the door.

It's like looking in the mirror: the same dark hair tumbling in waves to the same slim shoulders; the same narrow face and hazel eyes; the same-shaped mouth with full lips. A woman stands in front of me, hands on hips, eyes assessing, her mouth twitching in a half-smile. 'About bloody time!' she says and then, 'Hello Sis.'

Like a sleepwalker, I step towards her. She rushes at me and we cling to each other as if we're never letting go. I feel wetness on my cheeks and sobs of happiness building up inside me. She's shaking too; I can feel her whole body, pressed tightly against mine, quivering like a plucked guitar string. We hug and cry, both of us, for a very long time. Mel is first to recover. 'Phew!' she says, pulling back and wiping away the tears smearing her cheek. 'That was emotional. I need a drink.'

'Me too.' I brush away my own tears with an embarrassed laugh. 'Tea or coffee?'

'I hope you've got something a damn sight stronger than those,' she mutters, a gleam in her eyes. 'I'd say a family reunion calls for wine, at least. Actually, I've a bottle in the car if you don't have any here.'

'I have,' I grin back at her and fish a bottle out of the fridge. 'I was just joking. I knew what you meant. How did you find me? How long have you been looking? Where have you been?' I shake my head. 'God, there are so many questions.'

She nods. 'I know. I have questions too. Wine first though. I've had a long drive and I need fortifying.'

'Where have you driven from?' I ask. She purses her lips and points to the bottle. I chuckle and pour us both large glasses. It's difficult not to stare at her and I see she's having the same problem. We're both drinking in every detail of each other. She looks amazing – chic and well-groomed, in a beautifully-cut, burnt orange dress and a casual, cream jacket. Her clothes alone look like they cost a fortune. Add in her beautiful, cream Gucci bag and those elegant Ferramo shoes, carelessly kicked off by the front door, and I conclude that Melanie is clearly doing well. Beside her, I feel silly and a bit awkward in my pyjamas. *Don't be ridiculous. This is my sister. Who cares what I'm wearing?* Still, I can't help feeling a tiny bit intimidated by this glossy version of Mel.

'God, I thought you were going to faint when you saw me ... you were so bloody pale.'

I raise my eyebrows as I sit on the sofa beside my sister. 'It was just a teeny bit of a shock,' I reply drily, 'after all this time.' I grasp her hand. Her fingers feel cool in mine, strange and yet familiar. 'I always believed you were alive though. I had to.' Now is the time to start asking all the questions burning on my tongue but I'm overcome by a sudden reluctance to know. It feels like we're part of a wonderful piece of magic, brought together for just a few precious moments. I wonder if I'm dreaming but her hand feels real enough in mine. If I let the past intrude, it could all disappear ... *poof...* in a cloud of smoke, the spell broken.

'So, how have you been, Sass?'

I smile. 'I've been fine. Things were difficult after you vanished and Mum ...' I break off and bite my lip. Does she know about Mum?

She squeezes my hand. 'I know Mum died,' she says quietly. 'When I got back to England, I came looking for you both. That's when I found out about Mum and that you'd been taken into foster care. I had no idea where you'd gone or how to find you. It was tricky because I needed to stay under the radar. You're the only one who knows my real name ... and I need it to stay that way.'

I nod. I know all about keeping secrets. Her implicit request for silence doesn't seem strange to me and I assume it has something to do with Andrian. Instead, I focus on the first part of her statement.

'You've been living abroad. Where?'

She shrugs. 'Russia mostly. How about you?'

I notice how quickly she diverts attention away from herself and feel overwhelmed with sadness for her. What has she endured? I don't think I can bear to know. My voice rasps when I answer her question, emotion making it difficult to speak. 'Kent and then Suffolk. I didn't stray far.' I give her a brief history of my foster parents, university and my teaching career. This is safe territory. 'How did you manage to find me?'

'I have my ways ...' She winks and taps the side of her nose. Then, she laughs and, for the first time, I glimpse the girl she was, under all the gloss. 'Actually, I saw your photo in the paper. A heroine! Saving a child. That *had* to be you! You were always rescuing things when we were kids, do you remember?' I do. Any animal in trouble, I was there. She was too. Dad, Mel and I were regulars at the local vets with a succession of injured creatures – hedgehogs, birds and, one time, a feral cat which scratched my hands and arms so badly I had to have a tetanus shot. 'And obviously, I recognised you, even though they called you something different. But when I went to Suffolk looking for you, you'd disappeared. I asked at the school and was told you'd taken a leave of absence. So near and yet so far. I'd been so excited about finding you and then I'd lost you again.'

'So how have you managed to track me down here?' I ask.

'Ah well ... I'm not sure I can reveal my sources.' Her laugh sounds forced and I wait for her to continue.

'If you must know, it was via your old friend, Kaz. When I first came looking for you – that was about six or seven years ago – I was beyond distraught. Saskia Potter had vanished and I had no idea how to find her. Then, I remembered Kaz. You were so close as kids. If anyone knew where you were, she would. But I couldn't go and ask her. I just couldn't risk it. How did I know if I could trust her to keep quiet about me? I'd made a new life for myself – a good life – and ...' she regarded me solemnly, 'I've done some stuff I'm not proud of ... illegal things. If my true identity is discovered, I could go to prison.'

I stare at her, shocked by this revelation. 'You must have had reasons?' I hate that the pitch of my voice rises, turning the words into a question. My sister deserves unreserved loyalty.

'Maybe.' She gives a hard laugh. 'Anyway, instead of confronting her, I followed her for a bit, hoping she might lead me to you.' She frowns. 'But she didn't and I was stuck. There was nothing more I could do so I gave up, hoping that, one day, I'd get a lucky break. And then I did, with the news report, but by the time I'd managed to get to Suffolk, you'd gone and disappeared all over again. That puzzled me ... and terrified me too. You might've been snatched by our old friend, Andrian, or by some other weirdo. I couldn't understand why there wasn't publicity about it – a police investigation. But then I started to wonder if your vanishing act was your own choice. So, I resorted to my old strategy. Except, this time, I wasn't able to follow Kaz myself. I got my partner's son to do it; he was someone I could trust. Trouble is, he's not much more than a kid himself and certainly not a pro at detective work. He followed Kaz to Southwold and recognised you when you met at some café a few weeks back. Trouble was, he was so pleased with himself, he didn't think to follow you, rather than Kaz, at that point, to find out where you were staying. I gave him such a hard time over it. I told him he had to hang about in Southwold until he saw you again and make sure he got an address this time. That was this morning when he clocked you walking on the beach and managed to follow you back here.'

'Was he wearing a leather jacket?' I ask.

'You noticed him. He admitted as much. Poor kid. He's really not cut out for surveillance work. He wants to be a pilot. Anyway, he told me where you were and I came as fast as I could before you could bloody well go and disappear all over again! Hence my late arrival. Sorry about that. I guess I spooked you quite a bit, turning up at this time of night.'

It's all a lot to take in. I revert to something she said earlier. 'You mentioned a partner. Is that a work partner ... or something else?'

She rolls her eyes. 'Still nosy, aren't you? Actually, it's both.'

I grin. 'Details, please. Name?'

'Stevie.'

'Will I get a chance to meet him?'

'Her.' She barks the word defiantly, studying my reaction with narrowed eyes, daring me to display any kind of prejudice. 'It may surprise you, given my teenage history, but I prefer girls.'

My grip on her hand tightens. I feel so protective of her, this hard-edged sister who has cultivated an aggressive outer shell as a defence mechanism.

The teenage Melanie didn't give a toss about anything. 'I'm beyond happy that you have someone,' I say quietly. 'I'd love to meet her.'

She relaxes. 'We'll have to see. She knows about you ... and some of my past. Maybe, if it's not too dangerous. You know Andrian is still out there ... somewhere.'

'Yes.' I tell her everything then: my search for her in London; the police arrests; the text from Andrian; the shock meeting in Canterbury; and my recent attempts to uncover the true identity of Nick Georgiev. Cold fury burns in my sister's eyes. She sits up, instantly alert, when I tell her I think I've found him. 'I hired this investigator but I'm worried. Tonight, he was going to meet someone who used to be Andrian's right-hand man and I haven't heard anything since. He promised to update me when the meeting was over,' I say.

Mel frowns. 'Probably forgot ... or decided it was too late to call you. My philosophy is not to worry until you know there's something to worry about. He'll call in the morning.'

'I hope so ...' I picture Howard Jones' genial, round face, talking of his family. Despite my sister's pep talk, I can't help fretting that something bad has happened to him.

'I guess I'll have to get used to calling you Lily.' Mel's voice drags me back to the present.

'Yes.' I smile. 'And what do I call you?'

Her lips twist in a grimace and I see fire in those amber eyes. 'Ronnie,' she replies, 'short for Veronika – like the bogus company I was supposed to work for.' She gives a short laugh and downs the rest of the wine. 'Part of my plan for vengeance – to remind me to keep looking for Andrian Petrov until I find and destroy him ... like he tried to destroy me.' She slams down her glass, glaring at me, daring me to argue with her. 'I won't rest until I know the bastard's dead.'

I swallow in the face of her anger. 'I know how you feel,' I admit quietly. 'I sometimes feel that way too.'

She stares at me and I watch her rage ebb away, like a flame flickering into blackness and smoke. 'With respect,' she says at last, 'you *don't* know how I feel. You can't.'

'Tell me,' I murmur, reaching to fold my hand around hers. I snatch a glimpse of the pain deep within her soul, before she squeezes her eyes shut.

'I can't,' she replies.

CHAPTER 36

Mel

It was late when they finally called it a night but Mel couldn't sleep. She lay on her back in the cottage's second bedroom with her eyes open and brain buzzing. It had been a long, strange but incredible day, culminating in an emotional reunion with her baby sister. She hadn't expected to feel so rocked by it all. Long ago, she'd learnt to distance herself, shut down her emotions, put bad stuff behind her, focus on the present. But now, all those suppressed memories came tumbling back, a downpour of rotten apples. How *could* she tell her sister what she'd been through? In the end, she'd given Saskia the briefest of outlines of her life since leaving Norfolk – no specifics. Her sister didn't need to know. She wished *she* could forget ...

How excited she'd been, setting out for the bright lights of the city! And how naïve ... how stupid! Sass tried to warn her – her sister was always the sensible one – but she'd been too caught up in the glamour of it all, too eager to escape the drab monotony of life in Thorpe St Andrew. A good looking, young man called Stan met her off the train. He was Bulgarian, like Andrian, with a cheeky grin and arrogant demeanour. She noticed the way his leering eyes roved over her face and body and it excited her. As they drove to her lodgings, in a rackety, old van, she teased and flirted, confident in the power of her attraction. Too confident.

The first shock was the room in which she was expected to sleep. It was tiny with no beds – just mattresses on the floor. And she was expected to share with four other girls. They looked dour-faced, miserable creatures and barely glanced her way when she greeted them. This wasn't what she'd imagined at all! She pulled a face at Stan as he explained that the other girls spoke very little English. 'They haven't been here long,' he said with a shrug. 'You'll all be friends soon.'

There was one bathroom and a very small kitchen, also shared. The other rooms were all locked – 'out of bounds,' Stan told her with a wink – and she was instructed to stay in her room.

'But what about going out?' she asked, frowning. This wasn't what she'd signed up for.

He pretended not to hear. Then, he demanded her phone. There was something about his tone which brooked no refusal and she handed it over, even though alarm bells were sounding. She thought he was going to put his number in her contacts or something like that. 'Good girl.' He patted her arm and pocketed the phone. 'No going out.'

'Hey, what are you doing?' she cried but he ignored her. He barked something in Bulgarian to the other girls and then left. The front door slammed behind him.

'What the ...?' She turned back to her roommates. 'What the hell is going on here?' she blustered, determined to hide the fear burgeoning inside her. No response. They watched, waiting to see what she would do next, a mix of pity and indifference in their eyes. Hands on hips, she spun around. No way was she staying in this dump! She should have grabbed her phone back while she still had the chance. Losing it was a blow but she'd have to lump it. Picking up her case, she addressed the room once more. 'I'm leaving.' No-one answered so, with a toss of her hair and a final look of disdain, she flung open the door and headed out.

She got as far as the front door. It was locked. No matter how much she turned the handle and tugged, the door wouldn't budge. There was no key. She couldn't get out. Stirrings of panic seeped into her bloodstream; her heart hammered a frantic rhythm in her chest. The more she tried, the more the handle slipped in her sweaty hand. *Think, Mel.* Maybe there was another exit. She headed along the narrow hallway to the tiny kitchen where there *was* another door. But it was boarded up. There was no handle. *'No going out.'* Stan's guttural voice echoed in her brain. *Oh God!* Marching back to her room, she flung open the door. 'Key!' she cried. The girls were all lying on their mattresses, exactly where she'd left them, waiting for her return, she realised. 'Where's the fucking front door key?' They just stared at her. She glared back at them, one by one. 'Front door key?' she repeated, her voice shrill, as she mimed the action of turning a key and opening a door. 'I want to go out.'

'No key.' The response came from a pretty girl with very pale skin and short, black hair. 'No leave.'

'What do you mean? There *must* be a key. I want to go – now.' The girl shook her head. 'Are you saying we're ... *prisoners* here?' She choked back a sob on the word. How could this have happened? She needed to speak to Andrian; he'd sort it out. But she couldn't; her phone had been taken. 'Do any of you have a phone?' Again, she mimed her question. The girl who'd spoken before shook her head. 'No key. No phone,' she said, her voice flat. 'No go out.'

Thinking hard, Mel sat on her designated mattress. Somehow, she was going to get out of here. No question. But how? *The windows.* Even as the idea flickered into life, she guessed what she would find. Sure enough, when she tried each of the two tiny windows – one in the bedroom and one in the kitchen – both were locked. From the look of things, they both opened out onto a tiny, narrow corridor of a rear garden, protected on all sides by some type of security-style fencing. Even if she broke the glass and was able to wriggle through, there was no way out from there. The only exit was via the front door. When Stan came back, she'd try to slip past and get away before he realised what was happening. Her stomach churned. It wasn't much of a plan but, try as she might, she couldn't think of anything else. While she waited, she began to speculate. Why was she a prisoner? Why were all these girls being kept here? She'd read stories, and seen news reports, of girls kept as sex slaves. But that couldn't be happening to *her*. There had to be some mistake. She'd try talking to Stan again ... make him realise that she shouldn't be here. People would be looking for her. The thought brought momentary comfort ... until she realised no-one would look for her. Her mum? Probably hadn't even registered she'd left. Andrian? He wouldn't worry. He thought she was safely in London working for his friend, Stan. Saskia was just a schoolkid still. She wouldn't instigate a search for a sister who, as far as she knew, was working at a dream job and living it up in the city. The horror of her situation slowly dawned, chilling her to the core. Blinking back hopeless tears, she sat poised on the bed, muscles bunched in anticipation, ready to flee. There was no choice but to attempt escape. The alternative – what she might be forced to do – filled her with terror.

Suddenly, she needed to find out; she had to know what she was dealing with. Trying to keep her voice calm, she turned to the girl with short, black hair once more. 'Why are we here? Why are we prisoners?' This time, there was no response. The girl rolled over so she was facing the wall. Perhaps, she didn't understand. Mel tried again, this time turning to a girl who looked no more than about fourteen. 'Why are we locked in this place?' The girl stared back with dead, grey eyes. 'Why are we prisoners? Why are we being kept like this?' She asked each of the girls in turn but received only shrugs in response. For the first time, she noticed that one emaciated-looking girl had a large, purple bruise on the side of her face. Mel pointed at it. 'Did Stan do that to you?' she demanded. The girl shook her head. Asking questions was getting her nowhere and she lapsed into silence once more. She needed to be vigilant ... ready to seize her chance.

She didn't have to wait much longer. Male voices, speaking Bulgarian, she assumed. A laugh. The sound of a key turning in the lock. There were at least two of them. Mel stiffened and gripped the handle of her case. Quietly, she stood on the wrong side of the door so she would be concealed from view when it opened. The girls watched her. One of them, black hair, shook her head, an almost imperceptible movement. She held her breath.

The door opened and a man entered. She'd not seen him before. He was dark, swarthy-looking, with a short, black beard. As he stepped into the room, issuing an order to one of the girls, she slipped around the door. The other man was leaning by the wall, looking at his phone. 'Hey!' he yelled as she shot past him and yanked at the front door. Locked! They'd locked it behind them! Despair gripped her, just as something hammered the back of her head. Incredible pain and then, blackness ...

When she awoke, it was dusk. She was lying on her mattress, back in that room. Sitting up groggily, she looked around. Two of the girls were missing – the dark-haired one and the one with bleached blonde hair. Noises were coming from the other rooms. She could hear male voices, talking in Bulgarian. Other noises too. Grunts. Moans. She knew what they were.

'Good. You awake. Put this on.' The man with the beard had appeared in the doorway and he threw something at her. She held it up. It was a tiny, black, latex dress with a zip all the way down the front.

She threw it back at him and turned away. 'Go to hell!'

Immediately, his hand was gripping her arm, cruel fingers digging into her flesh. He raised his other hand, threatening to strike her. 'Put it on.' She stared up into his implacable face. That was the moment she realised she was completely out of choices ...

It was funny, Mel thought now, as she stared into the darkness, her sister in a room just across the hallway, how she remembered that day so vividly. So much of the other stuff had blurred into a series of fleeting images, smells, feelings. Those early days she'd been terrified, disgusted, filled with self-loathing. She'd longed for her home, her friends, her sister and prayed for rescue. But no-one came.

Over the following days and weeks, Mel discovered the other girls all came from Bulgaria too. The youngest, Svetla, was an orphan and had travelled to Britain with the men of her own volition, lured by the promise of a better life. Two of the others had already been on the streets. One had been handed over by a stepfather who wanted her out of the way. They all looked out for each other, as much as they could, and Mel was slowly accepted into their sisterhood.

Of course, she didn't stop scheming and plotting. There had to be a way out. And then the men would pay! As for the other girls, they seemed resigned to their fate. When she talked to them of escape, their faces glazed over.

'Where we escape to?' Ana asked. She was the one with short, black hair and spoke the best English. 'Nowhere.'

Mel had no answer. Instead, she watched and waited for her own chance. Four men formed their prison guard: Aleksandur, with the beard, Dimitri, Vasil, and Stan, who had met Mel from the train. The first three were thugs – brutes who regarded the girls as meat and took any excuse to give them a beating. Stan was different. He was kinder, smiled at them, always with the hint of apology in his eyes. Mel was clearly his favourite and she deliberately fostered the strange kind of friendship – the teasing flirtation – which burgeoned between them. He spoke good English and she felt that he looked out for her, as much as he was able. The other girls complained that he avoided giving her the worst 'clients' and she made sure he knew how grateful she was. He was a weak spot in the business and she was ruthless in manipulating it to her advantage.

The Bulgarians brought food, other necessities and a never-ending stream of men. Sometimes, the girls were taken to other venues and Mel soon realised those times would provide the best opportunities for escape. They were always accompanied by one of the Bulgarians and she waited until she was on her own with Vasil. He drove her to a flat somewhere east of London. She had no way of knowing exactly where she was, as the transport was the windowless back of a van. As he helped her out, she looked around, trying to get her bearings. She was on a rough-looking street, tall tower blocks on one side and a row of shops on the other. A gang of youths stood by a car to her right, cigarettes winking in the dusk. On her left, she noticed an alleyway leading off the street, tucked between a betting shop and a Chinese takeaway. Either were a possibility.

Vasil frowned as he looked at her. 'Where your shoes?' She wasn't wearing the customary stilettoes. Her feet were poised for getaway in the trainers she'd been wearing when she first arrived in London.

'The heel broke,' she shrugged. 'I didn't have any others.'

'Other girls have some,' he glared and wrenched her arm. 'You will pay for this.'

'I'm sorry.' She pretended to cower in front of him. 'Please don't hurt me.'

'Stupid bitch.' He eyed her with disgust and released her arm as he turned to lock the van. That was her chance. She sprinted towards the youths, yelling at the top of her voice, 'Help. I've been kidnapped. Help me.' Vasil was close behind, gaining on her as she reached them. 'Help me.'

The lads looked shocked and then awkward as they slouched away. She felt the back of her halter-neck top rip as she was yanked backwards. He had a knife in his hand, a fat, curved blade. The youths saw it too and were now scarpering in the opposite direction. There was no-one to help.

'Stupid bitch. You will pay for this,' he said again as he strong-armed her towards one of the blocks of flats. Later, after the clients had finished with her, he threw her, like a piece of used trash, into the back of the van and punched her in the jaw, knocking out two of her teeth. As she tried to slither beyond his reach, he crawled in behind her, pulled her up by her hair and rested the knife against her neck. 'Next time ...' He mimed slitting her throat.

There was a next time though. It was worth risking death to escape a twilight existence of fear and degradation. The second time, she'd climbed out of a first-floor bathroom window and let herself drop to the ground. The fall had hurt her ankle but she'd managed to hobble down two streets before she was caught. This time, it was Aleksandur and she was beaten unconscious. Back at the house, when she woke, she could hear men's voices raised in anger. The other girls looked worried.

'They argue about you ... what to do with you,' Ana told her. 'Aleksandur says get rid of bitch but Stan ... he stand up for you. They ring Andrian to ask what *he* want.'

Andrian! Her blood ran cold. So, he *was* involved in all this. She'd thought about it – a lot – but she hadn't wanted to believe it. Surely, he was ignorant of what Veronik Holdings really was, she'd reasoned. He was someone she trusted.

The voices quietened. The girls watched her, worry lines etched on their faces. Svetla said something in Bulgarian which included the name Bibi.

'Ssh!' Ana hushed her.

'Who's Bibi?' Mel asked. She was amazed her voice sounded so calm when her insides were writhing with terror. Now the threat of death was real, she realised just how much she wanted to live.

'Bibi ... girl used to live here.' Ana gestured to the mattress she was lying on.

'What happened to her?'

The girls exchanged uncomfortable looks. 'Not know,' Ana said eventually.

At that moment, the door opened. It was Stan. 'You come with me,' he barked. There was no gentleness in the way he forced her arms behind her back.

'Why? What's happening?'

'Come. Now.'

'Stan, please ...' Her appeal was no use. She felt the cold steel of handcuffs snapped around her wrists. 'No ... please!' He held her head between his hands as Vasil pressed a strip of industrial tape across her mouth, his cold, black eyes alight with mockery.

'Now you shut up, bitch!' he spat.

She was forced, struggling, out into the night, and to the rear of the van. Stan pulled the doors open and pushed her roughly inside. She stared at his implacable face, her eyes pleading for mercy. In response, he grinned and waved at his watching compatriots. Then, he leaned into the van. 'Ssh! Try not to worry. I will help you. Trust me.' As her eyes widened, he pulled back and the doors slammed her into blackness.

The engine coughed into life and the van lurched forward. She tried to wedge herself in a corner to prevent being thrown around too much but Stan was driving as if possessed by the devil. Her body constantly jolted and banged against metal but, at least, the instinct for self-preservation kept her too busy to think. Eventually, the van braked and slowed to a halt. She tensed, listening for the doors to open, but nothing happened. Her heartbeat drummed a frantic beat in the silence; she struggled to breathe behind the tape. The wait was worse than the journey. What was going to happen to her? Her hopes remained pinned on those few words mumbled at her in the van. Could she trust Stan? She'd soon find out.

Another vehicle was approaching. The van rocked as Stan opened his door and shut it behind him. The noise of the other vehicle grew louder and then ceased. Doors banged. The rumble of men's voices. She lay on the cold, hard floor, helpless, fear gagging in her throat. At last, the rear door of the van was thrown open. Outside, it was dark but the reflected light of the moon left her blinking.

'Get out Mel.' Stan's voice was gentler this time and she shuffled forwards, her heart still pounding. Pins and needles shot up her legs as she lowered herself out. They were nothing compared to the searing pain as the tape was ripped from her mouth.

'What's happening?' she gasped. 'What are you going to do to me?'

Stan was standing beside another man, a squat, rough-looking individual with an expressionless stare. 'This is friend,' he said. 'He help us. We both escape, you and me.'

'But why? How?' she asked, confused.

'They going to kill you and they kill me for helping you.' Stan replied. 'I had better offer.'

'What do you mean?'

'No time to explain. You have no papers so need hide. We have boxes.' He signalled the interior of the other van which was full of large, wooden crates marked *Fragile*. 'This box is empty. We put in van and you hide in there until it safe. Now, I take off handcuffs if you behave?' She nodded. What choice did she have? 'Good.' He moved behind her and fiddled a key into the lock. The shackles slid from her wrists and he handed her a water bottle. 'Soon as possible, I get you out. Good, yes?' He grinned, his teeth flashing white in the darkness. She bit her lip, thinking hard. Was this a stay of execution or something else? She didn't trust Stan but it looked as if he and his friend meant her no immediate harm. 'Quick. Back in van,' he barked.

She did as she was told. The men hoisted the empty crate in and slid it forwards until it was wedged against the cab. She wriggled inside. It was dusty and full of cobwebs. Stan called, 'Lower head!' The lid was pushed across and she was plunged in utter darkness once more. If she'd been uncomfortable before, it was now ten times worse. The sides of the crate were rough and she had to wriggle and contort her body to get into a crouched, lying position. The air inside smelt dank and musty and she started to fear suffocation. Outside, there were muffled grunts and thuds as more crates were shoved into the space. Then, she heard the rattle of the engine starting up. As they sprang forward, she fought back the panic rising within her. She could die in here! The crate juddered against the side of the van and her muscles were already starting to spasm with cramp. She clutched the water bottle between numb fingers. While they were moving, it was impossible to take a drink without spilling most of the liquid. The journey went on and on and she was exhausted, worn out both physically and mentally, by the day's events. Against all the odds, her eyelids fluttered closed and she sank into an uneasy sleep ...

CHAPTER 37

Lily

I spring awake, alert to the sounds of someone moving downstairs. *Mel.* Throwing off the duvet, I leap out of bed. The urge to see her consumes me. I have to make sure she's really here and last night wasn't just a dream.

'Morning.' The scent of freshly-filtered coffee fills the kitchen and I grin as I see my sister peering into a cupboard.

'You always were a lazy-bones in the morning,' she mutters as she retrieves two mugs.

'Your fault for keeping me up most of last night,' I retort. She's wearing denim shorts and a pale green T-shirt with a panda on the front. Her legs are lean and tanned and her feet are bare. With her dark hair tumbling carelessly over her shoulders and wearing no make-up, she looks amazing. I tell her as much.

'Well ...' She gives me a wink. 'The last few years haven't been so bad.'

'Oh?' I ask curiously. Last night, she was reluctant to tell me much about her adult life and I was equally reticent about asking. I learnt that she'd been imprisoned in London by a group of Bulgarians – the same ones who were later convicted – and that she'd later escaped to Russia. That's pretty much all she'd tell me. I watch her pour coffee into the mugs and wait for her to say more.

'For starters, I'm a widow.'

'You've been married?' I can't stop my jaw dropping.

'Don't look so shocked. Plenty of men have wanted to marry me!' She gives a self-deprecating laugh.

'Yes, but you mentioned your partner, Stevie ... a woman.'

'Mm ... well, she came along after Theo, my husband. He owned a shipping company and when he died of a heart attack, I was his beneficiary.'

'You *own* a shipping company?'

'That's right.' She nods. 'Conshard International. That's me. Well, technically, it belongs to a few people, but I have the controlling interest.'

'Is that what you do ... work in the shipping industry?'

'Not exactly. I took over from Theo for a while but it wasn't what I wanted to do. Stevie is in the business – that's how I met her – and she's taken my place on the board, much to the relief of the other directors. It's works well and enables me to do other things.'

'Such as ...?' I prompt.

'Rescuing animals. I run a small animal sanctuary. I love it.'

I smile. That seems more like the old Mel. We were both crazy about animals. I remember us begging Dad for a puppy when we were younger. He always said, 'We'll see.' We knew there was no chance of it happening but that didn't stop us trying. The thought of puppies reminds me of Charlotte. Her birthday is later this week and I forgot to ask Kaz to post her card and present for me. For a moment, I indulge myself with the thought of giving them to her personally. It dangles as a possibility, a chance to make Todd forget all about that Abigail woman ... Then, I realise Mel is staring at me curiously and I snap my attention away from silly daydreams. 'How on earth did you manage to snare a shipping magnate?' I ask. 'Tell me about your husband.'

She wrinkles her nose. 'Theo was one of the good guys. To be honest, when I finally got back to England and couldn't find you, my sole aim was to find myself a rich husband. To survive in Russia, I did a lot of things I'm not proud of. Bad stuff. Back here, I wanted money and respectability. I'd finally got my freedom but I wanted to feel safe. To be honest, I was pretty ruthless. My mantra was to use men as they'd used me. Poor Theo didn't stand a chance. He was a rich, childless widower and I knew exactly how to play him. Anyway, he fell in love with me, married me and spoilt me rotten.

We were together for four years and then he collapsed with a heart attack. Died the next day. He was sixty-eight.'

'Gosh, I'm sorry.' I'm trying to take it all in. 'Did you love him?'

'Such a romantic! What do *you* think?' She pulls a face. 'Actually, he was a very nice man and I *was* fond of him. I'd fallen on my feet and I wasn't going to take him for granted. Rest assured, I did my best to make him happy.' A wistful sigh escapes. 'I was genuinely upset when he died. Things were a bit dodgy with the company for a bit though. None of the directors approved of his decision to leave me the controlling interest ... but we're over that now. It all worked out in the end. Now, I'm starving. Shall I make some toast?' She opens cupboards again, looking for plates.

Again, I suspect there is much she's not telling me. 'I'm pleased that things turned out OK for you, Mel,' I say.

'Ronnie,' she reminds me.

'Sorry.' I carry on sipping at my coffee. 'Tell me about Russia.'

'I think that's enough for now. I need to eat or I'll keel over. I missed dinner last night in my rush to get here. And it's a beautiful day. We could go down onto the beach later ... like we used to when we were kids.'

'Sounds perfect. If you don't mind, I'll just grab a quick shower before breakfast.'

I return upstairs and notice my phone lying on the bedside table. *Howard Jones!* Thoughts of Mel had chased him from my head. I look at the screen but there's nothing from him. No missed calls or texts. There *is* a message from Kaz, though, telling me that Todd and Charlotte turned up at her house yesterday, asking about me, and urging me to ring him. 'He really loves you Sass,' she's written. The words send my heart into overdrive. The magazine photo and ensuing angst fade like a distant dream. My throat aches with longing but I can't call him. Not yet; not now. We'll both have to wait. I hug the thought to me and pray it won't be for too much longer.

Instead, I try calling Howard Jones but his phone remains dead. While I shower, I fret about him. Why have I still heard nothing? I can't help fearing the worst. I'll never forgive myself if something happened to him because of me. I'm still frowning as I head back downstairs. Mel is frying bacon.

'Who'd have thought it?' she chuckles, referring to the fact that she was hopeless in the kitchen when we were younger. 'Me ... cooking!' Then, she sees my face. 'What's wrong?'

I tell her and we eat the bacon, with toast and scrambled egg, in silence while we consider what might have happened to my investigator. 'Was your number on his phone?' Mel asks suddenly.

'Yes ... why?'

'And you used your real name, I assume?'

'Yes. He knew I was Lily Nichol.'

'If something *has* happened to him – and it's a big 'if' – it could mean that Andrian was on to him. Right now, he might have that phone in his possession ... And, if so, it's possible for him to trace you.'

'Oh God!' That would never have occurred to me. I want to leap up and start packing. Most of all, I want to get rid of my phone.

She places a hand on my arm and smiles. 'Don't panic. That's probably not the case at all. It's just best to be prepared.'

'OK.' I push my plate aside, no longer hungry. 'You're right. I guess it would be a good idea to lose my phone and move on from here. Can we go to your place?'

There's silence. I study her face for answers but have no idea what she's thinking. She's staring into the distance, her brow furrowed. While she deliberates, I slam plates into the dishwasher with impatient annoyance. There's no time to waste and I want to prod my sister from her inertia. 'Mel?' I say again. When she finally turns her hazel-eyed stare back to me, I see no reflection of my urgency. Instead, I glimpse excitement burning there.

'We *could* go to mine ...' she begins, '... but do you *really* want to spend your whole life running?'

I tense. *Why isn't she seeing the danger I could be in?* Irritation sharpens my voice. 'Of course not. That's why I hired an investigator and why I was trying to find proof that Nick Georgiev is Andrian Petrov ... so the police could arrest him.'

'Ivan Jankowitch,' she says.

'What?'

'Ivan Jankowitch. That's Andrian's real name.' She gives me a half-smile. 'I've been looking for him too.' I stare at her and realise there's an awful lot she's not telling me. 'Sass, if he knows where to find you ... and *we* know he's coming ... this could be our chance to end it, once and for all.'

'What? Phone the police, you mean?'

She hesitates. 'Not exactly. We still have no proof. I think we should wait it out ... see what happens.'

'Have you gone mad? He'll kill us!' I'm trying to remain as calm as my ice queen sister but fear is pounding my temples and all my instincts are screaming at me to flee.

'Look, Sass ...'

'Lily!' I snap.

'Lily ... I've waited a very long time to see that man get what he deserves. You have no idea. If Andrian *does* come here, looking for you ... that could be our chance to get a confession from him, find out what happened to Mum, finish him for good ...'

'Or he finishes us,' I interrupt. 'Let me get this straight. You want us to sit here like proverbial sitting ducks and wait for him to turn up? You *really* think we'll be able to trick him into telling us everything and then over-power him ... and the men he brings with him? You're completely mad. He'll just kill us and no-one will be any the wiser. No! I say we need to get moving.' I bang the frying pan into the dishwasher with a resounding clatter to reinforce my point.

'Hold up a minute, Sass ... Lily!' She stands and places a hand on my arm when I start heading out of the room. 'We *can* do this. Just hear me out. For a start, if he comes, I think he'll come alone. And I have a plan.'

I stop in my tracks. 'I'm listening.'

'Just sit down again for a minute, will you?' When I comply, she gives me a smile. 'Do you remember Magical Marvo, the magician at Pandora Whatsit's party, all those years ago?'

I shake my head at the bizarre question. 'Yes.' How could I forget? I remember Mel being obsessed with magic tricks after that. She even asked for a magician's set for Christmas and used to practise on me, wearing a black, nylon cloak and felt-covered, cardboard, top hat.

'Do you remember the end of the act when Marvo vanished and then reappeared in a fog of swirling smoke at the back of the hall?' I nod, completely bemused. 'Did you ever work out how he did it?'

I frown. 'No.' I'd always preferred to believe in the magic, the mystery of it all. I hadn't wanted to know – not like Mel, who always had to know how things worked. 'Look, we really don't have time for this ...' I stand once more.

'Please ...' She raises imploring eyes to mine and I return to my seat, cross with myself for being a soft touch and caving so easily. I listen, fascinated despite my irritation, as she reveals the secret behind Marvo's magic and then outlines the gist of her plan.

'I still think you're mad,' I say when she's finished. 'I'd be mad too if I even *began* to consider it.'

'Come on ... Lily ... it'll work ... I know it will.'

And, once again, after a bit more persuasion, I cave in.

***

We spend the next few hours talking through Mel's plan and bickering. I'm not happy. She is insisting on placing herself in serious danger. I'm not going to be entirely safe either but she's definitely the one putting her life on the line.

'You'll be doing me a favour,' she argues. 'I've waited too long to get my revenge on that bastard.' I continue to press for police involvement straight away but she says 'No, not yet. Wait until he shows up.'

We talk through all the possible scenarios. I'm the one who comes up with all the things which could go wrong; she's the one who suggests the solutions. We move furniture about in the sitting room to provide me with a good hiding place. 'See,' she grins, when we've finished, 'we make a brilliant double act.' I remain unconvinced. There's bound to be a problem I haven't considered. I say as much to Mel and that's when she takes my breath away. 'Actually,' she says, 'that's why you might need this.' I gasp in shock as she pulls a gun from the bag sitting beside her on the table.

I stare at it aghast. 'Holy crap!' I mutter. It's a small, black thing, about the size of her hand. She handles it with confidence and I wonder anew at the life my sister has led.

'It's a Sig P365,' she says. 'I'm going to show you how to use it ... just in case.'

Instinctively, I hide my hands behind my back. 'I can't shoot anyone,' I say. 'Not even Andrian. You're scaring me, Mel. Put it away.'

'Don't be a baby!' Her tone is matter-of-fact as she retrieves something else from her bag. 'Hopefully, you won't have to fire it. It's for emergencies only. I don't want to think of you being unprotected.'

'How did you even come to *own* a gun?' My sister is not at all the same person I knew seventeen years earlier.

'It's a long story. I'll fill you in when this is all over. Now, I want to show you how to load it. This is the magazine.' She shows me the second item taken from her bag and slots it into place. 'You hold the gun like this and slide your index finger in front of the trigger. Then, you pull back.' She pulls the trigger until it clicks. 'See ... it's easy. You try it.' She forces the gun into my right hand. It's surprisingly light and easy to hold.

'It can't go off, can it?'

'Nope. Now slide your index finger further in. That's it. Now pull.' I do as she instructs with the gun pointed towards the floor. 'Excellent. You see how easy it is. Now try aiming at that picture on the wall.' Rapidly gaining confidence, I practise firing the gun at different targets she selects for me. 'There you go. You're a natural. Now, place the gun on the table.' She picks it up and releases the magazine.

'OK. So, here's how we load it. First, we check the chamber is clear by fully retracting the slide like this.' She demonstrates. 'Then, you insert the loaded magazine.' She pushes it in until it clicks into position. 'Now, we press down this catch lever here and the slide releases forward, chambering a cartridge. This, here, is the safety catch.' She shows me. 'Leave this on unless you need to fire.' She hands me the gun again. 'Now, I want you to picture Andrian coming towards you. Your life is in danger.' I want to laugh but this is deadly serious. Instead, I do as she says. 'If you fire for real, there's a bit of a kickback. You need to widen your stance a little, for balance, and you may want to use your left hand to support your right, to keep the barrel level.' She watches me critically as I adjust my position. 'That's it. If you think your life is in danger, or mine, for that matter, don't hesitate. This is how you disengage the safety. And now, you're ready to fire.' She puts the safety catch back on. 'You try, but keep the barrel facing down while you do it ... that's it ... and again.' At last, she's satisfied and allows me to put the gun down. My hands are clammy with sweat.

'There's no way I can do this,' I protest. 'I'd be shaking like a leaf.'

'You won't have to.' She pats my arm gently. 'This is just a precaution. The gun is ready to fire as soon as you release the safety. That's all you need to remember. I've got every faith in you.'

'I wish I did.' I mutter. 'Have *you* shot anyone?' Her face shuts down instantly and she regards me blankly. 'Oh God, Mel, have you actually killed anyone?'

'Ronnie,' she says. 'You keep forgetting.' She turns away, leaving the question unanswered. I don't ask again.

***

To ensure the success of her plan, Mel has to go out and make some purchases. I want to go with her but she says no. We can't be seen together. Someone may already be watching. That's another reason she wants to go out. She'll know if we're under surveillance, she says. While she's gone, there is nothing to do but wait. Minutes crawl like they do in a dentist's reception area. I keep checking my phone but there's nothing from Howard Jones. A feeling of dread settles first in my stomach, a cancerous thing, steadily growing and gripping my entire body.

After approximately two hours, she returns. 'Good news,' she says cheerfully. 'Didn't see anyone lurking in the shadows so I think we're good.' Although it's only the early part of the afternoon, she pulls the curtains closed.

'What are you doing?'

'Making sure no one knows there's two of us here. I need to move my car away from here too. Any suggestions?'

I think for a moment. 'I'm pretty sure the house next door is empty. The Clarksons own that one too and rent it out ... Kaz's parents,' I add when she shoots me a questioning glance. 'I think Kaz said it would be occupied from next weekend. In the meantime, you could park in their drive.'

She disappears for a few minutes and, by the time she returns, I've put together some sandwiches. While we eat, I ask Mel about Russia. She's told me of her rescue by the mysterious Stan and I want to know what happened next.

She gives a short, mirthless laugh. 'I was betrayed – that's what happened. I thought he genuinely cared for me, that we were going to make a new life together. What a joke! We arrived in Moscow and he drove me to a posh suburb called Rublyovka ... and handed me over. I now belonged to a man called Egor Kuznetsov, an aide to Vladimir Putin. Believe me, there's no escape from a place like that! Mind you, it wasn't so bad. Egor had eclectic tastes and I was one of several girls, all different nationalities. It was a bit like being at court, all of us jostling for the position of favourite, trying to keep out of trouble and, most of all, to stay on the right side of his wife, Olga. But, it *was* a life of luxury. We had beautiful clothes, excellent food and were treated like exotic birds in a gilded cage. I was there for five years.'

'What happened? How did you get out?'

'He died ... and, just like that ...' She clicks her fingers '... it was all over. Olga threw us all out with just the clothes on our back. It was pretty tough ...' I see the pain in her face and my heart aches for her. 'We stuck together for a bit – me and the other girls – but stuff happened. Two of them wound up dead. I don't know what happened to the others. Because I spoke English, I was useful to a guy named Yuri Veselov. He was an arms dealer.'

'Oh.' Now the gun makes sense. I'm not sure what to say to that so I ask, 'Does that mean you can speak Russian?'

'*Konechno.* Of course. I lived there for the best part of twelve years in total. Knowing the language was essential to survival. I had to learn fast.'

'You say he was an *arms* dealer? What did you have to do?'

Her face darkens. 'Best we don't talk about it. At the time, it was the only lifeline available to me and I took it.' For a brief moment, I see a shadow flicker in her eyes. Then, she turns away and pulls idly at a loose thread dangling from her shorts, hiding her face from me. Whatever secrets she shares, it won't change how I feel about her. She's had to do what was necessary to survive. I lean across and hug her to me, flooded with a rush of protectiveness. She gives me a brief, hard squeeze and then withdraws. I see that she's recovered her composure.

'Anyway,' she continues, 'eventually I parted company with Yuri and was able to buy myself some papers, in the name of Veronika Harper. Harper was Mum's maiden name, if you remember. And that's basically it. I still have contacts in Russia – that's how I got the Sig – but, otherwise, my life now is my own. I have money, I've found you, I'm content ... except for some unfinished business.' She gets up and peers around the curtain. I sense the restlessness in her and the excitement. She misses it, I think. She misses the adrenalin rush of danger. I remember her sense of adventure as a small girl. She was the one who wanted to go on the more extreme fairground rides, who always had to test boundaries and get into trouble. Despite everything, she has thrived and I can't help being immensely proud of her.

'Right, time to show you my purchases and to do some practising,' she says, tossing the two carrier bags in my direction. I peer inside. The first one holds two identical, navy, cotton short pyjama sets.'

'One for you and one for me,' she grins. 'We'll be just like twins!'

In the other bag is a black, woollen blanket. 'What's this for?' I ask, pulling it out of its cellophane wrapper.

'I'll show you.'

She demonstrates how it's to be used and I watch, awestruck. 'Wow! How did you do that?' I gasp. 'That was amazing!'

'Magic.' She taps the side of her nose. 'Told you it would come in handy one day. While I was out shopping, I had a few more ideas which I think may work better.' She takes me through her latest plan, step by step. Then, we act it out ... over and over ... testing for different eventualities. The more we do it, the more I grow into my role. I like this plan better and I say so. Mel's first plan involved her taking all the risk; in this one, we have more equal roles. I'm surprising myself. Some of Mel's confidence must be rubbing off on me.

'How are you going to explain the gun to the police?'

She gives me a look. 'If necessary, we'll say it belongs to Andrian. Hopefully, they won't need to know anything about it. Whatever ...' She shrugs her slim shoulders and yawns. '... I'll think of something ... I always do.' She winks. 'I'm pretty bushed and we could have a busy night. If you don't mind, I'm going to take a quick nap.'

'But what about Andrian? What if he comes while you're sleeping?'

'He won't. If he comes, it'll be night time, after dark. He won't want to risk being seen.'

'OK.' I wish I had her confidence. She disappears up the stairs and I'm alone once more. The space seems empty without her energy and I switch on the TV in an attempt to fill the void. An old episode of *Murder She Wrote* is finishing and I watch, unseeing, as the credits roll. The news is next and I start to plan what I'll cook for tea. Mel was adamant that we shouldn't go out today, that we shouldn't be seen together, so I try to picture what's left in the cupboards and fridge from my shopping trip two days ago when I'd stocked up. There's a pack of pasta and a tin of tomatoes ... maybe an onion and some bacon leftover from breakfast this morning. I could put something edible together from that. I decide to check and head to the kitchen. Dithering about what to cook absorbs my attention and I spend some while raiding the fridge and the cupboards. The task relaxes me and I can pretend things are normal. I confess I'm feeling a bit inferior to my super-confident sister and I want to impress her. The range of available ingredients is just too limited, though, and I settle on a spaghetti carbonara. Decision made, I'm fidgety once more. Everything is quiet upstairs as I return to the sitting-room. I hope Mel is managing to get some rest. Me – I couldn't even begin to think about sleep. My body is as tight as an overwound clock. Pictures from the local news are now showing on the TV and my focus drifts back to the screen. Then, I gasp. There, in front of me, is the round, genial face of Howard Jones. The sound is turned down and, rigid with horror, I watch words scroll beneath his photograph:

Man in car fireball death near A12 at Kelvedon is identified as Howard Jones, 52. Police are appealing for witnesses.

Frantically, I rummage for the remote and turn up the sound. A sombre-looking police inspector is saying that the incident took place in the early hours of this morning. A witness saw the fireball in the distance and called the emergency services. As yet, they have no news as to the cause of the accident. Investigations are continuing.

The screen switches to a report on a series of smash and grab burglaries in Chelmsford town centre and I switch the TV off. My hands are shaking. Poor Howard! I try to process my thoughts logically but they tumble like random symbols on a slot machine. *Was it an accident? Did he die because of me? How much do the police know? Who has his phone? Do his wife and family know anything? Did he die in the blaze or was he already dead? Was Andrian involved?* Grabbing my phone, I search for more information. I find a report but details are sketchy and I learn nothing new.

For a while, I sit, staring at nothing, thinking hard. More than ever, I'm convinced Mel is right. Andrian is coming for me. Taking a deep breath, I resolve to screw my courage to the sticking place. It's time to end this thing once and for all. I owe it to Mel, to my mum, to myself and now, to Howard Jones. This time, Andrian's not going to get away with it ...

***

Mel enjoys the carbonara and compliments me on my culinary skills. I'm amazed at her appetite. She eats heartily, with no sign of nerves at what may lay ahead. I'm not at all hungry. The thought of food sickens me but I don't want to admit that to Mel. While she eats, she talks through the plan once more. 'Preparation is everything,' she says. Talking about it doesn't help my appetite. 'If he's coming tonight, it will be in the small hours – somewhere between one and four in the morning. I'll keep watch and wake you if it happens. You can just relax and get your beauty sleep,' she grins. *Relax? As if!*

We chat some more as the evening wears on, both dressed ready for action in our new matching pyjamas. I'm wracked with guilt over Howard Jones and Mel tries to pacify me. I ask her opinion on the questions tormenting me since learning of his death but, like me, she can only guess at the answers. To distract me, she asks more questions, this time about me, and I find myself telling her all about Todd. I try to stay cool and composed when I talk about him but she's not fooled.

'You go all gooey-eyed whenever you mention his name,' she teases. 'Is he really that great?'

I feign casualness and shrug. 'Time will tell.'

She screws up her face. 'I don't get it, though. If you're that close, why didn't you tell him everything? Why did you just run off? Maybe, he'd have been able to help.'

'It wasn't his problem.'

She purses her lips at me. 'God, we're more alike than I thought! That's how I was ... before Stevie. Now, I think that doesn't seem very fair to the poor guy. If he cares about you as much as you obviously like him, I'm sure he'd want to help.'

'I know he would,' I answer. 'But I didn't want to put him in any danger.'

She shakes her head. 'You're an idiot.' It seems weird whispering with her in the gloom. Mel has insisted we keep our voices low. 'If I was Andrian, I'd do an early drive-by,' she told me, 'and then a stealthy reconnoitre around the property, checking for a point of entry. We don't want him hearing two people.' I shudder. The mere thought of him driving past is enough to bring me out in a cold sweat. 'Ssh!' Suddenly, she raises her finger to her lips. We both freeze, listening. *Footsteps.* The unmistakeable crunch of gravel. Mel signals for me to go and hide and, while I creep towards the sitting room, there's a sharp rap at the door. The sound jolts me into action and my heart is pounding as I rush to my designated hiding place. Before I go further, I pause to listen.

Another knock, even more assertive, demanding entry. *Strange.* At no time in our discussions had Mel thought Andrian would knock at the door. 'He'll come at the dead of night,' she'd said, 'and he'll come alone. This is personal for him.' Another thought strikes me. It could be the police. I'm about to whisper as much to Mel when I hear her unlock the door and open it. I hold my breath. There's a beat of silence while my imagination draws a kaleidoscope of conclusions. Then, I hear my sister's voice.

'Who the fuck are you?' she drawls.

CHAPTER 38

Todd
Earlier that day ...

Monday – the start of another mundane, working week. As he drove to the office, Todd turned up the radio and sang along to Bon Jovi, belting it out at the top of his voice. The sky was a bright, cerulean blue and a beautiful day was forecast. Charlotte was back to her old self and as chirpy as usual when he'd dropped her off at school. The prospect of having her live with him had blossomed in his mind over the weekend and he was excited. It felt like his life had taken a turn for the better. Then, Lee had phoned. Todd could tell straight away from his voice that his friend's outing with his estranged wife over the weekend had gone well.

'We had a brilliant day, thanks mate,' he said in response to Todd's query.

'And ...?'

There was an embarrassed chuckle. 'Well, she invited me to stay for tea and help put the kids to bed. We talked for a bit and ... one thing led to another ... and I ended up staying over. She's agreed to give things another go.'

'Yes!' Todd fist-pumped the air, earning him a sharp look from the woman driver in the next lane to him at a set of traffic lights. 'That's fantastic, Lee. I'm so pleased for you both.'

'Honestly, I couldn't be happier. I'm not going to take things for granted anymore. And I want you to know that we both appreciate your support.

You're a good mate. We won't forget it.' There was a pause. 'Have you made any progress in finding Lily?'

'I'm not sure yet. Watch this space and keep your fingers crossed.'

'I will, mate. Have a good day.'

Todd was still smiling as he entered the office. Humming to himself, he switched on the computer and checked his diary. Not too bad. Should be OK for an early getaway. He was planning on checking out that cottage in Brancaster. The more he thought about it, the more he was convinced that Lily might be hiding there. Why else would Kaz have been so bothered about it? There was no address on the flier but he'd found the same cottage on the website and now had an exact location. He was closing in. Andy Schofield would be proud of him.

'Someone's in a happy mood.' Abi stood in the doorway of his office with raised eyebrows. 'A good weekend?'

'Great, thanks. How about you?'

'Fine. I hate to spoil your day but the boss wants to see you. There's a problem with the Rawlinson merger and he's scheduled an emergency meeting with them at their premises in Cambridge for this afternoon. Just thought I'd give you a heads up. He wants me to go too.'

'Damn.' His good mood evaporated. The Rawlinson merger with another independent printing company called Glemstock had been agreed and signed a few months back. It had been a tricky negotiation between the two rival owners and their respective solicitors. Todd had been relieved when an agreement was finally reached but, clearly, it wasn't a done deal. 'Does it have to be today? I had plans.' He glowered across at her.

'Hey, don't shoot the messenger! Just giving you fair warning. Take it up with Nathan.'

'I will.'

Unfortunately, though, the problem with the Rawlinson merger turned out to be a series of problems and, as the company's solicitors, Braithwaite and Hart were obliged to help resolve the issues. Todd had no option but to abandon his protests and resign himself to a late night. There was still a chance he could head out to Brancaster after the meeting. Just in case, he insisted on taking his own car to Cambridge, leaving Nathan and Abi to travel together. The meeting was scheduled for 3:30 p.m. to allow time beforehand to consider the legal implications of the latest series of proposals from the merger company. It was going to be tight; there was a lot to do. On the bright side, though, this was the stuff he actually enjoyed doing – troubleshooting, thinking on his feet, dealing with clients. At least, his working day wouldn't be boring. He only hoped it wouldn't go on too long.

***

Todd took a crafty look at his watch as he sipped his third cup of coffee of the meeting. 6:30 p.m. and still going strong. His Brancaster plan was fading fast. It would be, at best, a two-hour drive from Cambridge. If the meeting lasted much longer, it would mean arriving after dark. There were no guarantees he'd find Lily when he got there and he didn't want to freak anyone out by turning up in the dead of night. When Isaac Rawlinson raised yet another objection to some of the finer details of the merger, he struggled to stifle a sigh of frustration. It was looking like it was going to be a long night. He managed to deal with Isaac's point succinctly and, in doing so, tried to inject a note of finality into the proceedings – something which earned him a frown of disapproval from Nathan Hart. However, it worked. Just like that, papers were signed and the meeting was over. Todd got away as quickly as he could and headed for his car at a run. He just about had enough time.

The roads were reasonably clear and it was almost 8:45 p.m. when his satnav told him he'd reached his destination. Dusk was just beginning to creep around the edges of the sky and he crawled along the street, peering left and right. Nice-looking houses – medium-sized family homes, set back from the road; decent cars parked in driveways. None of them were the holiday cottage. As he headed slowly northwards, he glimpsed a sign outside one place proclaiming it as a holiday let. Not the right one. His eyes prickled with weariness but he didn't want to blink in case he missed something important.

Then, he saw it – a house painted pale blue. The sign said Fisherman's Cottage. He'd arrived ... but there was a flashy, silver BMW convertible parked out front. His heart sank. It wasn't Lily's car; other people were staying there. Groaning with frustration, he looked for a place to turn around. 'There's still a chance she could be there,' he told himself. He would knock at the door and make sure. As he drove past the next house, the driveway was empty. He craned his neck to peer across and caught a flash of something blue. Was that a car tucked back alongside the house? A shot of adrenalin rushed through his body. He needed another look. It could be a car … and one the exact same shade as Lily's blue Honda Civic.

He pulled in, further along, and switched off the engine. *Stay calm. Don't get your hopes up. It might be nothing.* He strode back up the street. Bracing himself, he rounded the tall hedge which shielded most of the house and there it was, tucked right back, almost invisible from the road – Lily's car. He halted and tried to calm the sudden onset of nerves. There was no movement in the house. Nothing to suggest anyone was there. The curtains in the front windows were all drawn. He took a deep breath. Only one way to find out. He walked up to the front door. It was painted white with a black, wrought-iron knocker. Raising his hand, he gripped hold and rapped it firmly, twice, against the woodwork. No answer. He stood listening before knocking again, a little harder this time. Still nothing.

He was about to turn on his heel and take a look around the back when he heard a bolt being slid across. The door was pushed open and there was Lily, with dark hair, not blonde, as beautiful as ever. His breath caught in his throat and he stood there grinning, drinking in the sight of her … except that there was something amiss. This wasn't Lily. It was someone else, almost identical. The face was harder; the hazel eyes lacked her warmth. She stood in the doorway, leaning against the frame on one side, giving him a cool, assessing stare. Then, she spoke and it definitely wasn't Lily.

'Who the fuck are you?' she said.

CHAPTER 39

Lily

I hesitate at the tone of Mel's voice. Whoever is at the door, it isn't Andrian. My ears strain to hear the response.

'I'm guessing you must be Melanie.' A man's voice, deep, velvety and instantly recognisable. *Todd!*

I utter a strangled squeal and make a charge for the door, stopping abruptly when I see Mel's raised hand. 'You'd better come in. Quick!' she urges and steps outside to scan the vicinity of the cottage.

Todd brushes past her and into the hallway. I'm poised at the base of the stairs and, as he faces me, I launch myself into his arms. He enfolds me in his warmth and I feel his heart thudding in his chest.

'Lily,' he murmurs against my head and his arms tighten.

'I'm sorry.' My voice is muffled by his shirt. I pull my head away to look up at him and his lips meet mine, urgent and demanding.

'I guess this must be Todd.' Mel's voice is as dry as sandpaper. 'I'll give you a minute, but we need to talk.'

I'm aware of her squeezing past us into the living room and then all I can think about is the man I'm kissing as if my life depends on it. He's the first to pull away. 'I've missed you so much.' There's a catch in his voice, a vulnerability which snags at my heart.

'I'm sorry,' I say again. 'I missed you too.'

'Had we better ... er?' He gestures towards the living room and I sigh. I want to prolong this moment, keep reality at bay for just a little longer, but he's right.

'I guess so.'

Mel is sitting on a chair flicking through a magazine. We sit on the sofa diagonally opposite, still holding hands. 'Well, this is a turn up,' she says, eyebrows raised.

'You found me,' I whisper to Todd, snuggling closer.

He puts his arm around me. 'I was never going to stop looking until I did,' he replies.

'Oh please!' Mel rolls her eyes. 'This is all very touching but it means we have a problem.' She looks directly at Todd. 'I'm really sorry ... I know you've only just got here but you need to leave. And please don't mention me or Sa ... Lily to anyone. Do you understand?'

He returns her fierce stare with a level look. 'Are you going to tell me what all this is about?'

'Sorry, but there's no time. Lily will phone you tomorrow.' Her eyes burn into mine and I know exactly what she's thinking. Todd being here is a complication we don't need. Everything else can wait.

I swallow. I can't bear the thought of him leaving but I know he must. Gently, I reach up to cradle his face with my hands. 'She's right.' My eyes beg him to understand. 'I love you so much, Todd, but you can't stay here. I promise I'll phone you tomorrow.'

His eyes are tender as he pulls my hands away. 'I love you too, Lily. That's why I'm not leaving. I can't risk losing you again.'

'Oh, for God's sake!' Mel splutters. She stands abruptly. 'Look, I'll give you five minutes. Make sure he leaves, Lily!' With a toss of her hair, she stalks from the room.

'She's your sister, right? And you *are* Saskia Potter?' Although he phrases it as a question, I know he knows. It's how he found me. He pulls me back into his arms. 'Oh Lily, why didn't you tell me?' The answer is complicated and I'm not even sure I know what it is anymore. When I don't respond, he continues. 'Look, we haven't got long before Godzilla returns.' Despite everything, I giggle at his description of my sister. 'You need to tell me what's going on.'

I take a deep breath. The truth. Only the truth from now on. With my head leaning on his shoulder and inhaling the musky, masculine scent of him, I tell him about Andrian Petrov and how I've been running from him since I was fifteen years old. I remind him of the way my face was splashed all over the newspapers, almost three months ago, and my fear that Andrian would recognise and find me. 'I couldn't take the risk ...so I ran,' I say. 'I didn't know what else to do.' His grasp of me grows tighter. 'But I'm tired of running. And one *good* thing came from the news attention. Mel found me.' I pause to savour the wonder of it, all over again. Then, I quickly tell him the rest: about Nick Georgiev; how I told the police but they could find no proof he was Andrian; about hiring an investigator. I falter when I describe what I saw on the news earlier. 'I think Andrian may have killed him.' I shiver and steal a glance at Todd's face. He's frowning, staring into the distance. 'If so, and it is a *big* if, it's possible Andrian now has Howard Jones' phone which has my number on it. There's a chance, just a small one ...' I squeeze his hand, '... that he *could* use it to trace my whereabouts.'

'What?' Todd swivels to study my face, his own features twisted in horror at my words. 'Have you told the police? Why are you still here? Lily, you could be in danger. We need to leave straight away.'

'That was my first thought.' I now regret my impulse to tell him the truth. How on earth am I going to reassure him and persuade him to leave? I plough on. 'But, then, I'll still be running. I'll never be free of him. Todd, I need to finish it ... get on with my life ... and this could be my chance.'

He shakes his head. 'Not like this.' He extricates his arm and jumps up, trying to pull me with him. 'Look, let's discuss this some place away from here. This Andrian could be on his way right now.'

'That's why *you* need to leave, pronto.' Mel is back, standing in the doorway, a mug in her hand.

Todd ceases pacing and glares at her, hands on hips. 'We *all* need to leave.'

'Look Todd ...' I stand too. 'It's all hypothetical at the moment. There's a very good chance Andrian doesn't know I'm here. But, if he does, Mel and I have a plan. It's brilliant. If it works, Andrian will be locked away for a very long time.'

'*If* it works! Why on earth would you even consider anything which could put your lives at risk? If you think this guy, Andrian, was involved in the investigator's death, you *need* to tell the police and ...'

'Todd, with respect, *you* need to butt out,' Mel interrupts. 'If we call the police now, nothing will happen. Andrian will back off and wait until the heat dies down. My sister will still be in peril. He's a very dangerous man. I know that to my cost.'

'Todd, please,' I implore, 'it's the only way. We know ...'

He's already shaking his head. 'No, it isn't. Any plan which leaves you two alone and unprotected is far too dangerous, in my opinion.'

'You don't know what you're talking about!' Mel scoffs. 'And, unfortunately for you, you have no say in this. This is *our* decision.'

Todd turns back to me. 'Look,' he says. 'I only want to help. Tell me your plan.'

Mel purses her lips. 'We're wasting time.'

'Please, Mel.' This stand-off is going nowhere. I can see by the look on Todd's face that he's not going to capitulate. 'Just tell him. Maybe, he'll think of something we've missed.'

She scowls at me but, grudgingly, outlines the gist of our plan. The way she tells it, I have to admit, it doesn't sound that plausible. She hasn't mentioned the gun ... or the stunt we're hoping to pull off. I know that's because she doesn't trust him. Todd listens, his stance aggressive, his brow furrowed with scepticism.

Before he can renew his argument for us to leave, I take a big breath. 'Look, Todd, you have to trust us. There's a bit more to our plan than Mel's letting on. For various reasons, she can't tell you everything. If you love me, you have to believe me when I tell you that I think it'll work. And I've thought of a way you can help, if you'd like to.' That takes my sister by surprise. So far, she's been the one with all the ideas. Swiftly, before either of them can disagree, I describe the role I have in mind for Todd and am rewarded by a grudging half-smile from Mel.

'Good thinking,' she says. 'That *would* be a help, if Todd is prepared to do it.'

We both turn to Todd. His hands have moved from his hips and are now clenching and unclenching at his side. 'I don't like it,' he says, his face set in grim lines. 'I don't like any of it. I still think, at the very least, you should phone the police and get them involved.'

'We can't phone the police. Not yet.' My voice has an air of finality. 'It has to be our way. We need a decision, Todd. Are you going to help us or not?' I watch the play of emotions across his face. Then, he shakes his head. He's going to refuse and despair washes over me. I can't think of anything else to convince him.

He exhales loudly, throwing up his hands in exasperation. 'I'll agree on one condition.'

'What's that?' I ask.

'If I think either of you *are* in danger, I'm calling the police straight away. No arguments.'

I look at Mel. She nods. 'That's fine. We will need the police. We just don't want them there too soon.'

'Thank you, Todd. Remember, there's a very good chance he won't come.' I take a step towards him. With another sigh, he gathers me in his arms once more.

'Please don't take any risks,' he murmurs into my hair. 'I can't lose you, Lily. It would destroy me.'

'You're not going to lose me. We've got our whole lives ahead of us. I love you.' His lips meet mine and I feel the desperation in his kiss. I cling to him as if I'm drowning. How I wish things were different!

Mel coughs and, reluctantly, we release each other. She has her phone in her hand and Todd pulls his from his jacket pocket. We all exchange numbers like kids in a playground. 'OK. This is how we're going to play it,' she says. 'Remember, Andrian may be watching the house. We don't know. Lily will open the door and say goodbye to you on the doorstep. You can even give each other another snog if you want.' She pulls a face at me before turning to Todd. 'You need to make it clear you're leaving. Say something about seeing her tomorrow ... that kind of thing. Then, get in your car and drive away. Park up somewhere – not around here – and double back. You've *got* to make sure you're not seen. Remember, if he clocks you, that puts *you* in danger. You don't want to end up like Howard Jones.' She pauses and my stomach clenches. 'Find somewhere safe to hide where you can still see the house,' Mel continues. 'And, for God's sake, be careful.' She nods towards the front door and gives me a nudge. 'Over to you.'

I grip Todd's hand once more and lead him away. The front door is pushed open and Todd pulls me to him. 'This is the one part of the plan I like,' he whispers in my ear and then his lips lock onto mine and I forget everything else. We stand like that for a long time, with our arms wrapped around each other, in our own, private world. Reluctantly, my eyes flicker open. It's dark now and the only light is coming from our hallway. Stars are bright studs in the black canvas above our heads and I pick out some of the familiar constellations, remembering the night we stood together in his garden. 'A good night for star spotting,' he whispers, following my gaze.

'You keep your attention on the task in hand,' I whisper back, smiling against the stubble on his cheek. I pull away. 'Bye then,' I call in a louder voice.

'Bye gorgeous.' He takes a step down the path into the darkness. 'I'll call you tomorrow.' He blows me a kiss and heads towards his car. I see the flash as he unlocks it. The interior is flooded with light and he slides behind the wheel. The engine fires up. I watch, with a lump in my throat, as his hand raises in farewell and he drives away.

Mel is sipping from her mug as I return to the sitting room. She purses her lips. 'I hope we can trust him.'

'Of course, we can!' I retort.

She smiles and stands, stretching her back like a cat. 'I'll go and fetch you a coffee.' As she passes me, she squeezes my arm. 'He's pretty stubborn ...' she says.

I roll my eyes. 'I know. I didn't think we'd ever manage to convince him to leave.'

She smiles. 'But he seems like a good guy.'

'He is,' I reply.

CHAPTER 40

Mel

Mel perched on a chair by her bed, wide-eyed in the darkness. The creaks and groans of the cottage were heightened by her vigil. Every whine, every rustle, every sound outside made her body shriek to attention. It was going to be a long night.

Lily had sat with her until past midnight. Dressed in their matching pyjamas, their dark hair loose, with no make-up, they did look incredibly alike. Her own hair had been slightly longer and she'd made Lily cut it. She'd also removed the burgundy nail polish on her toes. It was all about the details. Lily had wanted to stay up longer but Mel had insisted she went to bed. 'He might not come,' she'd argued. 'There's no point us both having a sleepless night. If I get to the point where I can't keep my eyes open, I'll wake you and you can take over.' There was no way that was going to happen but her sister didn't know that.

'OK,' Lily conceded. 'I can't imagine I'll be able to sleep though.'

Mel had given her forty minutes and then crept into her bedroom. Her sister was lying on her side, eyes closed, breathing softly. So much for not being able to sleep! Watching Lily lying there, so innocent and vulnerable, filled her with a tenderness she'd not felt for a very long time. A memory came flooding back ...

She was about seven and Saskia had not long started school. Whilst playing a game of hopscotch with some friends, her radar picked up her sister's distress, over on the little kids' playground. She charged across to find Saskia crying and some kids jeering at her, calling her a baby. They soon scarpered when Mel appeared, all guns blazing. That same, fierce protectiveness coursed through her veins as she watched her sleeping sister – just how it used to be. As a child, she'd always looked out for her younger sibling. Then, she grew up and went through a spell of resenting being the eldest. Her own life was tough enough, after Dad died, without having the added responsibility of looking after anyone else. She was selfish. Whilst she never stopped loving her sister, she was desperate to move away. Her longing for excitement and opportunity made her forget what was important. And she left Saskia behind without a moment's thought. Never again, she vowed silently, as she backed from the room.

Resuming her watch from the chair in her bedroom, she wondered how Todd was faring. He was wearing a suit, she recalled – not really suitable attire for night ops. The thought made her smile. Doubtless, he was cold and uncomfortable but there … he was the one who insisted upon helping. She could see why her sister was so smitten. He was very good looking, if you liked that kind of thing. Tall, dark, great body, carelessly sexy. Yes, he ticked all the boxes. What endeared him to her, though, was the unmistakeable love shining in his eyes when he looked at Saskia. He wouldn't let them down tonight. He had too much to lose.

Her thoughts turned, as they so often did these days, to her own partner, Stevie – small, blonde, quiet, calm, completely opposite in temperament to her. When they first met, via Conshard International, Mel knew she was abrasive, mistrustful and self-absorbed, unwilling and unable to let anyone else in. Gradually, in time, they developed a friendship based upon mutual respect. Stevie was clever and always one step ahead in their business dealings. Mel came to rely upon her advice and to trust her instincts. When her husband Theo died, the depth of her grief had taken her by surprise. Now, she realised, her bereavement had brought back feelings she'd buried when her father was killed. For a while, she was a mess. Many accused her of putting on an act but she didn't give a toss what they thought. It was Stevie's quiet sympathy and support which had helped most. Slowly, her rough edges of hurt and betrayal had softened and the friendship had grown into love. Now, she trusted Stevie with her life and knew how lucky she was to have found someone like that. Stevie didn't know everything about her past – not by a long chalk – but Mel had divulged much of it, over time, piece by agonising piece. There were secrets she could never tell, not to anyone. Heartache and shame burnt too fiercely.

She hoped Stevie wasn't worrying too much about her. Probably, she should've called but she didn't want to be forced into the position of lying. Instead, she'd sent a couple of upbeat texts and promised to call the following day. Yesterday, when she was hastily throwing clothes into a case, Stevie had offered to accompany her but she'd refused. She and Saskia needed time and space alone to pick up the lost threads of each other's lives, she'd argued, and Stevie was fine with that. Turned out, it was lucky she'd come alone, given what Saskia had told her about Andrian. Ever since she'd returned from Russia, she'd been trying to track him down and now he may be about to fall into her lap. How she hoped that would happen! Killing the bastard was too good for him. For so long, she'd imagined catching up with Andrian, confronting him, shooting him so that he died slowly, in great pain. But now, with her sister in the picture, she'd have to be content with handing him over to the police. Her lust for revenge would hardly be satisfied but her sister's safety was paramount. First though, she needed him to show up.

Rolling her shoulders, she stood once more and paced a few times around the room. It was now 1:35 a.m. Time for something to happen. Her phone, clutched in her hand, remained mute. Outside, the blackness stretched, calm and undisturbed. Once again, she returned to the chair. 'Come on!' she muttered under her breath. Despite what her sister believed, the thought of facing Andrian again did scare her. The thought of him failing to appear, though, was even worse.

Fingers tingled as the phone vibrated against her skin. Leaping up, she looked at the screen. *Todd.* 'Yes?' Her voice was a breathless whisper.

'I think he's here. A dark blue van has just pulled in about fifty metres away.' There was silence.

'Is it him?'

'I'm not sure. It *is* pretty dark out here, you know.'

Smartarse! 'Tell me what's happening.'

'Nothing as yet. The van has stopped. Lights are off. Whoever is in there is still in there. No, wait a minute. The driver's door is opening. Could be him. I caught a glimpse from his interior light. Tall, more than six foot ... does that sound right?' His voice lowered to the merest hint of sound. 'He's heading this way. Looks like he's alone. I didn't see anyone else in the van.'

'That's good.' Typical of Andrian's arrogance. Of course, he'd be able to handle a girl on his own.

'Yes. Improves the odds.' Todd's voice was calm. 'He's now going up your drive and ... it looks like he's heading around the back.'

'Great. Thanks. Stay there.' She ended the call and ran to wake Lily. 'He's here!' Lily was instantly alert and out of bed. 'Have you got your phone?'

Lily nodded and stared, wide-eyed, at Mel. 'Be careful,' she whispered.

'You too.'

She disappeared, a wraith creeping down the stairs. Mel returned to her room and took some deep breaths. *Stay cool. You can do this.*

Once again, she waited, alone, in the dark, listening. A crack. The smallest of sounds but she knew it was him. Another crack and a tiny thud. He was cutting the glass out of a downstairs window. The utility room. When she'd considered how he might gain entry, that's what she'd thought. Timing. That's what she had to get right now. He mustn't suspect anything. *Don't scare him off. Make sure he's inside the house.* A louder thud. That was enough. Time to move ...

'Is anyone there?' she called from the landing. The quaver in her voice wasn't an act. She switched on the hallway light and took a cautious step down the stairs. When she reached the bottom, she picked up the umbrella she'd left there and held it in front of her. 'Who's there?' she called again, mostly to let Andrian know where she was heading. She found the switch on the wall and illuminated the sitting room. There was a creak on the floor behind her and she had to steel herself to maintain her gaze to the front. 'I have a weapon.' The air shifted behind her and an arm grabbed her by the throat. She felt the umbrella yanked from her grasp.

'That's not going to do you a whole lot of good.' The same, harsh, nasal voice. Her whole body quivered with loathing.

'Andrian!' She injected all the shock she could muster into his name and managed to pull herself free, spinning so she was between him and the doorway. 'How?' She turned to face him. 'What are you doing here?'

He was smiling, a cruel, mocking twist of his thin lips. 'Little Saskia, we meet again.' He was dressed all in black: jeans, sweater, trainers and gloves. In his right hand, he held a knife. 'It's good to see you.'

'I can't say the same,' she replied. Her voice shook. 'What are you going to do?'

'What I should have done all those years ago. Such a waste. Still so lovely.' He reached to touch her hair and she took a step back. She was now level with the sofa.

'You're going to kill me?'

He pulled a sympathetic face. 'Not right now but I'm afraid so. You're going to disappear, just like your sister and just as I promised. You're a loose end and, anyway, you deserve it for meddling in my affairs and giving me so much trouble.' He shook his head in mock sadness. 'How can I forgive that?'

'Mel!' she exclaimed. 'What happened to her? What did you do to her?'

He chuckled. 'She was a lot of trouble. In the end, I had to make sure that she vanished. Poof!' He snapped his fingers. 'Just like that.'

She gasped and her face crumpled in pain. 'Did you *kill* my sister? Are you saying she's dead?'

'I'm afraid so. Personally, I would've loved the pleasure but I find it best to get others to do the dirty work.'

'Oh no!' She started to sob, her hands across her face, edging slightly closer to the sofa so she was leaning against it. 'And now you're going to get someone to kill me?'

'Sadly, yes. When you … disappear … I have to be certain I have an alibi. I'm not happy that the police have been investigating me recently. I suspect that is your doing, am I right?' She nodded. There was no point denying it. 'And that investigator too. So foolish. Tut, tut.' He waggled a gloved finger at her, the cruel smile once more playing on his lips.

'How did you find me?'

'Too easy. Your number was there on the investigator's phone. All we had to do was to put a trace on it. I have technical people who find that kind of thing child's play. Before that, though, I was closing in. It was most helpful seeing your picture in the newspapers and then your boyfriend was doing an excellent job leading me to you. Very touching, earlier, by the way … that scene on the doorstep. Almost brought a tear to my eye.'

'You're a monster!' Mel snapped.

'No, little Saskia. I'm now a very respected businessman.' His smile widened. 'And a happily married man. I'm good at what I do but sometimes, regrettably, I have to make tough decisions.'

'Was my mum one of those *tough decisions*?'

His lips twisted into a sneer. 'I did the world a favour. What a waste of space she was! I intended to marry her so I could legally stay in the country. When she refused ... stupid bitch ... my plans had to change. It made me laugh to watch your sister heading off to that great job I'd found for her. Call it a parting gift for Nerissa before I left. I was in no great hurry. It was fun seeing you worry. But then *you* disappeared and I found that letter you'd put in her bag. I realised that you knew more than you should ... so Andrian Petrov had to leave ... in a hurry. I was even forced to leave the country for a while. All because of you! It made me angry. Poor, useless Nerissa deserved what she got.'

'So, you killed her too?'

His hooded eyes glittered with malice. 'I would describe it as putting her out of her misery. And tying up loose ends. Now, fun as this is, it's time we were moving. What are you doing?'

Mel was sliding her hand along the back of the sofa. Her fingers touched the black blanket lying there and she tugged it towards her. 'I'm cold,' she said, her eyes fixed on Andrian's. With a challenging stare, she shook the blanket out, like a barrier, between them.

He shrugged. 'As I said, I'm not a monster. You can have your blanket. But don't even think about trying anything. There's no escape.' He held up the knife and took one step forwards.

That was it. The moment of truth. As Andrian reached out to grab her, Mel swirled the blanket high in front of her ...

CHAPTER 41

Lily

A bang; a bright flash; a puff of smoke. The blanket is lying in a heap on the floor. Mel has vanished.

'*Mamka mu!*' Andrian swears and leaps forward into the swirling fog. 'Where are you?'

'Right behind you.'

Startled, he spins around … and sees me, holding a gun, pointed right at him. 'Put the knife down,' I order.

I feel completely calm and hold the gun steady, aiming at his heart like Mel instructed me. Crouched in the chest behind the chair in the corner of the sitting room, I listened to Mel asking Andrian questions, prompting his confession. On my phone, I recorded every word. When Andrian said, 'It's time we were moving,' I pushed the semi-closed door of the chest and slipped out, crouched and ready. No hesitation. Then, I heard Mel say she was cold and I knew it was time. Peering around the edge of the chair, I watched her step into the doorway and hold the blanket high. It was so quick, so incredible! I wasn't expecting the fireworks – she hadn't mentioned those. The whole thing was slick and professional; the perfect illusion. I know that she's still in the cottage, busy dialling 999; Andrian has no idea. How I wish she could see his face! His shock is a sight to behold and he's regarding me as if I'm a ghost. His jaw hangs loose; his mouth is open; his eyes are muddy with confusion.

'How the fuck ...?'

I smile serenely. As Mel had promised, he's seeing what he expects to see. He doesn't know there are two of us. 'Put the knife down,' I repeat, my stance unwavering.

He recovers quickly and gives me a smile. I watch coldly as he makes a show of placing the knife on a nearby side table.

'Now push it away,' I order.

He follows my instruction and the knife clatters across the table and onto the floor behind it. Then, he turns back and holds out his hands, palms down, in a non-threatening manner. With his most charming smile, he says, 'Please ... put the gun down, Saskia. We both know you're not going to use it.'

'I wouldn't be so sure,' I reply. With a click, I flick off the safety catch. 'You just admitted you were going to kill me.'

He laughs. 'Don't be silly. You know me, Saskia ... I couldn't harm you, even if I wanted to.'

'I'm not an idiot, Andrian. Now, very slowly, I want you to lie, face down, on the carpet. Be extremely careful. If I think you're going to try anything, I will shoot you. That's a promise.' I'm pleased at the conviction in my voice. All that practising Mel made me do has really helped. By now, the police should be on their way. Hopefully, my act will not have to last much longer.

He ignores my instruction. Instead, he asks, 'Where did you get the gun?' as if we're having a conversation over coffee. Delaying tactics. He's going to try something. Mel warned me that might happen. My grip on the gun tightens and, for the first time, my hands feel clammy.

'You brought it with you. In the struggle, it fell to the floor and I managed to grab it.' His eyes narrow and I allow myself a small smile. 'That's what I shall tell the police.'

'And how are you going to phone the police, while still pointing that gun at me?' He smirks. 'Be careful, Saskia. That could give me the chance I need.' Then, he gives me a wink. 'I think we could call this a standoff. Time to reach a deal.'

'The police are already on their way. I called them as soon as I heard you taking out the utility room window. They'll be here any minute. Now, do as I say and get down on the floor.'

Once again, he shakes his head. 'You're not going to shoot me, Saskia. I know you.'

'You *don't* know me!' Fury erupts in my voice. *Stay calm.* 'Lie ...down ... on ... the ... floor!' This time, I enunciate every word, trying to re-establish control.

'Hush, little Saskia,' he murmurs and shuffles his right foot a tiny step forwards, testing my resolve.

'Do as I say, Andrian!' My hands are beginning to wobble and I take a deep breath. 'Don't move!'

He raises his eyebrows. 'Don't move ... or lie down? Which is it?' He's mocking me.

'I'm going to count to three,' I say harshly. Fear is making my mouth dry and I swallow. 'Face down, on the floor. One ... two ...'

I don't make it to three. With a manic grin, he lunges for me. No time to think. I fire the gun. Twice. In quick succession. I'm already ducking out of his reach as the second shot rings out.

The next few seconds pass as if in slow motion. Blood spurts into the space between us and a dark stain spreads across his chest. The impact stops him in his tracks and he crumples onto his knees, his face a mask of disbelief. 'You bitch!' he splutters, glassy-eyed, as he collapses onto the carpet. There's a crack as his head hits the stone surround of the fireplace. The gun drops from my trembling fingers and I stand, looking down at him, numb of all feeling.

Mel rushes, white-faced, into the room. 'Lily!' she cries. 'Oh, thank God you're alright.' She pulls me into her arms and squeezes me tightly.

'I shot him ...' I murmur. My knees feel weak. 'Is ... is he dead?'

Mel throws him a careless glance. 'Not sure,' she says. 'You had no choice. Remember that – it was him or you. The police are on their way but I guess I'd better call an ambulance.' She dials 999 once more and speaks to the operator. My legs start to wobble and I sink down onto the chair. The room swims around me. I blink, trying to regain my vision. Then, Mel is grabbing hold of my face between her hands, forcing my focus back to her. 'Listen to me, Sass. You did brilliantly. I wish it could've been me pulling the trigger ... I'm sorry you had to do it. And I wish I could stay with you but the police will be here in a minute. Stick to the plan and soon it will all be over.'

I nod, conscious of her urgency. We don't have long. 'The worst is already over,' I say. Mel squeezes my arm and pulls away. I watch as she kneels by Andrian's body and takes hold of his wrist.

'I think he's still alive.' She looks up and I can see that's not what she wanted. 'Not that he deserves to live. Look Sass, I'm going to have to go ...' She stops when we both hear a thump from beyond the kitchen. 'Ssh.' She puts her finger to her lips, retrieves her gun from the floor and tiptoes from the room. I strain to listen but can hear nothing. Did Andrian have someone with him? An accomplice? More than one? For a few seconds, panic flails. Then, I remember the knife. It's still behind the table, on the floor. I edge around Andrian's body and reach for it, all the while watching the doorway. The cold steel feels alien and sinister in my hand. I creep forwards ... and stop when I hear Mel call. 'It's OK, Sass.'

She reappears, still holding the gun, with Todd close behind her. He stops in the doorway and takes in the scene. When he sees me, relief floods his face and he strides across to gather me in his arms. 'I heard shots,' he gasps. 'I was so worried. I got here as soon as I could.' Holding me at arms-length, his brown eyes search my face. 'Are you sure you're OK?' I nod and give him a weak smile. 'So ... what the hell happened?' He turns to Mel. 'You didn't say anything about a gun!'

'It's Andrian's,' she lies briskly, using the blanket lying on the floor to wipe the handle, before returning it to me. I notice she's wearing gloves. They look incongruous teamed with her pyjamas. 'Take it,' she orders, 'and stand where you were when you shot him. Then, let it fall to the ground.'

'*You* shot him?' Todd's horrified gaze swivels in my direction.

'She had no choice. Andrian was armed.' Mel takes the knife from me, wipes the handle and puts it in Andrian's jacket pocket.

'But, in your plan, you said Lily would be hiding, recording the whole thing on her phone and calling the police! How come she was involved in ... this?' He gestures to Andrian lying motionless on the floor. Anger blazes in his eyes.

'Look, you and I need to get out of here. I'll explain everything but not now. The police will be here any minute.' As she talks, she continues to move about the room, carelessly draping the blanket over Andrian's prone form.

'We can't leave Lily like this!' he splutters.

'We have to.' She shoots him a look of exasperation. 'Lily's fine. She knows what to do.'

'I'm not leaving.' He puts his arm around my waist. 'You need support.'

'No.' I emerge from my stupor and my voice is urgent, brooking no argument. 'You can't be here when the police arrive. It will ruin everything. I'm fine. Go with Mel to your car and get away from here. Quickly! I'll call when I can.' When he's about to protest once more, I add, 'It's important, Todd ... please.'

He relents. I can see how reluctant he is to leave but Mel urges him forcibly through the back door. Then, I'm alone with Andrian ... waiting.

CHAPTER 42

Mel

Mel shoved her feet into the trainers by the back door and grabbed the bag of clothes she'd left hanging on a coat hook. She followed Todd as he skirted around the back of the house and continued his route behind the hedge which ran parallel with the lane. They kept low and moved fast, frequently stumbling in the undergrowth. Todd's long-legged stride meant Mel was almost running to keep up. He didn't speak, nor check to ensure she was still with him. Anger crackled in the tense set of his shoulders. In the distance, the sea rolled its steady, infinite course, a swishing backdrop to the hum of night time, oblivious to the two figures scurrying in the shadows.

Within minutes, they reached Todd's car and he rammed his body into the driver's seat. Without a word, she slipped in beside him, still clutching the bag of clothes, and stared out of the window as he drove away from Brancaster. He took the coastal road and pulled into an empty car park concealed by trees. After switching off the engine, he turned to face her, his jaw clenched. Ignoring him, she pulled on a hoodie, leggings and cap. He watched as she tied her hair into a ponytail and tucked it under the cap. She took her time, aware of his bristling, barely restrained fury. Only then, did she look in his direction.

'Lily's facing a murder charge because of you,' he exploded. 'Very convenient how you managed to work things so that *she* was the one in danger. And now *she's* the one in trouble.'

'Todd, I know you're angry ...' she soothed.

'How could you stitch your own sister up like this?'

His accusation stung. 'Look, before you start hurling abuse at me, you need to hear how it was ... what actually happened. Believe me, Lily shooting Andrian wasn't part of the plan.'

He raised his eyebrows. 'Go on then. Tell me everything. I want to know how this whole thing got so out of hand. I guess we've got plenty of time while Lily's with the police.' The acid in his voice seared her conscience. He had a point. It wasn't fair that Saskia was bearing the brunt of it all. It should've been her.

She nodded. 'You're right. I'm sorry.'

'Tell that to Lily!' Abruptly, he pushed open the door and stepped out of the car. 'I can't just sit here, doing nothing! I'm going for a walk. Are you coming?' He didn't wait for a reply.

'Todd!' She called, rushing to follow him. 'I thought you wanted to hear what happened?'

He puffed out his cheeks in an exasperated snort and spun on his heel. 'Go on then. Let's hear it.' As she reached him, he set off again, slower this time, down a narrow path which led to the beach.

When they reached level ground, she matched her stride to his, still silent, thinking hard. Where to begin? How could she explain the night's events without the rest of it, the whole story? The rhythmic roar of the waves called to her, suggesting a starting point. 'When we were kids, me and Saskia ... Lily ... used to love going to the seaside. Living in Norwich, we weren't far from the coast and that was always our choice of a weekend day out. We'd spend hours in the sea or building massive sandcastle creations or searching for shells. We loved it.' The moon was bright in the sky as they picked their way over to the damp sand, flat and newly washed. The tide was going out and they made a path of uneven footprints, the squelchy earth sucking at their shoes. 'But then our dad was killed ...'

She talked for a long while. Todd listened without comment. Sometimes, she skated over the details, much as she'd done when sharing the missing pieces of her life with her sister. 'Melanie is dead,' she said, her voice flat and emotionless. 'From now on, you can only call me Ronnie.'

'Why?' he asked. He didn't understand. Having managed to get back to England after all those years in Russia, why hadn't she gone to the police, told them her story and resumed her old life?

She stopped abruptly and stared out at the grey swell of the sea, white-tipped in the moonlight. No-one knew what she'd done ... not even Stevie ... especially not Stevie. The truth was that she had killed before – twice. The first was a total scumbag who had burst into her kitchen and shot down her defenceless friend Maria in cold blood before turning his gun on her. He wasn't aware of the pistol she kept taped under the table. She'd felt no compunction and no remorse when she'd blasted his chest open. But the second one haunted her dreams. He was just a young kid, caught up in something he had no place being a part of. It was a bad deal from the start. She'd begged Yuri to walk away from it. But he was greedy – too greedy. In the ensuing gun battle, it had cost him his life. As she fired in an attempt to run for cover, she'd seen the face of the boy caught in her crossfire, the terror in his wide-eyed stare as he slithered to the ground. She'd never forget it. Later, she'd discovered that the boy had not survived. Time had not diminished the guilt she felt.

She shook herself back to the present. Todd was waiting for her answer. She shrugged. 'Let's just say that, in order to survive, I lived for a long time on the wrong side of the law. I have no intention of going back to Russia to answer for my supposed crimes. I have a new identity and a new life. I intend to keep it that way.'

'So that's why Lily had to be the fall guy,' he mused, his anger returning afresh. 'Did she know it was being set up that way?'

'She wasn't *set up*,' she retorted crossly. 'Listen.' Her narrative took him back to her childhood and the magician at the birthday party when she and Saskia had been so young. 'I was fascinated when he vanished and reappeared from behind us. Do you know how the trick is done?'

He hunched his shoulders. 'I've never given it any thought.'

'Well, I had to find out. Of course, it spoils the magic ... knowing how it works ... but that's how I am. Obviously, his magic box has a secret compartment, big enough for him to hide in. I guessed that much. But I couldn't understand how he'd managed to get from the box to the back of the hall.'

'And?'

'The truth is he didn't. He was still in the box. The person who appeared at the back of the hall was his twin brother.' She smiled. 'It's obvious when you know the answer.'

'I guess it is.' He wasn't sure where this was going.

'Saskia and I look alike. When Andrian broke in, he thought I was Saskia, alone in the house. He had no reason to suspect it was me; he thinks I'm dead. Sass was able to hide and record our conversation. In it, he admitted everything. But I knew he would be armed and it would be difficult to overpower him. That's where the trick came in. When we'd got his confession, I managed to make him think I'd disappeared in a puff of smoke and Sass was there behind him, holding the gun. He didn't suspect a thing. That's how the illusion works – people always see what they expect to see. I was able to get out of earshot, call the police and be ready to help out if needed. She didn't need me though. She was fantastic.'

They walked on in silence. Todd appeared deep in thought and Mel was content to enjoy the cool freshness of the early morning breeze whipping around her cheeks. She still felt wired but the brisk walk was helping. Eventually, she spoke. 'We ought to be heading back. I want to make sure we're in the car when Sass calls. I've no idea how long that will be.'

'Lily,' he replied brusquely. 'Her name now is Lily.' He turned and stalked in the other direction. Once again, she fell into step beside him, waiting for him to speak to her. 'Where did the gun come from?' he asked at last.

She thought for a while before answering. Could she trust him? Probably not. He'd soon offer her up to the police if it meant saving Lily. But then, he wouldn't have to. She would put herself at the front of the queue. What the hell ... she might as well tell him the truth. 'It's mine. What can I say? I'm a bad girl!' When he didn't respond, she continued. 'I promised myself I'd never be vulnerable again, that I'd always be able to protect myself.' She kicked a pebble along the beach. 'Saskia ... Lily has spent all her adult life running from Andrian Petrov. I wasn't prepared to do that. If he came for me, I was going to be ready.'

Todd nodded. 'Thank you for telling me,' he said quietly. 'I get that.' He exhaled in a long sigh. 'I only hope that it really is over now. Lily could still face a murder charge.'

'When we left, Andrian was still alive so it wouldn't be murder. Anyway, they won't charge her with anything. Trust me. She'd already alerted them to the fact that Andrian was pretending to be a guy called Nick Georgiev. She'll tell them about hiring Howard Jones because she was so worried. She has no police record and a long history of being a victim. And remember, she has the phone recording. I reckon they'll be wanting to give her a medal.'

'I hope you're right. Poor Lily. I can't bear to think of her going through all this alone.'

She laid a hand on his arm. 'Listen, Todd. She's tougher than she looks. She's had to be. And she's not alone. She knows we're right there with her. Come on, I'll race you to the car.'

CHAPTER 43

Todd

Todd let Mel go on ahead and walked to the car at his own pace. Whilst her story had evoked his sympathy and grudging respect, his anger remained. Whatever had happened in the past, she'd knowingly exposed Lily to grave danger. It was hard to forgive something like that. Lily could've been killed. Bile rose in his throat at the thought. And now they had to wait to see what the police would make of it all ...

Mel was leaning against his old, green Golf, nonchalant, relaxed, looking at her phone. At his approach, she slipped it into her pocket and gave him a half smile. 'I guess you weren't in the mood for a run?'

'I guess not.' Tight-lipped, he unlocked the car. 'So, what's the plan now?' he growled. No doubt she had one.

'We wait,' she replied. 'When Sa ... Lily rings, you'll need to find out where she is and what's happened. Then, you go and pick her up.'

'What about you?'

She gave him a look. 'I don't exist, remember? That's why she'll ring *you*. Before you turned up, she was going to ring her friend, Kaz. If the coast is clear at the cottage, I'll pick up my stuff and my car and head home.'

'Convenient for you,' he muttered, an ironic twist to his mouth.

She sighed. 'Look Todd, you're going to have to get over it. Believe me, I don't like the thought of leaving my little sister to face all the repercussions of this, either. *She* was the one who insisted upon it, if you must know. If she needs me to do anything, she said she'd let me know ... and I'm sure I can rely on *you* to make sure of that,' she added drily. She swivelled in her seat to pin him with her stare. 'She loves you and you love her. You'll both get through this. I'm trusting you to look after her.' Her eyes misted over. 'I love my sister. She's the only family I've got. It kills me to walk away from her. But, hopefully, all this means that, one day, we can actually live *normal* lives and spend time with each other.'

The fervour of her tone melted the frosty edges around his heart. Averting his head, he rubbed his face with his hands and stared out of the window. There was a red tinge to the sky's moonlit panorama. Dawn was approaching. A new day. The first buds of hope tentatively began to surface. If Mel was right, it *could* mark the start of a new life together for him, Lily and Charlotte. A real life: doubtless messy and problem-ridden, but, for Lily, free from fear, with no more secrets, no more running. For that, he should be grateful to Mel, even while he struggled with the rest of it. And Lily wouldn't want him to be at odds with the sister she loved. Rolling his shoulders, he turned back to face Mel. She seemed deep in thought, staring into space. He cleared his throat.

'Look, we haven't got off to a good start. I suggest we try again.' He held out his hand. 'I'm Todd.'

He saw surprise flicker across her beautiful features, so like Lily's, before she grinned and gripped his hand. 'Call me Ronnie,' she said. 'It's lovely to meet you, Todd. I'm sure we'll be friends ... just so long as you don't mess with my sister!'

'No fear of that,' he retorted, matching the teasing lilt to her voice. 'I know what you're capable of!'

She nodded. 'Precisely.'

Awkward silence prevailed. To break it, he switched on the ignition and flicked his radio to a music channel. Classical. With a sigh, he leaned into his seat and closed his eyes, letting the soothing beauty of violins wash over him. The discordant buzz of his phone startled him back to action mode. 'Lily!' he exclaimed. 'How are ... things?'

'I'm OK.' Her voice sounded exhausted. 'Everyone's been very kind. The police have taken my statement and, for the moment, I'm free to leave. Can you come and pick me up please?'

'Of course. Right away.' He was already starting the engine. 'Where are you?'

'I'm at the police station in Hunstanton. I think there are police still at the cottage so can we go back to your place please? I can't face going back to … you know … at the moment.'

'Definitely. I'll be there as soon as I can. I love you.' He ended the call. 'Police are still at the cottage,' he said to Mel as he drove away from their parking spot.

'No problem. How's Lily doing?'

'She sounded tired but I think she's fine. The police are releasing her, at any rate. She wants to go back to mine.'

'That's good.' She gave Todd a smile. 'If you could drop me off somewhere on route, I'll make my own way from now on.'

'Don't be daft,' he replied. 'For the time being, you might as well come home with us … as long as you stay in the car or somewhere out of sight while I collect Lily from the police station.'

Her smile grew wider. 'That's kind of you, Todd. I think you're a bit of a softie at heart,' she teased.

'Not at all. I'm thinking of Lily. She'll want to see you.'

'Ah, right.' She was still smiling when they reached the outskirts of Hunstanton.

'Drop me off here,' she said. 'Best that I'm not seen in your car at the police station.' He pulled in along the seafront.

'Stay here and I'll pick you up when I've got Lily.'

'OK.'

The satnav directed him to Lynn Road and he soon found the station, an old-fashioned, red-bricked building. Lily was waiting in the front lobby. White-faced and dressed in an over-sized, baggy, blue jumper, she looked like a teenager. Wordlessly, she fell into his arms. 'Come on,' he said. 'Let's get out of here.'

'Where's Mel?' she asked, turning to scan the rear seat of the car.

Todd started the engine and headed back along Lynn Road. 'I dropped her off just along here,' he replied. 'We're going to pick her up and take her back home with us.'

'That's good.'

He sensed her body relax. 'She should be just around the corner,' he murmured, stretching across and squeezing her hand. They turned the bend and he slowed the car. 'That's funny ...' The street was empty. 'Perhaps it was further along ...' They drove the length of the road and stopped to turn around. 'Maybe, she found somewhere to have a coffee,' he suggested.

'At *this* time of the morning?' Lily frowned.

'I'll give her a ring,' he said, picking up his phone. After a few seconds, he put it down. 'It's gone straight to voicemail.' He looked at Lily. 'Now what do we do?'

She shrugged. 'I guess we head back without her. It surprised me, to be honest, when you said she was coming back with us. Was it her suggestion?'

'No, it was mine.'

'There you go. I think Mel probably had other ideas.' She settled back into her seat. 'She'll be fine. Mel's always been a law unto herself.'

He nodded, a wry smile dancing on his lips. 'You can say that again! And, by the way, it's not Mel – it's Ronnie.' Leaning across, he planted a gentle kiss on Lily's mouth. 'Now, let's go home.'

CHAPTER 44

Lily
2 months later

We're at the beach, Todd, Charlotte and I. The sun is glorious and it's taken a while to find a quiet spot, away from the crowds. The position we've chosen is perfect, nestling in the dunes but close enough to the water to satisfy Charlotte. Her energy is boundless and my swimsuit is still damp from our last foray into the waves. But now she's happily making a sand fortress with her dad, over where the sand is still damp enough. I watch from my vantage point. Their two dark, curly heads are bent together in concentration and Todd laughs suddenly at something she says. I find my phone and take a picture. I want to capture this moment forever. Those few old photographs of Mel and I at the beach with Mum and Dad were once all I had. Now, I have the freedom to build new memories.

There are only a few weeks left of the summer holiday and I'm looking forward to the start of the new term. It's taken a while and there's been a lot of uncertainty but my life is now settling back into a normal rhythm. This week, I learnt officially that Andrian will be charged with the murders of my mum and Howard Jones, as well as several other offences. He's still in hospital, recovering from his injuries. The police were satisfied that my actions were necessary and I was exonerated of all blame. I shot him twice. The first bullet caused most of the damage as it hit him in the chest. It missed his heart but caused massive bleeding and a severe pulmonary contusion.

According to his surgeons, he was lucky to survive it. The second bullet grazed his hip. His loss of consciousness was caused by the bang to his head when he fell. Already, that night seems a distant, surreal dream.

I haven't seen my sister since, but she phones me often and I'm getting used to calling her Ronnie. I've spoken to her partner, Stevie, a few times too. She seems lovely – warm and bubbly. I'm hoping I'll get to meet her soon ... and spend some proper time with my sister. The few days in Brancaster were far too brief to make up for years of absence.

Last night, after Charlotte was asleep, Todd and I lay on a rug outside, in each other's arms, gazing up at the stars. For the first time, I spoke freely to him about my life before. So much I'd kept hidden and it all came tumbling out, like sweets from a broken piñata. It felt good to share my secrets. Well, not quite all of them ... I didn't bother mentioning my schoolgirl crush on Darrell Parkinson.

We met up with Kaz, her husband, Tom, and their beautiful baby daughter last week and she told me that Darrell works on the ground staff at Norwich City Football Club. After her brief romance with him when they were still teenagers, she's remained good friends with both him and his wife, Lucy, and we've made tentative plans for a group meet up sometime soon. I hope I don't blush when I see him. He was my first love and, as such, holds a special place in my heart. I admitted as much to Kaz when we were on our own and she hooted with laughter.

'Not a chance,' she spluttered when I told her. 'Don't get me wrong, he's a really nice guy and all that but, compared to the total hunk that is Todd ... well, let's just say that I think you're one lucky lady!'

'You too. Tom's great!'

'Yeah, he's not too bad.' She looked fondly across at her husband who was laughing with Todd over a beer.

'And this little one is so adorable.' I cradled the baby in my arms. 'Little Saskia. I still can't believe her name. I cried when you told me.'

She smiled. 'What else could I call her? I have to call *you* Lily and I missed having a Saskia in my life. I didn't really have a choice.'

My eyes welled up as I stroked baby Saskia's downy, black hair. 'She's so beautiful,' I murmured. Emotion made it difficult to speak. I hadn't expected to feel such a powerful longing for my own baby, mine and Todd's, and I handed her back before I made a fool of myself. 'Just like her mum.'

Kaz nodded with contentment. 'Too right! Thank God she gets her looks from me!'

It had been a special day, like so many over the past few months. Todd and I had a wonderful week with Hugo, Vanessa, Simon and Manuela. It had seemed a lifetime since I'd last seen them and yet it was as if we'd never been apart. The guilt I'd felt about leaving them had been a terrible weight on my conscience and I'd been nervous about returning to Canterbury. I needn't have worried. In their loving, selfless way, they refused to listen to my apologies and said they blamed only themselves for not being there when I needed them. They are such special people and I'm so happy to have them back in my life.

Tomorrow, Todd is insisting on taking me for a weekend away. The destination is to be a surprise, he's told me. I'm trying to suppress lurking feelings of panic. I still don't like surprises.

***

We set off on Friday afternoon. It's the weekend of Reggie's wedding to Nick so Charlotte isn't with us. I'm feeling slightly uneasy as we drive along the A11, and, when we continue on towards Norwich, my nerves intensify. I realise where we're heading.

'You're very quiet,' Todd observes.

I don't reply. I feel sick. I'm not ready.

We pull in at a strange-looking bed and breakfast place on the outskirts of Thorpe St Andrew. It looks tired and scruffy. Weeds are sprouting in the gravel drive and the flower borders, although colourful, are wild and overgrown. I wonder why we're stopping here, of all places. 'We have reached our destination,' Todd says breezily. I feel like hitting him. How can he do this to me? Throwing open his car door, he whistles his way around to the boot. As he unloads our cases, an old woman hobbles across the gravel to meet us. She is almost as wide as she is tall, with corkscrew white hair and wearing a bright red apron. 'Todd!' Her arms are outstretched. 'You're here. It's wonderful to see you again!'

He bends down to hug her and grins at me. 'Are you going to get out of the car?'

'Is this Lily?' The old woman peers at me through the window as if I'm a scientific specimen. Reluctantly, I slide out of my seat.

'Yes, I'm Lily. Pleased to meet you.' I hold out my hand and give her a tight smile.

She turns back to Todd. 'Oh my, you didn't say how beautiful she was!' She raises fleshy hands to pull my shoulders towards her. 'I prayed he would find you, my dear. The poor boy seemed so lost.' I must look as confused as I'm feeling and she draws away again with an embarrassed laugh. 'But I'm forgetting … I haven't introduced myself. I'm Connie – Connie Cleverly. Todd stayed here a while ago when he was trying to track you down. I'm so happy he's brought you to see me.' She gives a little gasp. 'But what am I thinking … keeping you standing in the car park like this? Come in, come in. Here, let me take that.' She tries to wrestle a bag from Todd's grasp.

'I can manage thanks, Connie. It's my fault Lily's looking a bit shocked. I thought I'd make it a surprise, you see. She didn't know she was coming here.' He gives me his lopsided grin but I ignore him. What other surprises is he going to spring on me? Instead, I continue to smile politely at Connie, who looks anxious at the obvious tension between us. I follow her inside and up the stairs to the Dallas suite. She chatters all the while but I'm finding it difficult to focus on what she's telling me. My mind keeps racing ahead, trying to work out what else Todd has planned. I do my best to conceal my inner turmoil but Connie isn't fooled and, while she's unlocking the room door, she asks if I'm alright. 'Yes, thanks. I'm sorry, Connie. I'm not usually this befuddled. Blame Todd. Oh, this is lovely,' I say as she stands back to let me enter first. 'What a beautiful room!' It's spacious and, surprisingly, given the décor downstairs, modern in style. The crisp, white linen on the bed is enlivened by a stunning, multicoloured throw and matching cushions on a double sofa. A vase of alstroemeria sits on the chunky, grey dressing table and I'm touched by the gesture. 'And what lovely flowers! Indian Summer, aren't they?'

Connie gives a nod of approval, her face lighting up at my obvious pleasure. 'That's right. Well, I'll leave you to get unpacked. Dinner will be at seven, if that's convenient.'

'Can't wait,' Todd says. To me, he adds, 'Connie's cooking is amazing.' As she turns to leave, he calls, 'You will join us, won't you?'

'Oh.' She's a bit flustered. 'That would be lovely ... if you're sure?' Another anxious look in my direction. Feeling guilty, I reiterate Todd's invitation, even though I'm not sure we'll be staying. My instincts are screaming at me to get in the car and return to the emotional safety of home. Todd has some explaining to do.

'This is great, isn't it?' he beams at me after Connie has left, totally oblivious to my feelings.

I raise my hands in despair. 'You should've asked me,' I wail, plonking myself on the bed. 'You should've asked if I was ready to return here. I'm not.'

He sits beside me, as calm as ever, and takes my hand in his. 'What's worrying you?' he asks quietly.

My shoulders slump. It's difficult to put it into words. 'The past is the past. I don't want to go raking it all up again. I left Thorpe behind seventeen years ago and have never wanted to come back. There are too many painful memories here.'

He slides his arm around my shoulders. 'I'm sorry, Lily. You're right – I should've asked you.' We sit like that for a while. Eventually, he says, 'What do you want to do? Do you want to leave? Whatever you decide is fine by me.'

I take a juddering sigh. Why is he so reasonable? I'm spoiling for an argument but his capitulation has left me feeling like I should do the same – not what I want at all. The fight seeps out of me and I give him a weary nod. 'Well, we're here now and I guess Connie has gone to a lot of trouble for us.' I force a strained smile. 'And the room is lovely. Just so long as there are no more surprises?'

'Er ...' Guilt colours his face.

'Tell me,' I insist.

He reveals his plans, with promises that I can decide if I want to go through with them. Actually, now he's said what they are out loud, I feel better. We kiss and things improve from that point onwards. In his arms, I agree to give everything proper consideration and then spend a luxurious hour in a sumptuous, roll-topped bath.

The meal with Connie is a riot. She's hilarious, entertaining me and Todd all evening with countless stories. The food is excellent and, after I've consumed a few glasses of wine, I realise how much I'm enjoying myself. I squeeze Todd's hand under the table. With him by my side, I feel ready to face the demons of my past and I tell him so as we lay, once again, entwined in each other's arms much later that night.

The following morning, my rosy glow has disappeared and the nerves have returned. I can't face the delicious cooked breakfast Connie has prepared for us and push a piece of toast around my plate. Todd watches me with anxious eyes. 'I've booked for two nights,' he says, 'but we don't have to stay. Just say the word and we'll head home.'

I'm tempted. It would be so easy to run away again. But I know what Mel would say. A conversation we had in Brancaster, replays as if she were right there with me:

'Sass, you can't keep running.'

'I guess, but I'm not brave like you, Mel.'

'Rubbish. We're the same. If I'd had your choices, I'm sure I would've done the same as you. And, believe me, I tried to run.'

'Yes, but now ... you're so strong ...'

'We're both strong. We both did what we needed to do to survive. I know I'm ruthless − I've had to be − but you're just as tough. We've both had to make difficult choices and come through. You can do this.'

She's right. I've faced the worst and, now, it is time to deal with the rest of it. Todd may have forced the issue but it's my decision and I know, in a rush of clarity, that I am ready.

My new-found resolve notwithstanding, it's still an emotional day. First, we drive to Just a Snip to see Helen Batty. We both weep like babies. She looks just the same, her trademark pink hair short and spiky, and, after we stop blubbing, she pours us large gins. She launches into all the gossip from my missing years and I'm soon crying with laughter. I suspect Todd has phoned ahead and warned her that I might not be ready to talk about my past as she refrains from asking me questions, although I know she must be bursting with curiosity. So, when her monologue starts to dry up, I leap in and share snippets of my life since leaving Thorpe St Andrew.

'You've done well with this one,' she says, indicating Todd. 'He was like a man possessed when he came here, a few months back, searching for information about you. He was so single-minded that he even ignored my charms,' she cackles. 'Not that I blame him now that I've seen you. You're so beautiful, Saskia. I love your hair like that. It really suits you.' She's referring to its colour which is now back to Lily blonde.

'Lily – not Saskia any more,' I correct her gently.

'I'm not sure I'll ever get used to that. You *will* keep in touch, won't you?' She grips my hand and gives me a fierce look. 'No more disappearing off the face of the planet! I'm happy to do your hair for free, for old times' sake.'

'It's a deal,' I smile.

As I stand to leave, she says, 'I'm sorry, but I have to ask. Was there ever any news of poor Melanie?'

I hesitate. I can't tell her the truth but I don't want to lie either. 'I'm sure she's still alive,' I say carefully. 'Maybe, one day, I'll be able to bring her to see you.'

'Oh, I do hope so!' She clasps me to her in a fervent hug. 'Thank you so much for coming to see me, Lily. It means such a lot.'

'To me too.'

With the gin and the warmth of Helen's company buoying me up, we walk to the street where I used to live. This is the bit I've been dreading; I want to get it out of the way. Todd holds my hand and my fingers tighten their pressure as we approach. 'This is it,' I say and we stop outside a front door, now dark blue, with roses engraved in panes of frosted glass. When I lived there, this house was the poor relation in a street of modest, terraced houses. It now looks upbeat and freshly decorated, nothing like the shabby home I remember. Out front, there's a smart, brick weave driveway; tubs of pink begonias and trailing greenery frame a new front porch. It's difficult to picture our small, weed–ridden front garden. I was fifteen when I was last here. I picture myself slinking away to the train station in the half–light, terrified, not knowing what I'd find and if I'd return. I *did* come back, just once, to pack up my things, before I was taken to Happytrees. All that is a blur now. As I stare at the brick wall, where I used to play catch with a ball, my sharpest memories are happy ones, when our family was complete: Mel and I playing with other kids in the street; games of Monopoly on rainy days; favourite television programmes we watched together; the neighbour's Labrador we looked after when they went on holiday. I squeeze my eyelids shut, a half-smile on my lips, welcoming my long-lost reminiscences like old friends.

After a while, the images fade and I become aware of Todd, standing patiently beside me. I sense his anxiety, his protectiveness, and I smile to reassure him. The ordeal I'd feared hasn't materialised.

He smiles back. 'Do you remember Mavis Little?' he asks.

'Of course!' Her likeness pops up instantly: old, stooped, grey-haired and kind – so kind. She often found excuses to invite Mel and me for tea after Dad died and when Mum wasn't able to look after us. I don't know how she knew that food was scarce but nothing seemed to escape her eagle eyes. Mel and I used to laugh about her odd ways – her insistence on giving us tea in china cups and the mismatched clothes she used to wear – but we were both grateful. Mavis was more than a neighbour. She was a good friend to us both.

'I met her when I was looking for you. She's quite a character, isn't she? Do you fancy seeing if she's in?' Todd says.

'Yes.' I'm eager to thank her for everything she did.

Unlike others in the street, her house looks just the same, with paint flaking from the off-white, wooden window frames and two old terracotta pots, containing bay trees, by the front door. More memories drift in: the strange man with the funny eye who used to live next door; the ache of an empty stomach; standing in my scruffy, school uniform, waiting impatiently for Mavis to open the door. This time, it's Todd who knocks.

'Perhaps she's not in,' I suggest when there's no response.

Todd knocks again and this time we hear muttering from the other side of the door. 'Alright, alright, keep your hair on. I'm on my way.' Then, there she is, squinting up at us with suspicion. She's smaller than I remember, as if she's shrivelled a little with each passing year, and her straggly hair is now completely white. I watch as her eyes light up with recognition, for Todd, not me. 'It's you!' she exclaims, her voice breathless and wheezy. 'You've come back. Did you find her?' As she speaks, she turns to me and leans closer, peering intently at my face. As I watch, her mouth falls open. 'Saskia?' she murmurs. 'Saskia ...' She clutches at my hand, her grip surprisingly strong, as she pulls me towards her. 'Is it really you? Oh, my dear, I'm so happy to see you. I never thought I'd see the day ...' She turns to Todd who is grinning broadly. 'Thank you for bringing her. Oh, my goodness, you'd better come in. I want to hear everything. Both of you, come in, come in.' She hobbles back inside, leaning heavily on a stick, and we follow. Her house smells exactly the same as I remember, a curious mix of boiled vegetables and furniture polish. 'Oh, I wish I'd known you were coming. I'd have made biscuits. I don't bother to bake much these days, just for me. Oh, my goodness, I can't believe you're here. Sit down, sit down.' When she asks if we'd like a cup of tea, Todd offers to make it. 'Oh, go on then, young man,' she nods. 'I don't want to let this one out of my sight in case she vanishes all over again. Now, tell me everything!'

It's like the past twenty years have melted away and I'm back on her sofa, being interrogated. In those days, her questions had been about school and my plans for the future. Now, she wants to know every detail of what's happened to me since I left. I give her a brief outline, helped by having rehearsed it already that morning, and, when she asks about Mel, I repeat what I said to Helen.

'Oh, I do hope you're right. Now I've seen *you*, I could die happy if I knew *she* was safe. Poor girl ... and poor you, having to live without knowing.' I squirm, feeling uncomfortable with the half-truth I've told her. I long to tell Mavis all about my sister but it's not my secret to tell. To hide my discomfort, I jump up to help Todd when he finally appears with a tea tray.

She quizzes me further as we drink our tea, just as she always did. Mel and I used to laugh at how there was never any let up with Mavis. I manage to interrupt her questions long enough to thank her for her kindness when I was a teenager and I see she's pleased by my words. She becomes a little flustered and starts to fuss about moving the empty teacups.

'Let me do that.' Todd once again does the honours and Mavis smiles fondly at his retreating back.

'He's a good one,' she tells me, her tone confidential. 'Tell me, what are his intentions? Has he proposed yet?'

I blush at the blunt question. 'No.'

She frowns. 'Well, is he going to? You're not getting any younger. You need to get a move on if you want a family.'

I laugh. Experiencing Mavis' habitual bluntness is like putting on a worn pair of old slippers, familiar but certainly not soft and fluffy. 'Mavis, I'm thirty-two. There's plenty of time for that!'

'Plenty of time for what?' Todd asks upon his return.

I look at my watch as if trying to pretend we're discussing the lateness of the hour. Mavis is less discreet. 'Having children,' she replies, twinkling up at him. 'I was just saying that you don't want to leave it too long.'

'Mavis!' I exclaim, totally embarrassed now.

Todd sits beside her and grins at me. 'No arguments from me, Mavis,' he chuckles. 'I agree with you. She just has to say the word ...'

'Well, you have to get married first,' Mavis suggests primly.

'Of course.' Todd gives me a wink. 'I can't wait.'

I roll my eyes. He's incorrigible. Mavis now has the bit between her teeth. 'There you are!' She shoots me a look of triumph. 'He wants to marry you!'

'I'm sure that if Todd wants to propose, he'll ask me properly!' I retort. I can feel my cheeks are crimson. 'Oh my God ...' I stare in amazement as Todd drops to one knee in front of me.

'Lily Nichol ... Saskia Potter ...' His eyes, misty with love, hold mine. 'I adore you more than there are stars in the universe. Please marry me?'

I stare at him in total shock. I can't believe he's doing this, in front of Mavis Little, of *all* people! My immediate instinct is to give him a piece of my mind. But, then, I glimpse the nervousness in the tautness of his jaw, and the hopeful resignation in his eyes. I realise he's steeling himself for rejection and my objections melt away. 'Yes,' I whisper. 'Yes, I'd love to marry you.'

With a whoop of joy, he scoops me into his arms and his lips find mine. As our kiss becomes more passionate, I become aware of Mavis burbling, 'Goodness gracious, well I never!' over and over, with lots of noisy throat clearing.

Laughter fizzes in my chest until I can hold it back no longer. 'What a time and a place to ask me!' I splutter against Todd's cheek.

'Ah well, you see, I had to seize my chance.' He winks at our onlooker who, for once, is speechless at the turn of events. 'I was so afraid you'd turn me down if I asked you ... but I didn't think you'd *dare* say no to Mavis!'

EPILOGUE

Overhead lights snap off, plunging the room in blindness. Nervous giggles ripple and fade into throbbing silence. The walls shiver in anticipation.

A sudden explosion of light shakes the room. Thick smoke snakes in spirals as a creature shimmers into view – a man, resplendent in a swirling, multi-coloured cape and a tall, red hat like a pillar box.

'Behold!' he announces, his voice deep and hypnotic. 'You see before you ... Magical Marvo. Prepare to be amazed!' Beneath the cape, he whirls his arms. Slowly, with the artistry of many performances, he unfolds his long, thin fingers to reveal a squirming, white mouse. 'Ooh,' the children gasp.

'I can't believe you managed to find Magical Marvo, after all these years!' I whisper to my sister.

'Ssh,' she hisses back. 'You'll spoil it!'

'Watch carefully. I shall now make it disappear.' He turns his huge hands inward, fingers closing and reopening. The mouse is gone.

'And still doing the same old tricks,' I mutter. I sense Ronnie smiling in the darkness.

'For my next trick, I require an amazing assistant.' All three children shoot their hands into the air. 'Is there someone here called ... Charlotte?'

'Yes, me!' She squeals with delight and skips to Marvo's side, dark curls dancing in the spotlight. Her pink cheeks are flushed with excitement.

'Behold ... Charlotte!' Another flourish and more applause. 'Today, Charlotte will show you some true magic. She herself will disappear!'

'She's been so excited about this,' I whisper to Ronnie.

The magician wheels forward a large, black box emblazoned with 'The Magical Marvo' in gold letters. 'Charlotte will step inside the box.' He opens a forward-facing door so we can see the empty space inside. 'This is dangerous magic children.' He lowers his voice to a dramatic hum. 'Do *not* try this by yourselves. To successfully make a person vanish, a magician has to spend many years practising.' Charlotte wriggles in and sits, crouched, facing out, her sunflower yellow dress scrunched around her, her smile confident. 'Are you alright in there, Charlotte?' Marvo asks.

'Yes.'

'I'm going to close the door.' The audience watches. 'Don't worry.' Marvo waggles his long finger at us. 'She's still in there. I haven't said the magic words yet. Do you want to see?'

'Yes,' we call back.

The box opens to reveal Charlotte. She's giggling, knowing what is to come. Once more, he clicks the door shut and stands in front of the box. 'It's time to summon the magic.' He swings his cape, his movements now slightly stiff and jerky, like a marionette. 'Repeat these words after me. *Magical Marvo, make her go!*'

'Magical Marvo, make her go,' we chant.

Another wave of his arms. 'Now let's see. Has the magic worked?' With the theatre of his vast experience, he flings the door open. Charlotte is gone. We clap as Marvo bows. 'Thank you for your help everyone. That's the end of my performance. I hope you've enjoyed it.'

'Aren't you going to make her come back?' Ronnie calls. She gives me a sidelong glance to see if I remember.

'Charles Pilkington-Brown, Pandora's brother,' I whisper back.

She laughs. 'I'm not sure why he wanted Pandora back. She was such a pain in the ...' She stops when she catches Marvo glaring in her direction.

'Oh, would you like Charlotte to return?' He returns smoothly to his act. 'That would need a very powerful spell. I hadn't realised you wanted her to reappear. Oh, very well. I'll see what I can do.' He scratches his head, pretending to be thinking hard. 'Right. I've got it. You'll need to shout these words as loudly as you can if we're to summon the lovely Charlotte back with us. Repeat after me. *Marvo Mack, bring her back!*'

'Marvo Mack, bring her back!' we shout. The two young girls in the front row, Stevie's nieces, bounce up and down on their seats. Their dark hair is plaited and they're wearing matching, red ribbons. They remind me of the young Mel and Saskia.

The door opens once more and the white mouse scuttles out. Marvo scoops it up and drops it in his pocket before clasping his hands to his face. 'Oh no!' he moans. 'Wrong words.'

'Have you changed Charlotte into a mouse?' I ask, giving my sister a wink.

'No, no. I'm sure she's fine. Let's try again. I think I've got it this time. You'll need to shout these words as loudly as you can if we're to summon her back to us.' His arms sweep through the air, conducting his orchestra. '*Marvo Inkpot, show young Charlotte!*'

My sister and I both splutter with laughter as we repeat the words. '*That isn't as I remember it!*' Ronnie chuckles.

Out she steps, grinning broadly. As we cheer, she bows several times and allows Marvo to spin her around. 'An incredible performance of magic, young lady. Well done!' He joins in the applause.

After Charlotte has returned to her seat, Marvo continues his act. There are card tricks, some we saw before, but some new to us. He uses the two other girls, Ellie and Alice, to assist him in pulling an impossibly long string of silk hankies from his red hat. The three children are enthralled by the performance, just as we were twenty-five years ago.

'And now, for my final trick, I shall perform the most dangerous magic of all ... I shall make myself disappear. In a few moments, I shall get into the box. When you shout the magic words, I shall reappear from the back of the room.' Three small, dark heads peer around in unison and I smile at Ronnie, remembering the time when we did the same. 'The magic words this time are ... *Magical Marvo, it's time to go!*' He spends the obligatory few minutes rehearsing them. 'You've got to get it right or the magic might go wrong,' he informs us solemnly. 'Now, I need another helper. Perhaps one of the grown-ups ...' he surveys the group, '... you!' He points at my sister with a wry smile. 'What's your name?' he asks as she stands beside him.

'Scarlett.' She directs her words straight at me. 'Scarlett Starlight.' We all laugh.

'A lovely name. Now, Scarlett, I want you to check there's no trickery going on. Can you scrutinise the box please to make sure that this door is the only way out?' She walks around it, taking her time, inspecting every part of it. 'Do you want to check underneath?' She nods and he tilts the box forward so she can see. 'Can you confirm that this door is the only way out?'

'Yes,' she replies with a swish of her long, dark hair.

'Now, please stand close to the box as I go in so you can shut the door behind me. When I'm inside, I want you to count to three and then everyone must shout the magic words. Let's practise that, one more time.'

At last, he squeezes his frame into the box. Ronnie pushes the door shut and counts to three.

'Magical Marvo, it's time to go!' roar the children. There's a bang at the back of the room. We turn, as one, to see Marvo heading towards us, arms outstretched.

'It worked!' he calls. 'Well done everyone! You were amazing.' More applause. 'Now remember the name and tell your friends ... Magical Marvo! The best magician in the world!' A final bow and the lights dim. I squint to watch as Marvo wheels the box from the room. I see that it's heavier than before from the way his muscles strain in the faded coat. Otherwise, it's impossible to tell. It's a good trick. The three girls are chattering excitedly in the darkness and I reach for my sister, who has returned to my side, to clasp her hand in mine.

***

'That was amazing,' I say later to Ronnie. 'I can't believe you managed to track him down. It's a miracle he's still working!'

She smiles. 'He agreed to come out of retirement when I told him it was a trip down memory lane for us both. And for the money, of course.'

It's the first time I've seen my sister in over three months and we've been pretty much glued at the hip since Todd, Charlotte and I arrived, yesterday evening, for a long weekend stay. Stevie, her partner, is as lovely as she sounded on the phone – a small, pixie-like woman with kind eyes and a warm smile. She also has the organisational abilities of a sergeant-major and has planned a raft of activities for her two nieces and Charlotte to keep them busy for the duration. Much to my amusement, she's drafted Todd in as her assistant, leaving Ronnie and I plenty of quality time together.

Later, after the children are asleep, we all sit around the dining table, eating, drinking and laughing together. The conversation turns to Todd's novel. Earlier this week, he received a request for the full manuscript from an esteemed literary agent and we're keeping our fingers crossed for a publishing deal.

'What's it about?' Stevie asks and Todd summarises the plot without giving anything away.

'Is the missing girl found?' My sister looks at me as she poses the question.

'Now, that would be telling. You'll have to read the book,' Todd replies.

I smile. I've read the manuscript and loved it. His first two books are great but this is definitely his best. It's another crime thriller, fast-paced with lots of action, and Andy Schofield, naturally, saves the day when he finds the girl alive. Todd admitted that wasn't the ending he'd originally planned. 'But, after everything that's happened, the girl had to survive,' he said. 'There was no other option.'

What makes this book different is the greater focus on the victim herself. Her story is powerfully told and her voice resonates as a mantra for survival. 'I refuse to live my life as a victim,' she says in the narrative. 'I choose to be tougher, stronger, better than before. Don't waste your pity on me!'

'She sounds just like Ronnie,' I'd exclaimed when I'd finished reading.

'I can't deny it. She, and you, had to be my inspiration. There was a lot of editing after that night in Brancaster.'

Ronnie and I stay up late. Both of us are reluctant for the day to end and, eventually, Todd and Stevie leave us alone. I'm proud of my sister; she's so confident in her own skin, so fierce and strong despite all she has been through. She makes me believe that anything's possible. In my pocket, I have a photograph and my fingers close around it. It's the photo of us as children, so alike, both smiling, which used to break my heart. We're on Hunstanton beach, draped in towels, huddling together on the sand, laughing at something. When I show it to her, her composure cracks, just a little, and her eyes mist.

'I know Dad said something to make us laugh,' I say softly, 'but I've never been able to think what it was.'

She caresses our outlines with her finger. 'It was actually something *you* said. It wasn't even funny,' she replies. 'We were both freezing. Dad wanted to take our photo to remind us just how cold the sea can be. He said it might stop us pestering him to go in with us. I said something like, "Fat chance!" and then he did this funny dance, pretending to be really cold. He said, "You're making me shiver in my boots," and you piped up, "Daddy, you're not wearing any boots!" or something along those lines. We all cracked up and Dad took the snap.'

I stare at her. 'How have you remembered that so clearly?' I ask.

Her face clouds. 'Do you remember how we used to look through those family photos after Dad died? Just you and me. Well, when I was alone, in London and in Russia, I used to pretend you were there with me. I'd imagine us looking at each picture and, in my head, I'd talk to you about it, like we always did. I'd lost everything; those memories were all I had left.'

Tears fill my eyes. She sees and puts her arm around me. 'Don't be sad, you goon. I'm not. This is meant to be a happy time. Can I keep this photo?'

I hold her close. 'Of course. Promise me you'll *never* disappear from my life again.'

She grins and pulls a pack of cards from her pocket. 'I've been saving this for the right moment,' she says with a wink. 'Just an ordinary pack of playing cards. See?' I shoot her a questioning glance as she spreads them out. She waits for me to check and, at my nod, scoops them up. With long-practised expertise, she shuffles the cards, before splaying them face down. 'Now, pick a card ... any card,' she says. The shiny, red-patterned, plastic-coated surfaces wink in the lamplight. Baffled, I stare at her. 'Go on, do it!' she commands.

I reach to select a card just left of centre but, as I tug, I meet resistance. 'Are you sure you want *that* card?' she says. 'You can change your mind if you want.'

'No. I want that one.'

She sighs theatrically. 'Oh, alright then.' I extract the card from her grasp.

'Can I look at it?'

'If you must.'

I turn it over. 'Oh,' I gasp, wide-eyed. My amazing sister will never cease to surprise me. It's not a playing card at all, but an announcement, printed in a swirly, flowing font:

Scarlett Starlight has performed her final vanishing act.
There will be no encore.

***

ACKNOWLEDGEMENTS

This is a work of fiction. Real places in Norfolk, Suffolk and London are an integral backdrop to the narrative but I confess I've taken liberties, which I hope you can forgive, with geographical details and added imaginary locations of my own. There is also no mention of the coronavirus pandemic. This was a deliberate choice.

There are many people who have given me support and encouragement. Writing a novel, in my experience, is a journey beset with difficulty and self-doubt. I'm grateful for my friends from the writing communities on Twitter, Facebook and Instagram for their advice, morale-boosts, support and humour, which have kept me going through the tough spots. Similarly, thank you to some of my biggest supporters – Ros, Helen, Penny, Sandra, Rosy and Camilla – whose belief in me transcends my abilities, and to those loyal readers whose encouragement and praise fill me with joy.

The Vanishing Encore is my third novel and the theme of family is central to each of my books. My family are my biggest fans, cheerleaders and supporters. You are the best.

The thankless task of critiquing my manuscript has fallen to Sue, Sara, Mark, Kerry and Alex. You know how much I appreciate your insights, advice, comments and encouragement. *The Vanishing Encore* would be a lesser novel without them.

Rob, my book cover designer, has done his usual fantastic job. Thanks also, Rob, for your technical expertise. Alex: editor, proof-reader and website facilitator – you are a complete star.

Finally, and most importantly, I'd like to thank **you** for choosing to read *The Vanishing Encore*. I really hope you enjoyed it. If you did, please consider posting a review, however brief, which will help other readers to find this small book in that vast world library out there.

ABOUT THE AUTHOR

Carolyn Ruffles is the author of both contemporary and historical fiction laced with mystery, romance and suspense. She loves reading books which tell a compelling story: books with drama and emotional depth; books which keep her reading late into the night and then have a satisfying ending. That is what she strives to write. She is also fascinated by human interest stories – ordinary people embroiled in extraordinary situations and learning about themselves in the process.

 Having retired from teaching, she wrote her first book, *The Girl in the Scrapbook*, which was published in November, 2018. *Who To Trust*, followed in March 2020 and *The Vanishing Encore* is her third novel. If you wish to find out more about her and her books, she has a website https://carolynrufflesauthor.com. By signing up to her readers' list, you will receive the link to a free short story, *Memories Forgotten*, about a subject very close to her heart.

Carolyn lives in Norfolk with her husband Mark. When she is not reading or writing, she loves dog walking, playing badminton, gardening (in moderation – no weeding and a little light pruning is her preference) and looking after her two beautiful grandsons. She also loves spending time with family and friends, especially if there's a glass of wine involved!

Introduction

Welcome to the Original Doggy Milestone Series™ where you are encouraged to create those special moments with your dog. We have composed the milestones in a way that challenges you to set the stage before taking your photos.

Use props and make it fun - be creative in setting up your photos. Get family and friends involved - take it out with you - use it in different places and settings - have a play with it and most importantly, have a good time!

You can either hold the desired milestone spread open yourself - or have somebody hold it open as you take the snap.

If you would like to have the selected milestone book spread open and standing independently in your photos, you can use one or two large 'foldback' clips to hold the spread open.

Good luck and enjoy your photo fun.

I Love

My

Family...

...And My Family Loves Me

At The
Beach!

Having a **Wave** of a **Time**

With My Doggy Pals

IT'S...

I DIDN’T KNOW WHICH STICK YOU THREW

SO I
BOUGHT
BACK
ALL OF
THEM

They Say Diamonds Are a Girl's Best Friend

I Disagree! I'm The Only "Best Friend" Here!

I'm Going To Start Eating Healthy...

Next Week!

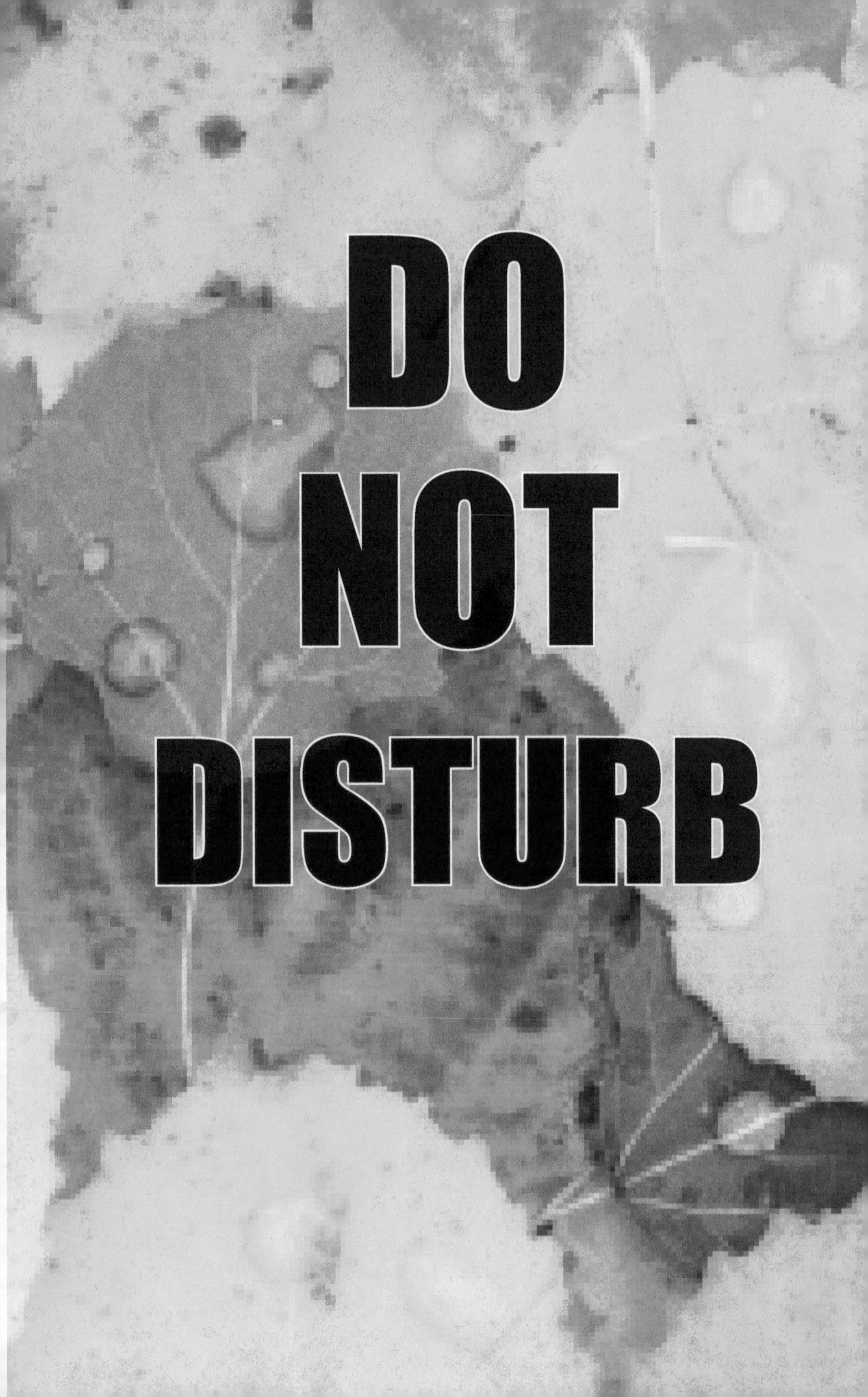
DO
NOT
DISTURB

PLAYING

IN THE

LEAVES

I Need a HUGe

Amount
of
Treats

To My Little Friend

CATCH ME IF YOU CAN!

KEEP CALM

WE'RE A TEAM

NASA

Wants

To Hire

Me

Because I'm a STAR!

OOPS!
I
Buried
Your
Stuff

...But I

Forgot

Where

Where

My Real Name Is

SUPER POOCH

Very
Incredible
Pup

I
DIDN'T
DO IT

I'll Just Be Over Here...

Looking

Fabulous

PLEASE

PLEASE

PRETTY
PLEEEASE

CAN I KEEP IT?

I'm On a SEAFOOD Diet